**Praise for *New York Times* bestselling author
Lori Foster**

"Storytelling at its best! Lori Foster should be on everyone's auto-buy list."
—#1 *New York Times* bestselling author
Sherrilyn Kenyon on *No Limits*

"Foster hits every note (or power chord) of the true alpha male hero."
—*Publishers Weekly* on *Bare It All*

"Count on Lori Foster for edgy, sexy romance."
—*New York Times* bestselling author
Jayne Ann Krentz on *No Limits*

**Praise for *New York Times* bestselling author
Tawny Weber**

"A great setup, sizzling attraction and wonderful characters all make *Risqué Business* by Tawny Weber impossible to put down."
—*RT Book Reviews*

"Forget the hot chocolate, the wool socks and the space heater—Tawny Weber's *Sex, Lies and Mistletoe* will keep you plenty warm this season."
—*USA TODAY*

Lori Foster is a *New York Times, USA TODAY* and *Publishers Weekly* bestselling author with books from a variety of publishers, including Berkley/ Jove, Kensington, St. Martin's, Harlequin and Silhouette. Lori has been a recipient of the prestigious *RT Book Reviews* Career Achievement Award for Series Romantic Fantasy, and for Contemporary Romance. For more about Lori, visit her website at lorifoster.com.

A *New York Times* and *USA TODAY* bestselling author of over thirty hot books, **Tawny Weber** has been writing sassy, sexy romances since her first Harlequin Blaze book was published in 2007. A fan of Johnny Depp, cupcakes and color coordination, she spends a lot of her time shopping for cute shoes, scrapbooking and hanging out on Facebook.

Readers can check out Tawny's books at her website, tawnyweber.com, or join her Red Hot Readers Club for goodies such as free reads, complete first-chapter excerpts, recipes, insider story info and much more. Look for her on Facebook at facebook.com/ tawnyweber.romanceauthor and follow her on Twitter, @TawnyWeber.

New York Times **Bestselling Author**

LORI FOSTER

SCANDALIZED!

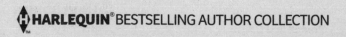

ISBN-13: 978-0-373-01023-3

Scandalized!
Copyright © 2015 by Harlequin Books S.A.

The publisher acknowledges the copyright holders of the individual works as follows:

Scandalized!
Copyright © 1997 by Lori Foster

Risqué Business
Copyright © 2008 by Tawny Weber

Recycling programs for this product may not exist in your area.

Printed in U.S.A.

www.Harlequin.com

CONTENTS

SCANDALIZED!

Lori Foster

With much gratitude to Anita Gunnufson
for all her medical assistance in this book.
I really enjoyed our long-distance calls.
And to Glenn Davis. I love you, Dad.

CHAPTER ONE

SHE WAS THE perfect woman to have his baby.

Tony Austin continued to stare, analyzing her features, considering the construction of her body. He'd already done so, of course, but now he was more thorough. She wasn't beautiful, but that was okay, because beauty wasn't essential to his plan. And she *was* striking, even arresting in her presence, her confidence and poise.

Though he tried to stop himself, his gaze was repeatedly drawn to her, and finally Olivia Anderson caught him looking. The small, curious smile she sent him took his breath away, but he shook his head, deciding his reaction was excitement for his plan and nothing else.

That was all it could be.

As always, she looked elegant. She wore a simple black dress and black heels, but that had little to do with his heightened interest. He had made a decision, and she was deeply involved in that decision whether she knew it yet or not. He rubbed his hands together, feeling his anticipation build.

He'd been acquainted with her for three years now as a business associate, and he knew she'd only attended his party as a means of furthering that association. Nothing in their relationship was of a personal nature—and he intended to keep it that way.

Just two days ago, she'd presented him with a pro-

posal to expand her business that would add one more
of her novelty lingerie shops to another Austin Crown
hotel. He hadn't given her an answer yet, but he would.
Tonight. And then he'd have a question of his own to
present.

For the first time in a very long time, he felt nervous
on the verge of making a business proposition. Then
Olivia started toward him with her determined, long-
legged, graceful stride and all he could think of was what
a beautiful baby they could create together.

He welcomed her with a smile.

HE'S GOING TO give it to me.

Olivia tingled with anticipation. Tony had been
watching her, almost studying her, all evening. And
there could only be one possible reason for that. The
sense of impending victory thrilled her.

His gaze held hers as she neared. There was that slight
tilting of his mouth—an unaffected sensual look that
she knew got all the single women and even the not-so-
single women excited. But Olivia would only get excited
if he gave her the news she wanted.

Her business was her life, and she didn't allow herself
the time or the desire for anything else. She was certain
he didn't, either. At least, not with her.

She was well aware of Tony's reputation with other
women, and it was the women building that reputation.
They claimed he was a spectacular lover, though how
many had firsthand knowledge she couldn't guess. He
appeared very circumspect to her. He never spoke of his
relationships. In fact, he seemed oblivious to the talk.

She tried to be oblivious as well; her only interest in
him was business related. But she had to admit there

were occasions when she couldn't quite stop her mind from wandering...

She stood mere inches from him and at five-eleven or so with her heels on she nearly looked him in the eye. They stood by the balcony doors, no one else within hearing distance, the ambience soft and intimate. Olivia dismissed her wayward thoughts and lifted her glass of soda to him in a mock salute. "Tony."

"Hello, Olivia." His voice was deeper than usual, his gaze more intent. "Are you enjoying yourself?"

He seemed almost watchful, and anticipatory, not wearing the cool persona he usually assumed in her company. She looked around at the newly decorated offices, pretending an interest she didn't feel. This party was to launch the renovation of his massive downtown hotel, which had been standing for decades. With its new upscale furnishings and classy decor, it was positioned to compete with other hotels where price was no obstacle. "Everything is lovely, Tony. Why wouldn't I enjoy myself?"

His lazy smile deepened, his gaze became probing. "I don't think you're much for parties. You seem preoccupied." He tilted his head slightly. "Anxious to get back to business matters?"

Olivia swallowed her immediate response and the last sip in her glass. She allowed her gaze to follow a passing couple, then said, "I was wondering if you'd come to a decision, yet. Of course, a party isn't exactly the place to discuss such things, but..." She looked back at him and caught him watching her closely. Again. "If you'd care to enlighten me?"

Tony chuckled and ignored her question. He excelled

at business games, but then, so did she. "Would you like something else to drink?"

"No, thank you," she replied.

"Had too much already?"

"Of soda? I think I can handle it. You however..." She circled his thick wrist with her fingers to bring his glass toward her and then she sniffed. But she didn't detect the fumes of alcohol. She frowned.

"I don't drink, either. Too many of my associates do, and I think someone has to stay sober to oversee things."

Olivia didn't want to show him her surprise, but she found herself doing just that. "So you never indulge?"

"An occasional glass of wine with dinner. Very occasional."

"I'm a teetotaler."

"Personal reasons?"

Olivia hesitated. It was funny how you could know a person for years and never say or do anything outside the realm of related business, then suddenly be discussing very intimate, personal topics. She didn't really mind, though. She'd always believed the better you knew your business associates the easier it would be to deal with them. It was her fondest wish to do a great many deals with Tony Austin. She finally nodded and answered, "Very personal. I detest alcohol."

"Maybe someday you'll tell me why."

"Maybe."

Tony was silent a moment. He appeared to be studying her drop-pearl earrings until suddenly he asked, "Do you have a five-year goal for yourself, Olivia? Or some long-term destination that you're working toward?"

Again, Olivia felt that touch of excitement and tried to quell it. He was showing an interest he'd never shown before, and that could only mean he approved her business management. Tony Austin was the epitome of business excellence. A person could learn everything she needed to know from him.

It was said Tony had doubled the Austin Crown hotel chain within three years of his father's death. Under Tony's guidance the hotels had grown from mediocre to posh and exclusive. Every upscale business convention around wanted to be on the receiving end of Crown's special treatment.

Tony Austin's employees loved him and praised his leadership. As a pioneer in the business world with one of the fastest growing hotel chains around, he was regularly featured in business magazines. Austin Crown hotels were located throughout the country and probably would soon be around the world.

Olivia watched now as he propped himself up against the wall, the breadth of his shoulders visible even beneath the elegant cut of his dark suit. He was a well-built man, she admitted to herself, in his early thirties, with more energy and determination than anyone she knew. Right now his brown hair, darker and richer than her own and with a spot more curl, had fallen forward over his brow, and his green eyes were intense on her features.

Olivia smiled. "Of course I have a plan. A very substantial plan. If you'd like, I could outline it for you."

To her surprise, Tony caught one of the servers milling through the crowd. "Miss Anderson and I will be in the inner office. Please bring us refreshments, non-alcoholic only, and see that we're not bothered unless it's absolutely necessary."

The server nodded, took their empty glasses and

walked away. Olivia felt her nerves tingle. *He's going to give it to me.* She hadn't expected this, hadn't expected Tony to want to discuss business tonight, but still…

Tony took her arm and began weaving through the crowd. Several people noticed, but she ignored them. Tony merely nodded to anyone who stared too long, but he was used to this. It was a fact he drew regular gossip from outsiders. After all, he was the local boy made good and there were always busybodies hoping to pick up a scrap of dirt. But they were in Willowbrook, Indiana, on Tony's home ground, and anyone who really knew him paid little heed to the rumors.

Olivia rehearsed her speech in her mind, preparing what she would say, how she would convince him to her way of thinking. She was busy wondering if she'd be able to shorten her five-year goal with his cooperation, when he tugged her into a dimly lit room that smelled of rich leather and Tony. Which, to her at least, was the scent of raw excitement. In this room she might get the break she'd been waiting for. All she had, all she would ever have, was her business. She'd given it everything she could, and it had given back all she had hoped for. Watching the business expand and grow was almost the same as having the life she really wanted. Almost.

TONY CLOSED THE door and leaned against it. It was funny, but before tonight he had never really noticed how lovely Olivia Anderson could be when she was excited, when she smiled…. Of course, he'd made note of and approved each one of her individual features. But he'd never before put them all together, taken them as the whole, and understood just how tempting an appearance she made.

Tonight she had her soft dark brown hair pinned back

in an elegant twist, though he knew it was nearly straight and fell to the tops of her shoulders. Olivia always looked elegant. She had more style and class than any woman he'd ever known. And it didn't matter that her eyes were dark brown, not green like his own. He liked her eyes. They showed her emotions clearly, showed the depth of her character and her passion. *Passion for her work, that is.*

He stepped away from the door and flipped on a single lamp that added a vague glow to the expansive room. It was cowardly of him, but he preferred to keep the lighting dim, to allow himself the cover of shadows while he presented her with his proposal. He said abruptly, "Have you ever been married, Olivia?"

She looked stunned by the question, but thankfully, not insulted. She shook her head. "No. Nor do I plan any such alliance in the near future."

"Alliance?" He found himself smiling again. She had the strangest way of looking at things, as if everything was a business venture.

Shrugging her shoulders, Olivia turned to find a chair, and sat down in one of a matching pair of chairs that sat adjacent to his massive desk. "My work is my life. I'm content that it stays that way."

Tony eased himself into the chair across from her, thoughtfully rubbing his chin. Though that was the answer he'd expected—anticipated—from her he was still a little disturbed. It wasn't right that a woman with her attributes, with her intelligence and personality, should spend her life alone.

"How old are you?"

She blinked, but she answered readily enough. "Twenty-six. Actually my five-year plan was only for-

mulated last year. By the time I'm thirty, I hope to have
created a very substantial business with at least three
more shops."

He waved that away. "You don't leave yourself much
room for a husband or children or any other personal
pursuits."

Frowning now, she surveyed him with a wary eye.
Tony knew he needed to retrench, to give her a bit more
room. The thing was, he'd never been a patient man.
When he wanted something, he wanted it now.

And he wanted a baby.

He reached out to take Olivia's hand, but she snatched
it back, then looked embarrassed that she'd done so.

"I don't understand the need for such personal questions. I assumed you were satisfied with our business
dealings…"

"More than satisfied. You run a very profitable business and your two existing shops have already benefited
my hotels. I don't see any problem in expanding them."

Olivia let out a breath and gifted him with a beautiful
smile. "Thank you. Obviously that's what I was hoping
to hear. I'll admit, though, you threw me with all that
personal stuff. I know it's important to understand your
associates, to make certain they won't suddenly change
their priorities and let their businesses flounder. If that
was your worry, let me assure you—"

"I'd like to have a baby."

His timely, or not so timely, interruption, left Olivia with her mouth hanging open and her brows lifted
high. It was a nice mouth, full and soft. He could see
her tongue, pink and moist and… She also had beautiful
skin, which of course would be a plus, along with her
excellent health and unbelievable ingenuity.

She cleared her throat, and with a small, nervous laugh, said, "I believe that might be an anatomical impossibility."

"Not if I can find the right woman to carry the babe."

She fell back in her seat, her hands braced on the arms of the chair, her mouth once again open. Right then, Tony decided to stop noticing her enticing mouth.

He was saved from having to say anything by the knock on the door. Tony waited until the server left the room and softly closed the door behind him before meeting Olivia's eyes again. She still looked stunned.

"I can practically hear your brain working, Olivia, and I want to assure you, before anything else, that this has nothing to do with your business. The third shop is yours, regardless. I'll sign the papers Monday morning and have a courier deliver them to you."

Olivia's mouth opened twice before she managed to say, "Thank you."

He poured her a glass of soda and handed it to her. "However, I would like to discuss something else with you."

"I gathered as much."

He grinned at her dry tone. "As I said, I want a baby. I have excellent people who can see to the daily running of my business now, so I no longer need to put in such long hours. I can more than afford to raise a child with every privilege, but not so many that the child is spoiled or doesn't understand the value of work. I'll be very careful to make sure the babe is raised with good morals and strong convictions, and—"

Olivia leaned forward in her seat and touched his arm. Tony liked her touch, felt it all the way to his stomach, and immediately cursed himself for reacting in a way he'd forbidden. Olivia, thankfully, seemed unaware of his plight.

"I have no doubt you'd be an excellent father, Tony."

He felt warmed to his soul by her praise. "Thank you."

"You're welcome. But what does all this have to do with me?"

His gaze flickered from her hand on his arm, to her face. "Why… I want you to be the mother."

He didn't get quite the reaction he'd expected. She covered her mouth with one graceful hand, and after a long, stunned pause, a nearly hysterical laugh emerged. Tony stood, caught her forearms and lifted her from her chair. "Olivia! Are you all right?"

She shook her head, and another giggle escaped. "Didn't I just make myself clear? Didn't I just say that my business was my life? I can't get married, certainly not to—"

"Married? Good God, I don't want to marry you!" He immediately realized how horrid that sounded, and quickly explained, "I just need you to carry my baby. After you've delivered it, you're free to do as you please. I'll make certain you can relocate any place you choose, but of course, you would have to relocate. I don't want any interference with raising my child, and neither of us would want a scandal. I thought the northwest would serve your purposes."

"You just want me to…"

"Carry the baby." He was still holding her arms and felt the way she tensed, the way her body trembled. He forced himself to release her. "As you said, it's anatomically impossible for me to do so, not that I have any desire to suffer through such a thing. God in all his wisdom knew men weren't cut out for such a trial. And I don't want you to think I'm being…well, untoward. There are medical procedures that would guarantee the planting of my sperm. Everything would be…"

She staggered back as if he'd struck her.

"I'm really messing this up, aren't I?" He ran his hand through his hair, then shrugged. "Believe it or not, this is the first time I've been uncertain of myself while presenting a business proposition. And that's exactly what this is, Olivia. A business deal." He waited, but when she remained silent, her eyes huge, he added, "Well? You could make this a little easier by saying…*something.*"

"I would. If I had any idea what to say."

He nodded, then slowly drew a deep breath. "You need time to think it over. Why don't we sit back down and I'll go over all my reasons for choosing you, all the benefits that will be yours if you agree, how I intend to handle the legalities involved, and—"

"That's an awful lot of ground to cover, especially considering it's near midnight. I put in a full day already, and plan to visit the office tomorrow morning." Her voice still sounded shaky, but she did resume her seat. Tony let out a short sigh of relief. She wasn't crying sexual harassment, she wasn't storming out. No, Olivia, bless her, was a reasonable woman. It was one of the qualities that had drawn him to her.

"First of all, you please me very much, Olivia. Not as a wife or for any other personal relationship, but as a gene donor. Your intelligence sometimes staggers me, especially given what few advantages you had in the world. The way you've excelled—"

"Excuse me?"

Tony lifted his brows, silently asking for clarification to her interruption.

"How, exactly, would you know anything about my advantages or disadvantages?"

Uh-oh. He could tell by the mulish set to her chin that he'd pricked her temper. He quickly thought about lying, then just as quickly discarded the idea. As he'd said, she was very intelligent. "I had you investigated. Now, just hear me out, then you'll understand how necessary it was for me to do so." He waited, and when she simply watched him, he began reciting his findings. "I know your parents, of moderate, low middle-class income, died in a river accident during a flood when you were only sixteen. I know you carried a full course load in college and kept a job at the same time, that you gained everything you now own by your own wits, without a single smidgen of aid from family or friends. In fact, there was no real family, and as far as I could discern, no close friends."

He continued, seeing her hold herself silent and still. She managed to look both proud and violated, and he lowered his tone even more, feeling his heart kick against his ribs. "You've never been involved with a man for any length of time other than during business to further your goals, you live a modest, understated lifestyle, apparently with quite a substantial savings account, and you keep to yourself. The only social gatherings you attend are business related."

She was quiet a long moment, and he felt regret, then determination.

"You've been very thorough."

"I had to make certain you would suit, Olivia. Please, try to understand. I don't want a woman who, after conceiving, will decide she wants to keep the baby, me, or both. Everything I learned about you proves you have absolutely no interest in tying yourself down right now or anytime in the near future. It was completely necessary that I find evidence to prove you wouldn't want a baby or a husband. And you don't, do you?"

She turned her head away to stare at the far wall. "That's right." After a shuddering breath, she glared at him again. "But I also have no interest in putting myself nine months behind. Carrying a child right now would sorely interrupt my schedule, not to mention what it would do to my reputation. I'd be gossiped about endlessly."

"Not so. Not if I promised to advance your five-year goal in one year. Not if I promised my backing to make certain you got a better start than you could ever have hoped to achieve, even in five years. Not if I have you relocated immediately, or provide for you to take an extended leave of absence."

"And you'd do all that?"

She was incredulous, but he didn't hesitate. "Of course. I'm very serious about this. I can afford to be generous, and I want the baby. Now. My birthday is November 14. Little more than a week away. By my following birthday, I want to be holding my own child. I'll be thirty-five then." He hesitated, a bit vulnerable in his feelings, but also knowing he needed to explain his desire fully to her.

"Thirty-five is getting up there. If I'm going to have a baby, it needs to be now. I'm still young enough to keep up with a toddler, but old enough to make wise decisions about the child's future. If I wait, even another year or two, I'll be close to forty before the child is born. I have to think long-term, of how my age will affect the child during his or her teenage years, when I'll be needed most."

She looked incredulous again, and her voice was strained when she asked, "You're worried about your... your biological clock?"

He felt disgruntled with the way she'd put it, but he nodded. "I suppose that's one way of looking at it."

"Why?"

"Why what?"

"Why do you want a child so badly? Why not just get a wife and do things the conventional way? And most of all, why me?"

Since she was still discussing it with him, Tony decided that was a good sign and took heart. He would win her over. After all, he had the advantage, being a man, and a more accomplished business dealer. He'd wrangled tougher deals than this when he'd first taken over the business.

But also true, he'd met few associates as tough as Olivia. It was one of the reasons he'd chosen her, one of the many things he admired about her.

He propped his elbows on his knees, leaned forward and forged on. "I want a child now because both my younger brother and sister have children. In fact, my brother only recently got his third child, a little boy, and it made me realize how much I was missing out on, how much I'll miss forever if I don't act soon. Don't get me wrong. I love being the doting uncle, getting to spoil the children and having them shout and jump around whenever I show up. It's good for the soul to be loved by a child, probably the biggest compliment a person can ever receive.

"But I have no real influence on the kids. And that's

as it should be. I'm not their father, I'm only an uncle, good for bringing gifts and giving occasional unimportant advice. I want to be the one doing the raising, leaving a part of myself behind."

Olivia smiled. "You're feeling your mortality?"

"I suppose. But that's not all of it. Being business minded, forming a successful company and being respected by your colleagues, that's nothing compared to raising a child. My brother and sister chose not to get too involved in the business, but they're raising wonderful, loving, beautiful children. And that's a much greater accomplishment than mine. I want to do something that matters that much." He faced her, holding her gaze, then added, "And I want to be loved the way they are. Unconditionally, completely."

"But no wife?"

"The kind of relationship my brother and sister have with their spouses doesn't come easy, I'm finding." He was so relieved she hadn't mocked him that he smiled. It was proving much easier to talk to Olivia than he had thought. Without thinking about it, he'd bared his heart as he had never done with any other person. "It's almost like they're one with the other. They share everything, support each other, and they have fun together. Honest, guilt-free fun. They seem to know each other's thoughts sometimes, they're so in tune.

"It amazes me. At times, I'm even jealous. I think it would be unbelievable to have that kind of relationship, and after seeing it, I don't think I could settle for anything less. But I haven't found a woman who would suit, and to tell you the truth, I'm sick of looking. Most women can't tolerate the amount of time I dedicate to the business, unless they're businesswomen also. But then, most of them are so wrapped up in company policies, in proving themselves in the male-dominant corporate world, they don't have time for me, much less a child."

He saw her flinch, and realized she'd taken the criticism personally. "Olivia. I don't mean to condemn. I realize it's more difficult for women than men, that the same rules seldom apply. And I understand the need to get ahead. I was the same way until recently."

"Until your business no longer required quite so much attention."

"That's right." He wouldn't apologize for accomplishing his goals. He'd earned his time off. "You know, there's a downside to being successful. I always get the feeling women are sizing up my bank account instead of me."

Olivia gawked. "Don't you have any idea how attractive you are? How personable you are?" She waved a hand in the air. "How...*sensual* you are? Believe me, with or without your hotel chain, you'd have women chasing after you."

Settling back in his chair, he whispered, "Not you."

Olivia looked as if she wanted to bite off her tongue, but no way would Tony let her take the words back, nor would he fill the silence for her. He suddenly felt predatory, and she was his prey. He could feel the surge of energy her words had given him, supplying an interest he hadn't felt in too long. It was invigorating, though he did his best to ignore the feelings and concentrate on his goals. Her compliments weren't necessary to his plan— but they did fill him with male satisfaction.

He waited, his expectation extreme, to see what she would say next.

Her gaze never wavered. "Well, no. As I said, I have

other goals in mind besides chasing down a man, regardless of his appeal."

Tony narrowed his eyes, watching her squirm as he pondered her words, then he smiled. "That's one of the reasons I chose you. Not once have you ever looked at me in a sexual way."

Olivia blinked again. "I don't think…"

"You know what I mean. I don't have to worry about you accepting my proposition with ulterior motives of trapping me, because you don't particularly want me." He waited, then asked, "Right?"

"Ah…right."

"But you are perfect to suit me. As I said, I admire your intelligence. With the two of us as parents, I know my son or daughter won't be lacking in that regard. You're also possessed of a great deal of savvy, something else to admire. You're healthy as a horse. I checked back as far as the last two years, and you haven't missed a single day of work. You have a kind and generous nature—everyone who knows you said so. And you're suitably built."

"Suitably built?"

She sounded as though she were strangling, and his gaze dropped to her legs. "Attractively built," he explained, allowing his gaze to linger for a moment. "Your legs are shapely, your shoulders squared, your back straight. You're large boned, not overly frail, but still very feminine. You're not prone to excess weight, but you are…sturdy. If I had a daughter, I wouldn't have to worry about her being too tiny, something I abhor in women. But she would make a very nice appearance. You always do."

Without his mind's permission, his gaze moved to her

breasts, outlined so nicely by the black knit dress she wore. Tony heard her say, "I'm small busted."

He managed a shrug when at the moment he felt far from indifferent, then had to force himself to look up at her face. Her look was challenging, and he grinned at her small show of vanity. "Not at all. You're...fine. Besides, if I have a son, it certainly won't matter, and if I have a daughter, I won't have to worry about all the young men chasing after her before I'm prepared to deal with it."

She gave an uncertain smile at his wit, then looked away, as if considering all he'd said. He felt his stomach cramping in anxiety. And something more. It was so damn ridiculous, but the more he talked with her, the more he liked her. She hadn't reacted as most women would have, she hadn't reeled in shock or shouted in dismay. She hadn't looked particularly insulted, either. She did look a bit disoriented, though. And somewhat contemplative.

He didn't want to, but he said, "Why don't you think about it? Take the weekend, and get back to me on Monday. If you agree, we can contact the doctor I've spoken with and have everything taken care of well before my birthday."

She winced. "A clinical procedure, you said?"

"Yes." He hastened to reassure her. "But from what I understand, it's not bad. I deliver my sperm—"

One slim eyebrow quirked. "Deliver your sperm?"

"Yes." He knew his face was heating and felt like a fool.

"How exactly is that accomplished?"

"Never mind." The order was ground out from between his teeth, and she chuckled. He'd never before seen her sense of humor; usually it was her determination to get ahead that she presented at a business meeting. He felt a touch of warmth at the sound of her laughter, then gave her an exasperated look and continued. "I deliver my sperm and they…well, I suppose it's much like visiting your gynecologist. Only instead of doing whatever it is they usually do, my sperm will be artificially planted—inseminated, it's called—and then we'll wait to see if it takes."

Olivia chewed her lips, then said slowly, "It sounds rather distasteful."

"I'll admit it isn't quite the way nature intended a woman to be impregnated, but it is certainly less personal, which is the main objective."

"Why?"

Her pointed look and bald question confused him. "Why what?"

"Why does it have to be so impersonal? Why can't you just…do it?"

"Do it?"

She made a sound of disgust. "Just impregnate the woman of your choice by nature's design."

He knew what she was asking, and felt an instant, unwanted tightening in his loins. Lust, damnable lust. He swallowed. "I want this to be as much of a business dealing as possible. Getting naked…" He felt himself harden and had to clear his throat. "Making love to a woman isn't at all a business proposition. It's very personal."

Olivia seemed relaxed now, arrogantly so, and somehow determined. Tony knew she was aware of his unease, and planned to take advantage of it—as any good businesswoman would do. She nodded, a pseudo show of understanding. Then she smiled. "I see."

He felt a twinge of anger at her for prodding him. "I should hope so."

"I believe I'll take your advice and think all this over. You said you don't want to hear from me until Monday?"

"I…" He had no idea what had come over her. She wasn't acting the way he'd expected, she wasn't even acting in a way he could have guessed or anticipated. He felt stymied. "You don't have to wait if you come to a decision before then."

"I think I probably will make up my mind before then. How about if I give you my decision tomorrow evening?"

He nodded, stiff-backed now, and forced a smile. He knew by her amused expression that she wasn't fooled, and that she was thoroughly enjoying his discomfort. "I'll give you my home number."

"No. I got the feeling you didn't want the fertile woman who would serve your needs to intrude on your life." He started to speak, but she forestalled him, her tone not nearly so sarcastic now. "Why don't I just give you my number instead—my privacy isn't nearly as threatened as your own. You can call me. Say, seven o'clock tomorrow?"

With her small chin raised, her straight nose in the air, she looked as proud and gutsy and almost as arrogant as he. She looked magnificent to him, and he merely nodded, distracted by thoughts of her feminine body rounded by his babe. They would make a beautiful, healthy child together. He reached out and touched her chin. "I wouldn't mind if the baby was a boy or a girl. I don't remember if I told you that."

She smiled, and seemed to relax again despite herself. "You didn't. But I had the impression it wouldn't matter." Then she went to his desk and picked up the gold pen from the marble holder and scrawled her home number across the desk pad.

"I had your number in my files."

"This way, you won't have to look it up."

He felt awkward now, but Olivia didn't seem to be suffering any such problems. She gave him a small salute.

"I'll be going home now. It's getting late, and I do have quite a bit to think over."

"I'll be a good father, Olivia." He hadn't meant to say that. He hadn't planned on trying to convince her what a good person he was. But he wanted the baby so badly, now, before he got any older, before he was left all alone in the world.

Again, she didn't mock him.

"I never doubted it." She looked almost sad, which didn't make any sense. "Tomorrow at seven, Tony." And then she was gone.

CHAPTER TWO

OLIVIA LAY IN bed that night, despising herself. She was a fraud and a manipulator and the worst kind of person for taking advantage of another. Tony had no idea the type of woman he was dealing with.

She'd known since she was sixteen that she would never have children. For her, it was physically impossible.

In the hospital, only hours before Olivia's mother had slipped away, she had explained about the condition that robbed her daughter of that particular function. Olivia wasn't a whole woman, could never lead a whole life. Having children was as beyond her as it was for Tony. And so she'd made her business her life. It was the only life she'd ever have.

Swallowing hard, Olivia felt the sting of tears as she recalled going to the hospital as a very young girl, her belly cramping painfully, the bleeding. It had been horrible, being examined by a male doctor. Beyond the pain, she'd felt violated and mortified. And then there were the days after when her mother and father had been so quiet, so withdrawn. She hated hospitals now, and she wouldn't go to the doctor unless it was absolutely necessary.

She thought she'd successfully put the past behind her, that she'd buried the wishes that couldn't come true. But now, with Tony's proposition, they all came flooding back. She wanted to be loved, to have children, to be desired by a special man who would accept her as a sensual woman.

She couldn't do anything about the first two wishes, but the third was a possibility.

It was rumored that Tony was an exceptional lover. She couldn't deny that the information had given her a few private fantasies of her own. After all, despite everything, she was still a woman, and on occasion, she'd seen him strictly as a man. But intimacy was something she'd neither expected nor wanted from Tony.

Until she'd heard his plan.

And now it was all she could think about. Tony obviously admired her, and that was something. It wasn't love, but it was a far cry from a totally detached sexual experience. She cared about Tony, thought he was a beautiful person and a very sexy man. And he wanted her as the mother of his child.

That was a precious gift all on its own, the highest of compliments.

Tony didn't have to know that she'd never be able to conceive a child, that she was infertile. She could insist on doing things the "natural" way, allow him to try his manly best for a couple of weeks, then confess it wasn't happening. He'd go on his way, none the wiser, find another woman, and have his baby by his designated time. She had not a single doubt of his eventual success. There were numerous women out there who would be more than willing to oblige him.

But he'd approached her, and she couldn't quite send him on his way. Not yet. Hearing him discuss his sperm in such a casual way, and talk of impregnating her as if he was referring to buying her coffee, had been somehow very arousing. Long dormant feelings had seemed to swell without her consent, and when she'd pictured him "supplying" his sperm, pictured the process necessary to such a deed, she'd felt a sexual heat at the image, along with an emotional tenderness that he wanted a child so badly. Together, the two feelings had conspired against her better sense.

She'd read every article she could ever find on him, and they were numerous. She'd tried to follow in his footsteps, as impossible as that seemed, because he was too dynamic, too overwhelming. And also, he loved his family, when she didn't even have a family to claim.

He was a good man, in every sense of the word. And she planned to corrupt him for her own purposes.

She was a fraud, but she wouldn't actually be hurting anyone. Other than herself.

IT HAD PROVED to be a long night and an even longer day. By seven o'clock, Olivia was so nervous her heart threatened to beat right out of her chest. When her phone rang, a good three minutes after seven, she jumped a foot. She forced herself to wait through four rings, feeling juvenile but determined not to look overanxious, and then she answered.

"Hello?"

"Olivia? It's Tony."

Just that, nothing more. She cleared her throat. "Hello." Her voice squeaked, but she didn't hang up. She could do this; she would grab the opportunity. But of course, she wouldn't accept anything from him, other than the additional shop he'd already agreed to. She would suffer no guilt for taking monetary advantage of him. She would only use his body, and only for a brief time.

"Hi." There was a long pause. "Have you made up your mind?"

She bit her lip, then took a deep breath. "I have. But I… I have a few stipulations I'd like to discuss."

She heard his indrawn breath. "Does that mean you'll do it?"

"Yes. But with a few—"

"I heard you. A few stipulations. Whatever it is, it's yours!"

His joy was impossible to ignore. The man was thrilled to be getting what he believed would eventually be his baby. Olivia swallowed her guilt and girded herself. "You probably ought to know what I want before you agree to it."

"I can afford whatever it is. I know you're not a greedy woman. You won't leave me bankrupt."

"I want to forget the doctor."

Deathly quiet. "Excuse me?"

Olivia knew she had thrown that out there awfully quick, but if she hadn't, she might never have said it at all. "I don't want to go through a doctor. I want… I want to do things naturally."

"Naturally?"

He sounded completely stupefied, and she nearly growled in frustration. "Yes, dammit! As in you and me, together, the way nature intended."

Not a single sound now. "Tony?"

"I'm here."

Olivia waited. Strangely enough, she could hear Tony trying to sort his thoughts as clearly as she could hear her own heart pounding.

Finally he said, "Would you mind telling me why?"

Olivia shook her head, realized how stupid that was and closed her eyes. "Of course not. I just…"

"No, wait. This isn't a conversation for the phone. Are you busy?"

"Now?"

"Yes, now. Believe me, I don't want to have to sleep on this without understanding."

"Of course not." Olivia looked around her apartment, hoping for inspiration, but found only the same quiet environment that always surrounded her. "I could meet you somewhere."

"No, I'll pick you up. I know where you live. It's—"

"It's in your records."

"Yes. I'll be there as soon as I can."

The phone clicked in her ear, and to Olivia it sounded like the beginning of a drumroll. Oh boy, too late to change her mind now. Then, because she had no idea how far away Tony was or how soon he would arrive, she rushed from the room to find something appropriate to wear.

When she reached her closet, she stopped, feeling ridiculous. What in the world would be considered proper dress for telling a man you'd agree to have his baby, but only if he'd pleasure you in the bargain?

Especially when you knew you were cheating him, and he wouldn't get a damn thing out of the deal, least of all, what he really wanted. A baby.

TONY STARED AT her apartment door, started to knock, then lowered his hand. Dammit all, why couldn't women ever do anything the simple way? He'd offered Olivia a straightforward, up-front deal, and she'd had to go and muddy the waters by asking that he actually attend her. Not that it would be a hardship, but he didn't want to get involved. He'd made his plans and he didn't want to deviate from them.

Still, Olivia Anderson—business barracuda and proprietor of two sensual, sexy lingerie shops—wanted to make love with him.

Who would have ever thought she'd ask for such a thing? She was always an enigma, a mix of styles and personalities, but even so, this development had thrown him for a loop. He'd sometimes wondered, when he'd been in her shop and seen the very stimulating garments she carried, if *she* ever wore any of those little bits of nothing, if she spoiled her body with silks and lace. It hadn't seemed likely. But now...

She had him totally confused, and he didn't like it one bit. He also didn't want to have to start looking for a new mother. Time was running out. He wasn't getting any younger, and if he didn't act soon, he'd be past the age of thirty-five when he brought his baby home.

No. He'd chosen her, dammit, and he wouldn't give up without at least trying to reason with her.

He ran a hand through his hair, then knocked sharply on the door. Immediately three doors opened. Olivia and two neighbors stared at him, the latter with narrowed eyes and curious expressions. Just what he needed, an engrossed audience.

Olivia tried for a smile, but it wasn't her best effort. "Come on inside."

"No." He shook his head, glaring at the neighbors. An elderly couple now stood at one door, and a younger woman with curlers in her hair at the other; they glared right back at him. Tony turned his gaze back to Olivia. "Let's go for a drive instead."

Olivia hesitated, seemingly oblivious to the onlookers, then finally said, "All right. Just let me grab my jacket."

Tony cursed under his breath. This was exactly what he'd wanted to avoid. He didn't need anyone speculating on his relationship with Olivia, because he'd never intended to have a relationship with her. In his simple, uncomplicated, male-inspired plan, he would have given her the address of the doctor and then heard from her later to learn if she'd conceived. He certainly hadn't intended to stand in her doorway providing entertainment to the masses. Not that three people could be considered a mass, but with their eyes glued to him, he felt very uncomfortable.

Olivia finally produced herself. She stepped outside the door, turned to make certain it was locked, then dropped her keys into her pocket. "I'm ready."

Then, as if on cue, she turned to the neighbors and nodded to each one in turn. "Hello, Hilda, Leroy, Emma. This is Tony Austin. Hopefully I'll be opening another of my shops in his hotel chain. Isn't that marvelous?"

Everyone nodded, their suspicions visibly dissipating and en masse they began to sing Olivia's praises. Tony did his best to make an exit, but he had to spend several minutes nodding in agreement before he could leave.

As they walked out of the building onto the street, he said, "That's the last time for that."

"What?"

"Meeting at your apartment. It gives rise to too much speculation. If we're not careful, we'll have that scandal yet."

He opened the door to his car for Olivia, but she didn't get in. "Does that mean you intend to meet with me again? You will agree with my terms?"

Pushy woman. Why had he never realized before just how pushy she could be? Savvy was one thing, pushy was another. He summoned his most noncommittal tone. "We'll see." He practically tossed her into the passenger seat, before going around to his own side.

"There's really not a whole lot to see, Tony. I don't like the idea of the clinical approach, that's all. If you can't see your way clear to actually touch me, then there's nothing to talk about."

He clenched his hands on the steering wheel. He clenched his teeth. He even clenched his thighs, but still, her words affected him. Touch her? He'd like to touch her all right—now, this very minute, with his hands, his mouth, his entire body. But he wouldn't. Oh, no. Touching was bad. Touching would only lead to more touching, and then he'd be in over his head and…

"Tony?"

"How about doing me a favor, Olivia? How about keeping your thoughts to yourself for a few minutes until we get off the road and then we'll discuss your…terms."

"All right."

She sounded too damn agreeable and that rankled, but at least she kept her words behind her teeth for all of five minutes, giving him a blessed chance to gain control of his libido. Then she asked in a very tentative voice, "Have you considered the possibility that I won't conceive? After all, there's no guarantee that I'll prove to be…fertile ground for you to…plant your seed. How much time are you willing to devote to trying to get me pregnant?"

Fertile ground? Plant his seed? Tony's five minutes of calm were suddenly shot to hell. How was it such bland, ridiculous terms sounded sexier than the most erotic whispered words he'd ever heard? Perhaps it was because of the envisioned result. He'd never before considered a woman carrying his child, and that must be the reason every word out of her mouth aroused him to the point of pain.

He cleared his throat and kept his gaze steady on the darkened road. "The doctor mentioned that several attempts may be necessary before the insemination takes."

"But doing it naturally? Is there a projected time span on that?"

He felt strangled. "I never actually asked him that."

"Perhaps you should."

Out of sheer necessity, he pulled the car off the main street and onto a small dirt road that led to a dead end. When Tony was younger, he and his brother had come here to make out with girls. In those days there was a wide cornfield, but it had been replaced by a small park with a street lamp. Obviously things had changed, but the premise was the same. Isolation.

Despite the fact that he was sweating, he left the car running, for it was a cold night in early November. He killed the lights, though, giving himself some illusionary concealment. When he turned to face her, he already had his mouth open to start his argument, but he was brought up short by the picture she presented.

Moonlight poured over her, revealing the sheen of dark hair, the shape of her ears, her high arched brows. Her eyelashes left long feathery shadows on her cheeks and shielded her eyes from his gaze. Her hands were folded in her lap. She appeared somehow very unsure of herself…

vulnerable. It wasn't a look he was used to, not from her. She lifted her gaze to his face, and once again he felt that deep frustration.

It wasn't that Olivia was beautiful. She was by far the most elegant woman he'd ever known, but she wasn't classically beautiful. He had dated more attractive women, made love to them, had long-standing affairs with them that had left him numb. But Olivia was the only woman whose personality, intelligence and disposition were attractive enough to entice him into asking her to carry his child. That was something. More than something, actually, when you figured it was usually looks that drew a man first, and the other, more important features of a woman that kept him drawn.

When he remained quiet, she said, "I know what I'm asking seems absurd. After all, you could have any woman you want, and after knowing you for so long, it's obvious you don't particularly want me. That's okay, because up until you mentioned your plan, I hadn't really thought about wanting you, either.

"But you see, I've made my career everything." Her hands twisted in her lap and her voice shook. "Just as you don't want any involvements now, neither do I. That's why the idea seems so perfect. I haven't taken the time or the effort to get to know very many men, and almost never on an intimate level. But starting a relationship isn't something I want, either. So I thought, maybe we could both get what we wanted."

Tony searched her face, feeling dumbfounded. Surely she wasn't suggesting what he thought she was. "I want a baby. What is it you want, Olivia?"

She turned her head away from him and looked out the window. Sounding so unlike herself, she whispered in a small voice, "I want a wild, hot, never-to-be-forgotten affair. For two weeks. If during that time I conceive, the baby will become yours, and we'll go on with the rest of your plans. If I don't conceive, I'll be on my way and you can find another woman who, hopefully, will prove more fertile. You won't owe me a thing. In fact, I'll consider myself well paid."

"*Well paid?* As in sex? You make yourself sound like a..."

"Like a woman who's desperate? I suppose I am." She finally met his gaze, her eyes huge and so very dark in the dim light. "I want to know what it's like to be with a man. But it has to be a man I trust, both with my safety and my health. I'm afraid you fit that bill."

The way she'd worded that had him frowning. "Olivia, you're not a virgin, are you?"

"No, but close." She held up two slim fingers.

"You've had sex with two different men?"

"No, I've had sex twice. With the same man, or boy rather. Neither time necessarily inspired an encore, but the second time I allowed myself to be convinced. I suppose I was hoping he'd improved from the week before, but he hadn't."

Tony found himself smiling. Olivia wanted to have sex with him, but she planned to keep a score card? "What did he do that was so wrong?"

"I'm not certain I know what was wrong, since I haven't yet experienced it *right,* but we were both practically fully clothed, cramped into the backseat of his car, and he grunted a lot. And by a lot, I mean for all of about three minutes. Continuously."

"Well..." Tony suppressed a laugh and tried to look serious. "I suppose I can improve on that, anyway."

"I should certainly hope so."

Tony couldn't help but chuckle at her serious tone. "I can't recall ever having a woman come right out and ask me to perform to her satisfaction. You're downright scary, do you know that?"

"I don't mean to be. And I don't mean to belittle that guy. We were in college, and he was majoring in football. It was probably my fault for not being more discriminating my first and second time, but even then I was very involved in getting ahead. Choosing an ideal mate simply took more energy than I wanted to give. At the time, it hadn't occurred to me to tell him specifically what I did and didn't like, which probably would have made things better. But now, since you've presented yourself on the proverbial silver platter, I can hope the results will be much more to my liking. After all, you have a reputation for fulfilling such expectations."

Reputation? He didn't even want to get into that with her. If she'd been listening to gossip... Well, at least the gossip appeared to have been flattering. He gave a groan that was loud and rife with confusion. "I just don't know, Olivia. I mean, this could all backfire."

She was all business, not moved in the least by his dramatic display of frustration. "You're afraid I'll be privy to your awesome technique, decide I can't possibly live without it or you and want to stake a marital claim?"

Actually she was pretty close to the mark. Not that he believed his technique was really all that awesome. But he knew women too often associated sex with love. He'd have to make it clear to her...

"I understand how you feel, Tony. I was concerned also, only for opposite reasons. Right now, you only want a baby, but as you see the woman who will give you your child grow, as you see the changes in her body—from you and your baby—are you certain you won't transfer your affection for the child to the mother?"

He stared stupidly. "I hadn't planned to watch any changes."

"No? But I understood, from books I read long ago, that the changes were the most fascinating part. You won't want to feel your baby kick? You won't want to be in on any prenatal pictures taken? I saw a documentary on TV once that was incredible. The ultrasound showed every small movement the baby made. You could even count toes and fingers."

His head began to pound with the growing complications. "I think… I think I may have more to think about."

"I'm sorry. Now I've confused you."

"You haven't confused me. It's just that I hadn't even considered prenatal observation. All my thoughts had been directed solely on the baby after its birth. But of course I'd want to see and feel the changes." He studied her closely. "You wouldn't mind?"

"Mind what?"

"If I watched you closely? If I observed all the changes in your body while my baby grew and if I examined those changes, took part in them?"

She was silent again, her fingers worrying the edge of her coat. Then she shook her head and in a hushed tone, she replied, "No. I wouldn't mind. If that was what you wanted—and if I got pregnant."

"Olivia, there's no reason to doubt you will. You're a healthy young woman, in the prime of your childbearing years. I've already been checked, and the doctor assures me I should possess sufficient potency to see the job done."

Olivia drew a deep breath and then held out her hand. "So. Do we have a deal?"

He was so aroused, he knew his hand would shake like the skinny branches on the naked tree shadowing the park, but he took her small palm in his anyway. His voice was little more than a croak when he said, "A deal."

"When do we start?"

She may as well have said, *when do you want to see me naked and touch me and come inside me,* because the effect was the same. He had trouble drawing a breath as images too erotic to bear shot through his already muddled brain. It took all his masculine power to bring himself back in order. "I suppose you should find out when you're…" He gulped, then forged manfully onward. "When you're most fertile. Do you, ah, keep track of such things?"

"Of course. All women do, if they don't want to be taken by surprise. How about if I let you know, then we'll see what works for both of us?"

It irritated him no end that she could speak so calmly after practically ordering him to pleasure her, to make certain he loved her in a way she would never forget. His brain was busy concentrating on the myriad ways he'd see the job done; he could barely form coherent words, damn her. "That's fine."

"I'll look at my calendar, find out exactly when I'm most likely to conceive, and then I'll call you."

"And you will take my home number now, Olivia. I don't want to miss your call if I'm not in the office when…when you're ready."

Her smile now was confident and made his insides twist. "Whatever you say, Tony."

Tony merely gulped, wondering if she would say that

when she was naked beneath him, her thighs open, her womb ready to receive him and his sperm, her body his. He kept silent, words well beyond him, and determined to see the job done as quickly as possible. It was the only way to save his sanity.

OLIVIA SPENT THE rest of the weekend boning up on fertility procedures. Though she didn't really have a regular cycle that could be timed and knew there was no chance she'd get pregnant, she thought it would still be easier to do things in the proper course, just so Tony wouldn't get suspicious. She had to be able to claim a day her period would be due, so Tony wouldn't think they'd been precipitous in their efforts.

When she decided to claim her best time would be that weekend, she suffered through a mixture of anticipation, guilt and plain old self-doubt. But she shook off her insecurities. Monday, after the new contract arrived, just as Tony had said it would, she used it as an excuse to get in touch with him.

She rushed the contract past her lawyer, insisting he give it top priority. If he thought her request unusual, he didn't say so. He returned it, with a few minor changes, the next day. Olivia forced herself to take another day to look it over, but she okay'd it without her usual relentless perusal, then picked up the phone to set up a business luncheon through Tony's secretary. It was only Wednesday morning, four days after she'd gotten Tony's agreement, and already it felt like forever since the deal had been made.

Just as she hoped, his secretary came back with the news that Tony could make time to see her at their usual restaurant. They'd met there before to discuss business, but today was different. Olivia left her office with the contract in her briefcase, along with a book on fertility and an anticipatory smile on her face.

TONY WAS ALREADY seated when she arrived. He'd chosen an isolated table at the back of the restaurant, away from prying eyes and ears. Olivia silently approved his choice, and forced herself to greet him in a normal, businesslike manner. Tony stood until she was seated, his eyes never leaving her, then waited while the waitress handed them menus. Very few things, including excitement, ever dampened her appetite so she ordered a lunch of rich soup and a salad.

Tony surveyed her a moment longer, then asked, "You have a problem with the agreement I sent you?"

Olivia waved away his concern. "We only made a few minor alterations."

"You always have alterations, Olivia, but I'd rarely call them minor."

She grinned. He was right, after all. She was a shark, but proud of it. "You can't expect me to blindly accept rules of your making, now can you, Tony? The revised contract will suit my purpose much better, as you'll see."

He gave her a small smile. "I don't doubt I'll approve it. I seldom win with you."

The way he said that, with a touch of pride, confused her. Could he have been telling the complete truth, not just trying to gain her acceptance of his plan? Did he truly admire her business skills? She felt warmed by the very idea, especially since most of her other male associates either seemed intimidated by her or resentful of her confidence.

She sent Tony a cheeky grin and said, "You win all

too often, anyway. Losing on occasion is good for your character."

"But winning's more fun." Then he held up a hand. "In this case, though, you didn't have to bother your lawyer. I already told you I'd give you whatever you wanted."

"No."

"Beg your pardon?"

Olivia wanted to make her point perfectly clear. Her conscience was nagging her enough about manipulating him emotionally. She certainly couldn't do so professionally, too. "I want this latest agreement to stand on its own, Tony. It doesn't have anything to do with…the other. Look over the agreement, judge it the same way you would any other, then get back to me."

"And you'll relent if I don't approve of your changes?"

"Absolutely not." She gave him another grin. "But I fully expect to have to work for them if they're not to your liking."

He looked amused, his chin propped in his palm, his elbow on the table. Then his gaze dropped to his napkin and he said, "Do you have anything else to discuss with me, Olivia?"

It was more than obvious what he was asking. She set down her salad fork and then pushed her plate to the side. After hefting her briefcase into her lap, she pulled out a slim volume on fertility and flipped the book open to the page she had marked.

Tony merely stared, his slouched position not so slouched now.

"I've been reading up on our latest subject, and it seems this weekend will be my most promising time.

According to this book, I should be ovulating on Saturday, give or take a day."

"So you're due in two weeks? Right at the end of the deadline you set?"

Her two-week time limit. Get her pregnant by then, or the deal was off. She almost groaned at her own audacity.

"That's right. Two weeks exactly." Actually she'd pulled that ridiculous number out of the air, just as she'd done with the deadline. She wouldn't conceive, not with only one ovary. And her periods were irregular, often nonexistent, so there was no true time frame. You couldn't get pregnant if you didn't ovulate, which was a fact she'd been living with for a very long time.

It was pure coincidence that she'd set up her most fertile time to fall precisely within her deadline. She glanced up and wished she wore reading glasses, just to provide her with a bit of camouflage. But despite her embarrassment, she was determined to follow through. Tony had been more than a little reluctant to agree to her terms, and if this was to be her one big romantic rendezvous, she wanted his wholehearted involvement. She *needed* his wholehearted involvement. As with any deal, success required planning. And Olivia had formulated her plan well. By the time she was finished with him, Tony would be beyond ready; he'd be anxious.

She braced herself and said, "I think I can get a few days away. How about you?"

"A few days?"

"Well of course." Olivia frowned at him. "According to the book, an extended amount of time might be necessary. Listen to this. *The couple should have intercourse at least twice with an interval of six hours be-*

tween. You see? There's no reason to do it if we aren't going to do it with proper enthusiasm. Things like this can't be rushed."

"I, ah…"

"There's something else, too."

Tony raised his brows, not deigning and frankly not able to verbalize at this point.

Olivia forged on. "It also mentions you should do without sex until then to allow your sperm count to build to a higher level." She paused, taking a small sip of her tea, then pinning him with her gaze. She felt horribly deceptive, but determined just the same. This was to be *her* time, and hers alone. "You should be celibate until we're together. Will that be a problem?"

"Olivia…"

She hurried to explain, wanting him to understand the supposed reasoning behind her request. It wouldn't do for him to know her remarks were prompted by a possessive attitude, rather than a legitimate concern. "You don't want to deplete your sperm, Tony, now do you?"

"No."

"Good." Olivia didn't want to admit to the relief she felt, and she certainly didn't want Tony to witness it, so she busied herself by smoothing back another page. Tony looked down and his eyes narrowed at the number of lines she'd highlighted. Olivia quickly tried to close the book, but Tony's finger got in the way.

"What's this? Other interesting facts you've made note of?" His voice sounded deeper than usual, and a little hoarse.

Olivia was very careful not to look at him. "A few."

"They apply to us?" When she only nodded, he said, "Please, enlighten me."

"Perhaps it would be better to wait until later—"

"But I'm dying of curiosity."

His mocking tone brought her head up. "All right." She held the book before her and made a show of clearing her throat. She'd bluffed her way through more than one difficult situation without losing her poise. "It also says, *For further assurance of success the woman should lie still on her back for several minutes, preferably with the man still inside her, with her legs bent at the knee to allow a pool of sperm to remain near the cervix.*"

Tony had just taken a sip from his glass as Olivia began her discourse. When he choked, spewing water across the small table, Olivia leaned over and pounded on his back, nearly unseating him. He caught her hand and stared at her, his face turning ruddy, until she finally subsided and pulled away.

Olivia felt satisfied with his reaction. If she could keep him off guard, he wouldn't stand a chance of dissecting her motivation and discovering her perfidy. "Surely you know all this already? It was your idea after all."

"No." He vehemently shook his head. "My idea did not include *staying still inside you for several minutes.*"

"You find the idea repellent?" She did her best to look affronted, knowing his problem now didn't stem from distaste, but rather from the intimate level of the conversation—and possibly his response to it. "You would prefer, of course, that I lie on a sterile table while a damn white-coated doctor probed me with a syringe?"

"Olivia..." He reached across the table and took her hand again. "I don't think you have any idea how all of this is affecting me. I'm only a man, you know, and I'm not accustomed to this sort of conversation."

His hand felt warm and dry and very large. Olivia closed her eyes, then experienced another wave of guilt. She was twitting him mercilessly for her own benefit, and he was having difficulty surviving it. "I'm sorry. I shouldn't carry on. The truth is," she added, hoping just a touch of honesty would help smooth over the situation, "I'm a little uncomfortable, too. I'm trying to be as straightforward and open about this as I can, so that we can look at it in a purely businesslike fashion."

"I know, and I understand." He hesitated, then released her fingers and leaned back in his chair. His gaze seemed hot, and very intense. "But I don't think it's going to work, Olivia."

CHAPTER THREE

HER HEART SKIPPED a beat and a swelling sensation of near panic threatened to suffocate her. Had she pushed him too far? "You want to call it off?"

"No!" He abandoned his casual pose and was again leaning toward her. "No, I just don't think I'm going to be able to look at this as anything *but* personal. I've thought about it a lot over the past few days and I don't believe it's at all possible to sleep with a woman—a woman I know and admire—and pretend that it isn't the least bit intimate. I do think we can get past that, though, if we both try."

"I'm not sure I understand." At least he wasn't canceling on her, and that was all that really mattered.

"I think we should look at this as something of an adventure. So long as we limit our socializing to the… ah…process, we should be able to keep things in perspective."

"I see. No friendly visits between appointments."

"Exactly. We'll meet when we have to in order to see things through, but the rest of the time our relationship, such as it is, will remain the same."

"Which is strictly business."

"Yes."

Olivia toyed with her fork. For some ridiculous reason she felt insulted. Her tone was a touch acerbic when she remarked, "That serves my purposes just fine. I'll enjoy you while you employ all your manly skills to impregnate me." A mental image formed with her words, and she had to catch her breath. "As to the rest, if you'll recall, I don't have time for frivolous dating."

He curled his hand into a fist and searched her face, looking as if he wanted to say more, but then he shook his head, and said, "All right, we're agreed then. And this weekend is fine for me, also. Should we begin Friday evening?"

"I'll be at the Southend location that day, but I'll finish up about six."

"That's good for me." He reached out to straighten his knife and fork, and Olivia saw that his hand was shaking. She shook, too, in impatience. "I'll make arrangements for us somewhere private, then meet you there. That way, no one will see us together, which I think is important. We need to maintain our social distance."

It was the physical closeness that interested Olivia, not the social distance, so she nodded. "I'd just as soon no one suspected us of enhancing our relationship, too. I don't want to start any nasty gossip and end up in a scandal."

He chuckled. "At least you wouldn't have to worry about your folks catching wind of it. My entire family lives nearby, and they all think they need to straighten out my life. Anytime the mere hint of a scandal surfaces, I find them all at my door ready and willing to butt right in."

"And what we're conspiring to do goes beyond the 'hint' stage. It *defines* the word *scandalous*."

"Which means my family would have a field day."

Olivia was fascinated. She'd often wondered what

kind of upbringing Tony had, especially in light of the fact she had no family at all. He was such a good person, she supposed his family had to be pretty good, too. "So they have no idea what you're planning? I mean, with the baby and all?"

"Hell no. My family is old-fashioned. They definitely believe in doing things in the right order."

"Marriage first?"

"Yep." He grinned again, that ready grin that made all the ladies of his acquaintance smile in yearning. "They've been very diligent in trying to get me married off. Every damn one of them has produced at least three prospective brides. I can't make them understand that I'd prefer to do the choosing myself when I decide the time is right."

Olivia suddenly realized they'd already broken their new set of rules. Learning about Tony's family definitely went beyond business and was dangerous besides; the more she knew about him, the more fascinating he seemed. It had taken her no time at all to become accustomed to wanting him, to accepting him as a desirable man. Every day, every minute it seemed, her feelings for him grew. She began to wonder if those feelings hadn't been there all along, waiting to be noticed.

It was a very scary prospect. She couldn't afford, professionally or emotionally, to get overly involved with him. So she changed the subject, away from his family, and tried to dwell on something less intimate.

Their soup was delivered and throughout the rest of the lunch they discussed Olivia's new shop and Tony's proposed agreement. To his credit, Tony argued fiercely, but Olivia wore him down. The meal ended with Tony promising to have his lawyer okay everything and return the finalized papers to her very soon.

They stood on the curb outside the restaurant, the lunchtime crowd flowing around them, and Tony touched her arm. "Friday at six."

"I'll be ready."

He started to move toward his car, then halted and turned back to her. "I hope you know what you've gotten yourself into."

Olivia never wavered. As with all her decisions, she didn't allow room for regrets. She held his gaze and nodded.

"Good. Because I think we'll barely make it inside the door before I'll lose my control. You've pushed a lot on this deal, lady, more than any before. You've demanded that I give you pleasure, and that I spend a great deal of time doing it." He reached up and flicked a finger over her cheek, so very briefly. "Friday night, you're liable to find I have a few demands of my own."

Olivia watched him stride away, and then as a smile spread over her face, she whispered, "Oh, I do hope so, Tony, I really do."

DISGUSTED WITH HERSELF, Olivia knew she wasn't going to get any real work done. She'd spent Friday afternoon having her legs waxed and her nails manicured, then left the shop early to go home and shower and change. She'd meant to get back in time to do some inventory, but she'd lingered over choosing an outfit, trying to find something simple and attractive, while not wanting to display too obviously her wish to be appealing. By the time she returned to the shop, she had only a little time before Tony was due to pick her up.

After saying good-night to her store manager, she settled down to look over the most recent batch of applications for new jobs, thanks to Tony. She'd already decided to promote one woman to manager of the new store, but then she had to fill that woman's position. Olivia was fortunate in always having found excellent employees. She'd learned from Tony that you got what you paid for, and she'd always been generous with her benefits.

As soon as thoughts of Tony entered her mind, she started daydreaming again. She should have bought a new outfit for today, she thought, looking down at her simple beige wool skirt and matching tunic. The top had a row of pearl buttons that started just above her breasts and ended at the hem. As she imagined Tony undoing those buttons, one by one, she shivered.

She'd tossed aside her normal panty hose in favor of silky stockings with a pale rose satin garter, a big seller for the shops. She had even dabbed on perfume in very naughty places. Her pumps were midheeled and made her legs extra long and shapely. To balance the effect, she'd left her hair loose, parted in the middle, and it fell to rest against the top of her shoulders. She was so nervous, she'd long since chewed off any lipstick she might have applied, and decided against fussing with more.

She'd probably feel more confident, she thought, if she'd worn something daring, something sinful and sexy. Her selection of underclothes often gave her confidence, especially when no one knew she was wearing them.

She walked to a rack and picked up a teddy that fairly screamed enticement with rosette patterns of lace across the breasts and between the legs. She fingered the material, feeling it slide through her hands. She drew in a deep, shuddering breath imagining it sliding through Tony's hands.

When she heard the bell over the door chime, even though the Closed sign was up, she jerked, then quickly spun around to face the door.

Tony walked in, his hands shoved deep into the pockets of his dress pants, and she could only stare. His gaze connected with hers, and he started forward with a steady, determined stride. He didn't stop at the counter, but came to the rack where she stood, her lips parted, the teddy still in her hand.

His eyes moved over her, lingering on the teddy, and he asked, "Are we alone here?"

She nodded. "I was just finishing up—"

He laid a finger against her lips. There was no smile on his mouth, no welcome in his eyes. He looked intent and determined and very hungry. He slid his hand into her hair and cupped her head, stepping closer until his pant legs brushed her skirt. And then he kissed her.

IT HAD BEEN worth the wait.

He couldn't remember ever feeling so anxious for a woman. It was the teasing, he was certain, that had brought him low. Olivia, in her usual forceful, decisive way, had seduced him most thoroughly. Odd, but he hadn't ever thought of her business manner carrying over into something so personal. He knew so damn little about her personal life.

Such as whether or not she really ever wore a garment as sexy as the teddy in her hand.

That was something he could soon find out. Because it was obvious she used the same tack of gaining what she wanted whether it was business or pleasure. And she wanted him.

That thought had plagued him all week, and it had been all he could do to maintain a touch of control over himself. What he needed, he thought, was a long, hot, intimate evening alone with her. And then he'd be able to get her out of his system and put her, and his purpose for being with her, in proper perspective. But damn, she tasted good.

He knew he should pull back, give her time to catch her breath, but she wasn't fighting him, wasn't behaving in a particularly shocked manner. She merely stood there and gave him free rein. He slanted his mouth over hers again, then lightly coasted his tongue over her bottom lip. She groaned.

Apart from the one hand he had in her hair and his mouth, Tony didn't touch her. Olivia's hands remained at her sides, almost as if she was afraid to move them. He leaned back and stared down at her face. Her dark brown eyes were half closed, the thick lashes seeming to weigh them down. Her lips were still parted, and her cheeks were flushed. He liked that.

"We're going back to my house."

She blinked twice, then cleared her throat. "I assumed you'd rent a place…"

"My home is very private. And I don't want to be running around town. Too many people know me. Besides, today is my birthday. Someone might decide to surprise me with a bottle of champagne or some such nonsense, and once we're alone, I don't want to be disturbed."

Her eyes widened. "Happy birthday. I didn't realize… You should be celebrating with someone special."

He started to tell her she was special, almost too special, but he bit back the words. "It's okay. More than okay." He bent to kiss her very quickly. She looked disappointed when he pulled away. "I can't think of a better way to spend the day. You're giving me the best gift imaginable."

No sooner did he say it, than he realized she might misunderstand. So he quickly clarified, "A baby, I mean."

"I knew what you meant."

But he was lying, to both her and himself. Right now, he wanted her so much, thoughts of conception were taking a backseat to good old-fashioned lust. He still wanted his baby, very much, but he found himself hoping it would take a couple of tries before they found success. He wanted—needed—to expend all his desire for her so he could concentrate on other, more important things.

Olivia looked slightly rattled, which was new for her. She reached behind herself to feel for a hanger, then slipped the teddy onto it and back on the rack. Tony looked around, taking in the ambience of the shop. He'd been in them all, of course, but still, she never ceased to amaze him with her organization and natural ability for merchandising.

She did a remarkable amount of business, and it was easy to see why.

Everything was displayed in a way that bespoke intimacy with a touch of class. Mannequins were shyly posed in every corner, their perfect forms draped in soft pastel shades of silk and satin, musky scents filled the air from the perfume rack and the shelves of sachets. Every inch of space was utilized to the best advantage, so nothing looked crowded or busy.

Olivia cleared her throat, drawing his attention. "I

was thinking of ordering more of these," she said, indicating the teddys. "I knew they'd be a big seller, but this week we went through more than even I had anticipated. They're just so comfortable."

"And incredibly sexy?"

She nodded. That Olivia felt the need for small talk proved her nervousness, and Tony didn't want her nervous. He also couldn't stop himself from asking the question of the day. "How do you know they're comfortable, Olivia? Do you wear these things?" He reached over and caught at the lace edging the leg of the teddy, then rubbed his thumb over it.

Straightening her spine, a gesture of defiance he was beginning to recognize, she nodded. "Of course I do. I've personally tried everything I sell."

Tony took another quick survey of the shop, and this time his gaze landed on a midnight black bra and panty set, the bra designed to merely cup the fullness of the breast, leaving the nipples exposed, and the panties with a very convenient open seam. He felt his stomach constrict, and knew he had to get her out of the shop before his libido exploded. "Are you ready to go?"

Appearing as flustered as he felt, she nodded and reached behind the counter for her coat. Tony helped her slip it on, then took her arm to guide her out. She was trembling, and he wanted to reassure her somehow, but as she locked up the shop, he saw that her nipples were peaked against the soft wool of her tunic, and any coherent conversation escaped him. He wanted to touch her breasts, to see if they felt as soft as they looked. He wanted to taste her, all of her, and he wanted to give her the pleasure she'd requested.

At first, it had seemed like a tall order, and a bit in-

timidating. No woman had ever come right out and told
him to give her the level of satisfaction she expected.
It was enough to shrivel many a man. But he wasn't a
man to cower under pressure, and the more he'd thought
of it—and ways to see the job done—the more excited
he'd become by the prospect. Going head-to-head with
Olivia during business always exhilarated him. Doing
so in bed would be even better. He felt challenged for
the first time in a long time, and what red-blooded male
could resist a challenge?

Besides, he decided, as they drove from the parking
garage, if he didn't get it right the first time, he'd have
plenty of time to keep trying. That thought brought a
grin.

"What?"

He glanced at Olivia and realized she was watching
him. She looked wary now, and a little self-conscious.
"Hey, you're not having second thoughts, are you?"

"No, but I'll admit that grin of yours is a little un-
nerving."

He heard the slight tremor in her tone and reached
over to take her hand from her lap. "I'm just…"

"Eager?"

"That's a very appropriate word." He grinned again.
"What about you?"

She drew a quavering breath, then whispered, "Yes."

Tony had to put both hands on the wheel. Never had
one simple word affected him so strongly. He wanted
to speed, to race to his house, but the streets were con-
gested with holiday shoppers. With Thanksgiving less
than two weeks away, it seemed as if everyone had a
reason to be out on a Friday evening. Curse them all.

"How far do we have to go?"

"It's about a twenty-minute drive." Twenty minutes that would seem like two hours. "Are you hungry?"

"No."

"Are you sure? I could stop at a drive-through."

She glared at him. "No. I am not hungry."

He liked the idea that she was as anxious to get under way as he. They stopped at a traffic light and he said, "Well, then how about scooting over here and giving me another kiss? It's the truth, I desperately need something to tide me over."

Her chest rose and fell in several deep breaths, then she scooted. Tony caught her mouth, pressing her back against the seat and this time skipping the teasing. He slid his tongue into her mouth and stroked her deeply. Olivia's hands came up to rest on his shoulders, and then curled to pull him closer.

The light changed, and at a snail's pace, traffic moved.

They continued to kiss and cuddle and touch at every opportunity, and Tony knew they were making each other just a bit crazy. But he didn't call a halt to the touching, and finally, after excruciating frustration, he pulled into his long driveway. It had taken twenty-five minutes, and every minute had been a form of inventive foreplay. Olivia had her eyes closed and appeared to be concentrating on breathing. Her coat lay open, her knees pressed tightly together, and her hands, where they rested on the seat on either side of her, shook.

Tony said very softly, "We're here."

She slowly sat forward and surveyed his home through bleary eyes. She was quiet for long seconds, then whispered, "Oh, Tony. It's beautiful."

He was pleased with her praise. "I had it built a few

years ago. I made certain as many trees were left as possible."

"It almost seems a part of the landscape."

That had been his intention. Built of stone and wood and slate, the house blended in with the background, sprawling wide with only one level, and surrounded by oaks and pines and dogwoods. "Now, with the trees bare, you can see the house better. But in the spring and summer, it's nearly hidden."

He hit the remote to open the garage door, then drove inside. The four-car garage held only one other car, and was very quiet.

When he opened Olivia's door for her and she stepped out, he couldn't help but kiss her again. And this time, since they were assured of privacy, he gave his eager hands the freedom to roam. His palms coasted over her back, feeling her warmth even through the thickness of her coat, then scooped low to cuddle her soft rounded buttocks.

Olivia sucked in a deep breath and moaned when he brought her flush with his body. He knew she could feel his erection, knew she was reacting to it, and with every rapid pulse beat of his body, he thought: this is Olivia, the cool businesswoman, the shark, and she's pressing against me, trembling and wanting more. It was wonderful and strange and so exciting he almost couldn't bear it. He felt his body harden even more, felt himself expanding, growing. He felt ready to burst.

He back-stepped her toward the door leading into his house. Now that he was this close, he certainly didn't want to make love to her in the garage. But when he lifted his head, his eyes were immediately drawn to her heaving breasts, and he saw again her stiff little nipples.

Her coat was open down the front, and he pushed it farther aside, then gently cupped her breasts, shaping them, weighing them in his palms. She was soft and warm and her nipples were pressed achingly against the fabric. She tilted her head back against the garage wall and made a small sound of pleasure and need.

Before he could give his mind time to approve his actions, he unbuttoned three small pearl buttons, and peeled aside the soft wool material. Her bra was lace and satin, a pale coffee color, but so sheer he could see the entire outline of her. It nearly sent him over the edge. He brushed his thumb over her nipple, gently, teasing, and watched her tremble. He lost control.

He growled low in his throat, pulled the bra down so it was cupped beneath her pale breast, pushing her up, seeming to offer her to his mouth, and then he brushed his thumb over her again. She panted as he toyed with her, building the suspense, the excitement.

"Tony."

It was her small, pleading voice that brought him around. He couldn't wait much longer to taste her, but neither should he be rushing things. He kept his eyes on her beautiful body, on the breast he'd bared, then wrapped his arm around her waist to guide her inside. He reached for the doorknob and turned it, then jerked when he heard a screamed, *"Surprise!"*

He looked up and saw his entire family, balloons in the background, streamers floating around. It took everyone a second to realize the misfortune of the entire scene, and then little by little, expressions changed. He saw his mother gasp, his grandfather chuckle. His brother was now wearing a wide grin.

His own face must have looked stunned, and he

couldn't find the wherewithal to move. Both he and Olivia seemed frozen to the spot. Then he saw his six-year-old nephew turn his gaze to Olivia, and watched as his sister-in-law rushed over and slapped both hands over her son's eyes. Tony came reluctantly to his senses. He slammed the door shut, then tried to get his mind to function in some semblance of order so he could figure out what to do.

"Oh my God."

He glanced down at Olivia, her hands covering her face, her shoulders shaking. She said again, "Oh my God." Her breast was still uncovered, and more than anything, he wanted to taste that small pink nipple. He wished his family elsewhere, but when he heard the sudden roar of hysterical laughter inside, he knew not a single damn one of them would budge. Meddling bunch of irritants.

"Oh my God."

Tony frowned, his gaze still on that taunting nipple. He was beginning to feel like Pavlov's dog. "Are you praying or cursing?"

She peeked at him from between her fingers, her expression as evil as any he'd ever seen. Through gritted teeth, she said, "You promised me privacy, Tony. There must be fifty people in there."

"No. If everyone's present, and I suspect by the low roar that they are, there's ten, maybe twelve total. It only seems like more because a portion of them are kids. Noisy kids." She dropped her hands and glared at him. She seemed totally oblivious to the fact that her body was bared. Tony, still retaining a death grip on the doorknob in case anyone tried to open it, reached over to cup her with his free hand. She jerked.

"Tony."

How her voice could change from cold and angry to soft and pleading so quickly, he didn't know. "One small taste, Olivia, okay? Then I can sort the rest of this out."

She didn't appear to understand, which was probably the only reason she didn't protest.

Tony shook his head, then bent down and slowly drew his tongue around her nipple. She gasped, and he gently sucked her into his mouth, holding her captive with his teeth. Her flesh was hot and sweet and her nipple was so taut it pained him. He licked his tongue over her, flicking, teasing, making her nipple strain even more. When she moaned, he suckled, holding her close to his body.

Olivia's hands settled in his hair just as a discreet knock sounded on the door. "You might as well come in, Tony. I sent the kids into the kitchen for some punch."

Tony cursed, dropped his forehead to Olivia's chest, then felt himself rudely pushed aside as she frantically tried to right her bra and button herself up. "Calm down, Olivia, it's all right."

From the other side of the door, he heard his brother say, "Yeah, Olivia. It's all right. We're glad you're here for the party."

Tony growled. "Go away, John!"

"All right. But I'll be back in two minutes if you don't present yourself. Both of you."

Now that she was decently covered, Olivia sent her gaze searching around the garage, and Tony realized she was hoping to find a means of escape. "Forget it. They won't let me leave, therefore, you're stuck, too."

"But you don't want this," she wailed, her hands twisting together at her waist. "This is your family, Tony, part of your private life, and I don't want to intrude. We both agreed I wouldn't intrude."

Tony sighed, knowing she was right, but also accepting the inevitable. "I'll find some way to throw my family off the scent. Just play it cool. As far as they need to know, we're business associates and nothing more."

Olivia's look told him how stupid she thought that idea was. "Play it cool? After what they saw us doing?" She shook her head. "No. I'm not going in there."

"Olivia..."

"They *saw* us!"

He shrugged. "It's none of their damn business. If anyone gets impertinent with you, tell them to bug off. Or better still, just tell me, and I'll handle them."

She didn't look at all convinced, and Tony touched her face. "I've seen you at work, lady. You can easily handle a few curious relatives. You're a shark, remember? Now pull yourself together."

She drew a deep breath and gave an uncertain nod. Tony dropped his gaze to her mouth, then had to swallow a curse. His fingertips slid over her lower lip. "Do you have any idea how frustrated I am right now? How badly I'm hurting?"

Olivia seemed to regain some of her aplomb. "No more than I am, I assume. After all, this was my idea. You, as I recall, were very reluctant to agree."

"I was an idiot." He turned to the door again. "I suppose I can suffer through a few hours. How long can a family birthday party last anyway?"

OLIVIA TRIED FOR a serene smile as Tony's family lined up to meet her. Tony waited until he had everyone's attention, then said with astounding sincerity, "Everyone, this is Olivia Anderson. She's a business associate. She owns the lingerie shops Sugar and Spice in the hotels, and today we were working on finalizing the placement of one more."

Olivia held her breath, but no one called him on the obvious cover-up. Then Tony began pointing out people, too many of them for Olivia to keep straight, though she was usually very good with names and faces. The men seemed inclined to leave her be, their interest caught by a football game someone had turned on. Other than a wave in her direction when Tony introduced her, and a few ribald comments to Tony and the kind of *business* he conducted, they stayed on or near the family-room couch and the large-screen television.

The women, however, hovered. They were anxious to talk to her, and Tony, with little more than an apologetic glance, abandoned her when the men called him to watch a play. Sue, Tony's mother, invited her to join the women and children in the kitchen.

To Olivia's surprise, no one was the least bit unpleasant, despite what had happened. "I'm sorry if we've upset your plans," Sue said. "Tony, of course, didn't know we'd planned a party. And we didn't know Tony had made other arrangements."

Tony's sister, Kate, and sister-in-law, Lisa, both chuckled. Kate said, "If you could have seen his face! Well, we certainly did surprise him."

Olivia couldn't help but smile. Both women were very adept at keeping busy in the kitchen, and dodging the kids who ran in and out. "It was rather awkward."

Lisa laughed. "For us, too. Of course, John is just like Tony, and never lets a chance go by to goad his brother."

"And they both goad me. Endlessly!" Kate shook her

head. "But now I have enough ammunition to twit Tony for a good month."

Olivia decided, even though their comments weren't malicious, it was time to change the subject. She didn't want to have to explain her business with Tony. "Could I help you do something?"

Sue was arranging ham slices on a platter, Kate was putting glasses and napkins on a tray, and Lisa was trying to balance a tiny infant in one arm and dish up potato salad with the other. She turned with a relieved smile when Olivia made her offer.

"If you wouldn't mind holding the baby, that would be a big help."

Olivia balked. "I, uh, how about I help with the food instead? I've never held an infant before."

"Piece of cake, believe me. And he's such a good baby, he won't give you any problems."

Before Olivia could form another denial, the baby was nestled in her arms. His mother had wrapped him in a soft blue blanket, and other than one tiny hand and a small, pink face, the child was completely covered. Olivia cuddled him carefully when he squirmed, settling himself with a small sigh that parted his pursed lips and made Olivia smile.

She felt a pain in her chest that had nothing to do with physical ailments and everything to do with a breaking heart.

One by one, the women left the kitchen to carry the trays into the dining room, and Olivia welcomed the privacy. She couldn't recall ever holding such a small baby before, and her curiosity was extreme. She carefully pushed the blanket back from the baby's head, then rubbed her cheek against his crown. So soft, she thought, wondering at the silky cap of hair. And the scents. Never had she smelled anything so sweet, so touching, as a baby. She wanted to breathe his scent all day. She had her nose close to him, gently nuzzling him, when Tony walked in.

"What are you doing?"

Olivia jerked at the alarm in his tone. She didn't have time to answer him, though, not that she would have told him she was smelling the baby. Lisa came back in then and thanked her. "I'll put him in his crib now that the other kids are all sitting down to eat. I worry when they're all running around that they'll wake him up. You know how kids are."

Olivia didn't know, but she could see Tony hadn't liked her holding the baby. Lisa left the room, and Tony whispered, "Do you think it's a good idea for you to do that?"

Olivia knew exactly what he meant. He was concerned she'd start wanting a baby herself if she held one. She could have told him it was too late for that worry, that it didn't matter. She could want forever and never get what she wished. At least, she couldn't get a baby. Now passion, it seemed Tony was ready to give her that in huge doses. What she'd felt during the ride and in his garage… It was almost everything she'd ever wanted with a man. Everything but the real emotion. Everything but love.

It angered her that he was pushing her and worrying about something that would never be, but she held in her words of resentment and instead, she shrugged. "Would you have rather I'd refused? What excuse would I give?"

He tunneled his fingers through his hair, then looked

toward the dining room. "Come on. They're waiting for me to eat."

"This is going to be impossible, isn't it, Tony?"

"No. Everything's fine."

He didn't sound at all convincing, and Olivia had to wonder if John or Kate had already been teasing him. When they entered the dining room, Olivia looked around. She hadn't had the chance to actually see the inside of Tony's house, but now that she could look, she wasn't at all surprised. Everything, every dish, every piece of furniture, the wallpaper, all showed excellent taste, but without the blatant stamp of wealth. Tony never flaunted his financial success, and other than the size of the sprawling house, it showed only a sense of comfort and functional ease.

The house was very open. Each room seemed to flow into the next, and there were windows everywhere. The furniture was all highly polished mahogany. As little Maggie, who Olivia guessed to be around three, walked to her seat with one hand on the buffet, she left small smudge marks in her wake. Tony only scooped her up and tossed her in the air. The little girl giggled, wrapped her pudgy arms around Tony's neck and planted a very wet kiss on the side of his nose. He pretended to chew on her belly, then sat her in her booster seat and took his own chair next to Olivia. The rest of the children yelled for his attention.

The pain in her chest intensified.

She so desperately wanted this one sumptuous, sensuous affair. The whole purpose was to help her fill a void, because her life was destined to be a lonely one, without children and without a man who loved her. But she was getting more than she bargained for. She hadn't wanted to be shown all she was missing, to find more voids, to have firsthand knowledge of what could never be hers.

As she watched Tony laugh and play with the children, she knew it was too late for her. Perhaps this would yet turn out to be the wild fling she'd anticipated, but it would also leave her lonelier than ever before.

Dinner was a wonderful, riotous affair with children laughing, grown-ups talking and food being continuously resupplied. The kids quickly realized Olivia was a new face and, therefore, easy to entertain. Despite her growing melancholy, she laughed at their antics, listened to their stories, and when one child came over and tugged on her skirt, she didn't even flinch over the stain left behind. The child wanted to be lifted, and Olivia obliged. But the small hand was still holding her skirt, and when the child went up, so did her hem.

She hurried to right herself, pushing her skirt back down. But it was obvious everyone had seen the top of her stocking and the paler strip of flesh on her upper thigh. John grinned, Lisa gave him a playful smack to keep him from speaking, and Sue quickly began talking about Christmas shopping.

Olivia glanced at Tony and saw he had his eyes closed, looking close to prayer. Despite his brother's chuckles, it took him a few moments to collect his control. And then he sent Olivia a smile that made promises and threats at the same time.

After that, Tony did his best to deflect the kids from her. Olivia understood his reasoning, but no one else did. And all in all, everyone accepted her. They attempted to make her a part of their family, and for the short while it could last, Olivia loved it. Every few minutes, someone stood to check on the sleeping infant, whose crib they could see in the family room through the archway. The men took more turns than the women did, and Olivia saw that Tony, more than anyone, was interested in peeking in on the little one.

Olivia was being smothered by the sense of familial camaraderie. As welcoming as they all were, she felt like an interloper. And when she spied the pile of gaily wrapped birthday presents in the corner, she knew she couldn't stay.

She excused herself, asking directions to the powder room, then quickly located a phone. It happened to be in Tony's bedroom, or so she assumed judging from the open closet door and the lingering scent of his cologne... and his body. Again, she found herself breathing deeply, then shook her head and forced her mind to clear. She perched on the side of the bed to call for a cab.

She was still sitting there minutes later when Tony found her.

CHAPTER FOUR

TONY SLIPPED INTO the room and quietly closed the door. Olivia looked up and their gazes touched, hers wide, his narrowed. He crossed his arms over his chest and kept his voice very low. "Hiding?"

"What do you think?"

"No. I don't think you'd hide. So what are you doing?"

Olivia came to her feet, feeling like a fool, like a sneaky fool. But she refused to be intimidated. "I called a cab. I think it's past time I went home."

Tony didn't say anything at first, just leaned back against the door. Then he closed his eyes and groaned. "You're going to make me wait another day, aren't you, Olivia?"

Her heartbeat jumped at the husky way he said that, and at the restrained hunger she heard in his tone. "This…this isn't the right time, Tony. You know that. Right now, I feel equal parts ridiculous and embarrassed."

His gaze pinned her, hot and intent. "I could make you forget your hesitation real fast, honey."

I'll just bet you could. It wasn't easy, but Olivia shook her head. "If I leave now, they might not suspect anything—"

"Olivia, they saw me kissing your breast. I think they're already a bit suspicious."

She felt the blood pound in her veins, but kept her gaze steady. "You weren't kissing my breast."

"I wanted to be."

Olivia curled her hands into fists and tried to calm her breathing. "They might decide that was just a temporary loss of control if I leave now. If I stay until they're all gone, they'll assume we're spending the night together, and that's what we wanted to avoid." She gentled her tone and asked, "No speculation, no gossip. No scandals. Remember?"

"Yeah, but—"

A knock sounded at the door, and John's jovial voice called out, "Everything okay in there?"

Tony closed his eyes, a look of annoyance etched in his features. "I'm going to kill him."

Olivia thought she might help.

"We'll be out in just a second, John. And if you dare knock on the damn door again, I'm going to knock on you."

"Hey! I just wanted to tell you they're ready to cut the cake."

"So you told me. Now disappear, will you?"

Olivia rubbed her forehead, knowing she'd fumbled again, that she'd only made matters worse. Good grief, Tony's brother was fetching them from the bedroom. "How that man produced such a beautiful, sweet baby, I don't know."

To her surprise, Tony laughed. "John's all right. Believe me, if he understood the situation, he wouldn't be hassling me."

"No?"

Tony slowly shook his head, then went to her and pulled her against his chest. "No. He'd be sympathetic as hell." He tilted her head back and growled, "I want you, Olivia."

Her stomach curled at his words. "Tomorrow?"

Tony placed damp kisses across her cheek, her throat. He touched the corner of her mouth with his tongue. "Early? You're not going to make me wait until evening, are you?"

Olivia thought she might agree to anything with him stroking her back and kissing her so softly. "Where?"

"Hell, I don't know. But I'll think of something before morning, okay? I'll pick you up. About ten o'clock?"

"That'll be fine." She forced herself to forget how sensual and romantic everything seemed with Tony, and to concentrate on their purpose. She had to keep in mind that this was temporary, that Tony didn't really want her, not for keeps. He only wanted to use her, just as she would use him. "I don't want you to worry, Tony. We still have time. I'm supposed to be very fertile for the next couple of days."

She'd barely finished with the words before he was giving her a real kiss, his tongue moving against her own, his teeth nipping. It was a kiss meant to last her through the night. Unfortunately she could still feel the heat in her cheeks when she was forced to walk back into the dining room. She was grateful that the lights had been turned out, and the candles on the cake were lit. She saw John standing by the light switch and knew he was responsible for the darkness. John gave Tony a wink, and Olivia decided he might not be so bad after all.

Kate's two girls, Angie and Allison, ages four and five, fought over who could sing the loudest during the requisite "Happy Birthday," and John's son, six-year-old Luke, wanted to cut and serve the cake. Though Olivia explained that she had to leave, they all insisted she eat a piece of cake first and enjoy a scoop of ice cream. Olivia couldn't remember the last time she'd had, or attended, a birthday party. It might have been fun today if she'd actually been a part of it, rather than a reluctant intruder.

She didn't want anyone to know she'd called a cab. She thought it might seem less awkward if everyone thought she was driving herself home, so she had her coat on and her purse in her hand when she saw the cab's lights coming down the long driveway. To her surprise, the kids all wanted to give her hugs goodbye, the parents all uttered enthusiastic wishes to see her again soon, and to her chagrin, Tony's mother invited her to Thanksgiving dinner. Olivia muttered a lame, "Thank you, but I'll have to see," along with something about a busy schedule, and then she rushed out the door, wanting only to escape the onslaught of emotions. Tony caught her on the last step of the porch.

"I'm sorry, Olivia. I know this wasn't easy for you." He glanced at the cab and cursed. "I should be driving you home."

"I don't mind the cab, Tony, and you can't very well leave your own birthday party."

He reached for his wallet, and she narrowed her eyes. "What do you think you're doing?"

"At least let me pay for the cab—"

"Absolutely not and I won't hear another word on it." She used her most inflexible tone, the one that got contracts altered and had suppliers promising early deliveries. "I'm not your responsibility."

His sigh was long and filled with irritation. "Will you do me a favor then, and at least call me when you get home?"

Olivia stared. She was used to taking care of herself and his request seemed more than absurd. "Why?"

"So I know you made it home okay."

"Tony, you can't start feeling responsible for me. That's breaking one of the rules, isn't it? I'm a big girl, and I know how to manage on my own. So don't worry."

"Call me."

He was insistent, using his own invaluable, corporate tone, and she could tell by his stubborn stance he wasn't going to relent. She didn't think it was a good idea, but she gave in anyway. "Okay. But only this once."

"Thanks." He was grinning hugely.

"You're not a gracious winner, Tony."

"I haven't won yet. Hell, I've still got a whole room full of relatives who are going to burst with rapid-fire questions as soon as I step back inside. Now that you're gone and therefore can't be offended, they'll revert to their normal unrestrained selves."

She knew he was teasing, knew he was very close to his family, and for that reason she suffered not a single twinge of guilt for leaving him to his fate. She stepped into the cab, and Tony came to lean inside, ignoring the cabdriver and giving her a quick kiss.

"Tomorrow, Olivia. Then I'll win."

He was taunting her, but she only grinned. It was in her nature to give as good as she got, so when he started to pull away, she caught his neck and drew him back for another kiss, this one much longer and hotter than the first. And while he was trying to catch his breath, she whispered, "We'll both win."

Tony chuckled. But as he stepped away from the cab, they both looked up. And there at the front door, huddled together as if for a kindergarten class picture, stood all of Tony's family. And even with only the moon for light, Olivia could see the wide grins on all their faces.

TONY GLANCED AT the clock, but it was only seven in the morning, and he had no real reason to get up, not when he wouldn't be seeing Olivia until ten. So he lingered in bed, thinking about her, about all that had happened the night before. Her vulnerability around his family stirred feelings he didn't want to acknowledge—especially when concentrating on the lust she engendered was so much more satisfying.

Not one single minute had passed during the night when he could completely put Olivia and her allure from his mind. It was ridiculous, but he wanted her more now than he'd ever wanted any woman. Of course, she was so different from any other woman he knew. She made demands, but she also gave freely of herself. She was a veritable shark whenever they did business, but she ran her business fairly, and with a generous hand toward her workers. It was a belief he subscribed to: Treat your employees honestly, and you get honesty and loyalty in return.

They actually had a lot in common.

And yet there was a multitude of reasons why he couldn't get overly involved with her. The very things he admired about her made her most unsuitable for an emotional relationship. He wanted a baby, pure and simple, someone to love him, and someone he could love without restrictions or qualifications. The baby would be his, only his, and Tony planned to smother the child with all the love he had inside him.

Olivia wanted a thriving business. She'd admitted she had no desire, no time for a family. She'd agreed to have his baby as part of a business deal, and while her agreement thrilled him, it also reemphasized the fact that business was still her main objective in life, while a baby was now his. He'd have to do his best to remember that.

The house was chilly when he finally rose and went to put on coffee. Naked except for a pair of snug cotton boxers, he felt the gooseflesh rise on his arms, but he ignored it. He needed a little cooling off if he was to deal with Olivia in a rational way.

He went into the bathroom and splashed water over his beard-rough face, then brushed his teeth while he waited for the coffee. Today, he thought, staring at his own contemplative expression in the mirror, he would get this business with Olivia back on an even keel. No more mingling with family, no more seeing her with a baby cuddled in her arms and an expression on her face that tore at his guts. He would view her with a detached eye and a reminder in his brain that she was a means to an end. They'd made an agreement, and it could be nothing more.

Not if he expected to escape this ordeal completely intact, with his heart whole and his mind sane.

He'd just poured his first cup of coffee when the doorbell rang. Padding barefoot into the living room, he leaned down to peer through the peephole and saw Olivia standing on his doorstep. A quick glance at the clock showed it to be only seven forty-five, and his first thought was that she was here to cancel, that something had come up and she had to go out of town; it wasn't uncommon in her business. Every muscle in his body protested.

He jerked the door open, forgetting for the moment that he wasn't even close to being dressed. Olivia took a long moment to stare at his chest, then down the length of his body before she lifted her gaze to his face.

"You're rather hairy, aren't you?"

"I'll shave."

Her lips quirked in a quick grin. "Your chest?"

If it would keep her from canceling. He only shrugged.

Tentatively she reached out and touched him, laying her palm flat where his heart beat in unsteady cadence. She stroked him, feeling him, tangling her fingers in his body hair. With a breathless whisper, she said, "I like it."

Tony didn't answer. He wasn't certain he could answer. And then she looked up at him, her eyes huge and bright. "I couldn't wait."

He felt the bottom drop out of his stomach. His hand shook as he set the cup of coffee on the entry table, then reached for her and pulled her inside. He needed to make certain he'd understood. "Olivia?"

She started to chatter. "I know you said ten, but we're both off today, right? And I'm really not used to this, being aroused and yet having to wait. It's terribly difficult. I couldn't sleep last night..."

"Me, either."

He couldn't believe she was here, looking shy and determined and he wanted her as much as he'd ever wanted anything in his life. Everything he'd just been telling himself about keeping his emotional distance vanished. He couldn't quite pry his hands from her shoulders, couldn't force himself to take an emotional step back. He felt her softness beneath the coat, the way she straightened her shoulders to face him. Ah, that small show of bravado, so like her, so endearing. So damn sexy.

The brisk morning air coming through the open door did little to impress him. As he felt himself harden, his pulse quicken, Olivia pushed the door shut behind her, then set an overnight bag on the floor. His gaze dropped to it, and she rushed to explain. "I... Well, I felt a little risqué this morning. And it stands to reason your house should be safe now. I mean, lightning doesn't strike twice in the same spot, right?"

He had no answer for that, not when he could see the heated need in her eyes, the way her lips trembled.

She swallowed hard. "I don't want you to think I'm intruding for the whole night, but I needed to bring something to wear for later... If we're going to spend the whole day together."

Before he could reassure her, she shook her head and started again, her tone anxious. "I'm making a mess of this. Remember, the book said we should wait a few hours then try again, and I thought..."

"Shh." He could barely restrain himself from lifting her and carrying her to his room. She had this strange mix of timidity and boldness that made him crazy with wanting. "Let me shower real quick and..."

"No." She shook her head and her dark hair fell over her shoulders, looking soft and silky. "I've waited long enough, Tony. I don't want to wait a single second more."

She was staring down at his body, her gaze resting on his blatant erection clearly defined within his soft cotton boxers. Another quarter inch, one more soft sound from her, and the boxers wouldn't cover him at all. He wanted her to touch him, he wanted... Feeling desperate, he said, "I have to at least shave, honey. I don't want to scratch you."

For a reply, she began unbuttoning her coat, and as each button slid free, his heartbeat accelerated. First he saw soft pale flesh; her throat, her upper chest, the gentle swells of her breasts. But as the coat began to part, he realized she wasn't dressed at all, that she was covered only by the teddy he'd admired the day before in her shop.

He'd had to know, he thought frantically, staring at her body, more perfect than any mannequin. She had a gentle grace that was made to wear such feminine items. He'd questioned whether she really wore the articles she carried, and now she'd proven to him that she did—with perfection. And suddenly it was too much.

Gripping the lapels of the coat in his fists, he shoved it over her shoulders and let it fall free to land unnoticed on the floor, abruptly ending her slow unveiling. Drawn by the sight of her, cheeks flushed, eyes anxious, he scooped her into his arms. He felt her slender thighs against his forearm, her soft breasts against his chest, her lips touching his throat, and he groaned. The bedroom was definitely too far away and he took three long steps to the living-room couch and landed there with her tucked close to his side. His mouth was on hers before she could protest, if that had been her intent. And his hands began exploring every soft swell and heated hollow. He moved too fast, he knew it, but he couldn't seem to stop himself.

She shuddered when his palm smoothed over her silky bottom, sliding between her buttocks, exploring her from behind. He dipped between her thighs to frantically finger the three small silver snaps there. They easily popped free at his prodding, and then his fingers were touching her warmth, gliding over softly swelled flesh, over crisp feminine curls. He stroked, feeling her wetness, her growing heat. The feel of her made him wonder why he didn't explode. He could hear her rapid breathing in his ears, feel her fingertips clenching tight on his shoulders.

He groaned, moving his mouth from hers, wanting to taste her skin, to breathe in her scent. She was soft everywhere, from her loose hair that brushed over his cheeks, to her arms that held him tight, to her slender thighs that willingly parted as he continued to cautiously explore her, exciting her, readying her.

Finding a puckered nipple beneath the sheer material of the teddy, he dampened it with his tongue, then looked at his handiwork. She showed pink and erect through the material. He suckled, flicking with his tongue, and Olivia arched her back, her panting, urgent breaths driving him on. He nipped and she gasped. With his big hand still between her thighs, he slid one long finger over her, again and again, finding her most sensitive flesh and plying it in much the same way he did her nipple, then pressing deep inside her, stroking. She made a high, keening sound. She was tight and wet and so hot Tony couldn't stand it another moment; he knew she was ready.

With frenzied motions, he shoved his shorts down and situated himself between her thighs. For one moment, their gazes met, and her look, that unique look of vulnerability and need and demand, pushed him over the edge. He covered her mouth with his own, thrusting his tongue past her lips just as his erection pressed inside her body.

There was a small amount of resistance as her body slowly loosened to accept his length, his size. And then with one even, rough thrust he slid deep, and even that, something beyond her control, appealed to him, made him that much more anxious to reach his final goal. He began moving, driving into her and then pulling away, hearing her panting breaths and feeling the way she tried to counter his moves, though the couch didn't allow her much freedom. He felt things he'd never felt before, as if he were a predatory animal, dominant, determined to stake a primal claim.

Pinning her beneath him so she couldn't move, he slid one hand beneath her hips and lifted, forcing her to take all of him, giving her no way to resist him at all. He briefly worried when she groaned raggedly, but then she squeezed him tight, her muscles clamping around him like a hot fist, and she was slick and wet and she wanted him—wanted him enough to demand that he make love to her. His explosive climax obliterated all other thought.

He knew he shouted like a wild man, knew Olivia watched him with a fascinated type of awe. He threw his head back, sensations continuing to wash over him, draining him, filling him, making his muscles quiver until finally, after long seconds, he collapsed onto her, gasping for breath.

Her arms gently, hesitantly slipped around his neck and her fingers smoothed through his hair. And when he felt the light brushing of her lips over his temple, a touch so unbelievably sweet and innocent, he came to the realization that he'd just used her very badly, that he'd totally ignored all her stipulations of the deal they'd made. He'd forgotten all about the damn deal. Hell, he hadn't given her pleasure.

He hadn't given her anything except a man's lust.

OLIVIA FELT TONY TENSE, knew what was going through his mind, and tightened her arms. He relented enough that he stayed very close to her, but lifted his head. She felt ridiculously shy about meeting his gaze, but she forced herself to do just that, if for no other reason than to reassure him. She couldn't quite prevent the small smile curling her lips.

He blew out a disgusted breath. "I'm sorry."

Placing two fingers against his mouth, she meant only to silence him. But then he kissed her fingers, and her heart flipped and she ended up lifting her own head enough to kiss him in return. "Don't ruin this for me by making unnecessary apologies, Tony. Please."

She said the words against his mouth, and before she'd even finished, his tongue was stroking hers, his narrow, muscular pelvis pushing close again. She tingled all over, a renewed rush of warmth making her stomach curl.

"I already ruined things, honey. And you deserve much more than an apology."

That was the second time he'd called her "honey" and she loved it. There had never been a relationship in her life since her parents' death that warranted an endearment. She hadn't realized that she'd even been missing it. But hearing Tony say it now, hearing the gentleness in his tone, the affection, she decided she liked it very much.

Since he seemed determined to talk about it, Olivia asked, "Why exactly are you apologizing?"

"Because I lost my head. I gave you nothing."

"Not true." Oh how she loved feeling his hard, lean body pressed against hers, the contrast of his firm muscles and his hair-roughened legs and his warmth. She tightened her arms and rubbed her nose against his chest, loving his morning musky scent. He always smelled so good, so sexy. So like himself. It made her dizzy and weak to breathe his delicious scent. "I've never made anyone lose their head before, Tony. I think it's a rather nice feeling."

He gave a strangled laugh, then tangled his hands in her hair to make her look at him. "I'll take the blame, especially given the fact I've never made love to a woman without a condom before. Feeling you, Olivia, all of you, was a heady experience."

She felt stunned by his admission. "Never?"

"Nope. I've always been the cautious sort, even when I was just a kid. But you're to blame just a bit, too, showing up here in that getup." He ran one large palm down her side, rubbing the material that was now bunched at her waist. His voice dropped to a low rumble when he whispered, "I almost died when you opened your coat, and I knew I wouldn't be able to draw another breath without getting inside you first."

And he thought he hadn't given her anything? With her heart racing and her throat tight with emotion, she kissed him again, getting quickly used to the feel of his mouth on hers. When he lifted his head this time, she was very aware of his renewed erection and the way his arms were taut with muscles as he restrained himself, holding his chest away from her.

Tony watched her so closely, it was hard to speak, but she forced the words out, for some strange reason, wanting to tell him her thoughts. "I was half afraid you'd laugh, that I'd look ridiculous. Though I love wearing sexy things, no one sees me as a sexy woman."

"You're sexier than any woman has a right to be."

"Tony…" The things he said made her light-headed.

"It'll be our little secret, okay?" He began tracing the small red marks left behind from his morning whiskers.

That long finger moved over her throat, her breasts. He stopped at her nipples and lightly pinched, holding her between his finger and thumb. He watched her face as he tugged gently, plucking, rolling her flesh until she groaned. Olivia wanted nothing more than to make love with him again.

But Tony was suddenly lifting himself away. "I have to shower and shave," he said in deep, husky tones. "Despite what you say, I don't like leaving burns on your skin."

"No." She tried to protest, to hold him near, but he only stood up then lifted her again. The way he cradled her close to his heart was something else she could get used to.

"You can shower with me, Miss Anderson, then I'll see about attending you the right way."

"I loved the way you did things."

"You didn't come."

A flash of heat washed over her mostly naked body. He had such a blatant way of discussing things that excited her despite her embarrassment. "I... I enjoyed myself." She sounded defensive and added, "But I'm supposed to stay still for a while."

"I can promise you'll enjoy yourself more when I do things properly."

He seemed determined to fulfill her demands, when she now felt horrible for having made them. She didn't want this to be only about base satisfaction, a series of touches meant to excite, with no emotion involved. It was the emotion that she'd been craving for so long, that felt so good now. But there was no way she could say that to Tony, not after she'd told him she wanted to be privy to his excellent technique.

An idea came to mind, and as he stood her inside the shower stall, she said, "Aren't we supposed to wait two hours before doing this again? To give you time to…to replenish yourself?"

Tony stepped in behind her and began working the teddy up over her shoulders. When he finally tossed it outside the shower and stood looking at her completely bare, Olivia knew he'd have his way. He took a long time scrutinizing her, and that gave her a chance to look her fill also. He was such a gorgeous man, so solid, his body dark, his muscles tight.

She wondered if he enjoyed the sight of her near as much as she did him, but then he met her gaze and there was such heat in his green eyes, and more emotion than she could ever wish for, she forgot her own questions.

Tony inched closer to her until their bodies were touching from the waist down. His hard erection pressed into her belly, stealing her breath. His hands came up to cup her breasts. "You don't have to watch the clock, honey. I promise you, it'll take me at least that long to get my fill of looking at you and touching you."

Her heart thumped heavily and she could barely talk. "Tony?"

"It's called foreplay, Olivia. I intend to make up for the orgasm you missed—and then some. We've got all the time in the world."

Thirty minutes later, their still damp bodies tangled in the covers on his bed, Olivia knew she'd never survive two hours' worth of this. Tony was gently lathing one nipple while his fingers were busy drifting over her hip and belly, pausing every so often for an excruciating moment between her thighs to torment and tease her until she groaned and begged. He used her own wetness as a lubricant, sometimes pressing his fingers deep, stretching her, other times circling her opening, sliding over ultrasensitive flesh.

He laughed at her soft demands, his fingers gently plucking, rolling. "Easy, sweetheart. I promise, you'll appreciate being patient."

"No. No more, Tony. I can't stand it." There was a touch of tears in her voice, but she was too new to this, too unskilled to rationalize an ending that she'd never before experienced. Tony kissed her softly on her parted lips, then whispered, "Trust me now, okay?"

When she felt Tony's cheek, now smooth from his shave, glide over her abdomen, the only thought she had was of finding relief. Every nerve ending in her body felt taut, tingling. There was no room for modesty, for shyness.

His hands curved around her knees and she willingly allowed him to part her thighs wide, leaving her totally exposed to his gaze. She felt his warm, gentle breath, the damp touch of his tongue. And then his mouth closed around her, hot and wet, and his teeth carefully nibbled.

No, she'd never survive this. She arched upward, again begging, feeling the sensations so keenly she screamed. He tightened his hold on her buttocks, holding her steady, forcing her to submit to his torment.

And then it happened and she was only aware of unbelievable pleasure. Tony encouraged her, controlled her, and when the sensations finally began to ebb, he eased, soothing her until she calmed.

When she opened her eyes—a move requiring considerable effort—Tony was beside her again, his hand idly cupping her breast and a look of profound interest on his face. She blinked at him, not understanding that look, and he said without a single qualm, "You've never had an orgasm before, have you?"

Her only recourse seemed to be to close her eyes again. But Tony laughed and kissed her nose. "Don't hide from me, Olivia. Talk to me."

"We're not supposed to be talking."

"No? Well, don't worry. We'll get on to making love again soon. But answer me first."

Disgruntled by his personal question and his persistence, she said, "It never seemed particularly important before. Besides, I told you my two attempts at this failed."

"Your two attempts with a partner." His voice gentled. "That doesn't mean you couldn't have—"

Her eyes rounded when she realized where this questioning was going, and it seemed imperative to divert his attention. "Aren't you supposed to be...uh, excited right about now?"

His smile proved she hadn't fooled him one bit. But to answer her question, he lifted her limp hand, kissed the palm, then carried it to his erection, curling her fingers around him. For one brief instant, he held himself still, his eyes closing as her fingers flexed. Then he gave a wry grin. "I'm plenty excited. But I'm also enjoying you most thoroughly."

"You're embarrassing me, is what you're doing." She said it with a severe frown, but he only chuckled.

"Why? Because I'm feeling like the most accomplished lover around? You screamed, Olivia." He cupped her cheek and turned her face toward him. "Look at me, honey."

There was that endearment again. She opened her

eyes and stared at him. The tenderness in his gaze nearly undid her.

"I'm glad I could give you something you'd never had before. It makes this all seem very...special."

"Tony." She rolled toward him, wanting him again, right now, unwilling to wait another instant.

And then the doorbell rang, and she knew she might not have any choice.

Tony seemed inclined to ignore it at first, but the insistent pounding that came next had him cursing and rising from the bed. As he pulled on jeans, he surveyed her sprawled form, then cursed again. "Don't move. I'll be right back."

Olivia waited until he'd stomped out of the room before scrambling off the bed and wrapping the sheet around herself. She went to the door and opened it to peek, then crept down the hall enough to see who had come calling so early. Tony's brother, John, stood in the entryway, the baby in his arms, and a very worried expression on his face.

Though they spoke in hushed tones, Olivia was able to hear every word.

"I know this is the worst possible time, Tony..."

"You have no idea."

"Yes I do. I saw the car. I assume Olivia is here?"

Tony crossed his arms over his bare chest and said, "What do you want, John?"

"I'm sorry, I really am. And I swear I wouldn't be here if there was anyone else. But Mom and Kate went on a shopping spree this morning and won't be back for hours, and I have to take Lisa to the hospital. You know she wasn't feeling great yesterday—it's why we left early. And she's always so busy with the three kids, she stays exhausted. But she started running a high fever early last night, coughing and having a hard time breathing, and she's gotten sicker by the hour. I've never seen her like this." There was an edge of desperation in John's tone when he added, "I can't watch my three hellions in a hospital and be with her, too."

Tony immediately straightened, then took the baby from his arms. "Is Lisa going to be okay?"

John looked almost sick himself. "I don't know what's wrong with her, hopefully just the flu, but…"

"Don't give it another thought. Of course I'll take the kids. Where are the other two?"

"Waiting in the car with their mother. I didn't want to leave Lisa alone, and I wasn't certain if you were home." He leaned out the door and waved his hand to get the kids to come in. "I really appreciate this, Tony. I know you probably wish we'd all go…"

"Don't be stupid, John. Just take care of Lisa and keep me informed, okay?"

As John stepped out to gather up a packed diaper bag and some essentials for the other kids, Tony rushed around the corner into the hallway and almost ran into Olivia. He had the overnight bag she'd brought in his left hand while he held the baby in the crook of his right arm. He didn't question her snooping, only led the way into the bedroom. "You heard?"

Olivia could sense the worry in his tone and expression, and was reminded once again how close he was to his family. "Yes. What can I do to help?"

He shook his head. "I'm sorry, babe. Here, can you get dressed real quick?" He no sooner handed her the bag than he was rushing to the living room again to relieve John of the children and send him on his way.

Olivia closed the door and sighed. It seemed Tony was going to throw her out, which made sense considering he didn't want her around his family. But it still hurt. While they'd been making love, she'd entirely forgotten everything else in the world, including their twice-damned deal and all the reasons she couldn't feel what she was presently feeling.

Despite all her reasons for needing to stay detached from him, she wanted to stay and help; she wanted to stay, period. Very much.

Her body was still tingling, her heart still racing from Tony's sensual torment, but she managed to get her slacks and sweater on before he reopened the door. The baby was still nestled in his bare muscled arm, but that didn't stop him from coming toward her, then pulling her close with his free arm. "Damn, I can't believe my luck."

"Things do seem to be conspiring against us."

He brushed a kiss over her lips, then surprised her by asking, "Can you stay?"

Olivia blinked, not certain what to say.

"I know our plans have changed, hell, we might even have the kids all night. But… I don't feel right about all this. It worries me, Lisa coming down sick like that."

Olivia cupped his cheek, touched by his concern, and warmed by the way he'd included her. "You don't want to be alone?"

His jaw tightened and his eyes searched her face. He seemed reluctant to admit it even to himself, but then he nodded. "I guess that's about it."

"We're friends, Tony. Despite any other agreements, I'd like to believe that. And friends help friends. You don't have to worry that I'll read more into this than exists."

He stubbornly ignored her references to their situation, and asked, "Does that mean you'll stay, Olivia? Please?"

At that moment, she would have done anything for him, but of course, she couldn't tell him that. She looked up at him and smiled. "Yes, I'll stay. For as long as you need me."

CHAPTER FIVE

A LOOK OF relief washed over Tony's features, then he hugged her close again. "I believe the coffee is still in the pot. It might be a little strong now, but I could sure use a cup. And the kids are probably hungry. Kids are always hungry, right? So what do you say? You up to breakfast?"

At just that moment, two faces peeked around the door frame, and they were both very solemn. Olivia's heart swelled with emotion for these two small people who were obviously concerned about their mother. She forgot Tony for the moment, forgot that she didn't know anything about kids, and went down on her knees to meet the children at their level.

"Hello. Remember me?"

Six-year-old Luke stared at her with serious eyes, all the energy of yesterday conspicuously missing. "Sure we remember. It was just last night. You was kissing Uncle Tony in his garage."

Olivia felt her face turn pink, but she smiled. "Actually it was the other way around. Your uncle was kissing me."

Maggie, who at three seemed very small and delicate, popped her thumb from her mouth to say with great wisdom, "Uncle Tony likes kissin'. He kisses me lots, too."

And just that easily, Olivia found a rapport. She

reached out and tugged Maggie closer, and the little girl came willingly, wrapping one arm around Olivia's neck while holding tight to a tattered blanket with the other. Olivia perched the little girl on her knee. "Are you two hungry? I think your uncle was planning on making breakfast for us."

Maggie nodded, but Luke turned away. Tony stopped him with only a word. "Your mom will be fine, Luke, I promise."

"Dad looked awful scared."

Tony caught Olivia's arm and helped her to stand, then began steering them all toward the kitchen. "Not scared. Upset. There's a big difference. Your dad can't stand to see any of you sick or feeling bad. The fact that your mom is sick makes him feel almost as bad as she does. He wants to take care of all of you, just as your mom does. But he needs time alone with her now, so he can make certain the doctors don't flirt with her too much. He can't watch her if he's busy watching you two."

Luke didn't look as if he understood Tony's humor. "Mom is awful pretty."

"Yes, she is. And so you guys get to stay here with me."

"For how long?"

Tony stopped to stare at Luke, pretending a great affront. "Good grief, boy, you'll have Olivia thinking you don't like me."

Maggie twisted loose from Olivia's hold to say in a very firm voice, "We do so like Unca' Tony. We like him lots." And Olivia couldn't help but smile.

The chatter continued all the while Tony cooked, and with each second, Olivia became more enamored of Tony's familial commitments. The kids, despite their concern, were happy and comfortable to be with him. There was so much love in the air, she could fill her lungs with it. And Tony proved to be as adept at holding a child while cooking as any mother. Olivia wondered if he did so because he enjoyed holding the baby so much, or because he didn't want Olivia to hold him.

Unfortunately, as the day wore on, the latter proved to be true. Not once, even at the most hectic times, did Tony request her assistance with the baby. Not long after they'd finished breakfast John called to say Lisa had pneumonia and they'd be keeping her overnight. She was worn down from all the daily running she did, not to mention having given birth not that long before. And since she was staying at the hospital, John wanted to leave the kids with Tony so he could be free to stay with her.

Tony agreed, and surprisingly, once the kids were assured their mother would be fine and probably home the next day, they seemed thrilled by the idea of staying. Tony promised to bring in a tent that they could set up in front of the fireplace. Maggie asked, "Will Livvy get to sleep with us, too?"

It seemed Tony was caught speechless for a moment, then he said, "If she wants to. And it's Olivia, sweetheart, not Livvy."

"I don't mind, Tony. Actually it's a familiar nickname."

"You look kinda funny, Olivia." Luke watched her closely, and Olivia was amazed by the child's perception.

"I'm fine, Luke, honest." But hearing little Maggie call her by the same name her own mother and father had always used dredged up long forgotten feelings and left her shaken. And Tony seemed to notice. He held her hand and gave it a squeeze, then went to call his mother and sister to let them know what was going on. He hadn't wanted to tell them Lisa was sick until he knew for certain she'd be all right. Olivia gathered by the one-sided conversation that his mother offered to come and take the children, but Tony only thanked her. He said they had already made plans, and she could have them in the morning, but not before their "campout."

Finally, right after an early dinner, Luke and Maggie got bundled up from head to toe and went out back to play. Being children, they seemed impervious to the cold, but Tony insisted that it could only be for a short spell.

Even though the yard was isolated, with no other neighbors in sight, Tony still admonished both children to stay very close by. They could use the tire swing in the tree or play in the small playhouse he and John had built the preceding summer for just such visits. The infant, Shawn, lay sleeping on a blanket on the floor and Tony and Olivia were left relatively alone.

Tony dropped down beside her on the couch, then grinned. "Man, am I worn-out. Kids, in the plural, can really keep you hopping, can't they?"

She knew he had loved every single minute, that he wasn't really complaining. It had been there on his face, the way he smiled, the way he held the baby and teased Maggie and spoke to Luke.

She licked her lips nervously and slanted him a cautious look. "I would have been glad to help you out a little, you know." She said it tentatively, hoping to broach the topic without setting off any alarm bells.

But all he did was pat her thigh in a now familiar way. "You help a lot just by being here. Pneumonia. Can you imagine that? Lisa always seems so healthy. But John said the doctor told him it could bring you low in just a few hours."

"Will she have to stay in the hospital long?"

"No. She'll probably get to come home tomorrow. And Mom and Kate are already making plans to take turns helping her out until she's completely well again. John is swearing he's going to hire someone to come and clean for her from now on, but he said Lisa told him to forget it. She's funny about her house, likes to do things a certain way, you know?"

His statement didn't really require an answer, and Olivia couldn't have given him one anyway. "Your whole family really sticks together, don't they?"

He seemed surprised by her question. "Of course we do."

"I mean, even though Lisa isn't really part of your family..."

"She's married to John. She's the mother of my niece and nephews. She's part of the family."

And that was that, Olivia supposed. It would be so nice to belong to such a family. She said without thinking, "When Maggie called me Livvy... It, well, it reminded me of when I was a child. That was what my mother and father always called me. But I'd forgotten until she said it."

Tony wrapped one large hand around the back of her neck and tugged her closer. His lips touched her temple, and she could feel their movement against her skin as he spoke. "I figured it must have been something like that. I'm sorry, Olivia. You looked so damn sad."

"No. Not sad really." She tried her best to look cavalier over the subject, even so far as giving him a smile.

"It's been so long, I've forgotten what it's like to miss them. I guess I'm used to being alone."

It was a horrible lie, because who could actually get accustomed to spending her life alone? There was never anyone to share the triumphs, which made them seem almost hollow, and when the struggles to get ahead occasionally became too much, she had only herself to lean on.

Tony was staring at her in his intent, probing way and Olivia had the horrible suspicion he was reading her thoughts, knowing exactly what it was she concealed, and how empty she often felt.

He looked down at her hands, which were tightly pressed together in her lap, then covered them with one of his own. "Is that why you've isolated yourself?"

"I haven't."

His gaze snapped back to her face, as if struck that she would deny such an obvious thing. "Of course you have. You keep to yourself, don't date, don't form long-standing friendships. You put everything you have into the lingerie shops. It's almost like you're afraid of getting involved."

"I am not afraid." She didn't know what else she could say. She felt defensive, as if she had to explain her choice of lifestyle, but that was impossible. She would never be able to give Tony the truth.

"It's not natural for a woman like you to still be single, to not want some kind of commitment."

Despite herself, she stiffened. "A woman like me? What exactly is that supposed to mean?"

Tony closed his eyes and made a sound of frustration. "I'm sorry. I didn't mean that the way it sounded. It's just that… I never thought of you as you are. You al-

ways seemed pleasant enough, but so businesslike and…
well, detached. And here you are, a very warm, caring
woman, wearing sexy lingerie that makes me go a little
crazy and looking so damn sweet and vulnerable at the
most surprising times."

"Tony…" She didn't like being labeled vulnerable
any more than she liked feeling defensive.

"I don't understand you, Olivia, and I want to. I really do."

"But why?"

He quirked a smile. "Don't sound so panicked. I
promise, I'm not asking for orange blossoms and golden
rings. I just… I guess I like you more than I thought I
would."

"Sex has a way of making a man feel like that. Believe me, it will pass."

He reached out to wrap a lock of her hair around his
finger, then gently pulled until her face was closer to his.
His tone was low, his expression heated. "Honey, you
don't know enough about men and sex to make that assumption." He laid his palm warmly on her thigh, gently
squeezing. "And I'd say that nasty little comment deserves some form of retribution, wouldn't you?"

Olivia tried to pull away, but she couldn't get very far.
She wasn't afraid of Tony, but she didn't trust the look
in his eyes. He was pushing, and there was too much
she could never tell him.

"I didn't mean it to sound nasty, exactly." She was beginning to feel cornered, and that made her so very nervous. Then she went on the attack, hoping to force him to
back off. "Dammit, Tony, we agreed not to get personal,
right? And this discussion is getting very personal. You
want a baby from me, not my life history. Why don't we

talk about sex instead?" Trying to be subtle, she leaned into him, allowing her breasts to brush against his chest.

He allowed her closeness, but his expression didn't change. "Since I do want a baby from you, and you don't appear to be the woman I first thought you to be, I think your family history is very relevant." He continued to maintain his gentle hold on her hair as his hand left her thigh and curved around her waist.

She drew in a sharp breath when his fingers slipped upward to tease against the outer curves of her breast. She tried to squirm, to get his hand exactly where she wanted it, but he only grinned and continued to tease.

It was enough to set off her temper, and without thinking she jerked upright again. But Tony only pulled her back, using her hair as a leash.

Olivia gritted her teeth. "I'm not going to sit and let you practice your intimidation tactics. This isn't a boardroom."

"No, and it's not the bedroom, either. So stop trying to distract me with sex—believe me, we'll get back to that as soon as possible. Just tell me a little about your folks." He was still speaking in that soft, determined tone, and she could feel his stubbornness. The man had it in buckets.

It was apparent he wasn't going to give up, so she did. She just wasn't practiced enough to play this kind of game with a man. "Never say I don't know when to restructure my plans."

"And your plans were to run the show?"

"Something like that. But it's not important now."

Tony laughed softly, then turned her head toward him so he could kiss her mouth. His quick, soft peck turned into a lingering kiss, and he gave a low curse when he finally managed to pull himself away. "You're a fast learner, but I'm afraid I'm too curious to let you get away with it. Go ahead now. Tell me about your parents."

Her sigh was long, indicating her reluctance. "They were poor, not overly educated, and they worked harder than anybody I know." Speaking of them brought a tightness to her chest that always wanted to linger. She tried clearing her throat, but the discomfort remained. "Our furniture was usually tattered, but it was always clean. My mother kept an immaculate house."

"You were close with them?"

She simply couldn't remember—and it pained her. There were too many other memories in the way of the good times. "We didn't have much daily time to do things together. Whenever possible, my mother would make me a special cake, and my dad always kissed me good-night, no matter how late he got in. But they weren't always happy, which I suppose makes sense seeing how poor we were."

She drew a deep breath, the tightness now nearly choking her, and before she knew she would say the words, they tumbled out. "My parents loved me, they really did, and they tried to do the best for me that they could, but…sometimes they made mistakes."

Easing closer, Tony twined his fingers through her hair and began massaging her scalp. His nearness touched her, made some of the hurt from the memories fade.

He leaned down and placed a kiss on the bridge of her nose. "All parents make mistakes, honey. It's a built-in factor that you can't be a perfect parent."

Olivia only nodded, since she had no idea how other parents did things. But he had questions, and she wanted to give him his answers quickly, to get the telling over with so she could forget it all again. "I was an only child and we lived on the riverbank in a tiny little nothing town called Hattsburg, Mississippi. My mother worked at the local market, my father at the one factory in town. Sometimes…sometimes he drank too much. It was the way he escaped, my mom used to say."

Tony leaned into her, giving her silent comfort. She drew a deep breath and rushed through the rest of the story. "They died on the river, using a boat that couldn't have passed safety standards on its best day, but was especially hazardous in bad weather. The river had swelled from spring rains, and the boat capsized. My father was drunk and didn't use good judgment, the deputy said. He was knocked out when he went overboard and died before they reached the hospital. My mother had tried to save him, but the water was still frigid, and she suffered exposure and multiple injuries. And grief. She died in the hospital not too many days after my father."

She drew a deep breath, knowing the unwanted feelings would crowd her if she let them. She shook her head at herself, denying the feelings, the hurt. "I don't really miss them anymore, because I can hardly remember ever having a family. You're really pretty lucky, you know."

He was silent over that, and Olivia wondered if she'd said too much, if he was again having second thoughts about allowing her around his family. But then he tipped her chin up and without a word began nibbling lightly on her lips. She exchanged one set of concerns for another. "Tony… Don't tease me anymore. I swear, I don't think I can take it and there's no way we can do anything about it now."

"No, we can't. But I just like touching you. Don't

deny me that." He slipped his tongue into her mouth, holding her head steady with his hand still on the back of her neck.

"When…" She gasped as his head lifted and his hand covered her breast, then she started over. "When will we be able to try again?"

"My mother will pick the kids up in the morning. Do you have to be at work early?"

His fingers found her nipple, encouraging her to give the right answer. After a breathless moan, she said, "I can take the morning off."

"Good. I have to go in for a while in the afternoon, but I want you to go with me. There's something I want to show you."

Olivia would have questioned that, but he suddenly tunneled both hands into her hair and leaned her into the padded back of the couch, his mouth ravenous, moving over her face, her throat.

"God, I think I've been wanting you forever."

Olivia thrilled at the words. It was such a pleasant alternative, going from the distressing memories of her childhood to the newfound feelings of adult desire, her mind simply accepted the change with no lingering remorse. Then a small, outraged voice intruded, and she practically leapt off the couch.

"Sheeesh! You guys are gross."

Luke stood there, his hands on his narrow hips, his skinny legs braced wide apart and a look of total disgust on his face.

With a sigh that turned into a laugh, Tony asked, "What do you want, squirt?"

"I wanted you to come out and toss with me. Maggie can't catch nothin'."

Tony considered it a moment, but his gaze kept going to the baby. She could tell the idea of a game of catch was enticing for him, and yet he was going to refuse. Olivia rolled her eyes. "Go on, Tony. If the baby starts fussing, I'll come get you."

Cupping her cheek, Tony drifted his thumb over her lips and whispered, "I don't want to leave you alone."

Again, Luke complained. "You two are worse than Mom and Dad!"

Olivia couldn't help but laugh. "Will you go on, before Luke gets sick? He's starting to turn a funny shade of green."

That had Luke laughing and looking for a mirror so he could see for himself.

Olivia pushed at Tony's solid shoulders. "Go on. I'll be fine. I'll just watch a little television."

"You're sure?"

"I'm positive. Now go."

It was a cool November day, and Tony pulled on his down jacket before stepping out the back door. Olivia went to the window to watch. The kids laughed and tackled Tony as he tried to throw the ball, and they all three went down in a pile. Tony began tickling Luke, while at the same time he managed to toss Maggie in the air. Olivia felt something damp on her cheek, and when she went to brush it away, she realized it was a tear.

Why the sight of Tony's gorgeous, healthy body in play with two kids should make her cry, she didn't know. It wasn't as if he wouldn't eventually get the child he wanted—and obviously deserved. He'd make a remarkable father, and she envied him the opportunity to be a parent. But she wasn't actually hampering him, only slow-ing him down for a few weeks. And what was that when compared with a lifetime of having a child of your own?

She would have stood there watching them forever, but the baby started to fuss, and since Olivia assumed he couldn't be hungry, not after Tony had just given him a bottle before putting him down, she decided he might just want to be held.

She knew she did.

Being very careful, she lifted the baby in her arms, and like a small turtle, he stretched his head up to look at her. She grinned at his pouting expression. It was almost as if he were disgruntled at waking to unfamiliar surroundings. She cuddled him close and patted his back and listened to his lusty little yawn.

Sitting in the large padded chair not far from where little Shawn had been sleeping, she settled them both there. It was easy to relax while inhaling his unique, sweet baby scent. And Shawn seemed to like her, resting against her in a posture of trust, with his little head against her breasts, his legs tucked up against her belly. By instinct alone, she hummed a melody she knew and gently swayed in the chair, lulling him. Before long, she was yawning as well, and thinking that if she could never have a baby of her own, at least now she'd know what it was like to hold one.

TONY CAME IN carrying Maggie and listening to Luke tell him all the things he wanted for Christmas. It was an impressive list, and he was thinking Luke might be just a bit spoiled, then decided he'd buy him the expensive remote-control car he wanted. Grinning, he knew John would have a fit, but it didn't matter. That's what uncles were for—to indulge their nephews.

He stopped cold when he walked into the family room and found Olivia curled up in a chair with Shawn sleeping in her arms. Immediately he hushed Luke and Maggie, not wanting Olivia to awaken. In fact, he could have stood there for hours just looking at her.

It was such a revelation, discovering her like this and having his heart suddenly acknowledge all the things it had been denying. It seemed as if all his strength had just been stripped away, leaving him raw and unsteady.

This was what he wanted.

He wanted to come in from playing with the kids—his kids—and find his woman resting with his baby in her arms. He wanted to coddle her, to love her. He wanted an entire family to look after, not just a single baby. He wanted to share all his love, and have it returned. He wanted it all.

With his heart thundering and his stomach tight, he set little Maggie down and pulled Luke close. Speaking in hushed tones, he told the children, "I want you to get the bag your dad brought and find your pajamas, then go into the bathroom and wash up."

"Carry me." Maggie reached up again, but Tony shook his head.

"Not this time, munchkin. Luke, can you help Maggie with her clothes?"

"Sure. She sometimes puts her stuff on backwards."

Maggie frowned. "I'm only a little girl, so it's okay. Mommy says so."

Tony grinned. "And your mom is right." He gave Maggie a quick squeeze. "You can leave your clothes in the bathroom and I'll pick them up in a bit. Get ready for bed and I'll get the tent set up, okay?"

Luke sidled close to get his own hug. "Can we have marshmallows and chocolate?"

"I think I have some cocoa left. We'll check when you've finished up. Put your toothbrushes in the bathroom, though, so we don't forget to brush before we go to bed."

"It's not bedtime yet."

Tony patted Luke's head, hearing the touch of anxiety there. "Nope. We still have to read a story, too. But when it is time, I promise to sleep close by you, okay?"

Trying not to look too relieved, Luke nodded. "Maggie'll like that."

"Carry me."

Again Maggie lifted her arms to Tony, and he almost gave in. Then he shook his head. "Go on, imp. Luke will give you a hand."

She didn't look happy about it, but she let Luke take her hand and lead her down the hall. Tony felt a swell of pride at what good kids they were. He hoped, when Olivia finally conceived, that he'd be half as good a parent as his brother, John, was.

That thought had his stomach roiling again, and he went back in to look at Olivia. She hadn't moved a single muscle. He'd never thought it before, but looking at her now, relaxed with a small, content smile on her face, she was a very beautiful woman. He swallowed the lump of emotion in his throat, then carefully crept toward her chair.

She was obviously exhausted, the past two days wearing on her. He knew he'd slept little, and she'd confessed to the same problem. What they were doing, what they planned, it was enough to rattle a person's thoughts.

Seeing her in sleep, though, with all her pride and

stubbornness and the attitude she generally affected wiped away by total relaxation, proved to be a great insight. He'd always seen Olivia in one way, as if any woman could be one-dimensional. He should have known Olivia would be more complex than most.

Talking about her family had upset her, had left her struggling for words in a way he'd never witnessed before. Her pain had become his, and he'd found himself wanting only to distract her, to ease her. When he'd kissed her, it had been with the intent to console, but as always with Olivia since starting this strange bit of business, one touch had left him wanting another, and for a brief moment, he'd actually forgotten Maggie and Luke outside.

It was a good thing Luke had walked in when he did, because Tony didn't want her thinking everything between them was about sex, or even about getting a baby. As she'd told him earlier, they were friends. Certainly they were closer friends now than he'd ever envisioned them being, but he liked it, and he sensed a need in her to be reassured. He planned to do just that.

Little Shawn wiggled, then snuggled into her breast, and without opening her eyes, Olivia gently patted his back and made soft *shushing* sounds. Tony reached out and laid his hand over hers, hoping to convey so much with that one small gesture.

Olivia's eyes snapped open, but she didn't move or jar the baby in any way. It took her a moment to reorient herself, then she smiled. "Hi."

That one whispered word had his chest squeezing again. "Hi."

"He wanted to be held."

Her voice, pitched low and husky from sleep, rubbed over him like a caress. "So I see."

"He sleeps a lot, doesn't he?"

"He's still considered a newborn. I suppose," he whispered, staring into her dark eyes and wanting so much to hold her, "we should get a book on babies, one that tells you what to expect so we'll be prepared when ours is born."

A look of such intense pain filled her eyes he reached for her without thinking. "What is it, Olivia? Are you okay?"

She swallowed twice, then took a deep breath. "I'm okay. It's just… Tony, will you be very disappointed if I don't conceive? I mean, what if we try the agreed two weeks, and it just doesn't happen?"

"We'll keep trying." He was positive. He didn't want any other woman to birth his child. He wanted this woman.

"I… I don't know if that's a good idea. We agreed—"

He bridged his arms around her hips and laid his head against her thighs. Her hand touched his nape, then she threaded her fingers through his hair. "Tony?"

"Shh. You're borrowing trouble. Let's just wait and see what happens." He continued to hold her like that until he heard the kids start out of the bathroom. With a sigh, he sat up. "I guess I'd better get started on that tent. Will you camp out with us tonight?"

She shook her head. "I shouldn't. I didn't bring any pajamas or my toothbrush or any—"

"I have a silly pair of Mickey Mouse pajamas Kate bought for me one year as a joke. You can use those. And I have an extra toothbrush."

"You do? Should I ask why?"

Grinning, he came to his feet. "I'd rather you didn't."

Olivia frowned at him, and he decided he liked her small show of jealousy, even if he knew she would deny suffering such an emotion.

Being careful not to wake him, he lifted Shawn and returned him to his blanket. "Come on. You can help me pitch a tent."

Her frown left, and to his relief, she joined in wholeheartedly. It took them a half hour to get the tent assembled. They shoved all the furniture back so the tent sat in the middle of the room. Olivia lit a fire in the fireplace while Tony searched through his kitchen for marshmallows and cocoa. Shawn woke up and began fussing, and though Olivia wanted to help, she was hopeless at changing a diaper. Tony laughed at her efforts, then showed her the proper way to do it. Her intent fascination through the routine process had him grinning long after the job was done.

He knew she wanted to give Shawn his bottle, but she held back, pretending a great interest in the silly, rather long-winded story Maggie was telling her about a cartoon character on her favorite preschool show. Tony watched her surreptitiously, and a plan began to form.

Maybe, because of all she'd been through as a child, Olivia only thought she didn't want a family. Maybe he could convince her otherwise. As soon as the idea hit, he felt a sick sort of trepidation. Like any man, the thought of rejection was repugnant to him. And he knew he was being overly emotional about the whole thing, but this particular situation was one to inspire romantic notions. Being alone with a woman, acting as a family to three children, left his need for his own family with a sharpened edge.

But his original plan was much more realistic, and much easier to plan around. He *knew* he could love a child, that he could be a good father. He had the example of his own father, not to mention his brother and brother-in-law to go by. But a wife…that was a chancy matter. Could he really count on Olivia to restructure her life to fit a family into her busy schedule?

He decided what he needed was more time—time to watch her with the children, to be with her. He'd take her to the office tomorrow and show her the expansion plans beginning with the new Northwestern Crown. He'd planned to do that anyway, to judge her reaction to the site for her new lingerie shop.

In the meantime…

He went over to her, not really giving her a choice, and put Shawn in her lap. She opened her dark eyes wide and stared at him, looking hopeful, and a bit unsure of herself. Then he handed her the bottle of formula, and watched as Shawn began to fuss, and Olivia looked from him to the baby and back again.

"I think he's hungry, honey. Would you mind?"

"You want me to feed him?"

"Just keep the bottle up so he doesn't suck air, and keep a napkin under his chin because he tends to make a mess of it."

Looking as if she'd just been handed the world, Olivia carefully situated bottle and baby, then managed to listen as Maggie picked up where she'd been interrupted.

His heart seemed to swell, watching Olivia struggle with the baby. And more and more, he found himself wondering if keeping only the baby wouldn't mean giving up the better half of the deal.

CHAPTER SIX

AFTER SEVERAL STORIES and whispered giggles, Maggie and Luke finally fell asleep. It was way past their usual bedtime, but it had proven very difficult to get the kids to settle down. The combination of worrying about their mother, being in different surroundings and their general excitement, had all conspired to keep them wide-awake.

Tony had arranged everyone in a row, with Luke first, then himself, then Maggie, then Olivia. He would have preferred to have her right next to him, but he didn't trust himself, and he wasn't into self-torture. Now, at nearly midnight, Tony turned his head to look at Olivia, and even in the dim interior of the tent, he could see that her eyes were open. He reached across Maggie, who was taking up more room than one little three-year-old girl should, and slid one finger down Olivia's arm. Her eyes slanted in his direction, and she smiled. "They're asleep?"

He answered in the same hushed tone. "I do believe so."

"I've never slept on the floor before."

He grinned, then tugged on the sleeve of the pajamas she wore until she gave him her hand. "A lot of new experiences today, huh?"

When she bit her lip, he suppressed a laugh and said, "I was talking about wearing Micky Mouse pajamas.

And giving a baby a bottle. And camping out in the family room with a three-year-old snoring next to you."

Olivia flashed her own grin. "And here I thought you meant something entirely different."

"Are you enjoying yourself?"

Turning on her side to face him, she laced her fingers with his, and they allowed their arms to rest over Maggie. The little girl sighed in her sleep. "You know, I believe I am having fun. I'd always thought of you as a stuffy businessman, and here you are, an adventurer."

"Me, stuffy? You're the one who eats, drinks and sleeps business."

She gave him another cheeky grin. "I learned from you."

"Ah, so it's my fault you're so ruthless?" His grin belied any insult.

"I'm serious. I've always respected you very much. Everyone does. When I negotiated my first shop in your hotels, I'd already read everything I could find on you. And there was plenty. You're considered a golden boy, you know. You took a mediocre hotel chain and turned it around to one of the fastest growing, most recognizable names in the industry. You gave new meaning to the name Austin Crown."

It was unbelievable the amount of pride he felt hearing her sing his praises. Of course he'd heard it before, but it meant more coming from Olivia. And he decided he liked this, liked talking quietly in the dark, getting to know her better, letting her know him. He seldom volunteered information about himself, but now, it seemed the most natural thing in the world.

"When my father died, I knew I had to do something to distract myself. It wasn't an easy time, and he'd been a really fantastic father—the best. He'd taught me what I needed to know in the industry, but like John, he refused to neglect his family to devote the time necessary to make the business what it is today. Sometimes I wonder if he'd lived, exactly where I'd be right now."

She answered with absolute conviction. "You'd have had your own business. You're a very driven, success-oriented man. I'll bet you were an overachiever in school, too, weren't you?"

He laughed quietly, knowing she'd pegged him. "I suppose. And it's not that I regret the life I've led. But there could have been so much more." He knew she understood when she squeezed his hand.

"And there will be. Now. You'll have your own family, Tony, just wait. You've still got plenty of time to do anything you want to do. You're young and intelligent and very handsome, and—"

It disturbed him, having her talk about his life with her being no part of it. Though that had been his original plan, and could still work out to be the best solution, he instinctively balked at the thought of losing her. Interrupting her to halt the words, he teased, "Very handsome, hmm?"

"Quit fishing for compliments. You know what you look like. Why not be honest about it?"

The glow from the fireplace barely penetrated the thick canvas of the tent, leaving the outline of Olivia's body a mere shadow beneath her blanket. But her eyes, so wide and sweet, were as discernible as her slight smile. "That's one of the things I like about you, Olivia. You believe in honesty. You're outspoken and truthful to a fault. I don't have to guess at your motives."

He felt her sudden stillness, the way she seemed to

withdraw emotionally. She didn't say anything, though the tension was thick, and then she was trying to pull away. "We better get some sleep. As I told you, I didn't rest much last night."

He didn't understand the way her mood had abruptly altered, but he decided he wouldn't allow her to pull completely away from him. Rather than question her when she seemed so anxious, he merely replied to her statement. Holding tight to her fingers, he whispered, "I'm sorry you're tired, but I'm glad I didn't suffer alone." She had nothing to say to that, so he added, "Good night, sweetheart. If you need anything during the night, let me know."

Pillowing her head on her arm, she closed her eyes and very deliberately shut him out.

But she didn't take her hand away. And then he heard her whisper, "Good night, Tony."

IT WAS VERY early when Olivia felt a puff of moist breath against her cheek. She opened one eye and jerked in startled surprise before she recognized the faint outline of Maggie's face in the dim interior of the tent. "What is it?"

Maggie's nose touched her cheek and she realized the child was trying to see her clearly. "Livvy, I gotta pee."

"Oh." For a second, Olivia drew a blank. She glanced at Tony to see that Luke was practically lying on top of him, draped sideways over his chest. They'd put Shawn to sleep outside the tent, surrounded by the cushions off the couch so no one would accidentally get up in the night and step on him. Twice, she had heard him fuss, but both times Tony had quietly slipped from the tent to prepare the baby's bottle.

Olivia didn't want to wake him again for something so minor, but she honestly had no idea how to deal with Maggie's request. "Do you, uh…know how to go to the potty by yourself?"

She could barely see the bobbing of Maggie's head. "But you come wif me."

"Oh." Olivia was beginning to feel like an idiot. Of course the little girl wouldn't want to go on her own. The house was dark and unfamiliar. "Okay. But let's be quiet so we don't wake anyone up."

They crawled out of the tent, and Maggie caught at the hem of the Mickey Mouse pajama top, then held her arms in the air. "Carry me."

Since Maggie wasn't really asking, but insisting, Olivia lifted her sturdy little body and groped her way down the hall. The fluorescent bathroom light was bright and made them both squint. Olivia watched Maggie struggle with her nightgown, then she asked, "Do you…um, need any help?"

Shaking her head, Maggie said, "Stay wif me."

"Right. I won't go anywhere."

Maggie grinned at her, and Olivia felt rather complimented that her company had been required for such a female outing. Hadn't she seen plenty of women visit the "ladies' room" in groups? It was practically a tradition, and Maggie had just given her a part of it. She leaned against the wall and waited, and when Maggie had finished and again said, "Carry me," Olivia didn't hesitate. In fact, she found she liked having the small warm body clinging to her, trusting her.

They entered the tent without making a sound, but no sooner had she settled Maggie than she heard Tony say, "You have all the natural instincts, Olivia."

This time, the reference to something that could never be didn't bother her. In fact, she felt a reluctant grin and realized she felt good. Damn good. "Go to sleep, Tony."

"Yeah," Maggie said. "Go sleep, Tony." And within seconds, the tent was again filled with soft snoring.

TONY'S MOTHER SHOWED up at eight-thirty with a bag of doughnuts and the news that Lisa was feeling much improved, except for a great deal of lingering exhaustion. The penicillin had done its magic and she was more than anxious to see her children again.

"I'm going to take them to the hospital to visit her this morning," Sue said, "and they're hopeful she can come home this afternoon, after the doctor makes his rounds and checks her over."

"Isn't that rushing it a bit?" Tony asked. They were sitting at the dining-room table while Maggie and Luke gobbled doughnuts in the kitchen. Sue held Shawn, and every so often she'd make faces at him and babble in baby talk or nibble on his ears or feet. Tony glanced at Olivia and saw she was fascinated by his mother's behavior. In his family, no one felt the least hesitation in playing with a child—and acting like a fool in the process.

"She seemed to be doing okay to me, but of course, I'm not a doctor." Sue smiled at Olivia. "You know how it is with mothers. They can't bear to be away from their kids. Why, if they try to keep her another day while she's complaining and begging to leave, she's liable to make herself sick with worry. She's afraid the kids are terrorizing Tony. Of course, she didn't know he had you here to help him."

The sound of suggestion in his mother's tone couldn't

have been missed by a deaf man. Tony glanced at Olivia again, but she was only smiling. He felt…proud, dammit. Proud of the way Olivia had greeted his mother, her natural grace and composure. Being caught in your lover's house by your lover's mother wasn't something Olivia was used to. But she'd handled the situation remarkably well.

Dressed in casual khaki slacks with a sharp pleat and a black pullover sweater, she didn't look like a woman who had spent the night on the floor. She'd been up and dressed when he opened his eyes, and that had annoyed him. Usually the idea of facing a woman in the morning was an unpleasant prospect, but with Olivia, he'd wanted to see her sleeping in his house. He'd wanted to make her coffee and awaken her with a kiss. Instead she was the one who had prepared the coffee, and all traces of peaceful rest had been washed from her big brown eyes before he'd even crawled from the tent. She was again the composed, elegant lady he'd come to know through business, and while he appreciated the picture she made, he wanted to see that softer, more accessible side of her more often.

Olivia laughed at his mother's comments, and Tony could only stare, wanting her again. Always wanting her. The woman didn't have to do more than walk toward him and he got hard.

"Tony did all the work, Sue. I'm afraid I haven't had much experience with children. But please, tell Lisa that the kids were adorable. I very much enjoyed myself."

It was at that moment Maggie appeared at Olivia's side. Her face and hands were sticky with doughnut glaze, and without missing a beat, Olivia picked up a napkin and began wiping off the worst of it. Maggie grinned and said, "Carry me, Livvy."

Olivia bent down to scoop Maggie into her lap. "And where are we going?"

"Potty."

Turning to Sue, she said, "Excuse me just a moment."

She'd done that so naturally, without any hesitation at all, Tony knew he was making progress. Toward what end, he wasn't certain, but he took great satisfaction from the progress just the same.

He didn't realize he was smiling as he watched her leave the room until his mother nudged him with her foot. "She's a natural."

He laughed. "I told her the same thing last night."

Sue made a big production of rearranging Shawn's blanket. "It's worked out nice that she was here yesterday when John came by."

"I could have managed on my own."

"You've never had all three kids overnight before."

"True. But we'd have muddled through. Actually Shawn was the easiest to look after. He still sleeps most of the day away." It was apparent his small talk hadn't distracted his mother one iota. She had that look about her that gave him pause and let him know she was set on a course.

"So…what was Olivia doing here?"

Never let it be said that his mother couldn't use subtlety when it was required. "Women have been in my house before."

"It's been a while, though. And Olivia, unless I miss my guess, isn't just another woman."

Their relationship was too complicated by far to explain to his mother. Especially since he didn't understand it himself. He decided to nip her curiosity and parental meddling in the bud, at least until he could sort out his own feelings. "Olivia is more into business than I am. She wants to get ahead, not stay at home."

"So? Plenty of women work these days and tend a family, too. And you're not exactly helpless. I think between the two of you..."

"Mom, you're way ahead of yourself. Olivia is very clear on the fact she doesn't want a husband or family. She told me that herself. She would be totally unsuitable as a wife, so stop trying to plot against me."

Sue glanced up at the doorway, then cleared her throat. Olivia stood there, her face pink with embarrassment and a stricken look in her eyes. Tony wanted to curse; he wanted to stand up and hold her close and swear he hadn't meant what he'd just said. But there was his mother to consider, and besides, he didn't know how much of what he'd said might be true.

Olivia took the problem out of his hands by forcing a smile, then retaking her seat. "I'm afraid he's right, Sue. I'm not marriage material. This is the closest I've ever come to playing house, and I'm not at all certain I was successful. Which is okay. I'm a businesswoman, with not a domestic bone in my body." She laughed, but Tony knew her laughs now, and this one wasn't genuine. "I'm not cut out for this sort of thing. But after watching Tony last night, I'm convinced he is. He should have a few children of his own."

His mother agreed, then made deliberate small talk, but the tension in the air refused to dissipate. Once again Olivia was invited for Thanksgiving dinner, but the invitation was left open. And when the children were done eating and had their teeth brushed, Sue bustled them toward the door.

Giving Tony a listen-to-your-mother look, she said, "Try to talk Olivia into coming for Thanksgiving." Then to Olivia, "It's very casual and relaxed. With all the kids, it couldn't be any other way. But now that I know the children don't bother you—"

Maggie spoke up and said, "We don't bother, Livvy. She likes us."

Olivia patted her head and smiled. "Of course I do."

So Luke added, "Then you'll come? Grandma makes lots of desserts."

That was obviously supposed to be enough inducement to tilt the scales. Tony laughed. "I'll see what I can do about persuading her, guys, okay?"

There was another round of hugs, and this time Olivia didn't look nearly so uncomfortable. And when he finally closed the door, Tony turned to her and gave his best wolfish grin. "Now, you."

"Me, what?"

"How did you get up so early today and put yourself together so well without making a sound?"

"Put myself together?"

"Yeah." He reached out to smooth his hand over her tidy hair. She'd pulled it back into a French braid that looked both casual and classic. She wore only the faintest touch of makeup—all that was needed with her dark lashes and brows and perfect complexion. "You sure don't look like a woman who camped on the floor of a tent last night."

"Oh." Olivia reached up and put her hands on his shoulders. With flat heels on, she stood just a few inches shorter than he. "I knew your mother was coming, and I thought it might be less awkward if I was up and about when she arrived."

"These are the clothes you had packed in that bag?"

"Yes. Not dressy, but suitable for just about anything."

Skimming his gaze down her body, he said, "You look wonderful. As always." Then his attention was drawn to her breasts, and he asked with increased interest, "Are you wearing sexy underwear again?"

"No."

"No?" She surprised him. "Why not? I thought you liked wearing that stuff. I was looking forward to you making me crazy again."

She cleared her throat. "I hadn't planned to spend the night. So just as I didn't pack a toothbrush, I didn't pack additional underthings."

"You didn't... Then what are you wearing underneath?"

"Nothing."

He froze for a heartbeat, then groaned and leaned down toward her mouth. "Next time, wake me before you get up."

Again, she surprised him. She pulled away and wrapped her arms around her stomach. "I don't think there should be a next time. This...spending the night, playing with children, morning visits with your mother—they weren't part of the deal, Tony."

He wanted to touch her, but her stance clearly warned him away. When he bent to try to read her expression, she kept her head averted. "I thought you enjoyed yourself."

Waving a hand to indicate the entire morning and night before, she said, "I wasn't supposed to be enjoy-

ing—" she waved her hand again "—all that. I was supposed to be enjoying…well…"

Tony grinned. "Ah. I've neglected my end of the bargain, haven't I? And I did promise to make it up to you."

She jerked away when he reached for her, her brows
lowered in a stern frown. "You did not disappoint me!
I meant…"

Tony caught her despite her resistance, then gently
eased her into his body. With his lips barely touching
hers, he said, "You don't even know what you're missing yet."

Again, she tried to protest, but he was done discussing issues he'd rather avoid, so he silenced her in the
best way known to man.

And this time, she voiced not a single complaint.

OLIVIA MOANED AS the sensations just kept building. Tony
was poised over her, in her, and his eyes held hers, touching her as intimately as his body did.

He was right. She hadn't known what she was missing.

One large warm hand curved around her buttocks,
then urged her into a rhythm. "Move with me, sweetheart. That's it." He groaned, his eyes briefly closing as
he fought for control. She loved that, loved watching him
struggle, loved knowing she had such an effect on him.

When he hooked his arms under her legs and lifted
them high, leaving her totally open and vulnerable, she
nearly panicked. He was so deep that her feelings of
pleasure were mixed with fear. Tony bent to press a kiss
to her lax mouth.

"Shh. It's all right." He thrust just a little harder,
watching her face. "Tell me if I hurt you."

"Tony…"

"Deep, honey, the book said deep. Remember? This was your idea."

She recalled sitting in the restaurant and taunting him about methods devised to better ensure conception. But what she felt now had nothing to do with receiving his sperm and everything to do with pleasure so intense it was frightening.

She felt the pressure build, felt Tony's heat washing over her, his scent filling her lungs, and she squeezed her eyes shut as her climax hit.

"Open your eyes!"

Tony's demand barely penetrated, but she managed to get her lids to lift, and then she connected with him in a way that went beyond the activities of their bodies. His eyes were bright, his face flushed, and as she watched he groaned, his jaw tight, his gaze locked to hers, and she knew he was experiencing his own explosive orgasm. She felt it with him, and her own again, and then he lowered himself, in slow degrees, to rest completely over her.

It seemed too much to bear, the emotional side to lovemaking, and she wondered that other people didn't find it too overwhelming. Tears came to her eyes, her breath starting to shudder, but thankfully, Tony was unaware, as he still struggled for his own breath. When he started to move away, she tightened her hold.

He wrapped his arms more firmly around her and pressed his face beside hers. "You're something else, you know that?"

She wondered if that was true. Was it always this way, or did they do something special? It certainly seemed special to her.

"What is it, honey?" Tony lifted away and smoothed her hair from her face. He noticed a tear and kissed it from her cheek, then smiled. "I can hear you thinking."

"That's impossible."

"Nope. I really can. You're worrying about something, aren't you?"

She noticed he wasn't apologizing this time for not doing it right. In fact, he looked downright smug, so she assumed this was how it was supposed to be. But... "It gets more intense every time."

"And that worries you?"

Shrugging her bare shoulders, she looked away from his astute gaze and mumbled, "Is it supposed to be like that?"

She could hear the smile in his tone. "Between us, yes."

"But not with other people?"

"Olivia." She knew she amused him and she frowned. He smoothed his thumb over her brow, making her relax again.

"Sex is different with everyone. It's certainly never been like this for me before, but it's nothing to worry about. Some people can be very cavalier about intimacy, but you're just not that way."

"Are you?"

He hesitated, then kissed her again. "I don't know. To me, sex is natural and not something to be ashamed of. But it was never just casual, either. I had to care for a woman. I didn't indulge in one-night stands. But...it was never quite like this. Not the way it is with you."

This time, Olivia couldn't look away. "Doesn't that bother you?"

His laugh made her jump, coming so unexpectedly. "No. It probably should, but…damn, I like it."

He forestalled all her other questions by rising from the bed, then looking down at her body. Rather than feeling embarrassment, she felt proud that he took pleasure in the sight of her. Then he reached down and smacked his open palm against her hip. "Come on, woman. Duty calls. I need to go into the office."

She stretched, not really wanting to leave his bed but knowing he was right. "I have to make a few calls, also."

"Will you come to my office with me?"

"Ah, the mysterious thing you have to show me. What is it, Tony?"

"You'll see when we get there."

Olivia rose and headed for the bathroom, amazed at how quickly she was getting used to being naked in front of a man. "I'll have to meet you there. I need to go home and shower properly and change, and check in at the office. I've got to hire a new manager now, you know."

She closed the bathroom door and reached for a washrag. When she saw the reflection of her own expression in the mirror—her smile, her look of contentment—she paused. She was such a fraud, and no doubt Tony would hate her if he ever knew.

She was about to contemplate the possibility of quitting the game before she got in too deep, and then Tony tapped on the door and said, "Come on, honey. Let's get going. If I get to the office soon, I can get my business done and make it an early day. Maybe we can do dinner tonight."

Of course, dinner was not part of the deal, either, but she desperately wanted to give in to him. And she knew by the way her heart jumped at the endearment, she was already in too deep to dig herself out.

She was falling in love with Tony.

CHAPTER SEVEN

THE CLICK OF her heels echoed across the faux marble foyer as she headed for the hallway leading to Tony's office. Out of all the Crowns, this was her favorite. Probably because it was in her own hometown; possibly because it was where Tony spent most of his time. This was the office he ran the business from.

She'd been here numerous times, for professional discussions, to meet associates, but never as Tony Austin's lover. Because of that, she'd dressed her best, choosing her most professional outfit. Not by look or by deed did she intend to start the scandalmongers talking. It would be difficult to deal with him in an impassive way, to pretend she hadn't lain naked with him just that morning—that he hadn't done those sinfully wicked, wonderfully arousing things to her.

That she hadn't done some of them back to him.

As she rounded the corner, she met familiar faces and nodded a polite greeting.

"Ms. Anderson," she heard from one woman, and, "How're you doing today, Ms. Anderson?" from a young man.

"Hello, Cathi, George. I'm well, thank you." She kept her responses brief, as was her norm. Tony was correct when he said she avoided even the simplest relationships. Interacting in a social sphere wasn't easy for her. She had to work much harder at such relationships than she did when in her business mode. Understanding social etiquette was so much more complicated than working a deal.

She hadn't been here since the night of the party, and she hadn't paid much attention to the remodeling at the time. But now she did. The carpeting was so soft, the colors so soothing and gracious, she couldn't help but admire them. She would have chosen something similar herself. It was just one more way they were alike, she and Tony.

She opened the glass door and walked to Martha's desk, then waited while Martha finished up a phone call.

Be businesslike, Olivia reminded herself, not wanting to take a chance on giving herself away. She was ridiculously nervous, as if she feared Martha would look at her and notice something different, see some sign of her new intimacy with Tony. Of course the woman wouldn't know; it was impossible. But already the situation was far more complicated than she'd ever thought it could be, and she couldn't help but fidget as she waited, staring around the office as if she'd never seen it before.

Finally Martha hung up the phone. "Ms. Anderson. How nice to see you again."

"Hello, Martha. I need to speak with Mr. Austin. Is he busy now?"

"He left instructions to notify him right away if you dropped in. Just let me buzz him."

Drat the man, Olivia thought. Couldn't he even remember his own deception? Tony had a long-standing rule: everyone needed an appointment to see him at the office except family and very close friends. Telling Martha such a thing, as if it didn't matter in the least if

Olivia interrupted his day, was as good as announcing their sexual relationship.

And then she remembered just how often she'd dropped by to discuss some contract dispute or other, and decided it didn't matter. She had never followed Tony's rules before, not when there was something she wanted.

Of course, usually what she wanted was a better deal, not Tony himself.

The office door opened and Tony stepped out, followed closely by his brother-in-law, Brian. She'd almost forgotten that Brian worked in the family business, but seeing him now, dressed in a dark suit and carrying a briefcase, jogged her memory. Two other men exited the office as well, and they all smiled at her. Olivia felt horribly conspicuous. Each of these men managed one of the Crowns; she remembered meeting them at Tony's party the night he'd propositioned her to have his baby.

Trying to work up her best professional expression proved almost impossible, especially given the fact that Tony stood there grinning in an intimate, very telling way. Surely the other men would notice, and then their secret would be revealed.

She was wondering how to react, what exactly to say, when Brian stepped forward and took her hand. "Olivia. It's nice to see you again. I hear you spent the weekend helping Tony babysit. Kate was so pleased. She judges everyone's character by how they treat our children, you know, and she claimed right up front you were a natural."

Olivia drew an appalled blank. Why did everyone keep saying she was a natural? She was hopelessly lost around kids and she knew it. And then it hit her.

Brian had just announced to the entire office that

she'd spent the weekend with Tony. She almost groaned and couldn't quite bring herself to look away from Brian and judge the reactions of the other men. Watching Brian, she had the suspicious feeling he'd just done her and Tony in on purpose.

The silence dragged on, and she forced a polite nod. "It was my pleasure," she said, and then flinched at the squeak in her voice.

Brian laughed. "There, you see? Who would consider entertaining three kids overnight a pleasure? Other than Tony, of course. He's a man meant to spawn a dozen, I swear."

Tony laughed. "A dozen? No, thank you. Three was a handful."

Olivia couldn't believe Tony just stood there, joking and laughing and letting the conversation deteriorate in such a way. Did he want everyone to know their business? What had happened to avoiding a scandal?

Brian still held her hand, and with a small tug, he regained her attention. "I keep telling Tony I get a turn now. With our two girls, he'd spend all his time playing house and attending tea parties." Brian cocked an eyebrow. "I don't suppose I can get you and Tony next weekend, can I? The girls would love it, and Kate and I could use the time alone."

Tony shook his head, still grinning, and pretended to stagger with Brian's suggestion. "Give us a month to recuperate, then we'll think about it."

A month? Olivia wouldn't even be seeing him in a month. Two weeks, and that was it. In fact, it was less than two weeks now, since they'd already started on the countdown, as it were.

The thought left her blank-brained for a moment

more, and saddened with the reminder that this wouldn't last, that it was so very temporary. When she finally gained enough wit to assess her surroundings, she saw that Tony was dismissing the other two men and saying his goodbyes to Brian. She glanced at Martha, but that busy lady was bent over her computer, typing away. Then she felt Tony's hand on her arm.

In the gentlest tone she'd ever heard from him, he said, "Come on. We'll talk in my office."

Unlike the outer office, this one had solid walls, not glass, and guaranteed privacy, and so she went willingly, needing a moment to gather herself. Tony led her to a padded leather chair and urged her into the seat, then knelt down before her.

"Are you all right?"

She wanted to say that she was fine, but she didn't feel fine. She felt downright wretched. "This is awful."

"What is?"

She gaped at him, refusing to believe he could be so obtuse. "The gossip is probably all over the hotel by now! Everyone will know."

"You're making too much of it, honey. So people will think we're dating? It's not a big deal."

"Not a big deal? You wanted to keep our association private, remember?"

"Our *relationship* is private. No one will know we're trying to conceive a child. And as far as the other, you're attractive, we work together. Why shouldn't people assume we'd share a date or two?"

Olivia bit her lip, his logic irrefutable. "I suppose you could be right."

"I know I am. And as long as my family already knows all about us, you might as well give in and come to Thanksgiving dinner. I'll never hear the end of it if you refuse."

She honestly didn't think she could survive another family get-together. "I really don't..."

Leaning close, Tony framed her face then placed a soft kiss on her lips. "I know it's hard on you, but I'll be there. And after a while, being with a big family won't bother you so much. You might even enjoy yourself. Besides, the kids are looking forward to seeing you again. And I know you enjoyed them."

"I did." Her answer emerged as a whisper. She was tempted, but also a little afraid. She was losing complete control of the situation, and that hadn't happened to her in years, not since she'd been a child. "I don't want everyone thinking we're seriously involved."

"They'll think whatever they choose whether you're there or not. At least this way, some of their curiosity will die."

"Do you really think so?"

"Sure. Right now they assume I've been trying to keep you a secret. This way, they'll think we're only dating."

Convincing her proved to be much too easy, and Olivia admitted to herself that she actually wanted to go. "I guess you're right. And when the two weeks are over and we stop seeing each other, everyone will just believe we've broken up."

Abruptly Tony came to his feet and stalked toward his desk. He stood there with his face turned away, one hand braced on the edge of the desk and his other hand pressed deep into his pants pocket. He was the perfect study of a man in deep thought, and Olivia wished she could decipher his mood.

Without looking at her, he asked, "How did you come up with this two-week time limit?"

On shaky ground now, she took a second to weigh her answer. "It seemed a reasonable amount of time. If I was going to conceive, it would probably happen by then."

"So you thought we'd just stop seeing each other, and if and when you turned up pregnant, you'd give me a quick call to break the news to me?"

It sounded very cold, having him spell it out that way. Of course, she knew she wouldn't conceive. "You agreed with that plan, Tony."

"Yeah, well now I don't like it." He glanced over his shoulder at her, then turned away again. "I think I have a better plan."

"And that is?" The mixed feelings of excitement and trepidation settled in her stomach.

"Let's continue to work at conception until we have positive news. If it takes three weeks, or four, what's the big deal? And this way, I'll be able to monitor every second of the pregnancy. You did agree to that, remember."

At that particular moment in time, Olivia wished with all her heart that she wasn't sterile. Spending more time with Tony, allowing him to be such a huge part of her life, would be next to perfection. But since she knew that couldn't happen, she was left floundering for an answer he could accept.

None came to mind, and she stared at his broad back, seeing the rigid set to his shoulders, until finally he asked, "Olivia?"

"There's no guarantee that it'll happen in four weeks, either, Tony. We have to have some time limit. That's only reasonable."

He turned to face her, his expression stern. "Then give me a month."

That was his corporate I'm-the-boss tone, demanding and expecting to be obeyed. She laughed because that tone had never once intimidated her. Teasing him now, she said, "You feel you can come up with sufficient potency in a month, do you?"

He grinned, too, as if her mood had lightened his own. Then his eyes narrowed. "Come here, honey. I have something to show you."

There was a determined set to his jaw, a look of challenge, and Olivia's curiosity carried her quickly to the desk. Spread out over the mahogany surface was a variety of photographs depicting a very posh hotel. "This is a new purchase?"

"Yes." Tony moved the pictures around so she could see them all clearly. "What do you think?"

Olivia studied the photos. There was an immense, elegant banquet room done in white and gold. One picture showed a pool that seemed to be outdoors, surrounded as it was with foliage and trees and what appeared to be a waterfall, but in fact it was centered within a large glass enclosure. Some of the photos showed ornate chandeliers hanging from many ceilings, and everything seemed to be accented in gold.

"It's beautiful."

"The building itself is actually ancient, and we've kept most of the historic qualities, which will be a draw on their own. But inside, it's been renovated a great deal. It'll be supported by a very upscale clientele, and it's where I thought you might relocate—if you choose—after the baby's born."

Her eyes widened and she took an automatic step back. Her stomach began to churn with a sick kind of dread. "I see."

Tony's jaw tightened and he ran a hand through his hair. "Actually the shop space is yours whether you conceive or not."

It took her only a second, and then she shook her head. "No. Our deal…"

"To hell with the deal!" He drew a deep breath and shook his head. "I'm sorry. I feel lousy about this. You see, I'd already considered offering you the space before I talked with you about the baby. But I kept it to myself because I thought it might be an incentive for you to accept my proposition. But now…well, you deserve the space. You're a good choice for the Crown. Our guests always love your shops, so I know you'll do well."

Olivia felt her head swimming. She tried to think, but it seemed impossible. This had been a horrendous morning all the way around. "I don't know. It's such a drastic move…"

"It's a move up. A large expansion for your business. The sales potential here will be incredible." He waited a heartbeat, then added, "Of course, the added shop will keep you busy. Having locations so far apart will be time-consuming, leaving little time for anything but work. But that shouldn't be a problem for you."

She glanced up at the way he said that. His gaze bore into her, hot and intent, waiting. But she didn't know what it was he waited for. Then he insisted, "That's what you want, right?"

"I… Yes. I want to grow." Despite everything, she felt a flutter of excitement. The new hotel was exactly the kind of place she eventually wanted to occupy. *Eventually.*

But she knew why Tony was offering it to her. He wanted her to be so busy she wouldn't be able to interfere in his and the baby's life. That hurt. She lifted her chin and gave him a level look. "It's a fantastic opportunity, Tony. But I don't want to get in over my head. The Northwest is so far away…"

"Seattle, to be exact."

He was watching her closely again, his arms crossed over his chest, and she had the feeling he was assessing her in some way. "Seattle." She stepped away, walking around his office to buy herself some time. It was actually an ideal situation, because she'd need to be away from Tony. She had no doubt that once the two weeks was over—and she would somehow have to keep it at two weeks—she would have a terrible time facing him, seeing him and pretending nothing had ever happened between them. The added work would help keep her mind off Tony, off what they had shared. But Seattle!

"I hadn't really considered this in great detail. After all, I've had other things on my mind." She flashed him a quick, nervous smile, which he thankfully returned.

"You can have some time to think about it if you want."

Time. Everything always came down to more time. Or the lack of it. "Yes, thank you." The relief she felt was plainly obvious in her tone.

He put his hand to his jaw, studying her a moment, then went to his office door and turned the lock. It caught with a soft *snick.* When he started toward her again, she could see the intent in his green eyes and she backed up until her bottom hit the desk.

He stopped before her, watching her, waiting. Then, lifting his hands to her shoulders, he gently turned her away from him until she faced the desk. Slipping her purse from her shoulder and setting it on the floor, he said, "Brace your hands flat on my desk."

She obeyed him without thought, her pulse beginning to race. "Tony?"

"I said I wanted to show you two things, honey, remember?"

"I remember." The trembling in her voice should have embarrassed her, but she was too concerned with the way his hands were busy lifting her skirt to pay much attention to anything else. "Tony, I don't think…"

"Shh. There's this quaint custom called a 'nooner.' I think you'll like it."

His fingers slid along the back of her thighs, higher, until they touched the lace edging on her panties. "But, what if Martha knocks?"

"Martha went to lunch," he said, his tone now husky and deep as he squeezed and petted her bottom. "I don't have any appointments, and at the moment, I'm feeling particularly *potent*." He lightly bit her ear to punctuate that statement.

"Um. I see." His palm slid around to her belly, then dipped into her panties, and she automatically parted her legs. "We can't very well waste your potency, now can we?"

He chuckled, his open mouth pressed to the back of her neck, warm and damp and hungry. And with her heart rapping sharply against her ribs and the sound of his zipper hissing in the quiet of the room, she decided every quaint custom should get its due. And right now, she liked this one very much.

THANKSGIVING DAY ROLLED around quickly, but Olivia no longer felt any apprehension at joining Tony's family. Over the past two weeks, she'd come to know them all very well. They'd somehow managed to run into her repeatedly, one or the other of them having shown up at her shop whenever she was there ordering, or interviewing new managers for the new location.

It had started with his sister, Kate, who dropped in with the supposed intention of buying lingerie. She did leave with a couple of purchases, but most of her time there was spent chatting with Olivia, getting to know her better and sharing little details of her life.

Kate came again later that week with Lisa, and laughed as she described Brian's reaction to the lingerie Kate had bought.

"I guess I must have let things get a little stale, because when he saw me in that satin teddy with all the cleavage, he nearly fell off the bed."

Lisa joined in the laughter and ordered herself the same teddy in a different color, but Olivia blushed to have such an intimate scene discussed in her presence. In fact, she was blushing most of the time that Lisa and Kate stayed to visit, trying on numerous things and including her in all their "girl talk," as they called it. They didn't pry, didn't ask her anything personal about Tony, but they certainly talked about him.

If there was anything she'd wanted to know, they had the answer, and seemed to relish telling her.

"Tony's played patriarch since our father's death," Kate said, her voice becoming a little more solemn. "He's set himself up in a difficult role, and I for one think he deserves a little fun."

Olivia wondered if she fell under the heading of

"fun." Kate and Lisa seemed to think so, given the way they included her.

"It hurt Tony even more than it did the rest of us," Kate continued. "He was the oldest and, even though Dad was always fair, there was a special bond between the two of them. John never had any real interest in the hotels, at least not to the extent Tony did, so it just happened that Tony and Dad spent more time together."

"When he died," Lisa added, "John was so concerned for Tony. But Tony being Tony, he hid whatever grief he felt and dived headfirst into turning the business around. I think he did it as much to keep himself busy as to watch the company grow."

"And he almost cut women out completely. Before that, he'd seemed determined to find a wife. He wanted to be married like the rest of us, and he gave different women a fair chance, though even I'll admit he really hooked up with some impossible choices. Tony is such an idiomatic man, arrogant, but kind. And always in charge. It would take a strong woman to satisfy him."

Lisa laughed, then nudged Kate in the shoulder. "He used to claim he was looking for the perfect woman."

Kate grinned. "And we'd tell him we were already taken."

All three women laughed, and Olivia began to feel some sort of kinship with them. Without thinking, she said, "Well, unfortunately, I'm as far from perfect as he could possibly get."

Kate shook her head. "The idea of perfection exists only in the perspective of the person who's looking— and what that person is looking for. Besides, love has a way of finding perfection in the most unlikely places."

"And anyway," Lisa said, choosing another pair of

"barely there" panties, "you and Tony are having fun, he's dating again and the kids all love you. For right now, that's more than enough, don't you think?"

Olivia avoided the context of the question, and said only, "I'm glad the kids approve of me."

"They adore you," Kate insisted. "And the way those kids worship their uncle Tony, that's a big requirement for any relationship he might have."

Of course, Olivia hadn't told them that her relationship with Tony had a set purpose and a time limit. He'd said to take it one day at a time, and she was doing just that, enjoying herself and storing away the memories so she would never be truly alone again. But her two weeks were rapidly coming to an end, and it wouldn't be fair of her to continue in the deception.

A FEW DAYS later at a different Sugar and Spice location, she was going over some backstock with one of her managers when Brian and John showed up. They looked around the shop with undiluted interest. John appeared to be enthralled, but Brian, unbelievably, had a dark flush to his lean cheeks. Olivia hid her smile.

"So," John called out, striding toward her with his cocky walk and self-assured grin. "There's the lady who's managed to single-handedly put a honeymoon into the daily workweek."

Olivia felt her own cheeks heat, and slanted a look at Brian. But he had paused by a rack of a sheer lace camisoles and seemed to be engrossed in examining them.

"Hello, John."

He pulled her close and gave her a big kiss on the cheek. "I do love this place of yours, Livvy, I really do."

He'd affected Maggie's pet name for her, as had all

the children. She felt flustered by such an effusive welcome, and tried to gather herself. "I'm glad you approve. Do you have business in the hotel today?"

"Nope. Brian and I are Christmas shopping. Since the ladies have been hanging out here so much, we figured you'd know which things they've shown an interest in."

"Well, yes." There were several items the women had liked, but had hesitated to purchase because they were a bit pricey. She hesitated herself, uncertain of how much they wanted to spend.

Brian took care of that worry for her. "Whatever she wants, I'll buy it."

John laughed at that firm statement. "Poor Brian. Kate has really got you tied up now, doesn't she?"

"You don't see me complaining, do you?"

John gave a mock frown. "I don't know if I like hearing this about my little sister."

"Your sister's not so little anymore, and whatever tendencies ran through the Austin men, she inherited her fair share."

John cast Olivia a look. "Now, Brian, you'll go and spook Livvy if you say things like that."

Olivia had no idea what they were talking about, but she was beginning to get used to the way the men razzed each other. She shrugged and said, "Not at all."

"There, you see? Anyone who knows Tony at all already knows he's a driven man. Just stands to reason that drive would cover every part of his life."

Understanding hit her, and she tightened her lips to hide her smile. Yes, Tony was a "driven" man, always excelling at whatever he did—including lovemaking. She certainly had no complaints there.

Feeling a little risqué herself, she asked, "So it's a family trait, is it?"

John laughed. "Indeed it is. So you see, you with your nifty little shops fit right in. And like all the Austins, Tony goes after what he wants—and doesn't give up until he gets it." She didn't have time to reply to that since he quickly rubbed his hands together and asked, "Now. What does Lisa want? I can hardly wait."

Brian snorted. "Are you sure this shouldn't be *your* Christmas gift?"

Both men paused as if they'd just had the same thought, then reached out to shake hands. "I'll pick what I want, and you pick what you want. At least this year, you won't give me an ugly tie."

"That was a silk tie, you idiot, and very expensive."

"It didn't match anything I own."

The men continued to argue as they each chose what the other would give them for a holiday gift. John picked out a satin Victorian-style corset, then grinned. "I'm going to be a very happy boy on Christmas morning."

Brian held up the gift John would give to him, a snow-white, stretch-lace teddy with attached garters. "Me, too."

The men were so outrageous that Olivia ended up laughing with them and feeling entirely at her ease. Before their shopping spree was over, they'd purchased numerous gifts for their wives, several for themselves, and instructed Olivia to point their wives in the direction of the more risqué items if they mentioned wondering what to get for their husbands. Olivia promised to do just that.

Her manager and the additional clerk had their hands full gift wrapping all the purchases.

They were such an open, loving family, the men so

dedicated to their wives, all of them functioning with such unity. And they kept including her. Despite her intentions to stay detached, she found herself feeling a part of things, and actually looking forward to visiting with them again.

This would be the first Thanksgiving she hadn't spent alone since her parents had died, and she was suffering a mix of melancholy and excitement.

TONY ARRIVED RIGHT at three to collect her. She'd dressed up a little more than usual, wanting to make the most of the day, and when she let him in, he gave a low whistle. "Honey, you'd make the perfect dessert tonight."

With his gaze ranging over her body, she knew the dress had been worth the extra expense. Made of soft black cashmere, it fit her body perfectly, the off-the-shoulder design making it just a bit daring. The hem ended a good two inches above her knees, and she wore heels, which put her on eye level with Tony.

He caught her hand and pulled her close, then bent to press a kiss to her collarbone. "Tony…"

He lifted one hand and palmed her breast, but paused when she sucked in a deep breath. "Did I hurt you?"

She shook her head, unable to catch her breath with him gently kneading her. She felt especially sensitive tonight, her breasts almost painfully tight.

"Your nipples are already hard and I've barely touched you." Tony groaned softly. "What I wouldn't give for an extra hour right now." Reluctantly he released her.

When she turned away to get her coat, he cursed, then mumbled, "If we weren't expected…"

"But we are." She grinned, though she felt every bit as

urgent as he did. Even if she had a lifetime, rather than just a few more days, she'd never get enough of having him want her. She shook herself, refusing to think of the self-appointed time limit now. She didn't want anything to spoil this day.

A light snow had started that morning and now, as they stepped outside, Olivia saw that everything was coated in pristine white. The naked tree branches shimmered with it, and it clung to everything, including Tony's dark hair. After he opened the car door for her, she reached up and brushed his cheeks, her fingertips lingering.

"Olivia." Tony leaned down and gave her a melting kiss that should have thawed the snow. He lifted his head, searched her face, then bent to her mouth again. Olivia forgot the weather, forgot that they might be late, and wondered if they could go back inside again. Then they heard a tapping sound, like knuckles rapping on glass, and they looked up.

At the front door to the apartment building, her neighbors stood watching, huge grins on their faces. When Olivia laughed, they all waved.

"Like Snow White, they're seeing you off with the prince?"

"Hmm. You consider yourself a prince, do you?"

Tony waited for her to get in, then went around to the driver's side. After he'd started the car, he turned to her. "I only meant they're awfully protective of you."

Olivia had to agree on that. "And it's so strange, considering that I've kept to myself. I'm friendly, and I don't go out of my way to avoid them, but neither have I ever sought them out."

"You don't have to. There's just something about

you, a genuine feeling, that makes people trust you. And today, with the world what it is, trust is everything."

She looked away. "It's sometimes foolish to trust anyone."

"I trust you."

Oh, why did he have to do this now? "Tony, don't. I don't want to talk about important issues or discuss anything heavy. I just… I want to have fun today."

Glancing at her, he reached for her hand. "And you have fun with my family?"

"I really do. They're all crazy and happy and so accepting, it's impossible not to have fun around them."

She could tell he wanted to say more, but he held his peace. "Okay. But tomorrow we have to talk."

Not really wanting to, but seeing no way around it, she nodded. They would have to talk. Time was running out, and Tony deserved to be set free.

They spent the rest of the drive in silence, holding hands and watching the snow fall.

When they reached his mother's place, Tony walked her to the front door, his arm around her shoulders. The house was decorated with bright Christmas lights, and a hearty wreath hung on the door. Tony tipped up her chin and kissed her. "Smile, sweetheart. Today is just for eating and visiting and, later, making love. Agreed?"

"Of course." She laughed as he pretended to be surprised by her quick agreement.

"Have I spoiled you, Olivia?"

"Shamefully."

"So you'd planned on seducing me later?"

"I had every intention of doing so, yes."

His hand slipped under her coat and lightly caressed her waist. "Does this mean you're wearing something sexy and scandalous and guaranteed to drive me nuts under this dress?"

With wide-eyed innocence, she said, "Of course not."

He frowned, and just as the door started to open, she whispered, "I'm not wearing anything at all."

CHAPTER EIGHT

OLIVIA FELT THE first cramps right after dinner, but she ignored them. She was used to such pain, knew it was only her body reminding her that she wasn't what a woman should be. Since she'd had her first period when she was eleven, she'd suffered the cramps. Not normal period cramps, because there was nothing normal about her body's functions.

Sometimes the pains were pretty bad, other times only annoying, but she always managed to function despite their existence, ignoring them until they went away. Except when she'd been a child, and that was when her parents had taken her to the hospital.

She couldn't remember what actual medical term had been given to her condition, but it had to do with her ovaries and the fact they didn't function properly. She'd had surgery to remove a horribly painful mass, and lost one of her ovaries in the process. Since then she was so irregular, she sometimes went several months without menstruating.

Her mother had explained that she likely wouldn't have any children, and Olivia understood why. You couldn't very well conceive with only one ovary, especially if you didn't ovulate. She wasn't totally ignorant about her bodily functions.

There were times when she would have gone to the

doctor, just to make certain her pain was normal, for her. But being examined by a man when she was still so innocent and shy had made her dread the thought of even a routine visit.

Now, as John made a jest and everyone laughed, Olivia was about to smile when she felt another cramp and winced instead. Tony leaned toward her. "Are you all right?"

He'd kept his voice low, thankfully. She didn't want to disrupt everyone's good time. "I'm fine. I think I just ate a little too much."

He grinned. "Me, too. I had one too many desserts." He leaned closer still, his lips touching her ear. "You'll have to help me work off some calories later. Got any ideas?"

At the moment, all she wanted was a pain pill. She patted his arm and got up from the table. "I'll think on it. Excuse me, please." Picking up her purse, she was aware of Tony's frowning gaze following her.

When she reached the powder room, she fished out two over-the-counter pain tablets and swallowed them, then leaned against the sink. The pain was a little more acute this time than it normally was. She wondered if the fact that she'd become sexually active had any bearing on it.

She waited a few minutes more, then left the room, only to find Tony standing there waiting for her. He searched her face with his gaze. "What is it, Olivia? What's wrong?"

What was one more lie? She tried surreptitiously to hug her stomach. "I'm feeling a little under the weather, Tony. Maybe I'm catching a cold."

Reaching out, he felt her forehead and then nodded.

"You feel a little warm. Why don't we go ahead and leave?"

"No." She didn't want this day to end, not when there were so few days left. "I'm all right."

"You don't look all right, honey. You look like you're in pain."

"It's nothing, I promise."

She sounded a touch too desperate, which made Tony study her a little more thoroughly. "All right. But I want you to sit down and take it easy."

"The women are all helping to clean up the kitchen."

"No, they're not. The men have decided to do it. Now go rest somewhere, okay? And promise me, if you start to feel any worse, you'll let me know."

"I will," she lied, determined to stay for the duration of the family get-together.

But an hour later, the cramps were getting to be too much to ignore, and she couldn't put off leaving any longer. She glanced at Tony and he immediately stood, as if he'd only been waiting for a signal from her. It amazed her that he seemed to read her so easily, that he knew her thoughts and her feelings.

He did a wonderful job of excusing their early departure. Olivia knew, judging by the grin on John's face and the wink Kate sent to her, that everyone thought they were leaving so they could be alone.

When they got into his car, Olivia found that Tony had a similar idea. "I'll take you to my house. I can look after you if you *are* getting sick."

Appalled by such an idea, Olivia shook her head and tried to think of a viable reason to refuse his generous offer. Tending her when she was sick had never been part of the deal. "I'd rather go home, Tony. I'll be more comfortable there."

He glanced at her, then nodded. "All right. I'll grab a few things from my house and stay with you."

Until now she'd managed to avoid having him spend the night or any length of time in her apartment. Generally she met him at the door, and within minutes they would leave. She wanted her home to feel the same once their time together was over, and she knew that would be impossible if he slept in her bed or ate in her kitchen or showered in her bathroom. She would be reminded of him everywhere she looked, and she couldn't let that happen.

She reached over and touched his arm. "Tony, I'm sorry. I really am. But I'd rather be alone. Whenever I've been sick—"

"But you're never sick! You haven't missed a day of work in years."

True. But the cramps had never been this bad before. She bit her lip and looked out her side window. "I'll be more comfortable by myself."

There was an awful silence and she knew she'd hurt him when that had never been her intent. She felt choked by remorse, but there was no way out, no way to make up for all she'd done, all the lies she'd told.

Finally Tony said very quietly, "I'll take you home. But I want your promise you'll call me if you need anything."

"Of course."

They both knew she was lying.

OLIVIA FINALLY ACCEPTED that something was seriously wrong. The pain had nagged her off and on since she'd

come home, and she'd started to bleed. Not heavily, but
still, it was an unusual occurrence with her periods so
horribly irregular. Then suddenly, at midnight, the pain
seemed to explode. She didn't think she could drive herself to the hospital, but as much as she hated to admit
it, she needed to go.

This pain no longer seemed familiar; it was nothing like what she was used to dealing with, so sharp
she could barely breathe. She had a vague recollection
of similar pain when she'd been a child, but it was too
hard, feeling as she did, to remember if the two situations were at all the same.

She couldn't disrupt Tony, not after he'd called to
check on her and she'd more or less told him not to
bother. She'd been curt, as much from the pain as from
the struggle to keep from giving in and telling him she
needed him. She'd used him enough as it was, and now
she didn't know who to turn to.

When she decided she couldn't wait a moment longer,
she pulled a coat on over her pajamas. Bent over, holding her middle, she went into the hallway and knocked
on Hilda's door. As usual, one knock had every door
on that floor opening, and soon all her neighbors were
there, fussing over her, fretting. Very quickly, Hilda re-
appeared fully clothed, car keys in her hand.

Held between Hilda and kindly old Leroy, Olivia
made her way outside. Hilda spoke to those who followed. "I'll call and let everyone know when we've made
it to the hospital. If I don't call within a half hour, send
a car after us. That snow is really starting to pile up."

Olivia curled into the backseat, and then felt the tears
start. It wasn't the pain, but the simple truth that she had
good friends and hadn't realized it. Even while avoid-

ing relationships, she'd still managed to form a few. She was only lying to herself when she claimed to be all alone. She was so touched by the sudden revelation, she couldn't halt the tears.

"It's all right, Olivia. Don't worry. I'll have you there in no time." The woman drove like a snail, but Olivia knew Hilda hated the snow. "When we get there, do you want me to call that boyfriend of yours?"

Olivia smiled, hearing Tony referred to as a boyfriend. There was nothing boyish about him, and he was now so much more than a friend. "No. Don't bother him, Hilda. I'll call him myself, later."

"He'd want to be with you, you know."

And then he'd find out what a fraud she was. "No. Please. I don't want to worry him."

Hilda didn't answer.

When they arrived at the hospital, Hilda ran inside, demanding attention, as Olivia struggled to get out of the car. Before she'd even set both feet on the ground, two nurses were there, assisting her into a wheelchair and rushing her in. The questions flew at her, one right after the other, but she was in so much pain she could barely answer. After that, she lost track of events as they ran an endless series of tests.

When a doctor came in and asked her if she might possibly be pregnant, she told him no and briefly explained what she knew of her own medical history. He wrote notes, smiled at her, then went about ordering a pregnancy test. Olivia balked at the idea. She wasn't up to creeping into the bathroom and utilizing their little plastic cups, especially for something that seemed totally unnecessary. But she was too sick to argue. She did as the doctor asked, then crawled back onto the narrow metal bed.

A few minutes later, the doctor leaned against the side rail and gave her a wry look. "Well, Ms. Anderson, it seems you are indeed pregnant."

Olivia stared. "That's impossible."

"I assure you, it isn't." He smiled benignly and went on. "I'd like to do an ultrasound. It will tell us exactly what's going on, why you're having so much pain and bleeding."

Olivia felt numb. Pregnant? She couldn't be pregnant. "But I only have one ovary."

"One is all it takes. Granted, your chances were decreased, but still—it happens."

"But I almost never have periods!"

He patted her hand and stood. "Let's do the ultrasound and then go from there, okay? Try not to worry."

Worry? She was too dumbfounded to worry. And then it hit her and she almost shouted with pleasure. She was pregnant! She would have her own baby, Tony's baby. The pain seemed to lessen with the knowledge, but it was still a reminder that all was not well, and she began praying, wanting this baby so badly she would have promised anything to hold on to it.

It was quite a while before the doctor was standing beside her again. He was a nice enough man, she thought, surprised that she actually felt comfortable with him. In fact, she was anxious to speak with him, to hear how her baby was faring.

He spoke in specific terms for her, making the situation very clear. She wasn't far enough along for the ultrasound to show the baby, but the test confirmed that she had a large cyst on her one remaining ovary—and it had ruptured.

She immediately began to panic, remembering what had happened when she was so young, remembering the surgery, losing an ovary… The doctor pulled up a chair and took her hand.

"Your ovary did rupture, and until your placenta is large enough and produces enough progesterone to maintain the pregnancy, I'll need to give you progesterone and hope it works. Things could still go wrong, and you could lose the baby, but there's no reason to start borrowing trouble yet."

Olivia had never considered herself a weak person. She drew on her strength now, mustering her courage. "I don't need to borrow trouble. It seems I have enough as it is."

"I gather you want to keep the baby."

"Oh, very much! I just never dreamed…"

"When did you lose your other ovary?"

"I was twelve. Not long after I'd started my period. I understood I wouldn't be able to get pregnant. And since my cycle seemed so haywire…"

"It was a common misconception years ago that a woman couldn't conceive with only one ovary, but as you see it is definitely possible." He grinned at her, and she grinned back.

"Yes." Hugging her arms around herself, she asked, "What now?"

"I'd like to keep you here until we can run a few more tests, rule out the possibility of a tubal pregnancy, make certain everything is as it should be. Also, I'd like you to come back a couple of times for blood tests. We'll check the hormone level, which should double in two days if everything is okay. We'll run the test again, just to make sure everything checks out."

He wrote a few notes on her chart, then asked, "Do you have an obstetrician in mind?"

"No." She was in a daze, answering questions she'd never imagined hearing.

"I can recommend someone if you'd like. You should see him right away, then set up frequent appointments until you get past the first three months."

"And after the first three months?"

"Well, then, the risk is greatly reduced."

Olivia hung on to that thought long after the doctor had left. He'd given her codeine for the pain, and it was tolerable now, but she couldn't rest. Her hand remained on her belly, and she couldn't seem to stop crying.

With a little luck and a lot of care, she was going to have a baby.

And there was no way she'd ever give her baby up to anyone—not even Tony.

Olivia worried that thought over and over in her mind, but it always came down to the same thing. She'd have to tell Tony the truth now. She wouldn't keep the baby from him, but neither would she give it up. He had a right to know. She knew he would be a wonderful father, even if he didn't have the situation he wanted, even if he was enraged by her deception.

For one brief, insane moment, she wondered whether Tony would go so far as to offer to marry her, just to get the baby. It was possible, but she wouldn't let that happen. She wasn't the average woman with the average pregnancy. She was more like a miracle. What would it do to Tony if he married her and she lost the baby? Just the thought had her squeezing her abdomen in a protective embrace; still, it was a very real possibility.

No. Tony needed to find a healthy woman who could give him as many children as he wanted, not just a miracle baby with risks. She'd confess to him, and she would set him free.

It turned out to be the longest night of her life—and the most joyous. A baby, she just couldn't believe she was having a baby.

OLIVIA ARRIVED HOME the next afternoon to a ringing phone. She was feeling much better, more like herself, and she rushed to answer before the caller hung up.

Breathless, weak from her painful ordeal and a sleepless night, she gasped out, "Hello?"

"Where the hell have you been?"

Oh my. She straightened, staring at the receiver in her hand. Tony was in quite a temper. Olivia bit her lip and tried to think of what to say to him.

"Olivia?" There was an edge of near panic to his tone. "Dammit, I'm sorry." He gave a long sigh and she could hear his frustration, could almost see him running his hand through his dark hair. "I was worried, honey. Where were you?"

"I, uh, I had to go out for a little while."

"I've been calling since early this morning. I wanted to make certain you were feeling all right."

That left her blank. She thought they'd agreed he wouldn't call to check on her. "I'm feeling much better. Tony? Are you busy right now?"

"I'm at the office. Why? Do you need something? You *are* still sick, aren't you?"

He sounded so anxious, she rushed to reassure him.

"No, I just…" Her voice dropped as she was overcome with dread, but it was better to get it over with. "We need to talk."

Silence greeted her, and she bit her lip. "Tony?"

"This sounds like a heavy-duty brush-off, Olivia. Is it?"

How could she answer that? How could she possibly explain? She heard him curse, then curse again. "I'll come on over now."

"What?" She didn't want him in her apartment; she wasn't ready to face him. Her night in the hospital had left her looking wan and feeling lifeless. She'd planned to shower and clean up and meet him somewhere. "Why don't we just do lunch?"

"To hell with that. If we need to talk, we'll talk now. Whatever it is you've got planned, I'd rather get it over with. I'll be there in half an hour." He hung up and Olivia sank back onto the couch.

Half an hour to prepare herself. It wasn't much time, but then, from the moment Tony had propositioned her, there hadn't been enough time. She didn't know if a lifetime would be enough.

TONY RAPPED SHARPLY on the door, feeling his frustration ready to explode. The other doors opened, but this time he didn't even look to see who was watching him. He'd almost gotten used to her nosy neighbors who appeared each and every time he came to pick her up. But he was in no mood to be polite right now.

He slammed his fist on the door. "Open up, Olivia."

It didn't matter to him that his behavior was somewhat juvenile. She was dumping him, he was sure of it. *Damn her.* How could she make a decision like this, when he hadn't even made up his own mind about things? He'd thought they were getting closer, thought they might have been able to work through all the difficulties. He'd considered the possibility of offering her a compromise....

But no. She was done giving him time... He raised his hand to bang on the door again, just as it swung in. There stood Olivia.

He opened his mouth, but in the next instant whatever acerbic comment he might have made was forgotten. She looked awful—pale and drawn and tired. Concern immediately replaced all his other emotions. He pushed his way in, forcing her back, closing the door on the curious gazes of her neighbors.

"Olivia?" He caught her shoulders in his hands. "Are you all right, honey?"

"I'm fine." She tried to inch away from him, and he felt his anger renewed. He knew he had to get control of himself. He'd never been concerned with that before. He rarely lost his temper, and never with a woman. He'd never had a relationship with a woman outside the family that had warranted that much emotion. With Olivia, though, he was off balance, bombarded with unique feelings and apprehensions.

He bent to meet her at eye level. "Tell me what's wrong."

She twined her fingers together. "This is very difficult for me. I'm still in shock myself. But... I wanted you to know as soon as possible."

This didn't sound like a rehearsed brush-off. He dropped his hands, but when she staggered slightly, he caught her arm and led her to her couch. "Here, sit down."

She did, and he sat right next to her. "Now just tell me whatever it is. Are you sick?"

"I... I was. Last night." He started to question her, but she said quickly, "And I'm okay now. I promise. It's just that..." Her eyes were huge and dark and filled with uncertainty. Then a small smile flitted over her lips, and she covered her mouth with one trembling hand and whispered, "I'm pregnant."

Tony blinked. Of all the things he'd expected, all the horrible words he imagined... Elation welled, burst. He gave a shout, watching as Olivia blinked back tears, then pulled her close for a hug, rocking her and trying to contain himself. "Don't cry, sweetheart, it'll be all right. I promise."

She was afraid, he understood that now. And he didn't blame her. It was a scary thing to have a baby, but especially so for her, a woman who until recently had never had any dealings with children at all.

Though she was nearly as tall as he, and, as he'd pointed out to her in one of his less auspicious moments, very sturdy, she felt small and frail. He cradled her close, and then she started to cry in earnest. Could it be she didn't want their time to end? He tipped her chin up and watched as she hiccuped, then wiped her eyes with her fist.

He knew there was a ridiculously tender smile on his face, but he couldn't help himself. She was so sweet, so vulnerable. And then she said in a surprisingly steady tone, "You can't have it."

He tilted his head. "What?"

"You can't have my baby."

He searched her face as realization dawned. She couldn't possibly mean what it had sounded like. "We can discuss—"

"No." She came to her feet, one hand braced on the arm of the couch as if to steady herself. "I have to explain something to you, Tony. When I agreed to your plan, it was because I believed I couldn't have children. When I was very young, I lost an ovary due to a condition called PCO, polycystic ovaries. My periods have never been normal, or even close to regular, and so I didn't think I could conceive. I believed I could make love with you without any risk of pregnancy, otherwise I never would have agreed to give you the baby."

He was frozen with shock, what she was saying too unbelievable to accept. "Then why...?"

She laughed harshly, and again covered her mouth. "Look at yourself. You're a very desirable man. You'd never shown any interest in me before, and most of my reasoning was true. I wanted to know what lovemaking was all about, with a man I admired and could trust."

"You lied to me?"

She choked on a sob. "Yes."

Slowly, feeling as if his body wouldn't function properly, Tony came to his feet. She hadn't dressed today as she normally did. Today she was wearing a long casual caftan, and her feet were bare; her hair was brushed but unstyled. Every time he thought he'd figured her out, she changed.

And this change was killing him.

"You used me for sex."

Wrapping her arms around her middle, she nodded. "I'm so sorry."

"Sorry?" His voice had risen to a shout, and she flinched. It hit him then: she was pregnant. With his baby. He didn't want to upset her, not knowing what it might do to the baby, and he fought hard to regain some calm. "This is why you kept telling me you might not conceive."

"Yes."

"And why you insisted on the two-week time period."

Again, she said only, "Yes."

"But everything backfired on you. Because you are pregnant?"

"I am. It's definite." Her lips trembled when she drew in a deep breath. "I wouldn't have realized it on my own for some time yet, but then I got…sick, and the doctor did a test, an accurate test, and now I know I'm going to have a baby."

His jaw tightened. "Must have been one hell of a shock for you."

Instinctively she placed her hand on her belly. "It was." And there was that small smile again, as if she was glad, but trying desperately to keep her happiness to herself.

"So," he asked, not really wanting to, but having to know, "how do I fit into all this? It is my baby, too."

She turned away and walked to an end table, straightening a lamp shade, flicking at a speck of dust. He looked around and realized he hated her apartment. It was so like the business persona she presented to the world—detached, immaculate, no softness or giving anywhere. The place could have been empty and not seemed any less cold.

"I want you to take part in everything, if you want to."

Barking a rough laugh, he caught her shoulder and turned her back to face him. "If I *want* to?" Her eyes opened wide and he almost shook her. "I was the one who *wanted* the baby, not you! You had the grand five-year plan, remember?"

Hands curled into fists, she jerked away. "Only because I didn't think I could have a baby! But I can, and I want this one."

"What about work? How are you going to raise a baby by yourself?" He knew he was being unfair, asking her questions she couldn't possibly have found the answers to yet, but at the moment, it didn't matter. He wanted to hurt her just as she'd hurt him.

And judging by the stricken look on her face, he had.

He tilted his head back and closed his eyes, silently counting to ten. Then he faced her. "Olivia, be reasonable. Do you have any idea how difficult it is to be a single parent?"

"I suppose I'll find out, won't I?"

He almost laughed, she looked so much like herself, digging in, ready to do battle. He rubbed his chin and studied her. "I could take you to court, you know? I can provide for the baby in a way you never could. I can give him things, my time and attention..."

"What if it's a girl?"

"You don't remember me telling you it wouldn't matter? I thought I was clear on that."

Abruptly she dropped back onto the couch, her face in her hands. "Don't do this, Tony. Don't make things more difficult for me. Please!"

His chest hurt, seeing her look so defeated. All her bravado had just vanished in a heartbeat. He sat beside her and awkwardly tried to find the right words. "I *will* be a part of the baby's life, Olivia."

She jerked around to face him, her expression anxious and fierce. "Of course you will be! I wouldn't keep you from him. Or her, or..." She paused, and then grinned past her tears. "Oh, Tony, I'm having a baby!"

She was crying and laughing, and he couldn't help but hug her to him. She started babbling, her words almost indistinguishable mingled as they were with her sobs.

Keeping her face close to his chest, she said, "I never, ever thought this was possible. And I swear, I'll be a good mother. I didn't mean for this to happen, and I know it wasn't what you wanted. It wasn't even what I wanted. But I won't tie you down. I promise. You can see the baby whenever you want, be as close to it as you want. Your life doesn't have to change, just because I want to remain the baby's mother. I'll figure out some way to keep my business going and take care of the baby, too. And you'll be the father, so you can—"

"Watch the baby for you while you go on about your business?" They had agreed the baby would be his, but now she planned to keep the baby, and use him again to make it easier on herself? He leaned back, holding her away from him.

She swallowed in the face of his renewed anger. "That wasn't what I was going to say."

"No? But you're seeing yourself with only half a problem, right? After all, I can support you both while you go about your plans to expand the business. And whenever the baby is inconvenient, I'll be a built-in babysitter. How could I ever refuse, when I'd wanted this child so much?"

She seemed to go perfectly still, not breathing, not moving so much as an eyelash. Then a placid, business smile came to her mouth, and he didn't like it, didn't like the way she'd pulled herself together and back into that protective shell of hers. It was the way she always looked during a business meeting, the look that had led him to believe she had no sensitivities, no vulnerabilities. He knew now that it was a sham.

Her back was very straight, her chin lifted when she said, "You thought I'd start using you that way? Not at all. I need nothing from you. I've never needed anything from anyone. The baby and I will be just fine."

"Olivia…"

"I think you should go now."

"We're not through talking."

"Yes, we are. I've told you all I have to tell you. Whether or not you choose to take part in the baby's life is up to you now."

He glared at her, his jaw so tight it ached. "You know damn good and well I want this baby."

"Fine." She stood, managing to look somehow regal and serene despite her obvious fatigue and whatever illness had plagued her. "When he or she is born, I'll let you know."

Then she went to the door and opened it, waiting for him to leave.

And he did, only because he was so angry, he was afraid he'd upset her again if he stayed, and he couldn't believe that would be good for the baby. Feeling numb and sick to his stomach, he stomped out to his car and then sat there. Damn her, she'd thrown him for a loop this time.

He realized there was still so much he didn't know about her—and despite everything, he wanted to know. She'd actually had some sort of surgery when she was young that made her believe she couldn't get pregnant.

And she'd pretended otherwise just so she could make love with him.

It seemed absurd, especially now that she'd been trapped by her own ridiculous plan. But he wasn't giving up yet. Olivia always wanted to run things, in business

and in private. It was part of her nature to take charge
and make all the decisions. She was pushy and arrogant
and in the general course of things, very fair-minded.

But not this time.

Damn, he knew he should have stuck to his original
plan. He should never have gotten involved on a personal
level with Olivia Anderson. He hadn't gotten the baby
he wanted so badly; he hadn't gotten anything at all.

Nothing except a broken heart.

CHAPTER NINE

"So when are you going to marry her?"

Slowly, wishing he didn't have to deal with this right now, Tony laid his papers aside. "I'm not."

John placed both palms on his desk and leaned forward to glare at him. "And why the hell not? She's perfect for you."

Perfect? Nothing felt perfect. It had been two weeks since he'd seen Olivia. He'd tried dropping in on her shops a couple of times, hoping to appear casual about seeing her since his pride was still bruised. He would have conjured up a business excuse, but in truth, he'd half hoped that seeing him again would give her a change of heart, that she would want him again, even though she was pregnant. But she hadn't been there.

He'd called her once or twice, but each time he'd gotten her voicemail. No doubt she was busy organizing things for the new shop she would open.

And that thought made him angry all over again.

He glanced up at John, then back to his desk full of files, trying subtly to give the hint that he was busy. "It's none of your business, John."

"You've been moping around long enough. Hell, Mom's worried about you, Kate's worried about you. Why don't you just accept the inevitable and admit you love her?"

"Because she lied to me, that's why!" He hadn't meant to shout, but he'd had no one to talk to, and he was ready to explode with the effort of trying to understand Olivia and his own feelings.

John straightened, looking startled by Tony's display of temper. "Lied to you about what?"

Wishing he'd kept his mouth shut now, Tony shook his head. "Why don't you mind your own business?"

Instead John propped a hip against the desk. "Was it a big lie, or just a little lie? Now don't glare at me. I'm trying to help."

"If you want to help, find me a woman as perfect as Lisa."

A look of stunned disbelief crossed John's face, then he burst into hysterical laughter. "Lisa? Perfect? You've got to be kidding."

"She's perfect for you. The two of you never fight. And I know damn well she'd never lie to you."

"We fight all the time, actually. I enjoy it. And it gives me a good excuse to make up to her." He winked, which confounded Tony. "As far as lying… Lisa would never lie to me. But I lied to her once, and it was a doozy."

Tony laid aside the file he'd just picked up and stared. "When was this?"

"Before we were married. Almost ruined things, and that's a fact. But Lisa, bless her heart, didn't give up on me. She got madder than hell, then she schemed, and before I knew it, I was apologizing and begging her to marry me. As it turned out, she wasn't so upset over what I'd lied about, as she was that I'd lied at all. Is that true with you and Livvy?"

Tony considered the question a moment. Was he mad that Olivia had used him for sex, or that she didn't appear to want him now? He figured he could forgive her anything if she loved him, but… He shook his head, not really coming up with an answer. "I don't suppose you'd care to tell me what you lied to Lisa about?"

"Actually…no." He grinned. "It's history, and now I'd never lie to her about anything any more than I'd ever hurt her."

"But you two fight?" Tony was intrigued by the idea; he'd always thought his brother had the perfect marriage.

"All the time. Hell, you know me, Tony. Did you really think anyone could live with me without losing their temper on occasion?"

"And Kate and Brian?"

"They've had their share of whoppers. Kate can be a real pain, you know that. And she claims Brian is far from perfect. If you love Olivia, it won't matter."

Tony narrowed his eyes, considering what John said, but the big difference was that Olivia didn't appear to love him. "I don't know."

John slammed a palm on the desk. "I don't get it! She's a sexy lady. Smart. Sweet. The kids love her. The women love her."

Tony ignored him, going back to his papers and pretending a great interest in them, even though his eyes wouldn't seem to focus on a single line.

John crossed his arms over his chest and glared. "She is sexy, you know. Very sexy."

The paper crumpled in Tony's fist. He slanted his gaze up at his younger brother and asked in a growl, "Just what do you think you're doing, noticing if she's sexy or not?"

"Do I look blind? Olivia is one of those intriguing cool-on-the-outside, burning-up-on-the-inside kind of ladies. Every guy who looks at her knows it. It's just that usually a guy's too afraid to get close enough to her to see just how sexy she is. She can be damn formidable as I remember it. Of course, after you got her to soften up a bit, it's more noticeable."

"Oh, that's just dandy." She no longer wanted him, but he'd managed to show the world how appealing she was? He didn't need to hear that.

"You don't have to worry about me or Brian. You know we're both well satisfied in our own marital bargains, but..."

"Brian, too?"

"He's not blind, either, big brother."

Tony threw the papers aside and shoved his chair back, then took an aggressive step toward John. He felt ready to chew nails, but John only shook his head.

"Look at you. This is pathetic. Give up and tell her you love her and you want her back."

Tony narrowed his eyes and against his best intentions, blurted, "She dumped me, you ass. Not the other way around."

It was almost funny the look that flashed over John's face. Obviously this possibility hadn't occurred to him. He asked simply, "Why?"

Shaking his head and stalking around the office, Tony knew he'd already said too much. No way would he ever confide in anyone—even his brother—the extent of Olivia's perfidy. "Go away and leave me alone, John."

John didn't budge an inch. "I don't get it. She seemed crazy about you. I was sure of it."

Crazy about him? Tony stared, wondering if it could have been possible.

Then John demanded, "What did you do to her to

make her dump you? Did you yell at her over this lying business?"

This time he did laugh, but there was nothing humorous in the sound. What had he done? Made love to her, as per her request, giving her pleasure, giving her his baby.

Then he'd accused her of using him for money. It had been his anger talking, but still, he shouldn't have made such a ridiculous claim. Sex, yes, but Olivia would never use anyone for money. God, she'd spent her life proving her independence, isolating herself, facing each day alone.

But now she'd have the baby. His baby.

He cursed again, aiming his disgust at John. But it was a wasted effort. John only dropped into a chair and looked thoughtful. "I think we need to figure this one out."

"I need to get back to my work." He said it through gritted teeth, wanting privacy to wallow in his misery, but John shook his head.

"I don't understand why, if you want her, you don't just woo her."

"Woo her? *Woo* her? What kind of word is that?"

"An appropriate kind. Olivia must need something you haven't given her yet. When I was dating Lisa, I always thought I was saying the right thing, and it always turned out to be the wrong thing."

Brian opened the door just then and walked in to hear John's statement. He grinned. "You have a knack for saying the wrong thing. So what else is new?"

John turned and without a single hesitation, explained the situation to Brian. Tony threw up his hands and dropped back into the chair behind his desk. He listened as the two men discussed his life as if he weren't even in the room. Damn interfering…at least his mother and sister didn't know.

No sooner did he have the thought, than Kate came storming in.

"What did you do to Olivia?"

Tony leaned back in his chair and closed his eyes.

Again, John began to explain. Tony tried to tune them out, but then Kate said, "Oh. When I talked to her, she only said that they weren't seeing each other anymore."

"You talked to her?" Tony asked, sounding anxious in spite of himself. "When?"

"Just this morning. She sounds awful. Not at all like herself."

"What do you mean? Is she still sick?" He was aware of their looks, how they all exchanged glances, but at the moment, he didn't care.

"I don't know anything about her being sick, Tony. I assumed she was heartbroken. But then, I thought you had broken things off. I mean, it was obvious she was crazy about you."

There it was again. Tony leaned forward and said, "Why does everyone keep saying that! The woman dumped me."

"What did you do to her?" asked Kate and Brian together.

Tony had had enough. He came to his feet in a rush and said to the room at large, "I'm going out for lunch."

John grabbed his arm before he could leave the room. "I've always thought you were an intelligent man, Tony. But right now, you're acting pretty dumb. Don't sit around here sulking. Go fix things with her."

"And how am I supposed to do that?"

John slapped his shoulder and grinned. "As I said, you're smart. You'll think of something."

IT TOOK TONY a few more days to come up with a solid plan. But once he did, he couldn't believe he hadn't thought of it sooner. It was perfect, probably the only ploy that would work with Olivia.

He would appeal to her business ethics.

He tracked her down at the downtown shop where she was busy stringing white twinkle lights in the front store window that faced the lobby. She stood on a small stool, a smile on her face, looking beautiful and healthy and not at all like a woman pining away for a man. He almost balked, but then she looked up and met his gaze and her smile vanished. Her dark eyes took on a wary look.

He approached her and took her hand, helping her to step down from the stool. "Hello, Olivia."

"Tony. What brings you downtown?"

"I was looking for you, actually."

That wary look intensified and she nervously brushed her hands together. "Oh?"

"We have some things to discuss, I think. Don't you?" He kept his tone gentle, not wanting to upset her before it was absolutely necessary.

"I... I suppose we do." She turned and called to her assistant. "Finish hanging these lights, will you, Alicia? I'll be in my office."

Without a word to him, she started toward the back of the shop. This location was smaller than the one they'd met in before, but he liked it. There were the red bows and garlands strung around the shop and Tony wondered if she decorated her own home at all. Doubtful.

Her apartment was utilitarian to the point of being depressing.

This year, he hadn't decorated, either. It just hadn't seemed important.

She closed her office door after he'd stepped inside, then went to sit behind her desk. There was only one other chair in the room, a plain wooden chair, and Tony pulled it forward. "How have you been, Olivia? Kate mentioned that you seemed ill."

She looked frightened for a second, then she visibly relaxed. "Morning sickness, I'm afraid. Although it hits me at the oddest times, not just in the morning."

Perfect, Tony thought, knowing he couldn't have asked for a better opening. "Any other changes you're noticing?"

Looking anxious, she smiled and said, "You know, there are. Small things, but it's amazing how the baby is making itself known. Even though I'm not very far along yet."

"What kind of things?" He held her gaze, refusing to let her look away.

She flushed, then shook her head. "Nothing big. Just…little things."

"But I want to know." He added gently, "That was part of our deal, remember?"

Olivia stiffened at the reminder of their original bargain. "What are you talking about?"

It took all his control to look negligent, to hide his growing anticipation. If she guessed at his ulterior motives, she'd throw him out on his ear. He picked up a lacy slip lying on the desk and pretended to examine it. "You agreed to allow me to view all the changes—if you got pregnant. I realize now of course that you only made the deal because you thought it would never come to this. But I've given it a lot of thought. And I've decided you should be fair-minded about the whole thing."

Her face was pale now and her hands were clenched together. "I already told you how sorry I am about all that, Tony. But I'm keeping my baby."

"I'll want visitation."

"I offered it to you."

"And," he went on, as if she hadn't spoken, "I'll want to pay for half the baby's bills. As to that, I should pay for half your medical bills as well."

"No!" She was out of her seat in an instant and leaning over the desk to glare at him. "I told you, I want nothing from you."

"And I believe you. But it's my right to pay half."

"But it's my body, my baby!" Then she stumbled back, realizing what she'd said. Tony merely waited, and she drew several deep breaths. "Okay. It's your baby, too. And when it's born, if you want to take part of the pediatrician's expenses on yourself, that's fine. Why should we argue? But my bills are my own."

"I could take you to court, you know."

She gaped at him. "You'd sue me to get half my bills?"

He shrugged. "That, and to get you to honor the bargain we made."

Feeling behind herself for her chair, she dropped down and concentrated on taking several deep breaths. Her face was pale, her eyes huge. "You're going to take the baby from me?"

Tony felt like a monster. He stood up and went around the desk, then turned her chair toward him. Kneeling, he took her hands in his and held them tightly. "Do you honestly think I'd do that to you, Olivia?"

She shook her head and her hair tumbled over her shoulders. "No. But you said…"

"We made other deals, sweetheart." He kept his tone low and soothing. "Don't you remember?"

Her gaze became wary.

"I want to be a part of the pregnancy as well as the birth. You promised me I could observe all the little changes, watch you as the baby caused changes in your body. I want to do that, Olivia. I want to know every little thing that occurs."

"But…everything is different now."

"No. The only thing that's different is that you've admitted you lied to me, and you want to keep the baby. The rest of our agreement should stand." He squeezed her fingers again and stared into her stunned gaze. "It's the least you could do."

He could tell she was considering it, thinking about it. His gaze dropped to her breasts and he whispered, "I bought a book that detailed all the changes. One of the first things to happen is your breasts should get tender and swollen." He glanced up and was caught by her wide dark eyes. "I remember now, the last time we made love, you seemed especially sensitive."

Her chest heaved as she watched him, and then she nodded.

"Ah. So they are swollen?"

Licking her lips, she nodded again. "A little."

"And they're tender?"

"Yes." Her voice was a barely discernible whisper, husky and deep and shaky.

"I want to see."

"Tony…"

The way she groaned his name did things to him,

things that shouldn't be happening right now, not while he was trying so hard to get the upper hand. He rubbed his thumb over her knuckles and whispered to her. "Shh. It'll be all right. I'm just curious. You know how much this has meant to me. Can't you give me at least this much?"

"But I thought you'd find another woman."

The thought of touching anyone other than Olivia was somehow repugnant. He didn't want another woman. Even if he went the rest of his life without a child that would be solely his, he wouldn't want anyone but her. The idea was staggering, but true.

"No. I don't think that's necessary." He released her hands and stood, needing to put some space between them before he embarrassed himself by making declarations that would be better left unsaid. At least for now. "We'll have this baby, and that's enough to deal with. Hell, this is far more complicated than I'd ever intended."

He had his back to her and didn't hear her rise, but then she was touching him, and he turned. She stood looking up at him, her expression earnest. "I'm so sorry, Tony. Honestly. I never meant for any of this to happen. It seemed like such a simple plan to me."

Touching her cheek, he smiled. "Nothing about you is simple, honey. You're the most complex woman I know."

She looked crushed. "I've really messed things up for you, haven't I?"

She'd made him happier than he'd ever imagined being, but he didn't tell her that. "Things aren't just as I'd planned them, but I *will* get my child. I'll just be sharing it with you." He shoved his hands into his pockets to keep from touching her again. "But it would help if you'd abide by the agreement as much as possible. You knew from the start how I felt about things."

She nodded miserably, and he almost apologized for heaping on the guilt, but she deserved it for her deception. And it was the only way he could think of to reach his goal.

"Then you'll agree? You'll let me observe the changes and take part in everything?"

She turned away and wrapped her arms around herself. "What exactly do you mean by 'taking part'?"

"I want to attend your doctor appointments. If there are any sonograms taken, I want to be there so I can see whatever you see. When the doctor listens for a heartbeat, I want to hear it, too."

Her shoulders slumped in relief. "That's no problem."

"I also want to know about every spell of morning sickness. I want to see your ankles if they swell." Without his intention, his voice went husky. "And feel if your breasts are tender."

She shuddered, and he wanted her right then, so badly he could hardly breathe. "I've seen you before, Olivia, so it won't be a breach of your privacy. I've touched you…" He had to stop to draw his own breath, his lungs feeling constricted, his stomach tight with need. "I know your body, how it looks and how it feels. It'll be easy for me to see every tiny change. Will you let me?"

She nodded very slowly, and his pulse quickened. But he wanted to be sure. "Olivia?"

"Yes." She faced him, her cheeks flushed, her eyes bright. "Yes. That's the least I can do."

He recognized the signs of arousal in her expression and it took a moment before he was able to speak. "I can come over tonight."

"I'd rather…"

"I know. You don't want me in your apartment." She looked surprised, and he gave her a wry smile. "I realized after I left there the last time, you've always avoided having me in your home. That was because you had no intention of having my baby, of course, and you wanted to keep your life separate from mine. You didn't want me invading your inner sanctum."

With a guilty flush, she nodded.

"But now you are having my baby, and I will be visiting there, if for nothing else than to pick up the child. So it doesn't really matter anymore, does it?"

"I suppose not."

She looked reluctant as hell, and he almost grinned. *I've got you now,* he thought, knowing he was moving in on her, and knowing she didn't like it. He said, "How about six o'clock?"

"I suppose I should be finished by then."

"Good." He didn't want to go, but he decided to leave before she changed her mind. "I'll see you then."

OLIVIA STRAIGHTENED HER hair again, then stepped away from the mirror. Tony was five minutes late, and she was a nervous wreck. She couldn't believe he was doing this, but she was so glad. She'd missed Tony horribly, the days stretching on endlessly. She'd wanted so many times to tell Tony of all the little changes she'd noticed. Not even work had filled the void—a situation she had never encountered before.

Until now.

When the knock sounded on the door, she jumped, then raced to answer it. She didn't want to have to deal with her neighbors today; they'd been hovering over her

ever since that night at the hospital. While she appreciated their concern, she didn't want Tony to know about
the risks involved with the pregnancy.

But when she opened the door, Tony stood there surrounded by familiar faces. He gave her an ironic grin,
said goodbye to all her neighbors and stepped inside. As
she was closing the door again, Hilda called out, "You
take good care of her now, you hear? I don't want to be
making any more trips to the hospital."

Though she could have wished it otherwise, Olivia
knew Tony had heard every word. He stared at her, then
started to open the door again—to question Hilda she
was certain.

"Don't, Tony."

"What the hell was that about the hospital?"

She tried to think of some excuse to give him, but he
grabbed her shoulders and gave her a slight shake. "No
more lies, Olivia. Dammit, just once give me the truth."

She flinched at his tone, and at his right to doubt her.
"I'm sorry. I just didn't want to worry you."

"Worry me about what? Is the baby okay?"

"The baby is fine." She rushed past him to the end
table to pick up a recent sonogram picture. "This is the
baby."

Tony looked at the odd black and white picture,
frowned, then asked, "Where?"

Olivia laughed in delight because his reaction was so
much like her own had been. "You can't really see the
baby, it's so tiny. In fact, right now, it's only about half
an inch long. But did you know, by about eight weeks,
it will already be getting fingers and toes?"

Tony stared, then a huge smile broke out over his features. "Fingers and toes, huh?"

Olivia held up the picture and pointed out what she did know, showing Tony her womb and explaining the dark shadows as they'd been explained to her. "My doctor is very big on ultrasound, especially since I didn't believe I could conceive."

"Okay, start with that. What exactly happened to you? And how is it you got pregnant when you thought you couldn't?"

She was so thrilled to have someone to talk all this out with, she took Tony's hand to lead him to the couch before she could think better of it. She explained her specialized problem at length, and Tony asked a million questions.

"But what happened the other night? Why did you go to the hospital?"

Feeling her way carefully now, not wanting him to know of the risks involved, she said simply, "I had another cyst on my ovary. It was causing me some pain." And before he could question that, she added, "But that's a good thing, because otherwise I wouldn't have gone to the hospital, and I wouldn't have known I was pregnant. Heaven only knows how far along I would have gotten before I realized what was happening."

He searched her face, his concern obvious. "You're sure you're okay now?"

"I'm positive. They took very good care of me. I felt wretched for a few days, and if you check, you'll find I missed a few days of work. But now, other than the morning sickness, I feel great."

"You don't look pregnant."

He was staring down at her body, and she felt a flash of heat. Clearing her throat, she tried to distract herself from thinking things she had no business thinking. "According to the book I bought, I won't start picking up any real weight until after the first three months."

"But you said you've noticed signs?"

This was the tricky part. "My skin is different. I don't need to use as much moisturizer. My hair is different, too. I've had to switch shampoos to get it to lie right." She laughed. "I have unbelievable cravings, and I have to go to the bathroom more."

"And your breasts are swollen and tender."

"Well…yes." She had hoped to slip that in with all the rest, but he hadn't given her a chance.

He took her hand and pulled her to her feet. She stared up at him, feeling her heart pound, her temperature rise. In a low, tender voice he said, "I want to see, Olivia. Take your shirt off for me."

CHAPTER TEN

OLIVIA SWALLOWED HARD and closed her eyes. Not for the life of her could she unbutton the pale flannel blouse she wore. Then she felt Tony take her hand and her eyes flew open again.

"Let's go in the bedroom so you can lie down. It'll be easier for me to...examine you that way."

Examine her. Her heart was tripping, her stomach pulling tight, and yet she let him lead her to her bedroom—a place he'd never been before—without a single complaint. She knew, in her own heart, she wanted him to touch her, to look at her. But she didn't think she could admit such a thing. Not after how badly she'd blundered so far. It was a wonder Tony would even talk to her, much less want to touch her.

She sat on the edge of the bed when he gently pressed her down, and then his hands were on her shoulders, urging her back. She squeezed her eyes shut and she could hear her own breath.

His knuckles brushed against her as he slowly unbuttoned her top and parted the material. Her bra was new, sturdier than those she usually wore, and it had a front closure that Tony deftly flicked open. He brushed the cups aside and then she felt nothing but the cool air on her breasts.

"Olivia. Open your eyes."

She did, feeling foolish, and saw that he was just standing there, looking down at her, his gaze intent. She started to cover herself, but he caught her hands then sat beside her on the bed. "You are much fuller."

She could hear the amazement in his gravelly tone, and she said, "I'm going to breast-feed when the baby is born."

His gaze shot to her face. "Are you?"

"Yes. I've been reading a lot of books about it." Her own voice crackled and shook in nervousness and arousal, but she ignored it. Tony was interested in all this, and she did owe it to him to keep him apprised of everything.

He lifted a hand and with one finger followed the tracing of a light blue vein to the edge of her nipple. She sucked in a deep breath, but he seemed unaware of her predicament as he cupped her fully in his palm, weighing her. When his thumb touched her nipple she shuddered.

"You're a lot more sensitive, aren't you?" There was awe in his whispered question, and she could only nod her head.

"Olivia?" His hand rested low on her midriff now, and she watched as he unbuttoned her tan wool slacks and slid the zipper down. "I want to see all of you." He tugged her pants off, and when she saw how his hands shook she had to bite back a groan.

She lay there, legs slightly parted, her upper body framed by the shirt that still hung from her arms, while Tony's gaze, so hot and fierce, roamed all over her. When he bent to press his cheek to her belly, she couldn't stand it a second more. She curled up to wrap her arms around him, and the tears started.

"Shh. Sweetheart, don't cry."

He held her close, gently rocking, but the tears wouldn't stop. "What is it, Olivia? Did I hurt you?"

As if he ever would. She shook her head and squeezed him tighter.

"I need you, Livvy. I want to make love to you."

She didn't need any encouragement beyond that. She shifted so she could find his mouth, then kissed him hard, clasping his face between her hands and biting his lips.

He laughed, then groaned and in a heartbeat he was over her, kissing her everywhere, kicking off his shoes.... Olivia struggled with his shirt until finally he sat up and stripped off his own clothes. As he lowered himself on top of her again, he said, "Tell me if I hurt you."

"You won't. You couldn't. Please, Tony, I missed you so much."

His hand slid down her belly and started to stroke her, but she curled her fingers around his erection and he froze. "Damn, sweetheart, don't do that. I won't be able to..."

"I don't want you to. Just make love to me, Tony. Now."

His gaze locked on hers for a long moment, and then his fingers were parting her, preparing her. She was already wet and ready for him, and when he lifted his damp fingers to his mouth, she groaned, watching him lick the taste of her from his hand, seeing the heat in his eyes. She pulled him over her, kissing him wildly, opening her legs wide and he gently pushed inside her until she groaned and wrapped herself around him. It was excruciatingly sweet and slow and hot, and it was all she could do not to tell him she loved him. He held her face still and kissed her as she climaxed, letting her suck his tongue, then whispering to her in a voice so low she couldn't hear what he was saying. He pressed his face into her throat and gave a deep, hoarse groan, and she held him, stroking his back until his breathing had calmed.

TONY PUSHED HER damp hair away from her face, smoothed her eyebrows, and all the while, she could see him thinking. It was the awkward moment after, and she wanted to put it off, but there was no place to hide. Before he said it, she knew what was coming.

"Marry me."

Oh God, it hurt. She shook her head as fresh tears rolled down her cheeks, as much denying the words as denying him. "I can't."

"Why?"

She'd known he would ask. Tony didn't like being refused—for any reason. She looked at him squarely and went on the defensive. "Why do you want to marry me?"

He gave her a disgruntled frown and shoved himself away from her, sitting on the edge of the bed with his naked back to her. "We're having a baby, and I can't keep my hands off you. Don't you think marriage would be a good idea?"

The disappointment was crushing, but she kept her tone level, not letting him see how much his reply had hurt. "You planned all along for us to have a baby, but you didn't want to marry me. As I recall, you were appalled when I first misunderstood that to be your intention."

"That was when I thought the baby would be mine alone."

"I see." She scooted up in the bed and began refastening her clothing. Her bra left her stymied for a moment and required all her attention. As she buttoned her shirt, she watched him. "I've told you I'll share the baby with you. I would never deny you your child, or deny the child a father. And you'll make an excellent one. You can take on as big a role as you wish."

He started to say something fierce—she could tell by the frown on his face—but the knocking at her front door stopped him. His expression turned comical for a moment and then he cursed. "I don't believe this, I really don't. I'd have thought we'd be safe here, at your place."

He moved over on the bed as she jumped up and started pulling on her slacks. "At least we know it can't be my family this time."

Olivia shook her head, glad of the reprieve, regardless of who it was. "I can't imagine who would call on me."

Tony lounged back, gloriously naked and unconcerned by that fact. "That's right. You avoid all relationships, don't you?"

His sarcasm was especially sharp after the tender way he'd made love to her. She slanted him a look as she headed out of the room, then had to force herself to look away from the sight of his blatant masculinity.

"Do me a favor and stay put, okay?" She didn't wait for an answer, but pulled the bedroom door shut and went to see who was knocking. It had to be one of her neighbors, she thought, trying to smooth her hair and wipe her eyes dry at the same time. She was wrong. She opened the door to find a good portion of Tony's family standing in the hallway, exchanging pleasantries with her neighbors, who of course had opened their own doors to see who was visiting the building.

Kate was the first one to notice Olivia. Grabbing her

and giving her a big hug, Kate explained, "We were out shopping and realized we hadn't invited you to Christmas dinner yet."

Lisa stepped forward with John and Brian in tow, and Olivia had no choice but to move out of the way so they could enter. "The kids would love to see you again. They've been asking after you."

John grinned. "And Tony would love to see you, too, I'm sure."

Lisa poked her husband in the ribs. "John. You promised you'd behave yourself."

"I am behaving. I'm not telling her what a sullen ass Tony's been lately, am I?"

Olivia felt her stomach start to churn. It was always this way. The nausea would hit her at the most inopportune moments, usually when she was on her way to work or while she was at one of the shops, with customers all around.

Now, with Tony's family surrounding her, had to be the worst timing of all. She cringed, then laid a hand to her stomach, praying her belly would settle itself.

Kate stepped forward and put her arm around Olivia, misunderstanding her distress. "We don't mean to upset you, Olivia. But we really would love to have you. And in all honesty, the kids do ask after you. I think they miss you."

Olivia was thinking it couldn't get any worse when Tony came on the scene. "No fair, sis," he said, "using the kids as bait."

Everyone turned to stare at her bedroom doorway, where Tony stood wearing only his slacks—and those not properly fastened. It was no wonder John and Brian began to grin and Kate and Lisa looked at her with wide eyes. The questions would start any minute, questions Olivia didn't know how to answer. All at once, her stomach turned over and she knew she was going to vomit.

She clapped a hand to her mouth and ran.

Behind her, she could hear Kate's gasp and John's muttered, "What the hell?"

But mostly what she heard was Tony saying in a bland tone, "She's all right. It's just morning sickness. Excuse me, will you?"

HE CAUGHT THE bathroom door before she could slam it in his face, then quietly locked it for her while she dropped to her knees in front of the toilet. He winced as she gagged, his sympathy extreme. When she sat back on her heels, he flushed the toilet, dampened a washcloth in cool water and handed it to her.

"Are you okay now?"

"Go away." She sounded weak and croaky and he sat down behind her and pulled her against his chest. Taking the washcloth from her hand, he wiped her face for her, then laid it aside.

"Aren't you supposed to take deep breaths or something?"

"That's during labor, you idiot."

Tony grinned at her acerbic tone, weak though it was. "Well, I haven't gotten around to reading all the books you've evidently gone through. Give me a little time, okay?"

She groaned again and he barely managed to get the toilet lid up for her. This time when she finished, she glared at him and demanded, "Go away and leave me alone."

"Don't be silly, Olivia. So you're sick? I've seen worse, I promise."

She staggered to her feet and went to the sink where she splashed water on her face. "Yeah. Worse is waiting in the other room, and you can be the one to explain."

"What's to explain? We're having a baby. They'd have found out sooner or later anyway."

"You know it's more than that and you could have spoken to them when I wasn't around!"

They could hear the rush of whispered voices from his family, and Tony shook his head. "There's no hope for it now." He opened the door and took her hand, but she held back. "Don't be a coward."

Olivia would have happily detoured into her bedroom and locked the door, but Tony didn't release her hand. He dragged her into the living room, where everyone had taken a seat, and said to the room at large, "We're having a baby."

Kate was the first to shoot from her seat, squealing in happiness. "Tony, this is so fantastic! When is the wedding?"

And without missing a beat, he said, "There won't be one."

Everyone stilled, their smiles frozen. And then the first volley of righteous umbrage hit. Of course he had to marry her. What could he be thinking of? Hadn't he enjoyed enough freedom of late? And babies deserved two parents. Kate even went so far as to put her arm around Olivia and remain protectively at her side while she glared daggers at him.

It was laughable, he thought. His family should know him better than this, but obviously they'd switched loyalties somewhere through this farce of a courtship. Then he shook his head. No, it was only that they thought they would save him from his own poor judgment. He wished them luck in their efforts.

And poor Olivia. He could see she was beginning to fret over the way they crucified him. Obviously they didn't realize it was Olivia who'd shied away from marriage, and if he told them the truth of the matter, it would really put her on the spot. He couldn't do it.

But Olivia could.

She looked around at all of them, dazed by their reactions. Brian was shaking his head and trying to be reasonable, Kate kept squeezing Olivia and patting her hand, and John was red in the face, telling Tony what a mistake he was making. Lisa, the only quiet one, stood twisting her hands together, the perfect picture of concern.

"Tony asked me to marry him!" She had to practically shout to be heard, and then the room went silent.

John was the first to react. "So what's the problem then?"

Olivia looked to Tony for help, but he just crossed his arms over his chest and waited. He was as curious as anyone to hear her explanation.

"It's not as simple as that."

"When has love ever been simple?"

Lisa again smacked John. "It's their business, John. Maybe we should just leave them alone."

"But Tony wants to marry her! And she obviously cares about him." He paused, then looked at Olivia. "You do, don't you?"

"I...yes."

"Just not enough to marry him?"

"It's complicated!"

John snorted. "How complicated can it be? You care about Tony. He's crazy about you. Hell, he's been so maudlin all week, I thought I'd have to shoot him to put him out of my misery," he joked.

Olivia's gaze shot to Tony's face, and he gave her a grim smile. "I have been a miserable bastard."

Tears welled in her eyes. "Oh, Tony."

She looked cornered, and he hated it. Enough was enough. He walked across the room and jerked the front door open. "Why don't you all get lost, all right? She's having a terrible time of it with this morning sickness stuff, and now she has all of you badgering her. Give us some time alone."

Lisa patted Olivia's arm. "The morning sickness will pass in a few weeks. And the rest of being pregnant is a breeze in comparison."

Kate gave her a firm hug. "I had it all day long, too. Try nibbling dry crackers as soon as your stomach acts up. And don't worry about the tears. Both Lisa and I cried all the time when we were carrying."

Brian squeezed her shoulder. "Hope you're feeling better soon, hon. Try to make it for Christmas. Celebrating will take your mind off...other things."

Then only John was standing there, and Tony watched as he gave Olivia a stern look. "Whatever you think your reasons are, discuss them with him. Sometimes you find out the problems that worry you don't even exist." Then he gave her an affectionate kiss on the cheek and left.

The door closed with a resounding click, and the room was uncomfortably silent after that. For a moment, Tony didn't look at her. He kept his gaze on the door while he organized his thoughts. "You seemed surprised that I wasn't happy this past week."

Her response was trembling and uncertain. "I thought you'd still be too angry to be unhappy. Or if you were unhappy, I...well, was it because you thought I wouldn't involve you with the baby?"

Tony did turn to her then, and he made no effort to hide his anger. "The baby? I fell in love with you long before I knew you were carrying my baby. Hell, I think I may have been half in love with you for a long, long time. You were my first choice when I decided I wanted a baby. And then it didn't take me long to realize you were my *only* choice."

Her eyes were huge, her mouth open in a small O. Tony shook his head, amused by her astonishment. How could she not have realized how much he cared for her?

"Olivia, we just made love, and it didn't have a damn thing to do with the baby."

"No?"

Stalking toward her, he smiled and said, "Nope. I get near you and I want you. I think about you and I want you. Hell, you throw up in a toilet and I want you."

"You do?"

He nodded, still coming closer. "And it's not just sex. I want to hold you, talk to you, listen to you laugh. God, I love watching you negotiate a deal."

She laughed at that and he finally reached her, but he didn't touch her. He lowered his voice and admitted, "It makes me hot as hell seeing you in your shark mode, being demanding and unrelenting. Of course, it was almost the same watching you give little Shawn his bottle. And when you defended me just now to my family—you do funny things to my insides, lady."

"You love me?"

"Hell, yes. Isn't that what I've been saying?"

"Oh, Tony." To his chagrin, she started to cry. When he reached for her, she stepped away. "There's so much you have to know."

He sat on the couch and propped his feet up. "Then don't you think it's time you told me?"

She nodded uncertainly, and he patted the couch beside him. When she started to sit there, he caught her and tugged her into his lap instead, holding her close and tucking her face into his shoulder. "All right. Now talk. And don't leave anything out."

She did. She told him about her trip to the hospital, that the pregnancy was still at risk, that there was a good chance she'd never get pregnant again. Even if she was able to carry this baby full-term, it might be their only child.

She didn't look at him as she spoke, choosing to keep her face hidden against him. Tony was relieved. It was damn difficult keeping his anger hidden, but he wanted her to finish the story, to make certain there were no more secrets between them. When she grew silent and he didn't immediately respond, she turned stiff in his arms.

"Tony?" He heard the uncertainty, the vulnerability, and his anger doubled. But he remained silent.

"You're angry?" she persisted.

"I'm furious." And he was.

She gave a small sob, but he didn't relent. "How could you do this, plan to go through all this alone, leave me in the dark? Didn't you think, somewhere along the line, I'd earned your trust? Have I ever given you any reason to believe I'm such a shallow ass that I'd let you go through this alone? Damn you, Olivia, are you ever going to open up to me?"

She had gone very still just after he started his tirade, and now she whispered, "I just did."

"What?" He was almost too angry to make sense of her words.

"I just opened up to you. And I do trust you. I swear. It's just that I love you so much, I didn't want you to be burdened with a wife who couldn't give you what you want."

"And if what I want most is you?"

She pushed away so she could see his face. Her dark eyes were liquid with tears, her cheeks blotchy, and he loved her so much, he wanted to cry with her. "Olivia, I love you."

She sniffed and threw herself against him, squeezing his neck so tightly he couldn't breathe. He choked out a laugh and said, "Marry me."

"But you want a baby, too."

"We're having a baby."

"But what if…"

"Shh." He laid his finger against her lips. "No what-ifs. I love you. You love me. If something happens, we'll have other children. And if you can't carry them, we'll adopt. It doesn't matter. What matters is that I need you with me."

Olivia laughed and squeezed him again. "I want you, too. And this baby. I'm being so careful, following all the doctor's orders, taking my progesterone twice a day…"

"You have to take pills?"

She slanted him a look. "Don't ask. Just understand that my body needs to absorb it now to help the baby. After the first trimester, the risks aren't nearly so high."

He loved holding her like this, seeing her so animated. "You've really studied up on this, haven't you?"

She ducked her head. "I've been so afraid."

He held her face, making her look at him. "From now on, you'll tell me. We'll get through it together."

Smiling, she said, "Yes."

"And you'll marry me."

It was his I'm-in-charge-now voice, and Olivia said, "Yes, sir."

He grinned. "You've just made my family very happy."

"And you?"

"I've just gotten everything I ever wanted. Of course I'm happy."

Two years later

"SHOULD WE TAKE the diaper bag on the plane with us?"

Tony laughed. "I wouldn't leave home without it." He walked into the bedroom where Olivia was packing. Her body once again slim and beautiful, though it wouldn't be that way for long. "How are you feeling?"

She turned and gave him and their thirteen-month-old son, Devon, a big smile. "Fine. Anxious."

"No morning sickness?"

"It's the strangest thing, but this time I feel wonderful."

"Lisa and Kate swore each pregnancy was different for them, as well."

Devon reached for his mother and Tony transferred him into her waiting arms. There was no hesitancy on her part now as she cuddled him close and kissed him and breathed his scent. Devon laughed and kicked his pudgy legs.

"Do you think he'll like flying? Maybe I should wait a little longer before making the Seattle trip."

"You've waited long enough. Besides, we'll only be

there a week to look things over, and the woman you hired to manage the place is counting on seeing you. I have no doubt she's gone to great pains to impress you. And I did want to check in on the hotel anyway."

She laughed at him and shook her head. "You're worse than me. But running a business from across the country is easier than I'd thought it would be."

"With hotels, you have to adjust. Can't be everywhere at once."

"I know. And you taught me the secret long ago." She balanced Devon on her hip and went back to her packing. It sometimes amazed him the things she could now do one-handed. "As long as I hire good people, treat them well and expect the best from them, things, for the most part, run smoothly."

She bent to tuck a pair of shoes into the suitcase, and Tony couldn't stop himself from patting her rear. "Did I ever tell you how hot it makes me when you use that logical corporate tone?"

She cast him a look and said, "Why do you think I use it so often?"

"You always were a devious woman." He laughed when she playfully smacked him. Her earlier ploy was no longer a sensitive issue between them, especially since things had turned out so well. They had their baby, they had each other, and it was the best deal either of them had ever made.

* * * * *

RISQUÉ BUSINESS

Tawny Weber

"It takes courage to grow up
and become who you really are."
—e. e. cummings

To my parents,
who always encouraged me to be who I really am.

CHAPTER ONE

Her hot, desperate breaths echoed down the long, dark hallway. Terror coalesced into a black swirl of passion as his mouth slid down the concave silk of her belly. His fingers gripped her butt, lifting her for his pleasure, totally in control. He held complete dominance over her. Damp heat pooled between her legs, making her squirm in silent supplication. His fingers tightened, holding her prisoner, demanding she await his command.

Delaney Conner's own breath puffed out as the words blurred on the page. God, to be that woman! She'd already read this scene three times since she'd gotten Nick Angel's latest erotic thriller, but it still fascinated her. Fascinated, hell. She'd had two orgasms thanks to this chapter alone. Three, if she counted the memory it'd invoked in the shower.

She traced a finger over the face on the back cover. The author's eyes, vivid and piercing, promised an ability to live up to the heat between the pages. She wondered how much of the sexual appeal was the words themselves, and how much was knowing they'd been written by the man with the sexiest face she'd ever seen grace a book jacket.

"Professor Conner?"

With a gasp, Delaney tossed the book in her canvas tote as if it had spouted flames. Cheeks on fire, she plastered a look of ingenuous questioning on her face. Hopefully the rapid flutter of her eyelashes conveyed innocence, in addition to cooling off her cheeks.

"Mr. Sims, hello," Delaney said, her tone tight and stiff, as suited a professor at Rosewood.

Women like the heroines in Nick Angel's books, when busted having sex in public places, gave a wicked smile and made you envy their moxie. Her? She couldn't even read sexy books in public without blushing and worrying someone was going to rat her out for ill-advised reading choices. After all, reading was meant to be an educational pursuit, never for tawdry entertainment.

"I just wanted to say how much I got out of today's lecture. The evolution of character archetypes fascinates me."

Her discomfort dissipated as Delaney shifted into teaching mode. The two of them fell into a discussion of the topic, Delaney growing more animated and excited the more they talked. She loved it when a student grasped her concepts, loved even more seeing the spark of excitement in his eyes. Delaney wasn't an easy teacher by any means. She pushed her students, keeping her curriculum dynamic and challenging. But she prided herself on having the lowest failure rate of any other professor in the English department.

And her success would only help in her bid to become assistant head of the department. A plum promotion, it'd put her in the position to take over as department head within the next ten years. Exactly as she'd planned. And maybe, just maybe, it'd have the added bonus of actually getting her father's attention.

"Excuse me," said a husky voice.

Delaney and Sims moved aside to let a gorgeous

brunette pass. Stunning from the top of her perfectly straight hair to the bottom of her sleek black heels, even her little red suit screamed power. Now *she* was a perfect Nick Angel heroine. Sexy, savvy and confident.

They both watched the woman pass, Delaney envying her sense of presence and Sims obviously admiring her ass. While he gathered his composure, Delaney glanced at her watch.

Damn. Late again. With a quick goodbye to her student, she hurried down the hall to the dean's office.

She flew into the reception area. The tiny blonde at the desk looked like a kewpie doll. Flaxen curls, huge blue eyes and a round dimpled face hid a razor-sharp mind and a wicked sense of humor. She was Delaney's best friend, and the two women had bonded over an obsession with Johnny Depp, eighties rock music and their mutual love for romance novels, a top-secret subject here at the college. Rosewood was that uptight and narrow-minded.

It'd taken Delaney until last year to finally confide in Mindy Adams her deepest, darkest secret. She not only loved to read popular fiction, but unbeknownst to anyone other than Mindy, she also made a tidy income reviewing it for various magazines and newspapers. She'd heard a rumor that two years ago, the college had fired an art history professor when they'd discovered she modeled on the side. That her modeling had been of historical costumes in a magazine layout had seemed to make no difference to the dean. Delaney could only assume that he and the trustees saw it as frivolous and mocking.

So she kept her reviews top secret and used her middle name, Madison. She'd have been crazy not to.

"Am I too late? Is my father still here?" she asked, catching her breath.

"He's still here," Mindy responded slowly.

"What's wrong?" Delaney asked, still panting slightly.

"I just thought you might want to know, um—" Mindy hesitated, then sighed. "Did you notice that brunette leaving a few minutes ago?"

"She had a great laptop bag, with plenty of room for books and papers." She glanced at her own canvas bag, ratty and worn. She hated shopping, but she lusted after practical totes, especially in leather. Maybe after she got the promotion she'd treat herself to one like that.

"She was here about the position in your department."

Brow furrowed in confusion, Delaney stared. "My position?"

She hadn't ever considered there would be competition for it. She tilted her head in silent question and Mindy nudged a paper toward her. Delaney scanned the woman's resume.

"Nice, but not as strong as mine."

Mindy winced.

"I'd heard talk Professor Belkin wants someone who's going to attract attention," the girl said, referring to the head of the English department. "Attendance is down in the department and he's taking it personally. He seems to think a more attractive assistant head will help boost the numbers."

"A dynamic curriculum and strong teaching reputation aren't enough?"

They both knew it was a rhetorical question. Where Delaney might hide a mystery novel behind her textbook, Belkin was the kind of guy who hid a *Hustler* magazine behind his. The man was all about looks, the hotter, the better.

And even though the position was awarded by a hiring committee, he headed it. Which meant he had a lot of influence.

"I heard Belkin tell the dean he wanted someone with a lot of charisma and looks, who could not only handle the academic side of the job, but the PR angle he's planning to push," Mindy said to the top of her desk. She obviously couldn't meet her friend's eyes.

Delaney clenched her jaw to keep from screaming in frustration. Temper never helped, but imagining how good it would feel to throw her ratty bag across the room sure did.

Mindy took a deep breath and shot her a long, considering look, probably to make sure Delaney wasn't going to pitch a fit. Reassured, she tapped the magazine on the desk in front of her.

"Maybe if you'd consider a makeover…" she suggested hesitantly, not for the first time. Delaney was already shaking her head before the blonde continued. "You know, something to change the visual so maybe people will give you the attention you deserve?"

Delaney sighed. Spoken like a true girly girl. Mindy never left the house without lipstick, how could she be considered unbiased? Delaney figured it was because she'd grown up motherless that she'd never been inducted into the girly club.

"Why bother? I am who I am. Will mascara and a push-up bra make me someone else?" The thought made her cringe. Makeup, fancy clothes, they baffled her.

"No, but they'll get you noticed." Mindy waved the magazine in her hand. *Risqué*. Delaney rolled her eyes.

What a title. She looked at the tagline, "You're only as confident as you look." *Right.*

"Who needs that kind of attention?" Delaney groused. She tugged at the frayed hem of her tweed jacket and frowned. "What about that whole 'inner beauty being more important than outer beauty' thing?"

"It's a feel-good myth, like Santa Claus," Mindy deadpanned.

Delaney snorted.

"You've got looks under all that tweed. You've definitely got brains, and you're a nice person," Mindy mused. "You just need to learn to make the most of it all. Take my advice, read this magazine. It'll have you on the road to satisfaction. Better yet, I'll bet you even get laid."

Delaney snorted again.

"Unlike some people, I don't think sex is a cure-all." Well, she was alarmingly addicted to a certain author's books. But that had nothing to do with real life. Their only purpose was titillation. They had the reality level of SpongeBob SquarePants and even less emotional depth.

"How would you know? When was the last time you had sex?"

When Delaney opened her mouth to retort, Mindy shook her head. "With someone else actually in the room with you."

Damn. She clamped her lips closed.

"What good is another department-store makeup fiasco?" she asked instead. She'd tried that once in her teens and discovered being invisible was much preferable to being mocked.

"No, you need something much bigger." Mindy leaned over to push the magazine into her hands.

Delaney glanced at the cover, then at the dog-eared page. *Risqué?* "A makeover contest? You're kidding, right?"

"Not at all. It's a killer deal. Complete makeover. Hair, makeup, completely new wardrobe. Not some cheesy thing, either, it's custom created just for you. They even teach the winners how to maintain her new look."

"Why on earth would I want to do this?"

"It's your shot. You win, you'll see what a difference it makes."

Delaney tossed the magazine back on the desk with a roll of her eyes. "What's the point? I hardly think something as shallow as eye shadow and hairspray will cure my problems."

Mindy pulled a face, then shrugged. Delaney felt bad for hurting the other woman's feelings. Before she could apologize, Mindy slipped the magazine into her drawer. The alarm on her desk squawked a reminder.

"He's leaving in ten minutes. If you want to see him, you'd better go in now," Mindy reminded her.

Frowning, Delaney nodded her thanks, scooped up the tote and squared her shoulders.

She strode through the heavy doors, lifted her chin and took a deep breath. She'd originally intended to hint around that she'd appreciate his backing on her application. Now she'd have to be more direct. For once, she had to stand up for herself.

Of course, it would help if her father actually looked at her. Delaney cleared her throat, but he still didn't glance up from the papers he was signing.

"I need your help," Delaney stated quietly.

He lifted a finger, gesturing for her to wait. Preferably in silence.

She clutched the strap of her bag so hard the canvas hurt her fingers. She wished she had the nerve to throw it across the room, but years of lectures on why losing control never paid off flashed through her head. Temper, temper. Maybe if she recited that often enough, she'd stop imagining how good it might be to let loose and let him know exactly how she felt. But, as with most things nonacademic, imagining was the only way she'd experience the pleasure. Her mother had always been able to soothe away her temper, but once she'd gone, Delaney was on her own. Once, only once, she'd let her temper fly with her father. She'd been ten. He'd sent her away to boarding school as a result.

She glared at the top of his balding head. Tufts of red hair stuck out like chicken fluff. Didn't it just figure that along with his brilliant mind, she'd inherited the man's long, lanky body and god-awful hair? Where he came across as scholarly and authoritative, Delaney just looked like a carrot-topped Olive Oyl. Except given her miserable luck with men, instead of fighting over her, Popeye and Bluto would probably run off with each other.

"What kind of help?" Randolph Conner, Dean of Rosewood College and Delaney's only living relative, asked in a distracted tone when he finally glanced at her.

"Support," she informed him. "You know I applied for the assistant's position. Apparently Professor Belkin is changing the job requirements."

"He's merely expanding the job description," Dean Conner—as he preferred everyone, including his only daughter, to address him—said. He still didn't bother looking at her, so Delaney didn't bother hiding her angry expression. "Professor Belkin, as head of the English department, feels we need a strong, dynamic person in the position."

Frustration surged through her. For all the faculty noticed—her father included—she really was invisible. Delaney thrust out her chin and did the unthinkable— she questioned his motives.

"Is it because she's so attractive?" she asked.

"Wha...?" Dean Conner shot her a frown, his brows drawn together like a pair of bright red caterpillars. Finally, a reaction. "Who? Professor Tate? How does her appearance factor into anything? Who cares about all that physical fluff?"

And he meant it. A single parent, Randolph Conner had raised Delaney to value intelligence. Intellect, he deemed, was much more meaningful than something as fleeting and nebulous as society's current definition of beauty.

Of course, since most of the rest of society hadn't been raised with the same standard, that left Delaney at a slight disadvantage. She ground her teeth in frustration. And now it looked like brains weren't enough, either.

"Professor Tate is the woman who was just here, right?" Delaney took a deep breath and, despite the clenching in her gut, confronted him. "My qualifications, to say nothing of my seniority, are stronger."

Her father sighed, his deep, put-upon sigh that let her know she was wasting his valuable time. He used the same sigh when she'd wanted to learn how to ride a bike, had asked permission to go to school activities or wanted to get a pet. That sigh was so effective she still couldn't ride a bike and had the social skills of a pimply-faced twelve-year-old girl who'd been deprived of the love of a puppy.

"Delaney, you're missing the point. We need fresh blood in the English department. New ideas and a strong program."

She just stared. He obviously *wasn't* going to back her proposal. But she needed to hear it from him.

"Will you support my application?" she asked, her throat tight.

"As I said, we need fresh blood. Bright, energetic people who will bring excitement to the program. You're one of our most brilliant professors, Delaney. A strong benefit to the department." He fiddled with some papers on his desk, then met her eyes. He had that irritated "it's for your own good" look on his face. Her stomach did a somersault. "As a matter of fact, at Professor Belkin's recommendation, this next semester we're going to experiment with taking some of the classes to the Internet. We'd like you to handle them."

He handed her a course outline for the summer semester. She didn't have a single nonvirtual class.

Her breath caught in her chest and she abruptly sank into a chair. Tears, rarely allowed to surface, filled her eyes. She took the few seconds needed to gather control, knowing her father would prefer she delay her response rather than show any form of emotion he might have to acknowledge.

"If I'm such a benefit, why'd I just get demoted?" Not what she'd intended to say, but she found she didn't regret her outburst. After all, maybe if she spoke up for once, he'd listen to her.

Before he could put into words the irritation clear on his face, she jumped up to pace the room, the paper clenched in her fist. "Oh, sure, you can claim it's not an official demotion. But what the hell would you call it when my classes are suddenly all via cyberspace?"

If not for her brains, nobody would ever notice her. And now they'd found a way to get her brains without her actual physical presence. She resisted the urge to sniff to see if she smelled bad. Apparently that was her life's theme: Delaney Conner, the Invisible Woman.

She sucked in a shuddering breath and shoved a hand through her hair. Her fingers tangled in the knot she'd forgot she'd anchored in place with a pencil. With a wince, she untangled herself and tossed the pencil— along with a few carroty-red hairs she'd yanked out as well—on her father's desk.

He glanced at the pencil, then back at her. Then he sighed.

"I don't have time to debate this, Delaney. I'm due in a meeting in a few minutes and would like to review my notes. Please—" he waved toward the door "—we'll discuss it another time."

Her fists clenched at her sides, she watched him turn back to his papers. And just like that, he'd dismissed her. As usual. Delaney opened her mouth to tell him just where he could shove his meeting, to demand that he address her questions and really *actually* listen to her. Those damned tears welled up again, this time out of frustration that he couldn't—wouldn't—understand her. Value her. For once. She blinked the tears—and words—back, though. What was the point?

He'd never paid any attention to her before. Her intellectual achievements were expected, not celebrated. And to Randolph Conner, intellect was the only thing that mattered.

Her vision now blurred with anger, Delaney grabbed her purse and stormed out of the office.

She caught a glimpse of herself in the plateglass window. Long, skinny and…brown. She was a baggy mess. The heavy tweed of her ill-fitting suit sagged, her shoulder pads drooped. Just because the Conner family put no value on physical appeal didn't mean the rest of the world didn't. With a considering frown, she yanked at the waistband of her suit jacket to mimic a better fit. She captured the strands of hair flying around her face, then tucked them behind her ear. Her shoulders drooped. Still a mess. Definitely not what Belkin had in mind as a more visually appealing assistant.

Delaney ground her teeth. So what did she do? Give up? Go teach at a different school? Resign herself to invisibility?

Hell, no.

She stomped down the hall and planted herself in front of Mindy's desk.

"Makeover, huh?" she asked.

Mindy's blue eyes bugged out so much she looked like a squished Barbie doll.

"Really?" The girl scrambled to hand over the magazine, pages tearing in her haste to get it into Delaney's hands.

The glossy image promising a sexy, sophisticated change made Delaney pause. Then she lifted her chin. It was time she stopped letting her father decide what had value and what didn't. After all, that was probably the only way she'd ever learn to put any stock in herself. His assessment definitely wasn't working in her favor.

"Instead of a well-earned promotion, I've been invited to teach from the comfort of my own home," Delaney said with a sneer.

"Huh?"

"I'm taking over the Internet English curriculum."

"I didn't know we had an Internet English curriculum."

"We do now. And it's all mine. All the better to keep me invisible."

Delaney knew she sounded bitter, but she couldn't help it. She *was* bitter. And angry. And, not that she wanted to admit it, just a little desperate. After all, her career defined her and that definition had just taken a turn for the worse.

She glanced at the magazine again. *Risqué*. That was so not her. What chance did she have of winning? And would it really help? Belkin wanted visually appealing *and* charismatic. A few swipes of mascara and blush wouldn't give her that.

"Did I mention the hiring committee won't even look at the applications until the fall semester?" Mindy asked. "Even though Belkin's made his choice, it still has to go before the rest of the committee."

Delaney pursed her lips. That would give her six months. She considered for all of three seconds. Change? Or invisibility? Bottom line...invisibility sucked.

"I'm in," she declared, ignoring the warning blaring in her head, screaming that decisions made in anger never paid off. "How do I become visible?"

CHAPTER TWO

"You HAVE TO ADMIT, sex sells," Nick Angel declared, leaning back in the butter-soft leather chair and folding his hands behind his head. "And I sell it better than most."

"Sure, sure," Gary Masters, Nick's literary agent, agreed with a slow nod. "Nobody is saying you don't do great sex, Nicky. The thing is, this new editor wants more."

Nick puffed out a breath. This was the third meeting he'd had in two months over editorial changes. Nick wanted a solid relationship with this new editor. After all, he credited a great deal of his career success to his previous editor. Damned if he didn't wish she hadn't retired.

"More sex?" He frowned, then shrugged. As long as it didn't compromise the ratio of suspense in his books, he didn't mind more sex. He'd just cut back on that foreplay crap, hit them hard and fast with the hot-and-wild kink. "I can do that."

"Not more sex," Gary said, his voice a low rumble at odds with the sophisticated gloss of the office. "More emotion."

Nick dropped his feet to the floor and frowned. He'd come to New York to meet with Gary, sign his next round of publishing contracts and take in some R&R before heading back to San Francisco. From the way

Gary was tapping his pen against the stack of contracts on his desk, there was a little problem or five buried in those papers.

"He's suggesting more emotion?"

"More like demanding."

Son of a bitch. "Three books on the *New York Times* bestseller list and he wants to change the core of my work? You're kidding, right?"

"Look, you don't have to take the demand. We can counter the contract clause. Or we can shop you around. But…"

"But what?"

"Well, he's really pushing the point. He's backed it with plenty of industry facts, data and even some fan requests. You're starting to lose your female fan base, which composes over thirty percent of your sales, according to data."

Nick gave a bad-tempered grimace. He wrote erotic suspense, not romantic suspense. The only emotions in his books were fear, excitement and lust. Jaw clenched, he bounced his fist on his knee.

"Look, those numbers came from the publisher. How do you know they aren't skewed to their advantage?"

Gary raised a bushy brow. "In the first place, I'm not some green newbie without a clue—I checked with my own sources. In the second place, I've had even more mail here requesting you tone down the meaningless sex and give John Savage a softer side. The female fans want emotions. Even your reviewers are starting to band together about this. One just slammed your writing in a national magazine."

Nick shrugged his disinterest. Reviewers had their place, but it wasn't behind his computer keyboard. He wrote for himself first and foremost. If he'd caved to all the people who wanted him to write differently—hell, to be different—he'd have quit long ago.

"Don't scoff," Gary warned. "I know reviews don't mean anything to you, but this one has become a hot topic on the Internet. And your editor is freaking out. He's sure your next release will tank. In fact, he even messengered me a copy of the magazine with the reviewer's comments highlighted."

Nick frowned. "Who the hell is this guy?"

"Gal."

He rolled his eyes. Figured. Female reviewer, female fans. Leave it to women to demand more emotion. What was with them and their need to talk about, hell, to even believe in the fairy tale of love?

Nick sneered. He'd watched enough manipulation, pain and drama played out in the name of that nebulous love thing to know the reality. Emotions were simply a label for choices made in the moment. They were what people used to justify whatever it was they wanted to do.

Nick prided himself on his honesty, brutal though others might find it; he always stated in the beginning of any physical relationship that he didn't play the emotion game. And yet, like his character, John Savage, women always figured they could change him. The only ones not interested in changing him were the ones interested in using him.

Just like this damned reviewer. Probably thought she'd make a name for herself by slamming his work, thinking if he caved to her review, she'd be set.

"So some mouthy reviewer wants to use my books as a platform," Nick summed up with a shrug. "Let her try. It doesn't matter to me, I'm not changing. John Savage is a solid character. He's intense, he's a man's man. The last thing his stories need are foofy love stuff slopping around to mess him up."

"Actually, she has a solid reputation in publishing circles. She's gained quite a bit of notoriety over the last couple months, though."

"Based on trashing my books," Nick scoffed.

"Nah, trashing you was incidental. Her rise to fame is from a contest she just won. *Risqué* magazine ran the interview last month."

When he raised a brow, Gary lifted a file off the corner of his desk and handed it over. Nick flipped through the contents.

Risqué. One of the top women's periodicals in the country, it touted everything from sexual adventure to health and fashion. Huge doe eyes framed by a silky sweep of russet hair caught his attention. There was something in those carefully made-up eyes, a vulnerability, that tugged at him. Rather than dwelling on it, Nick ignored the glossy images and went straight for the text.

"Ms. Madison, don't you feel modern fiction leaves quite a bit to be desired?"

"Oh, no. There is so much fabulous writing in the bookstores today. New authors are to today's reader what Brontë was to her readers. Inspired, entertaining, talented."

"Brontë could be termed romance?"

"Definitely. But the other genres hold just as true."

"What about oh, say, erotica or suspense?"

"If those are your cup of tea, one of the best authors to read is Nick Angel. He's done a commendable job of combining both eroticism and suspense. You can't read his books without having a physical reaction. Definitely a pulse raiser."

Nick grinned. He wondered how often he'd raised her pulse.

"Then as a literary expert, you recommend Nick Angel?"

"If you want a commitment-free read, definitely."

Nick frowned.

"Commitment-free?"

"Well, his books are great, but not the kind you become emotionally invested in. The sex, while some of the hottest out there, is always distanced. There is very little empathy or reader involvement. It's like watching a fast-paced television program. A lot of impact in a short amount of space, but not enough depth to make the reader care much about the characters. It's similar to well-done pornography. Hot and sexy, yes—I'll be the first to say it totally draws you in for the sexual payoff. But that's all it is. Sex for the sake of titillation. It's too bad Angel is afraid of emotion. If he brought in some depth, his books would be amazing."

Afraid? Nick sneered. Who was afraid? Just because opening the door to emotions was the equivalent to being shoved into a pit of flesh-eating piranha…

"She compared my work to porn?" he asked, not

wanting to think about the other irritating—if blatantly untrue—accusation. It wasn't the first time someone had made the comparison to porn. But it was the first time it'd bothered him. It was probably those big brown eyes of hers.

"That's the part everyone latched on to." Gary's narrow fingers tapped a rhythm on the stack of contracts. Nick scanned the man's face. Angular, almost scholarly, the gray-haired agent looked like a wise monk. He had the heart of a shark and the industry knowledge of a wizard. It was thanks to him that Nick was where he was, career-wise. The guy knew his business.

He also barbecued a mean steak, kept Nick's mother off his back and had pulled Nick out of the nightmarish hell that had been his life after his wife had publicly humiliated him during their divorce. Nick owed him. Even more important, he trusted him.

"Look, I know you avoid emotions. And you have good reason, given your past," Gary said in a carefully measured tone. Nick just glared. He didn't want to talk about Angelina. The woman had lured him in, then ripped his life apart. Even after finding out about her affair, he'd been willing to work things out. She hadn't, though, as she'd proved when she'd hit the interview circuit to share with the world the deep, dark secrets of their marriage. And more to the point, their sex life. Thanks to her, his sales had skyrocketed in equal measure to his cgo deflating. Her point, he was sure, since she'd snagged a tidy share of his royalties. That'd been all Nick had needed to assure him that giving in to emotion was a one-way ticket to being screwed over.

"I don't avoid anything," he denied adamantly. "I just think this publicity stunt is a bunch of bullshit."

"Nick, just consider it. You know, give Savage a love interest. Make your editor happy. Appease some female fans. Head this off before it gets any bigger."

"My character is already established, Gary. I've already done eight books. It's obvious he's not an emotional kind of guy. He works, the stories work. You can't just go in, midseries, and rewrite his entire history and motivation. I'd lose my core readership."

"I think you need to consider some changes, then. Even if they aren't to the main character. Maybe a subplot?"

Nick tamped down the angry panic clutching at his gut. To write a character, he had to get into his head. The last thing he needed was to delve into an emotional pit.

He glanced at the folder, flipping through the stack of newspaper clippings. Instead of a picture next to her byline, this Delaney Madison had a book graphic. Odd. Most women he knew craved attention like they craved air. It was a necessity. Maybe it was a ploy to play up the makeover fame.

"Give me a chance to take care of this," he said, getting to his feet. Looming over his agent's desk from his six-two height, Nick rolled the folder and stuck it the back pocket of his jeans.

"What are you going to do?"

Nick headed for the door. His hand on the knob, he glanced back.

"I'm going to teach Ms. Madison to think twice before she messes with me. By the time I'm through with her, she'll publicly admit the way I do sex is just perfect."

"You know, you should try a different shade of eye shadow," Delaney mused, her chin resting on her hand as she stared across the restaurant table at Mindy. "Maybe something in a gray instead of brown. I think it'd bring out your eyes more."

Her glass of iced tea halfway to her mouth, Mindy stared, shock clear in her brown-shadowed eyes. Then she burst into laughter.

"You're loving this, aren't you?"

"Actually, I am," Delaney confirmed, lifting her own glass to toast her friend.

This was the makeover results, of course.

She glanced at her reflection in the restaurant's plate-eglass window. Even blunted in that poor excuse for a mirror, the change was still amazing. Her once wild carrot hair flowed in a smooth, russet bob, swinging a few inches above her shoulders. Cheekbones she hadn't realized she owned accented eyes made huge and mysterious by the wonders of cosmetics.

She'd actually won! Sure, she'd figured her essay on "The Inner *Risqué* Woman" would give her an edge. But after that first round, the entire contest had depended on chance. But thanks to a combination of her essay, her obvious need of a makeover and some awesome luck, here she was. All made over.

Right after the drawing at the beginning of April, they'd done the makeover in segments, briefly interviewing her and running a "before" photo in the May issue of *Risqué*. Then for their June issue, they'd spent two weeks showing her the ins and outs of doing her makeup and how to actually style her hair to look the same as they'd done. And best of all, she mused as she ran a finger over the buttery leather strap of her purse, was her new wardrobe.

The shock of winning *Risqué*'s contest was starting

to pass, but the shock of her own transformation was still fresh.

"I had no idea something as superfluous as makeup and fancy clothes could be so, well…"

"Sexy?" Mindy finished, grinning like a proud fairy godmother.

Delaney started to deny it. She'd never in her life aspired to be sexy. Oh, sure, she might have wished to be like the women Nick Angel wrote about. The kind that had a body worthy of using as an international weapon. But that'd always seemed as impossible as having tea with Frodo in Middle Earth. But now…

"Ladies, your salads will be right out. More tea?"

The women glanced up. Delaney's cheeks heated when she realized the waiter's attention was totally focused on her. Or, more specially, on her gel-bra enhanced cleavage. Again. This restaurant was a block from the college, and the guy had waited on Delaney at least a dozen times in the past. He'd never stared before. Maybe he was trying to figure out where she'd bought the new boobs?

Delaney squirmed while Mindy shooed him off.

"Yeah, maybe I'm feeling a little sexy," Delaney admitted when he was gone. "But it's a weird feeling. Uncomfortable. Like wearing a Halloween costume or pretending to be someone I'm not."

Mindy shook her head so hard her kewpie-doll curls shook loose. "Oh, no, this is totally you. You're a beautiful woman, I've told you that before. Now you have to admit it yourself because it's staring you in the face."

"As long as it gets me that promotion," Delaney muttered, waving her hand in dismissal. Not realizing he was there, she knocked her salad out of the waiter's hand as he tried to set it in front of her. He fumbled to catch it but half still ended up on the floor. With a dirty look he left, probably to get a broom. Apparently new boobs weren't enough to excuse clumsiness. Delaney glared at Mindy, who didn't bother to hide her snicker. "I told you, I'm not used to this."

Mindy tilted her chin as if to say "watch," and then gave the waiter two tables away a warm smile. He scurried right over. "Could you be a sweetie and take that salad back for a fresh one. And the sun is shining right through onto our table here, can you pull the shades down just a smidge, please?"

Delaney watched, awed as always, as Mindy wrapped the guy around her finger with a sweet smile and little flutter of her lashes. With a big grin to them both, he stepped over the spilled lunch and hurried to do Mindy's bidding, tugging the shade down on his way.

"Instant obedience," Delaney breathed. "Always. How do you do that? I thought maybe it was just a girly thing. But I'm wearing girly stuff now, all the way to my pastel panties, and I can't get that kind of attention."

"You'd better figure it out," Mindy warned with a little frown. "You know the makeover is only part of what you need to get the promotion. Belkin can't claim he's hiring on looks, even if he is. He's going to use the argument that he needs a charismatic, commanding assistant."

Delaney's jaw clenched. No. She'd gone through so much already, spent a month having her face and body analyzed like a freakish puzzle. She'd almost blown her anonymity when she'd slipped up in her "after" interview and told the *Risqué* people she was a book reviewer. The discussion turned to hot authors and next thing she knew, she'd opened her big mouth and critiqued Nick Angel's books. Since she'd entered the contest using her pseudonym, she'd been worried her face attached to it would blow her cover. But *Risqué* wasn't typical reading material for Rosewood's students or faculty. Heck, it wasn't even sold in bookstores or newsstands anywhere in the Santa Rosa area. It might be false confidence, but she figured her reviewing secret was safe.

She wanted that promotion. It was more than a job now. It was a symbol of her worth. To herself, to the college and to her father.

"You know," Mindy said, picking at her nails like she always did when she was nervous, "I might have a suggestion that'd help you with that."

"What?" Delaney asked slowly, eying the fingernails. As long as they stayed away from Mindy's mouth, the idea probably wasn't too crazy. It's when she started nibbling on those things that Delaney really worried.

"My brother is the station manager at the local TV station. He mentioned last week their morning show is thinking of expanding their summer programming to include a critic's corner." Delaney's stomach tightened when Mindy raised her hand to her mouth, pressing her thumbnail to her lip. "When I mentioned your name, Mike said he'd wait to post the job until I talked to you."

"Me?"

"They're looking for someone with a good handle on literature to do book reviews, discussions, that kind of thing," Mindy finished in a rush, the words falling around the fingernail she was now diligently chewing. "It's right up your alley. You do reviews already, love to read, and it'd be a great way to learn to become visible."

"A TV show?" She couldn't help it, she started laughing. "You're joking, right? Me, on TV?"

She hyperventilated at the idea of having her driver's license picture taken. Why on earth would she want to be on TV?

She'd make a complete ass of herself.

"It's a great idea," Mindy argued.

"No, it's a crazy idea. What if someone saw me? I'm trying to hide that I'm a reviewer, remember?"

"It's a San Francisco station, we don't even get it up here," Mindy assured her. "Besides, it's a morning show, on the air during school hours. Who'd see it?"

"My father?"

"Does he even own a TV?"

No, but that wasn't the point.

"Ahem."

Both women turned startled glances to the tall, angular man standing by their table glaring at the mess the waiter had yet to clear. He turned his glare to Delaney. His eyes widened briefly, then narrowed with consideration.

Delaney grimaced. Professor Belkin. Then she glanced past him and felt herself turn pale. Her father. She'd been avoiding him, easy enough now that the spring semester was over. This wasn't how she'd intended to tell him about the makeover.

She forced a smile on her suddenly stiff lips, but he didn't respond. He didn't even look at her, so engrossed was he in his discussion with a physics professor. Two feet away, and she was invisible to her own father. As usual.

"Ms. Adams, Professor. Perhaps they can bring you

a bib," Belkin said, his tone stiff and annoyed as he stepped over the scattered croutons.

He was obviously not impressed with her makeover, and even less with her dining skills. Delaney wanted to pick up a tomato and throw it at his departing head. Bet that would get his attention. It'd blow her ever-narrowing shot at the promotion, too. So she choked back her temper with a deep breath.

"TV?" she asked Mindy, blinking away the frustrated tears as she watched her father depart.

"Keep using your pseudonym," Mindy advised. "Let Delaney Madison become the woman you've always wanted to be. Imagine the shock value when you waltz into the hiring meeting and wow them all with your newly acquired charisma and command of the room."

The woman she'd always wanted to be? Her ultimate fantasy was to be a woman like the kind she loved to read about. Sexy, powerful, confident. The kind who could handle the most arrogant snobs and the hottest guys with the same panache.

Delaney knew there were a million reasons why TV was a crazy idea. But this was to improve her chances of getting the promotion. She'd thought the makeup would be enough, that it'd make her stand out. Obviously she needed a little more than a costume. She needed to learn to command attention. So she'd do TV and become Delaney Madison. Super Reviewer. Savvy, sexy and commanding.

Nobody was ruining this for her. No way, no how.

"SEX IS SECONDARY," Delaney insisted to Sean Logan, host of the morning show *Wake Up California*. Despite the fact that she was almost hyperventilating with nerves,

she managed a quick smile and strong, assured tone.
Nothing like a good literary argument to put her at ease.
After three weeks of her weekly fifteen-minute segment
on "Critic's Corner," she still hadn't gotten past the terror of being on camera.

"Yes, I want to be invested in a hot, wild love scene,"
she continued. "I want to feel just as turned-on as they
are when I read the character's actions. But unless I
care about them, unless I've already developed a con-
nection to them, it's just…well, bodies. Often messy,
rarely appealing."

"So what you're saying is you want emotionally
driven love scenes when you read?" Sean, the epitome
of the all-American boy grown up, asked as he shifted
in his chair.

"I'm saying all stories, to really draw in the reader,
benefit from an emotional depth the reader can empa-
thize with," Delaney clarified.

While Sean tugged his bottom lip and nodded, she
shifted in the hard wood chair, wishing she could take a
deep breath. She assured herself it wasn't nerves— after
three shows, she had to be getting over those by now,
didn't she?—but it was just the bite of leather where her
belt snugged around her waist. Why couldn't fashion
and comfort be synonymous? According to Mindy, her
skirt was the "latest fashion," which apparently meant
uncomfortably short and tight.

"Tell me the truth, Delaney," Sean said with a schmoozy
smile, leaning toward her like an old friend about to share
a secret. "Do you really buy in to all that romance…stuff?"

Delaney grinned at the last-second correction. Halfway through her first segment, she and Sean had gotten
past the formal Q&A they'd started with, and relaxed

into a casual conversation. Used to his technique now, she knew this was the sign to wrap up the chosen topic for this week's segment—the romance genre.

"Romance is what makes the world go 'round," she paraphrased. "The excitement of falling in love in all its varieties, the quest for happily ever after."

"You really believe that? That romance has that much of an impact on the world?"

"Relationships, by whatever terms they are defined, are what drive literature. Both period and modern," Delaney said, warming to her subject. "*Jane Eyre, Romeo and Juliet, Wuthering Heights,* they're all examples of romances that have strongly impacted our literary history."

Caught by something offstage, Sean's eyes went wide.

Delaney noted the muted explosion of murmurs and rustles. Well used to impatient students, she continued her lecture on romance novels through the ages without a hitch, but let her gaze shift to the ruckus on the main set.

Oh. My. God. Could a woman have an orgasm at just the sight of a man? Delaney tried to catch her breath, but she couldn't stop her racing thoughts long enough to remember how. Gorgeous. Pure male perfection.

Midnight hair, so black there were hints of blue from the bright studio lights, waved back from a face that would do a romance writer proud. Piercing eyes, a clear blue that made her feel as if he could see through her carefully applied mask all the way to her squirming insecure soul, narrowed when they met hers.

Delaney swallowed, sure the zap of sexual energy was just some weird reaction to the camera and lights. Or maybe an allergic reaction to the makeup. Did gel bras have a toxic effect when the skin got overheated?

"Well, well." With a quick look at the producer, Sean

gave a little nod, then said, "We have an unexpected guest joining us today. Ladies and gentlemen, Nick Angel."

Delaney barely kept her jaw from dropping. Her gaze shot back to the hunk joining them onstage. She stifled a little gasp as his eyes met hers, energy zinging between them like lightning.

No, she assured herself. Not between them. It had to be just her reaction. Men never got zingy around her.

When he joined them her stomach took a nosedive. All the zing on her side or not, it still scared the hell out of her. She had no idea how to channel this level of sexual attraction.

So she fell back on the tried and true, and pretended her body didn't exist. Shifting into brainiac mode, she processed his appearance, which consisted of jeans, a dress shirt and a black leather jacket, his attitude—defiance wrapped in charm—and his body language, which suggested "watch out, someone's gonna get it."

Damned if she didn't wish it were her.

CHAPTER THREE

DELANEY MENTALLY RECITED the works of early American poets to keep from drooling at the sight of Nick Angel, master of erotic suspense, just inches from her. If she'd thought he looked hot across the room, he was an inferno now. The pure masculine sexuality called to her like nothing she'd ever felt before. She wanted to peel his clothes off with her teeth. An image flashed through her mind of the two of them, a few feet of rope and a tub of double chocolate fudge ice cream.

"Nick, I'd like you to meet the newest addition to *Wake Up California,* Delaney Madison. Delaney, I believe you've read Nick's work."

Visions of ice cream melted as Delaney met Nick's piercing blue gaze. She froze at the look in those intense depths, then reminded herself this was the new Delaney. The made-over, sophisticated, worthy-of-attention Delaney.

Even if his gaze said he knew what she looked like naked, she was only imagining that he knew how nervous she was. Don't let them see you sweat, Mindy had lectured. Delaney recalled all her friend's advice on handling the on-air nerves and figured it applied even more now. As long as she kept her polished mask in place, she'd be fine.

For a woman who worshiped the written word, meeting an author was always a pleasure. To meet the author responsible for her last orgasm was both fabulous and a little embarrassing. Especially since the look in his eyes, that dark and sexy consideration, made her wonder if he knew he'd given her such pleasure. Probably. He had that much self-assurance.

The old Delaney would have been humiliated to face that considering look. She'd have run, no question about it. But the new Delaney? Delaney Madison, Super Reviewer? She drew back her shoulders, showing her gel-lifted breasts to their best advantage in her red silk blouse, and lifted a brow in challenge.

"It's a pleasure," she said, proud of her smooth tone. "I've read all of your books."

"Have you, now?" He arched one perfect brow, his smile predatory. Like a sexy, charming shark…ready to take one huge bite out of her ass. "And what did you think of them? Oh, wait, I think I've read your opinions already, haven't I?"

Not sure how to respond, Delaney licked her lips, disconcerted to see his eyes narrow as he followed the movement of her tongue. After a heartbeat, he raised his gaze to meet hers again. The dark heat of his look made her stomach clench.

"From the look on your face, Nick, you're not a fan of reviews?" she commented, falling back on her debate training to hide her nerves. "Or is it just reviewers who say things you don't want to hear?"

She watched with fascination the expressions shift on Nick's gorgeous face, from shock to amusement to appreciation.

"I have no problem with reviewers, or their reviews," Nick said, his voice rich and deep. Delaney knew she'd be hearing it in her sleep. "It's when they interject their unfounded prejudices into the review that I take issue."

"Such as asking for emotional depth from your stories?"

"That'd be a good example."

"But that's what your readers are asking for."

"They weren't until you stirred them up," he pointed out.

"Oh, please," she scoffed, nerves forgotten. "You're giving me credit for the readers' demanding emotions in your books? You think my one comment turned the opinion of thousands of readers?"

"Thousands?"

"I get mail."

"So do I."

"Did you want to compare sizes or something?"

Sean visibly choked back a laugh. Delaney saw him and the producer sending subtle, off-camera hand signals back and forth. Sean waved his hand to indicate heat, the producer indicating he wanted it fanned higher. Delaney smothered her panicked giggle. Higher, her ass, if things got any hotter in here, she'd melt all over Nick Angel's very muscular thighs.

Nick snagged her attention again, his grin quick and appreciative. She couldn't stop her answering smile.

"Seriously," Delaney said, leaning forward to emphasize her point. His gaze dropped, just for a second, to the view highlighted by her V-necked blouse. She gave a brief thanks for gel-bra enhanced cleavage and pretended she wasn't turned-on when his gaze returned to hers. "Don't you feel an obligation to your readers? So many I've heard from are clamoring for emotions to go with the wild ride you take them on. Doesn't that influence you at all?"

"I give them plenty of emotions. Fear, adrenaline, lust. Until you'd stirred this up, my fans were plenty satisfied. Especially with the sex," Nick declared. He paused and considered, then added, "A review before yours once said the only way someone could be dissatisfied reading my work was if they were sexually dysfunctional."

"So you're saying the only way someone would hate your work is if they had a sexual dysfunction?" Delaney let out a baffled laugh. "You're kidding, right?"

"Of course not. I never kid about sex." His words were teasing, but the underlying intensity proclaimed that he did, indeed, take sex very, very seriously. Delaney shifted in the hard chair, trying to ignore the damp warmth in her panties.

"That's why I stopped by," Nick continued. "Since I happen to disagree, strongly, with your view of how I handle sex, I figured we'd discuss the matter."

"You mean you're here to try and change my mind?"

"Or you can try and change mine."

She pursed her lips, trying to see the trap. There was one, she was sure of it.

"Chicken?" he murmured in a low, husky tone.

Hell, yeah. Delaney stared into his cocky face. He'd known she'd be intimidated. He'd come here with his sexy self, his arrogant attitude and his challenge, all with one intention. To intimidate her, make her look stupid.

She narrowed her eyes. He probably figured if he made her look dumb, he'd be able to refute her comments from the *Risqué* interview.

"Actually, no," she said slowly. "I've complete confidence in my evaluations. After years of reviewing, I believe the opinions I share generally reflect the public consensus."

"You're claiming to speak for the average reader?"

She considered that. She'd never been average anything, so the concept was intriguing. But she had consistently seen her reviews reflected in sales numbers, to say nothing of the mail she received. After a few seconds, she gave a slow nod.

"If you use the definition of average as the consensus of readers of the given genre, then yes. I'm comfortable saying that my reviews tend to fall into the norm."

His brows drew together in a frown. Delaney wondered if she'd stepped too far over into brainiac-land. She wet her suddenly dry lips and hoped she hadn't blown her cover.

Having anyone connect Delaney Madison, makeover winner and popular fiction reviewer with Dr. D. M. Conner, Associate English Professor, aka the invisible woman, was definitely not acceptable.

She had the feeling that whatever game Nick was playing could seriously jeopardize her anonymity and quite possibly ruin her shot at the promotion.

But she wasn't about to back down. There was something about the man that demanded she stand firm, give one hundred percent. She wished she could figure out what it was. That way she could figure out how to ignore it.

"If you're so sure of yourself," Nick drawled with a satisfied smile that told Delaney rather than stepping into brainiac-land, she'd actually stepped into his trap, "how about we place a little bet?"

NICK LEANED BACK in his chair, ignoring the heat of the camera lights, and grinned. As hot as the lights were, they had nothing on Delaney Madison's glare. The angry look suited her flame-colored hair, bringing a sweet flush to her porcelain skin. Huge doe eyes dominated a face that was all planes and angles, sharp rather than curved.

A man who prided himself on doing research, he'd been surprised at his misconception about the hot little reviewer. He'd read all her book reviews, and both her *Risqué* interview and the magazine's makeover feature.

Apparently he'd missed a few details. Number one, the woman was razor sharp. Number two, and definitely more important, she was sexy as hell. Her "before" shots had been mousy, but that was obviously part of the magazine's bid to play up the makeover. Ms. Madison was clearly one of those *über*-sexy ladies who had done the makeover thing to mix things up. He'd known plenty of women like her—easily bored, always looking for change. Their looks, their job, their men.

"What kind of bet did you have in mind?" the slick blond cohost asked. Nick could see the guy's mind working, trying to find a way to turn this into a ratings-buster event. Fine by him, the more people watching his triumph, the easier job Gary would have telling editorial to ditch the push for emotional crap in his books.

"I'm of the opinion that despite her obvious appeal, Ms. Madison doesn't speak for the average viewer," Nick restated. He didn't understand the surprise in her gaze, but her furrowed brow made it clear she disagreed with something he'd said.

"Over the past few weeks we've polled viewers on *Wake Up California*'s fabulous interactive Web site, www.wakeupca.com, and I'm sorry to say they don't seem to agree with your assessment. Delaney has a growing fan base," the cohost, Sean Something-or-other, challenged with a gleeful smirk.

Nick gave the host a long, dark look that had the guy visibly swallowing. Reminding himself why he was there, he barely managed to rein in his impatience. The last thing he'd planned was to give the hottie reviewer from hell any further ammunition to support her claims about his work.

"That's all well and good, for what it's worth," Nick said in a tone that made it clear how worthless he considered their little poll.

"I can understand your disquiet with my comments about your book," Delaney mused, her lips in a contemplative moue that reflected the bright lights. His gaze traced her lower lip, the full cushion of it inviting small, nibbling bites. "Nobody likes to have their intimacy issues brought to public attention. Then again, you don't seem like an insecure kind of guy who'd worry about that."

She shifted in her chair, her body language screaming *challenge.* The sweet curve of her breasts pressed against her silk blouse, showing the lace outline of her bra. But it was the expression in her eyes, that look of intelligent curiosity, that was the major turn-on. Nick's body reacted in tried-and-true fashion, desire spiking through his system.

Wait... Intimacy issues?

"I don't have intimacy issues."

"No? You're in an emotionally mature, committed relationship?"

The glint in those dark eyes made it clear she thought she'd cornered him.

"Is that how you equate intimacy? Commitment? I define it a little differently."

She ran her tongue, just the tip of it, over her bottom lip. His eyes followed the movement, even as he wondered if she'd accept his challenge. She gave an infinitesimal sigh. Obviously she knew she had to take up the gauntlet, but she wasn't thrilled.

"The dictionary's definition of *intimacy* is 'a close personal relationship, or knowledge resulting from a close relationship or study of a subject,'" she asserted.

"The dictionary also defines intimacy as a sexual act," Nick said, shutting her down with a wicked grin.

Her grimace, so slight the cameras probably didn't pick it up, showed she'd figured he'd use that response. Damn, he wasn't sure what was more appealing. Her curvy body and sexy lower lip, or her intelligence. He wanted nothing more than to debate semantics with her. While naked, of course.

"You're claiming, then, that sexual relationships without emotion are on the same level as emotionally committed sexual relationships?"

"Apples and oranges," he declared with a shrug. "But notice both are fruit."

"And you're only shopping for apples, apparently. Which is clear in your books. The singular focus on lust over love only seems to highlight a one-dimensional aspect of intimacy."

"I don't claim to write about intimacy," Nick defended. "I write erotic suspense. Heart-pounding excitement, both in plot and, yes, in the explicitly detailed sex scenes. Hardly one-dimensional."

She tugged the corner of her lower lip between pearly white teeth, obviously debating how far she wanted to take the conversation. Nick was becoming obsessed with that mouth.

"I hate to disagree with an author whose work I honestly admire a great deal," she said slowly. Then she gave a one-shouldered shrug that let him know that she was a woman who didn't back down from things, no matter how much she hated them. "But if you were to analyze your last…oh, let's say three books just to keep it current, then you'll find the sex scenes actually are one-dimensional."

She gave him what could almost be taken for an apologetic look and continued, "Predictable, even."

If she'd accused him of having a tiny dick, he couldn't have been more appalled.

"The hell they are." Nick growled. "I do kick-ass sex. It's hot, it's wild. I've never had a single complaint."

"We're actually talking about writing, not sex. Even though they are apparently similar in your world, I didn't review your sexual prowess."

"Anytime you want a shot at *that* review, you just let me know," he offered with his most wicked grin. His temper, always quick to flare, fizzled out.

The producer was practically dancing in place, his excitement clear as he mouthed crap like "great sexual tension" to the blond host. Nick ignored them, while Delaney actually seemed to be completely oblivious to the crew—and the charged atmosphere on the set. Or, he thought as his gaze dropped to her white-knuckled grip on the edge of her chair, was she just acting oblivious?

The woman was a mystery. There was something intriguing about the combination of innocence in her eyes and her sophisticated packaging.

The shaky breath she took assured him she wasn't

unaffected. A plan, wicked as hell, formed in the back of Nick's mind. This doe-eyed hottie had stirred up plenty of trouble for him. Oh, sure, he realized she'd only intended to criticize his writing, not him personally. But really, they were the same thing. And all that emotional crap was off-limits for both.

He tossed the plan around for flaws, but couldn't find any. Perfect. He could discredit her and have a little fun at the same time. He grinned. Seeing her eyes round nervously, Nick's smile widened. Oh, yeah. This little adventure was definitely going to pay off.

As SEAN AND Nick debated off-air the details of some contest to prove her worth as a reviewer, and the weather girl wowed the television audience with her well-endowed cloud banks, Delaney tried to catch her breath.

No matter what direction she'd tried to move the dialogue, Nick Angel, writer extraordinaire, had blocked her attempts and refocused. She'd like to think she'd have been better able to control the conversation if it weren't for the fact that the sex scenes from his last few books had kept flashing through her mind like a slideshow. Each one featuring Nick himself as the studly hero doing decadently hot, wild things to *her* body.

It was almost enough to make a woman long for erotica instead of romance. Almost.

Her fingers clenched and unclenched the nubby linen of her skirt. With a sigh, she noticed the roadmap of wrinkles creasing the oatmeal-hued fabric. Between nervously chewing off her lipstick and now mangling her skirt, she obviously wasn't handling this "new her" thing very well.

Her gaze flashed between the two men. Back and

forth, they debated ways to prove their points. Once again, even though she was the actual subject under discussion, she was invisible. Her frustration quieted her nervous fingers. Dammit, this makeover was supposed to give her empowerment, not simply shift her from completely invisible to pretty but ignorable.

Sucking in an irritated breath, Delaney pulled back her shoulders and pressed her hands flat to her thighs. If she wanted to be more like one of Nick Angel's heroines and snag her promotion, she couldn't fade into the background. Mindy and a library full of self-help books all advised speaking up. So she'd speak. Even if it meant the possibility of the "old her" coming out.

"Gentlemen, I think you're complicating this."

Well, what d'ya know? Her words, quietly spoken but with that underlying edge of authority she used with her students, grabbed the men's attention.

"Beg your pardon?" Sean asked.

"It'd be a much more encompassing answer if it simply addresses the issue at hand. Mr. Angel questions my ability to speak for the average reader, correct?"

Both men nodded, Sean with a frown, Nick with a gleam in his eyes. Delaney looked away from that laser-blue heat and took another girding breath.

"The easiest answer is for me to review a variety of books and post the reviews on the show's Web site. Create a poll with safeguards to ensure cheating isn't allowed, and invite readers to vote. We could add two other reviews, just to ensure anonymity and an unbiased vote. And then we'll know if the public agrees with my reviews or not."

"Take it to the public," Sean mused, his tone contemplative. He rubbed his chin as if he was considering the ramifications, but the fact that he was practically bouncing in his seat let her know she'd hit his happy spot.

"I think this would be a great way to prove the validity—" he cast a glance at Nick "—or lack thereof, of your reviews."

"Right, like that's a fair assessment," Nick scoffed.

"Oh, it would be," Delaney said sweetly. "As long as you choose the books."

His eyes narrowed. "I get to choose?"

"Sure. We'd need some solid parameters, of course. You know, books still available in print so viewers can get ahold of them, something like that. But I have no problem with you choosing the subject matter."

His grin, wickedly satisfied, assured her she'd have plenty of erotic reading coming her way.

"And when I'm done," she assured him, "I'll have proven that readers are looking for emotion. They want the thrill of the ride, yes. But they want to read knowing there are real feelings at stake."

"Quite the contrary," Nick said, leaning over to offer his hand to seal the deal. "I'm sure you'll have proved that the readers are savvy enough to take their thrills without a fake sugar coating."

With a quirk of her brow, Delaney put her hand in his larger one. Engulfed by the hard strength, she wondered if she'd just made a huge mistake. Or if she'd just guaranteed her loss of invisibility.

Either way, things weren't boring. That was for sure.

"The stakes?" he asked, the gleam in his eye making it clear he already had that worked out.

She tilted her head, indicating he name them.

"If your reviews don't win, you'll admit I'm right," Nick demanded. "And you'll admit it here on television."

Ahhh, a publicity stunt. He must be getting a lot of pressure because of her comments. She nodded slowly.

"Deal. And if my reviews do win…?"

"They won't."

She cocked a brow. "Good, you're confident enough that I won't win, so you shouldn't have any problem agreeing to write your next book to include a truly intimate relationship for John Savage."

She didn't know where it came from, maybe she really was channeling one of his heroines, but she leaned forward and with what she hoped was a wicked smile and a flutter of her lashes, she gave his knee a pat.

"I'll be happy to help you write those pesky love scenes, of course."

CHAPTER FOUR

A COMMERICAL BREAK LATER, the deal was sealed. The producer rubbed his hands together in glee, Sean had informed the viewers and Delaney drooped from exhaustion.

She left the testosterone-filled set and made her way down the narrow hallway. She reached her dressing-room door and turned the knob, only to find it locked. With a groan, she leaned against the opposite wall and let her head fall back.

She'd been in such a hurry to get away from Nick Angel and his overwhelming sexual charisma, she'd proposed the terms of the bet without thinking it through. She didn't know what worried her more, his agreeing or his wicked grin as he'd done so. Either way, she was in trouble.

"Forget something?"

She didn't even jump. She did, however, give a sigh before she opened her eyes.

The man was even more gorgeous in natural light. Standing there in the deserted hall, he had a look of expectation on his face. Before she could wonder why, she noticed her purse, dangling in all its feminine allure, from his fingers.

"Thank you," she murmured, taking it from him. But instead of getting her key, she let it fall to her side. The idea of inviting him into her dressing room was simply too much to consider.

She flicked a glance over him, as he stood there in all his masculine beauty. Had she ever met a sexier man? She'd seen plenty of handsome ones over the years, but none who'd exuded the level of sexual charisma Nick did. Definitely no man she'd dated came even close to his appeal.

She recalled that scene from his last book. The hero had cornered the heroine in a dark hallway. After pinning her to the wall, he'd told her in graphic detail the many ways he wanted to do her. Then he'd taken her in the hall, right in front of a plateglass window, with her leg wrapped around his waist.

Delaney eyed Nick's waist and wondered if her leg could reach that high. The heels would be a definite help. A shuddery breath caught in her throat as heat spiraled down her body. Warm heat pooled between her thighs, shocking her. She'd never been this turned-on. And never for a stranger, especially one with such obvious issues with intimacy and relationships.

It was his writing, she was sure. Like foreplay, it had already stirred up the sexual tension in her mind. And, after all, the mind was the largest and most important sexual organ. Next to the heart, of course.

"I wanted to bring you that," he said, indicating her purse, "and see if you were okay with the bet."

She shook off the sexual cobwebs from her thoughts and focused. The bet. Reviews. Her now very public reputation on the line.

"I'm fine with it as we outlined," she said slowly. From the look on his face, there was more going on than the simple bet she'd agreed to, though. "Has it changed in some way?"

"Nope. Logan announced it on the air, it's a done deal. You're going to review a half-dozen books of my choosing for the online poll and we'll see who the readers agree with."

The smug assurance in Nick's eyes made her even more determined to win. God, even the idea of trying to push herself forward made her nervous. But she'd do it. That's what this makeover was all about. To put herself out there. Learn to be visible.

With that little pep talk in mind, she gave Nick a questioning look, her nerves tight and wary. She felt as if he was waiting to pounce on her.

"Are you okay with the bet?" she asked.

He leaned in close, his breath minty warm on her face.

"I'm fine with it, for what it's worth. But I'd like to ramp it up a bit. You know, make it a little more…personal."

The way he said it, as if it were something that involved sliding naked over silk sheets, made her heart pound.

"Like what?" she breathed. More importantly, the formerly alert part of her brain pointed out, why?

"I was thinking along the lines of a side bet. You know, something private, just between the two of us."

"Were you now? Why would I want to do that?"

"Because you like to be right?"

Score one for him. She might have been physically invisible, but she was definitely not used to her opinions being shunned.

Not that she wanted him to know that. For once, a

man was looking at her as if he'd like to eat her up in long, slow, slurping bites. But that wasn't reason enough for her to make some stupid bet. Was it?

She ran her tongue over her lower lip. His gaze narrowed at the movement, like blue flames sending a spear of desire through her body.

Maybe it was. The rush of sexual energy and the power of having a man physically attracted to her—especially a man like Nick—made here realize she'd be an idiot to ignore the opportunity. The ideal her, the strong, sexy woman she was trying to become, wouldn't ignore it, she'd grab on with both hands and make it hers.

"The question is," he said softly as he reached out to trace her lower lip with his thumb, "just how far are you willing to go to prove you're right?"

The challenge was impossible to ignore. But he wasn't asking her to take a bet based on intellect. He was trying to move into a completely different arena. One she'd never played in. Who knew fear could give anticipation such a jagged edge.

"I know I'm right. Whether or not you're willing to admit it doesn't change my assurance of that fact."

"I love it when you talk all intellectual like that," he said, his body so close she could feel the heat from his chest through the smooth silk of her blouse. "You get this snooty, uptight tone going that's at odds with the sexy glint in your eyes."

"How do you know I'm not a snooty, uptight intellectual?" she asked with a little laugh.

Rather than the glib, offhand denial she'd expected, Nick's face turned serious. He stepped back and gave her a slow, intense once-over. From the bottom of her miserably aching feet in three-inch spectator pumps, to her waxed and lotioned legs to the "oh, my god, it's too short" skirt.

His eyes skimmed her hips, making her aware of curves she'd never realized she even had until she'd put on more fitted clothes. He slid a glance over the wide croc belt at her waist and then let his eyes rest on her breasts, which were outlined by the smooth red silk of her blouse. This gaze didn't linger long enough to make her uncomfortable, but there was definitely enough heat to warm her body with feminine awareness.

His eyes roamed her face. She wondered if it was a writer's thing, the way he catalogued her features in that semidetached way.

"You're smart, I'll give you that. But there's nothing snooty or uptight about the looks of you." His brows drew together and he gave a baffled little laugh. "If anything, under that sophisticated sheen, you give off an air of innocence."

"Maybe I am innocent. Maybe the sophistication is a sham."

He shook his head. "Nah, I've been around plenty of women. Enough to know when they are putting on an act and when they are genuine."

Delaney laughed, she must be better at this pretending stuff than she'd realized. Being taken as a natural sophisticate was both novel and bizarre. But it beat the hell out of him realizing she was really a brainy geek who couldn't have gotten a roomful of her peers to notice her if she'd sung "The Star-Spangled Banner" at the top of her lungs…while tap-dancing naked.

Exhilarated by his assessment, she sighed and let her body relax as much as possible while in such close proximity to the sexiest man alive.

"So what's the side bet?" she asked, unable to contain her curiosity. Not that she'd take it. That'd be insane. But, she had to admit in the privacy of her own mind, Nick Angel was the kind of guy who made a woman want to see how good "crazy" could feel.

"Either prove good sex needs emotions—" he paused, his voice pure liquid heat "—or admit the greatest sex in the world is purely physical."

"How?"

His stare said it all.

Delaney gasped. Sure, she was attracted to him. What woman with a pulse wouldn't be? And he'd given her some hot looks that coming from any other guy—to any other gal—she'd have imagined meant he might be interested. But her? And the sexiest man alive?

"You expect me to sleep with you?" she whispered, more a statement than a question. She'd already had sex with the man in her mind at least a dozen times since he'd walked on the set. But to actually *have* sex with him? She'd have to get naked. Really naked, as in he'd see the actual her beneath the makeup and gel bra. Hell, no.

"Can you think of any better way to prove your point?" he asked with a wicked laugh. The look on his face made it clear he was turned-on by the concept. Delaney narrowed her eyes. It had to be a trick. Guys didn't give her those long, sexy looks. Not unless they wanted something. Or, in Nick's case, wanted to distract her. Or worse, make her look like a fool.

Her shoulders tightened.

"Please," she said with a sniff. "I'm not having sexual relations with you just to win some stupid bet."

"Aren't you interested in learning firsthand what my version of intimacy is?"

personally had sex good enough to make her forget the way she felt when she first read *Lady Chatterley's Lover,* let alone something as important as her feelings. "But that's not what I'm talking about. I'm saying that true intimacy is more than slam, bam, thank you, ma'am."

"And I'm saying if the slamming is done right, *ma'am* is the one doing the thanking."

Delaney rolled her eyes.

"You're playing with words," she told him.

"Words are my specialty. They're not all I'm good at, though," he said with a cocky grin.

"Obviously," she murmured, not about to argue his sexual prowess. After all, the guy got her hot and wet just standing there. If he actually put some moves on, she'd probably melt into a whimpering puddle.

"So..." he said, his voice trailing off as he moved even closer. Heat radiated off his chest and an answering flame flickered low in her belly. "What do you say? A no-strings fling. Hot, wild sex."

He took that final step, bringing his body flush against hers. Delaney bit back a whimper at the sweet pressure of his chest against her aching nipples, his thigh, warm and hard, pressed between her legs.

He placed his hands on the wall on either side of her head and lowered his face until his mouth was within inches of hers. Delaney swallowed, unable to tear her gaze from the hypnotic blue depths of his. As though under an irresistible spell, she simply waited, both eager and terrified to see if he'd follow through.

When he did, it wasn't the deep, wild kiss she'd anticipated. Instead it was more of a tease. A soft brush of his lips over hers, warm, moist and gentle. Any other guy and she'd have termed it sweet.

His eyes still holding hers prisoner, Nick pulled back just a bit, his breath warming her mouth.

That was it? The hottest guy she'd ever had pressed against her and that was the kiss she'd inspired? Delaney wanted to grab his hair and yank him closer, ravage his mouth with hers. To kiss him with an intense, deep passion she hadn't even known existed.

"Just consider it," he murmured.

Her eyes narrowed, but before she could say anything, his mouth plunged again, this time taking hers with a fierceness that shot straight down to her belly. She gave herself over to the wild power of his kiss.

Heat flamed as he trailed one hand down the side of her neck, then traced the soft silk of her blouse. Over her collarbone, her shoulder and just barely brushing the side of her breast. Delaney shuddered as his fingers skimmed past her waist, his hand gripping her thigh. Need like she'd never felt before surged and she hitched her skirt, just enough for his hand to touch bare skin.

If her own boldness shocked her, his reaction blew her mind. Fingers clenched once, then he slipped his hand over her thigh, around until his fingers grazed the curve of her butt. Her body taking the lead, since for the first time in her life her brain had shut down, she shifted her leg to wrap it around his hard muscular thigh and give him better access. His groan was low and guttural against her mouth. He moved, just a bit, so his leg pressed against the throbbing that wet her panties. His kiss went deeper, his fingers cupping, squeezing her butt in rhythm with the dance of his tongue. Pressure wound in a tight little knot, strong and demanding. It was all she could do not to grind herself against him in search of relief.

The intensity of her reaction, her swift loss of control, scared Delaney. Not enough to stop, though. Not even close.

So she couldn't think, could barely react, when he pulled back. Not just his mouth, but his entire body. He stepped away, leaving her churned up, panting and cold where her flesh had felt the warmth of his.

"One month," he said in a husky whisper. "We give each other a month, totally focused on physical pleasure. In the end, you'll admit I'm right."

Still caught in a fog of desire, she almost agreed—was actually in the process of nodding—when his last words sank in. Right, her ass. All that kiss had proved was he knew how to use his mouth. She closed her eyes against the image that particular realization brought to mind and shook her head.

"You think I'll fall in love with you or something?" she accused. From her body's reaction, it would be easy to believe. But that was just physical. She knew herself too well. Nick Angel was so far beyond her type that there was no way her subconscious mind would ever open the emotional gates and let him in.

"God, no," he said with a laugh that ricocheted through the empty hallway. "You're too smart for that, and I'm definitely not loveable. Believe me, I've been told by enough women to be sure."

Still turned-on, but determined to act as blasé as he was, Delaney narrowed her eyes. Why no bitterness in his words? For all that her father ignored her, his love was never a question. Just his priorities. To be called unlovable would, well, basically suck. But Nick didn't seem to care at all. Maybe he really did believe that emotions were an indulgent fantasy.

And maybe she owed it to herself, and to all the readers out there clamoring for more depth from his books, to prove him wrong. She almost snickered. It was like her own version of a public service. And if she got the most incredible sex of her life out of the deal? Well, hey, sometimes a girl just had to do what a girl had to do.

"Lust versus intimacy. Which one is really more powerful? You know you're intrigued," he said, running his finger down the side of her neck. It was all she could do not to arch and purr. "Think about it. We'll go out Friday and you can let me know what you've decided."

Maybe it was his cocky tone—he was so sure she'd back down. Or his assured stance, hip cocked to one side as he gave her that half smile that screamed sexy-man-in-charge. Or maybe it was that little voice inside Delaney, demanding she totally embrace the new her, makeover and all. She'd wanted to stop being invisible…well, he definitely saw her now. Almost like she was the kind of woman he wrote about. Hot, sexy and commanding. Right down to the up-against-the-wall kiss in a hallway.

It could have simply been the overwhelming nature of the entire experience, but finally, she gave a slow nod.

"All I'm agreeing to is dinner on Friday," she told him.

His eyes lit with triumph, but he just nodded.

"And if you take the bet? What'll be the stakes?" he asked.

"You mean you haven't already figured that one out, too?"

"How about I give you the pleasure."

Delaney's mind was blank. She couldn't think of a single thing that didn't sound stupid. But she was so confident in her stand on romance that it really didn't matter, so she borrowed his cocky attitude and shrugged.

"Let's leave that open, why don't we? Winner sets the prize, within reasonable limits." She realized that sounded as if she'd already agreed, so she quickly tacked on, "If I take the bet, of course."

"You're on."

Nerves fought with anticipation as Delaney watched his face. His smile oozed satisfaction, like he'd just been promised a world-class orgasm.

And, she told herself, if they went through with this, she'd damned well have one.

As HE SAUNTERED out to his car, Nick realized he couldn't remember when he'd had that much fun with a woman. Considering they'd both been fully clothed, he was pretty sure it was a first. Even Angelina, for all her hold on him, had only pushed his buttons physically. Delaney made him think, made him want, made him laugh. It was a potent combination.

As much as he was looking forward to it, he hadn't really believed Delaney would take either of his bets. The most he'd hoped for was to shake her up, push those nerves a little so she'd think twice before messing with him.

He was sure he'd win the reviewing bet. Not because he didn't think she was a good reviewer—he'd done his research and had to admit, she rocked. But he'd pick the most controversial books out there, which would make it impossible for her to garner enough votes to win.

Once he'd met her, he'd realized she had a deep competitive streak. But there was a definite reticence layered over the top. He couldn't figure her out. But he planned to. Oh, yeah, he planned to devote a great deal of time to learning all of the luscious Ms. Madison's secrets.

Which was why he'd given in to impulse and cornered her for that side bet. If her agreement had been a surprise, the stakes had been a shock. She'd left them wide open.

He knew what he *wanted* to claim. The savvy businessman in him demanded he make her publicly refute her earlier reviews. The ever-curious writer in him wanted an in-depth interview, promising total honesty. He wanted to delve into her brain, to learn everything that made this enigmatic woman tick.

But Nick, the man, wanted nothing more than the pleasure of Delaney's body beneath his. Over his. Welcoming him into her glorious wet heat.

His body hardened again at the memory of how sweet her ass had felt in his hand.

Given the choices, the horny man always won out.

CHAPTER FIVE

"WHAT HAVE I gotten myself into," Delaney grumbled, not even trying to keep the irritation out of her tone. He'd cornered her, kissed her into a pitiful mound of panting hormones and played her like a master. Holy crap, the man had her wet and desperate, with his hand on her bare ass within an hour of their first meeting.

Nick Angel was a dangerous opponent.

"A dream come true?" Mindy responded absently.

Delaney stopped her agitated pacing to glare at her friend, who was curled up all comfy and secure on the couch with paperbacks piled around her. Mindy didn't notice, of course, since she was engrossed studying Nick's sexy photo on the back of a book.

"You call this a dream?" Delaney demanded, thrusting her hands through her hair. That her fingers slid through smooth as silk still shocked her, but not enough to stop her from freaking out.

Mindy heaved a sigh and set aside the book she'd been ogling. Like Delaney, she was still dressed in her yoga gear after their weekly class.

"Let me ask you a few questions, okay?"

Did she have a choice? Not willing to snap at her friend and risk upsetting her, Delaney waved a hand in agreement.

"When you met with the *Risqué* people, they asked

you about your vision, about who or what you wanted to be, remember?"

"Yeah, I said I wanted to be visible. To come across as assured and strong and—"

"And sexy. Like a heroine from a novel. The kind of woman who could wrap a guy around her little finger and make him beg."

Delaney scrunched up her nose and resolved to quit sharing so much with Mindy. The other woman had a rotten habit of throwing her words back in her face.

"Okay, yes, that was my vision. But that's what I wanted to look like. Looking doesn't instantly translate into being, you know."

Mindy lifted her index finger to her lip. But instead of biting down she shook her head, dropped her hand—unnibbled—back to her lap and squared her shoulders.

"This is your chance, Delaney. You keep taking these steps toward your goal, but you never take the final leap. You love the makeover, but you weren't willing to consider it until forced to for your career. You are an incredible reviewer, but weren't willing to even tell people you did it until you accidentally let it slip in your *Risqué* interview."

Where was this going? She wasn't sure but she knew she wasn't liking it. Struggling not to frown, Delaney dropped into her favorite chair and pulled a pillow onto her lap. Holding it across her belly like a security blanket, she tilted her head to indicate Mindy could continue.

"You've had the hots for this guy's writing for a long time now, right?"

Delaney's shoulders went stiff. Shit. She wasn't the youngest professor on staff at Rosewood College for nothing. She knew exactly where Mindy was going.

"You want things to happen, but you aren't proactive, you're reactive."

Ouch.

"You're taking too many psych classes," Delaney muttered.

"Well, duh, I'm a psych major. That doesn't change the fact that you have a golden opportunity here to fulfill your ultimate fantasy. You want to prove you're a strong, sexy woman? Take this guy up on his challenge. Then put him in his place."

"Oh, sure, like I'd have a chance at that."

"Why not? Look in the mirror, Delaney. You look like a woman who could bring a guy to his knees. You're hot. And Nick Angel obviously wants you."

The old Delaney would have rolled her eyes and scoffed at the impertinence of even *imagining* Nick Angel wanted her in his bed for any reason other than so he could win the bet. But the new Delaney, the one who'd pressed her damp, aching core to the hard muscles of his thigh in a desperate bid for release, believed he did want her, and was totally attracted to her. Oh, she knew the attraction was purely physical, based only on the made-over mask he'd seen. It didn't matter.

It was the wildest feeling. Intense, empowering and just a little scary.

"You wanted to be visible, now you are. Big-time. So what are you going to do about it?" Mindy challenged.

"Just because he's attracted to me doesn't give me the power, you know. He's basing this entire competition on a premise of lust versus intimacy."

"Do you believe in your stand?"

"Of course. Sex without intimacy is hollow. It might

be fast and hot, but it won't last. There's no common ground, nothing other than animal urges."

Mindy nodded, then she lifted Nick's latest release, his photo facing Delaney. Those wicked blue eyes stared back, making Delaney's stomach clench with lust. She recalled his voice, husky and low, as he'd verbally seduced her. The taste of him, hot and heady on her tongue. The feel of his hands as he'd explored her body. Sexual need surged, urging her to do whatever it took so she could feel the wet heat of his mouth again.

"Do you think you have enough in common with this guy to build intimacy?"

"I…" Her automatic denial trailed off. Intimacy required a bond beyond sex. Did they have anything in common to build that? They both loved books, obviously. She'd love to talk literature with him, to hear more about his writing process. And he wasn't intimidated by her intellect. If anything it appealed to him.

"From your silence, I'm going to take it you have enough to build on," Mindy said with a snicker. "So the only real problem is repercussions."

"Like what?"

"Like falling in love."

Delaney's mouth dropped open and, for the first time she could recall, her mind went blank with shock.

"You think he could fall in love with me?" she finally found the voice to ask.

Mindy frowned, then pink washed over her kewpie-doll cheeks. "I meant you falling in love with him," she muttered.

Delaney burst into laughter.

"Okay, you obviously think it's a crazy idea," Mindy

said in a huffy tone. "I don't know how you can be so sure it wouldn't happen, though."

Oh, sure, maybe if Delaney believed in fairy tales, she'd think it was possible. But she was too smart for that. "As hot, sexy and talented as Nick Angel is," she said between giggles, "he's definitely not the fall-in-love type. I promise, that's not going to be an issue."

Mindy huffed, then shrugged. "Then the only question left is can you go into a sexual relationship with this guy knowing that it's just physical? Doesn't that support his argument for lust?"

"Of course not," Delaney protested. "Lust is one-night stands. He's already doomed his argument by offering a month-long affair."

"So it's a win-win?"

Delaney considered. Winning the bet and cementing her reviewing career and becoming confident enough to assure herself she'd get her promotion. And potentially the most incredible sex in the world with the hottest man she'd ever seen.

"Definitely win-win," she agreed. It was like Christmas, her birthday and Valentine's Day all rolled into one sexually charged gift. How could she resist?

Thirty minutes later, she saw Mindy out and resisted the urge to beat her chest and give a Tarzan yell. Delaney Madison, Super Reviewer. Able to seduce a sexy author in a single bet. She felt as if she could take on Nick Angel, guarantee herself multiple orgasms and leap tall stacks of books in a single bound.

Riding that feeling, she easily ignored the scoffing voice in her head and made her way down the hall to her office.

Unlike the rest of her apartment, which was furnished

in kitschy hand-me-downs and flea-market finds, her office was pure business. The sleek, sexy lines of her chrome-and-glass desk were reflected in the curves of the sculpture on the floating shelf and the rounded ebony bookcases.

A low, overstuffed chair in nubby red silk sat in the corner, catching the morning light. Perfect for reading. There, she knew, was where she'd read the books Nick chose for their bet. When she read for pleasure, she inevitably chose the pillow-festooned couch or her bed. But no matter what stories Nick chose, reading them would be all business. After all, her reputation was on the line.

And, she realized as she dropped into the leather office chair to boot up her laptop, if her barely used feminine instincts were right, so was her virtue.

She wasn't risking either without doing her homework. Any good scholar knew that knowledge was in research. And if in the process of trying to figure out what kind of books Nick would have her read, she found hints on how to deal with him and best win her argument, that was great.

But mostly, she wanted to make damned sure if and when they ended up having sex together she was armed with as much information as she could find to show him an A-plus performance. Because after years of obsessing over the man's books, she'd be a total idiot to give up the chance to actually become like the women she'd fantasized about being.

BY FRIDAY NIGHT, Delaney felt like a schizophrenic. She'd alternated between excitement and terror over this evening so much, her nerves had whiplash. The only thing keeping her from cancelling was her assurance that she'd succeed. Delaney didn't know how much of her desire to win was ego and how much was belief in her stance. She just knew she had to win.

She'd spent her life honing her intellect. And that was her secret weapon. Because while she'd done her homework and learned everything she possibly could about Nick Angel, thanks to her makeover and her sexy new persona, Nick would have no clue who she really was. All he'd see was the mask.

And what a mask it was. Still not quite believing it was her, she glanced in the mirror Mindy had insisted she install by the door for last-minute wardrobe checks and blew out a breath. Nick wasn't the only one who was out of the loop. Delaney herself was having untold difficulties accepting that she was the sleek, sexy redhead with the tousled curls.

Smokey shadow defined her brown eyes, a hint of shimmer in the corners giving them extra sparkle. Only she'd recognize the glint in them as terror, rather than anticipation. She ran her tongue over her glossy burgundy mouth and had to force herself not to chew on her lip for fear of ruining the slick look Mindy had created.

With her do-me makeup and sexily tousled hair, she actually did justice to the tiny bottle-green silk dress with its baby-doll styling and jewel-encrusted bodice. She'd wanted black, thinking it'd be sophisticated, but Mindy had shot her down. The fast-talking blonde had insisted the rich grassy hue would make her stand out.

That had done more to convince Delaney than any argument about the season's hot hues or being told that black wouldn't suit her coloring. If she was going to win this bet, she'd have to command every second of Nick's attention, she told herself just as the doorbell rang.

Delaney pressed her hand to her stomach and took a deep breath. Using the same method Sean had taught her at the TV station, she focused on her breathing, letting the icy picks of terror melt away.

Huh. Who knew: "Critic's Corner" was already paying off. Maybe she wouldn't suck after all. With a giggle, she opened the door and forgot every bit of terror, worry and concern. A few thoughts of sucking did flitter through her mind, though.

Oh. My. God. The man looked so delicious, Delaney wanted to take tiny little bites of him. Her face flamed at the idea, so sexy and bold, and so unlike her.

"Hello, Delaney."

"Hi," she said quickly, hoping to distract him before he could comment on her heated cheeks.

She didn't need to worry, though, since he was busy looking at the rest of her. Apparently long, naked-to-midthigh legs rated tops on his inspection list. A sense of vanity she'd never felt before swept over her.

She was pretty sure she liked it, too. Delaney resisted the urge to tug at the hem of her dress; instead she gave Nick the same treatment.

He'd been sexy enough in the studio, but dressed for seduction? Holy cow. If she'd thought he'd go easy on her, take it slow, she'd been deluded. The man had one thing on his mind, and one thing only. Winning.

Thanks to her makeover education, she recognized his clothes as designer. She recalled the magazine stylist's explanation of how the cut and fit of material played into pricier clothes. Given the way the black fabric was caressing its way across his shoulders and the jeans cupped his…thighs, she figured they were worth a small fortune.

Her eyes met his. Instead of looking flustered at her obvious perusal, he sported a huge grin of appreciation.

"You're gorgeous," he said, his voice a husky purr that sent shivers down her spine.

Delaney lifted her chin and reminded herself to focus on the competition.

"I'm looking forward to this evening," he told her. "I hope you enjoy everything I've planned as much as I'm sure I will."

Definitely focused on the competition. It was a contest he apparently thought he had in the bag. Did he have that much faith in his hypothesis? Or was he just that sure he could overpower her with his charm and charisma?

Delaney frowned and tilted her head to the side, her curls bouncing on her cheek at the movement. Nick's eyes slid over her hair, almost like a caress. Soft, light, gentle.

This time it was easier to ignore her body's reaction. Sure, her nipples beaded and her stomach tightened. Maybe her breath quickened just a little at the idea of him running his fingers through her hair. But years of being physically invisible were about to pay off. All she had to do was remember he was drawn to her made-over persona, not the real her. If she kept that in mind, played the vamp and used some of the tricks she'd researched in the books on flirting and seduction, she'd be fine.

Fine, hell. She'd win. With one brow raised, she stepped forward, close enough to Nick to reach out and press one hand to the lapel of his jacket. Her heart raced at the feel of his sculpted chest beneath her fingers, but she kept the amused, slightly distant look on her face and made a tut-tutting sound.

"If you're trying to influence me, it won't work. I'm

still sure I'll win the reviewing bet," she told him with a smile. "But I am definitely looking forward to tonight… and seeing what you think will convince me to accept your side bet."

Nick laughed. "I can't say I didn't have convincing you in mind when I planned the evening. To be honest, it's been an intriguing challenge. I debated a number of ideas to use as proof that good sex is all physical."

He reached up and laid his hand over hers, holding it trapped between his larger one and the hard planes of his chest. Delaney's smile stiffened but she forced herself to keep it, and her hand, in place.

"The actual bet, if you remember, is to prove that emotions make sex better."

"Interesting paraphrase," he mused, his fingers curling into hers now. "My concept of the bet, of course, is that sex doesn't need the fluffy veneer of emotion to be incredible."

Delaney gave a little one-shouldered shrug and, needing the distance, slid her fingers out of his grasp.

"It's all moot unless you convince me to take the challenge, of course," she demurred. After all, she still hadn't agreed, not totally. If her body had any say in it, though, she'd be tossing him to the ground and doing it monkey-style before the night was out. But he didn't know that. She took comfort in the slight frown between his brows. Hopefully she was keeping him off balance.

"Ready?" she asked, lifting her heavy cloak off the back of the couch. The rich black wool was satin-lined, creating an elegant silhouette. Better yet, it would be warm. Perfect, since San Francisco nights were chilly, even in the summer.

"Ready," he agreed, placing the cloak on her shoulders. She stiffened, but he didn't do more than adjust the fabric, then step away.

He handed her an envelope. She pressed the thick card-stock between her fingers and shot him a questioning glance.

"Your reading list," he informed her with a wicked grin. "I thought I'd let you have a peek at it before I sent it to the producer."

Delaney ran her thumb under the flap and Nick's hand shot out to close over hers. She gasped as the hard warmth of his fingers made her tummy spin. He gave her a naughty look and shook his head.

"After," he said.

She ran her tongue over her lower lip, tasting the sweet flavor of her glistening lip gloss. *After?*

After what? Images of the two of them writhing together in ecstasy, their moans of pleasure filling the air, flashed through her mind. If the brain was the strongest sexual organ, she was already halfway to a mind-blowing orgasm with Nick. And that was just from looking at him.

Control, Delaney. She had to keep a cool head. He'd obviously given her the list, with the no-reading instructions, as part of his strategy to keep her off balance. Probably figured she'd be more susceptible to his naughty games this way.

With that in mind, she slanted him that slow "I'm gonna win" smile again and tilted her head. "I'm sure I'll have other things on my mind...after. But I'll leave this for later."

His blue eyes widened, then lit with appreciative heat. Before he could act on the smoldering promise, Delaney gestured to the door.

"Let's get started, hmm? I'd hate to be late."

NICK SMOTHERED HIS grin at the dare in the sexy redhead's eyes. From her attitude, she actually thought she had a shot at changing his mind about emotion. Ha, about as likely as his ex ever offering anyone unconditional love.

Like taking candy from a baby, this bet was in the bag.

The list of books he'd come up with were all guaranteed to push her buttons, both sexually and on the emotional level. He was sure she'd get all holier-than-thou with her reviews, turning off readers. Especially his readers, who would find out next week when he announced the review contest on his Web site. He was sure his fanbase would flock over and, after reading her uptight, emotionally demanding reviews, vote her down.

"By all means, let's begin," he agreed, eager to start the evening. After all, with the review bet sewn up, he could focus all his energy on the bet he really wanted to win. The one that would get the most intriguingly sexy woman he'd ever met into his bed. He gestured toward the door. "I have a car waiting."

Delaney gave him a small frown, as if she'd suddenly realized he was up to something. Her small pink tongue slid over a rich, bitable lip. He wanted to mimic the action, to see if the plump glossy flesh tasted as good as it looked.

"A car?"

"I figured you might enjoy wine with dinner. Afterwards I thought we'd stop at a club I enjoy, but it has a two-drink minimum. I have a strict policy about alcohol and driving. It's simpler to have a driver and car waiting. Then we can do whatever we want without limiting ourselves."

The long, slumberous look she gave him from those

huge eyes had him wishing he could drop to his knees, just for the pleasure of kissing his way up her body. Hardly a monk, he'd enjoyed the company of a variety of women over the years. But none, ever, had equally intrigued and challenged him, while making him hornier than a sixteen-year-old with a free run of his daddy's *Playboy* stash.

Control, Angel. Get a grip.

"I should probably warn you," he told Delaney in his standard first date warning as they left the apartment, "somehow everything in my life makes its way into my books. There's a good chance these bets will, too."

He waited for her reaction. Fawning excitement or outrage were typical.

But Delaney was anything but typical. She gave him a startled look, then laughed. Not a small, ladylike giggle. A deep, husky laugh that brought to mind black silk sheets, moonlight and champagne.

Nick's eyes narrowed on her face. She was gorgeous, of course. But when she laughed she lost that "don't touch me" air of sophistication.

"I take it you wouldn't object?" he asked, holding the elevator open for her.

She stepped in, then waited for him to join her before shaking her head, a smile still playing over those kissably soft lips.

"Object? Only if we end up being chased by nefarious evildoers with a goal to hurt us. Or—" she slanted him a slumberous look through her lashes "—if you make me the heroine and our storybook sex is impersonal, jaded and emotionless, used only to titillate rather than deepen the plot."

It took him half a second to decipher that. For a

woman who looked like one of the sexiest hotties he'd ever met, she sure talked like a brainiac. Not that Nick objected to smart women. It was that most smart women objected to him. He wasn't sure whether it was in response to his genre or his cynicism.

"I doubt we'll be chased," he offered, leaning against the metal wall of the elevator.

"And the sex?"

Nick ran his gaze over the silky shape of her body. Her skin, so much of it exposed by the simple lines of her green dress, glowed in invitation. His fingers itched to trace a path from her collarbone down to the edge of the bodice and her breasts.

Nick met her eyes. There was a hint of unease in the brown depths. Good.

"Well, I draw the line at chasing you for it," he said, and was horrified to realize he didn't actually mean it.

CHAPTER SIX

NICK WAS GOING CRAZY. Seriously, "ready to grab Delaney, toss her over his shoulder and haul her off to a dark corner," crazy. Maybe it was the atmosphere of the SupperClub, an upscale restaurant that featured both titillating wait staff and the novelty of serving the patrons on beds, rather than at tables. Or maybe it was the fact that the woman across from him seemed only interested in him as a writer, not as a man.

The dim light from the sculpted wall-sconce cast a soft glow on Delaney's hair, as she leaned back against the pillows. Her foot, bare except for the wash of deep burgundy polish on toes Nick wanted to nibble, bounced a slow rhythm on the blue satin bedcover.

Nick's gaze slid to the brushed iron of the headboard. He'd spent the last hour fantasizing about her gripping those iron bars while he drove her to screaming delight with just his tongue.

In preparing for this date, he'd realized he'd never actually set out to seduce a woman before. He glanced around the room and grimaced. Apparently he wasn't very good at it. He'd figured a restaurant made up entirely of beds would give him a leg up in convincing Delaney to take his bet. After all, what was more seductive than eating finger foods on a satin-covered mattress to get a gal thinking about other in-bed delights?

But he seemed to be the only one of them who was fixated on the bed...and on sex. He shifted, glad for the tray over his lap. Delaney, though, seemed oblivious to the sexual tension rippling through his system.

"You write sexually charged, sometimes terrifyingly brutal stories that embrace living life to the fullest. Why can't you open yourself to the idea that other genres have just as much to offer readers?" she asked after nodding her thanks to the waiter who had brought the dessert tray and refilled their wine.

"I'm not against other genres," Nick said, pulling a face, "But don't you think most are a little...formulaic?"

Delaney lifted a mini-éclair to her mouth and took a bite. The rich cream filling oozed around her fingers, making Nick's mouth water to lick it off. She swept cream off her lips in one wicked little swipe of her tongue.

"So you're one of those, hmm? A literary snob?" she asked. "I've met quite a few in my time, but I'm still surprised. The stories are really what it's all about, and being true to your characters. Really, isn't that one of the functions of fiction? To create worlds, lessons in story form, to draw people in and make them think? Yours definitely do all that."

Nick opened his mouth to retort, but couldn't marshal an argument, too turned-on and fascinated by watching her eat the tiny cake, how she savored every sensual bite. He'd bet Delaney had been hell on wheels on the debate team. Laughter rolled, quiet at first, then growing as he replayed her argument in his mind.

"You win," he acknowledged.

She pulled back, just a little, as if shocked by his response. Then her lips, gloriously slick and inviting, parted in what he could only term a bashful smile.

He shook his head. The more time he spent with Delaney, the more confused he became. At the beginning of this date—hell, just an hour ago when they'd sat down to dinner—he'd thought he had her pegged. Sexy, sophisticated and worldly, he'd figured she was all about her career.

But, he thought he was finally keying in on her true personality. An intellectual wrapped in fine silk, she was obviously used to lulling people into complacency with her looks. While a guy lost himself in the depth of her doe eyes or wondered if her hair would feel as silky on his thighs as it did between his fingers, her mind was skipping three steps ahead.

It was fascinating.

Then she tossed out that shy little smile and threw all his assumptions out the window.

Afraid he'd go nuts if he didn't get his hands on her soon, if only to dance, Nick tossed his napkin to the tray and lifted a brow.

"I'm ready, are you?"

DELANEY HAD TO swallow twice to wet her throat enough to speak. She'd been so caught up in the thrill of talking about books with Nick, she'd forgotten his real reasons for being here.

"Ready?" She hoped the wispy texture of her voice would pass as seductive, instead of terrified.

She'd forgotten the terror over the last hour or so. That was to Nick's credit, since her initial reaction on walking into the restaurant had been to gasp and run. She'd stomped it down, of course. She was sure his plan was to intimidate her with this side bet, to keep her all muddled and distracted so her reviews would fare poorly in the contest.

And he might have succeeded. After all, he was the most incredible distraction she could imagine. Hot, intensely sexual and, best of all, an incredible author. But she had a plan of her own. As long as she kept in mind that she was now the kind of woman Nick wrote about, her own fantasy self, she'd be fine. After all, she was in this to win. The review bet, the side bet and Nick's capitulation.

So instead of running at the sight of a room filled with beds, she'd rolled her eyes and asked him if this was how he usually got women into bed.

Because that's what the restaurant was. A large room filled with beds. It took pillow talk to a whole new level. But instead of being sleazy, as she'd have expected, the atmosphere was lushly sensual. Probably aided by the ongoing lingerie fashion show taking place center stage. Nothing like lying in bed watching a bunch of women strutting around in their undies to keep the focus on sex.

She wished she wasn't so easily influenced. As it was, she'd resorted to debating the merits of popular fiction in an effort to keep some semblance of control. It hadn't kept the images of climbing across the bed and straddling Nick's lap out of her head, but it'd kept her from acting on them.

"Do you dance?" he asked. "There's a club I think you'll like. Great music, a very…unique atmosphere."

All Delaney heard was the word *dancing*. Her hands, hidden by the tray across her lap, crushed her linen napkin. She never danced. At least, not in public. In private, alone, she loved nothing better than turning on the music full blast and losing herself in the rhythm.

She flipped through a mental summary of the probable results of refusing. With a quick clench of her jaw, she realized she had no choice. Refusal meant looking like a chicken. And worse, losing any advantage she'd made toward winning their bets. Which, after all, was why she was sitting on this bed with Nick.

She needed to keep that in mind instead of losing herself in the vivid blue of his eyes.

"You don't want to go dancing?" Nick guessed, his gaze narrowed and thoughtful. He wouldn't push her, she realized. Nor would he gloat. For all his charisma and charm, he was remarkably easygoing.

"I'm not much into modern music," she hedged instead of taking the escape route he offered.

"What kind of music do you prefer?"

Delaney hoped the dim lights hid the color washing over her cheeks. At the college, her stock answer would have been classical music, of course. She'd listened to enough to discuss it, and did, to a degree, enjoy it. But it wasn't her first preference.

"Hard rock," she murmured, waiting for his laugh.

A slow smile curved his lip instead.

She shook her head and gave him a playful swat on the arm. If she was tempted to let her fingers linger, to fondle the hard muscle beneath his black shirt, she kept it to herself. "I said hard rock, as in eighties hair bands. Not rock hard."

"I didn't say anything," he defended.

"But you were thinking it."

He just grinned. Then he lifted a hand. Their waiter was there immediately to take away their trays and Nick's credit card. Delaney shot the server a startled glance, then tossed her napkin on the tray with a smile of thanks.

"You'll like this club," he promised. "It's vintage rock, so I'm sure there'll be plenty you enjoy."

Goody. She offered what she hoped was a smile, but

felt like a sickly grimace, and took his hand to slide off the bed. She kept a hold of his hand for balance as she slid her feet back into the spiked heels that brought her eye level with Nick.

"I know you brought me here to push my buttons, and probably to set that sexual scene you've got plotted in your mind," she told him, "but I've got to admit, this is the most comfortable dining I've ever experienced."

From his frown, she'd nailed his motivation. While he signed the credit slip, Delaney didn't bother to roll her eyes at his surprise. It was almost as baffling to be treated like a desirable sex object as it was to have him underestimate her intellect.

"I admit I had our bet in mind when I booked the reservations. The atmosphere here—" he waved his hand to indicate the rich colors, decadently comfortable beds and half-clad women on stage "—is unquestionably sexual. But I don't want you to think I thought to manipulate you into following a plotline."

"Really?"

"Really," he said with a smile. "When you go to bed with me, it'll be your choice. I might have lain next to you on that bed and fantasized about how it'll feel, of the moves you'll use, of the ones I'll use. But I don't have a script. Besides, you have an incredible mind. Sex between us would be so much better with your input."

Something melted in Delaney's heart. A wall she hadn't known was there gave way as she realized how much he *did* respect her intelligence. He saw her as a desirable woman, but to him, that femininity wasn't exclusive of intellect.

His eyes met hers, the heat of his gaze burning through her. Already familiar images of the two of them, naked and sweaty, flashed through her head. She'd have denied having moves only a few days before, but her research had paid off. Now she had a whole list of things she'd love to try.

Who knew this was what it would take send her over the edge from considering Nick's bet to taking it. And all because he hadn't underestimated her intellect. In fact, he acted like it was a turn-on for him. How…novel. A guy who wanted the whole package, looks and brains. Except she knew the looks were a temporary mask. She had to keep that in mind so she wouldn't let herself think she could fall for him.

The concept, so huge she couldn't quite take it in, had Delaney swallowing. Seeing Nick was waiting for a reply, she murmured, "We'll have to see, won't we?"

Twenty minutes later, Delaney almost wished she had gone with her first instinct and told Nick to take her home so she could strip him naked and have her way with his body.

It couldn't have gone worse than walking into this club.

"What's this place called again?" she yelled into Nick's ear as they made their way through the throng of bodies. Hot, overly scented, writhing bodies. The music was a physical thing, pounding a beat through the floors, its rhythm echoed in the flashing neon lights. Dark, intense and edgy, it felt ripe with…something. She couldn't figure out what, though, except that it made her nervous.

Nick shot her a grin. "Fantasy Club," he clarified.

Delaney was glad for Nick's hand in hers since she was sure if they separated she'd never find him again. When they tried to get through, the crush of bodies was so heavy, they were pushed to the center of the dance floor.

"Shall we?" he asked with a laugh, pulling her against his body.

No! She wanted to scream and run, but Nick had his hands firmly on her hips, his body moving in easy time to the thudding beat of the music.

It was so crowded, she couldn't have pulled away without a major scene. Besides, with Nick's hands guiding her, she didn't have to worry about more than following his lead.

Shift, rub, slide. Hip against hip, thigh against thigh. Her body was stiff, barely moving beyond his directions. She didn't know what to do with her hands, so she clenched them over his biceps.

"Loosen up," he said, pulling her even closer. The beat shifted, slower, heavier. Letting go of her hips, he took her hands and placed them on his shoulders, then trailed his fingers back down her arms, so lightly over her waist she almost giggled, and back to her hips.

She felt like an idiot. Dance lessons hadn't been a part of her makeover, and thank God they weren't necessary for "Critic's Corner." Not wanting to see disdain in Nick's gaze, she looked around at the other dancers, sure they were staring. But nobody was. For all the attention anyone paid, it was—almost—like she and Nick were alone.

"What do a vibrator and soybeans have in common?" he asked.

"Huh?" Her gaze flew to his.

"They're both meat substitutes," he deadpanned.

Delaney's mouth dropped. He grinned. She couldn't help it, she started laughing.

"That was bad," she told him with a shake of her head.

"It made you relax," he said, satisfaction gleaming in

his eyes. "Just let the music flow, let your body move. It's not a test, not a contest. Just you and me, having fun."

Fun. Delaney took in a deep breath, forced her body to relax. Fun, as in her and Nick, their bodies pressed together. For the first time since they'd hit the dance floor, she became aware of how close they were. How good it felt. His thighs, so hard and solid, slid against hers in a way that suggested other kinds of rhythm. Their torsos didn't touch, but she could still feel his warmth. Answering heat curled low in her belly, tingling, winding tighter. Delaney focused on that feeling.

Her gaze locked with the vivid blue of his. There beneath the humor she could see a spark of desire. As he slid closer, his hip brushed hers, and she felt the proof of his interest. That he was getting turned-on by her and her lousy dancing skills actually relaxed her. For the first time, Delaney listened to the music, letting the feel of it, the rhythm and pulse, move through her body.

She shifted her hips, just a little wiggling undulation, and his eyes went dark. Her hands curled around the back of his neck, fingers sliding into his silky hair, and she shifted just a little closer. She wanted to taste him. She stared at his lips, wanting to feel them crushed against her mouth in passion.

Passion. Her gaze shifted away as reality clicked back in. The bet. They were here for a reason, and her playing tonsil hockey with Nick on the dance floor would only work in his favor, not hers.

Shoving aside her body's screams of protest, Delaney pulled back and gave him a little shrug. She waved her hand in front of her face and said, "It's so hot here. Can we get a drink?"

Nick gave her a long look, but didn't press the issue. "Sure. We'll go upstairs. I've got reservations."

Their progress was slow. When they finally moved past the bar, she noticed alcoves built off to the sides. Each one had some kind of filmy curtain closing it off, but was back-lit so the shadows of the people inside were clear.

Graphically clear, she realized as one of them pulled her shirt off and pressed her breasts to the guy's face.

Heat curled over Delaney's cheeks, an odd buzzing sounded in her ears. She'd never considered herself a voyeur before. But she couldn't pull her eyes away from the sexual display.

The woman pushed the guy backward, stood and gave a little shimmy to lift her skirt. Then she climbed on.

Delaney squinted, then gasped and tugged on Nick's hand.

"Don't they know they're in full view of everyone?" she asked, not caring if she sounded like a naive goody-goody. "That curtain doesn't hide anything."

He glanced at her, then followed her gaze to the alcoves where couples were silhouetted in various intimate poses.

"I'm sure they know. They probably don't care, though." Nick's eyes narrowed in speculation. "Why? Does it bother you?"

"I'm not the one with my bare butt flashing like that," she said with a feigned casual shrug. "If it doesn't bother them, it's definitely not a problem for me."

Unable to stop herself, she glanced at the couple again, their movements in sync with the pulse of the music and lights. It was almost like a performance.

"That's a part of the turn-on," she commented. "Knowing they're on display."

"That," he agreed after he gave his name to the gorilla

at the base of a gated staircase, "and the thrill of skirting the law. Indecent exposure, lewd and lascivious acts in public etcetera."

The bouncer, so big Delaney wanted to poke his bicep to see if it was real, opened the gate for them. She felt like Alice in an X-rated Wonderland. Nothing here was like she was used to back in her real world. Nick's long look at her made her feel as if it *was* her bare butt on display.

It was a look that brushed aside all the makeup, the carefully constructed facade, and delved right into her soul. He bent down, pressing his mouth to her ear. The soft heat of his breath sent a shiver down her back.

"That's lust," he said. His words were soft, but she heard them easily over the pounding music, the cacophony of voices. Even more, she felt them move through her body like a teasing finger, stirring up a grabby, desperate desire. "Raw, unbridled, 'don't give a damn who watches,' 'do me now' lust. That's what I write about. The erotic dance of a man and woman. The exploration to see how far they can take each other, how wild their senses will make them."

Ignoring the patient man mountain, Nick tilted his head to one side and gave her another of those long, sensual, bone-melting looks.

"You can concede now, if you'd like. Without the fling, no actual sex between us. Just admit that great sex is all about lust."

Delaney was so turned-on, it took a whole ten seconds before his words even penetrated the lust clouding her brain. This was all about the bet?

"You've got to be kidding, right?" she asked in shock. She'd never conceded in her life. She'd rarely lost, so the concept of just giving up and walking away was unfathomable. Of course, all her challenges had been in the realm of academics, so she was admittedly out of her comfort zone here. She glanced at the alcove again, the woman's head now thrown back as she moved fast and frenzied to her own beat, rather than the music.

Nick followed her gaze. "You sure? I honestly don't see how you'll find an argument to beat mine."

Delaney didn't, either. But she'd find a rebuttal. Eventually. For now, she just had to hold her own. And, of course, keep from jumping on Nick and begging him to relieve some of the sexual tension wound tight in her belly.

"I'm sure of my point," she said slowly, meeting his eyes. Again, there was no gloating or glee in his clear gaze, just a question, and maybe a lurking respect. "And while I'll give you credit for finding a lust-filled scenario, how do you know they're not a couple who simply get off on the idea of public sex? I don't think they'd appreciate our interrupting them to ask if this is their first date."

"Interesting argument." His grin was slow, wicked and tempting. With a nod, he waved her through the gate the bouncer still held and said, "Then let's continue to enjoy our date, shall we?"

NICK FOLLOWED DELANEY up the carpeted stairs, his gaze trailing down the enticing curve of her back, which was bare in her silky little dress, to the mouth-watering sway of her hips.

The look on her face when she'd seen the couple getting it on in the alcove had been priceless. Nick hadn't planned for that type of thing to happen, but he'd known there was a strong possibility. This club had a reputation for turning a blind eye to the patrons' proclivities, as long as there was a pseudo-out for the management, like claiming the alcoves were for conversation and the curtains afforded privacy.

He honestly hadn't intended to offer her the chance to call off their bet, but he'd felt like such a creep, hauling an innocent sheep through a throng of horny wolves, that he'd said it before thinking.

"Angel," he told the hostess when they reached the top of the stairs.

As his hand curved over the sweet, barely there curve of her hip as they followed the hostess, he was damned glad she'd thrown the offer back in his face.

Not that he felt intimacy or any of the drivel she purported to be so vital. But he had to admit, only to himself, he was more interested in Delaney than he'd been in any woman in the past.

Nick and Delaney murmured their thanks to the hostess as she indicated their seats. He glanced around and nodded. Perfect.

Their booth was secluded, back in the corner by a glassed-in balcony, with a clear view of the dance floor. The glass blocked the sound, so it was like watching a virtual orgy of bodies, all tangled together in a sexual rite.

He glanced at Delaney to see if she'd noticed, but she was gaping at the caged dancers on this floor. Four women, all well oiled and limber, strutted their stuff around chrome poles. Other than the automatic guy-appreciation of all the sleekly toned female skin, Nick was pretty indifferent to the show. But Delaney wasn't. Color washed her cheeks and her eyes were huge as she slid into the dimly lit booth.

Nick watched her give a little wiggle, like she was imagining herself wrapped around one of the poles, sliding up and down. He imagined what she'd look like, those glorious long legs bare and slick, and shifted in his seat. Damn. A roomful of half-naked women and he had no reaction, just the thought of Delaney's bare legs and he got hard. So much for indifference.

"Do you come here often?" Delaney asked in an obvious attempt to diffuse the sharp edges of sexual tension spiking around them. As soon as the words were out, she gave him a rueful look and rolled her eyes. "That's a pickup line, isn't it? Must be the atmosphere, putting clichés in my head."

Seated next to her on the bench seat, Nick looked at the meat market scene below and gave a laugh. She was right.

"I've only been here once before," he admitted. "It was for research. Hopefully the atmosphere didn't leak clichés into my writing."

She glanced around, a cute furrow creasing her brow. Then her mouth made a little O, the movement sending a shaft of lust straight through Nick. Which was more fascinating? Her mouth or her mind?

"*Hangman's Noose,* right?" She set the menu down and leaned forward, a move he'd come to recognize as her discussion pose. "It was brilliant. You used the setting in such a powerful way, creating drama and a… well, subtle terror. There was nothing clichéd about that book."

Oh, yeah, Nick grinned in pleasure. Her mind. Hands down. Of course, it didn't hurt that it came in such gorgeous packaging, that luscious mouth included. He reached out to trace a pattern on the back of her hand, noting the perfection of her manicure. Delaney was obviously a woman who knew how to put herself together.

"And yet you claimed the love scenes were…how did you put it? Emotionally flat?"

She pressed her lips together for a second. He thought it was out of shame until he saw the humor dancing in her eyes.

"To be accurate, I said they were erotically charged, but emotionally flat. You might pout less if you'd remember the first part, too."

Pout? Nick felt like patting his chest to see if he'd grown boobs. "I'm not a girl, I don't pout."

"What do you call it, then? You obviously got upset over my reviews, although why they'd catch your attention over reviews from the major newspapers and magazines baffles me. You were so bent out of shape, you traveled to the East Bay to confront me on TV." She arched a brow. "You even had that whole bet angle worked out before you even set foot on that soundstage."

"Not all of it," he admitted as his finger trailed up the soft skin of her arm to her shoulder, bare beneath the slender wispy silk strap. "If you recall, you're the one who came up with the actual parameters of the bet, how to decide a winner and all that."

"Just like you wanted me to."

Score another for her side. He didn't bother agreeing, since they both knew she was right. Instead he slid his wandering hand around the curve of her neck, letting her curls slide through his fingers.

"There's plenty of other things I want you to do," he murmured. "How about we see if you're open to any of those?"

Heat flashed in the brown depths of her eyes, like

melting chocolate. He waited to see if she'd pull back. Instead she licked her lips and tilted her head to one side, as if deciphering a puzzle. He could see her pulse as it beat a nervous staccato against the deliciously creamy flesh of her throat.

"Why don't you show me a few," she finally said in a soft, husky whisper.

Nick barely heard her over the noise in the club, but his body reacted instantly.

Without a word, his mouth swooped down to take hers, a slick slide over her glossy sweet lips. She tasted... perfect. He'd never felt anything so perfect. While he was still absorbing that shock, she turned voracious. One hand behind his head, the other curled into his chest, Delaney's mouth took over, sending him on a wild, edgy, pleasure-filled ride.

Nick grabbed on with both hands and made the most of her passion. His hands delved deep in her hair before he slid one down her body, slow and gentle. His fingers skimmed her breast, reveling in her swift intake of breath. His palm curved over the delicate indention of her waist, then slid down farther, to the luxurious wonder of her long, smooth leg.

Nick groaned against her mouth as his hand curled over her bare thigh. She squirmed so her leg angled toward him, sliding the other along his calf. He pressed closer, shifting his body to shield them from the rest of the room. Her hands gripped his shoulders, kneading his skin like a contented cat. He wanted to see if he could make her bare those claws, drive her wild until passion overcame that sexy brain of hers.

Suddenly obsessed with making her want him as much as he wanted her, Nick deepened the kiss. While he explored the delicate depths of her mouth, his hand slid up her leg. The heavy fabric of her beaded dress was in sharp contrast to her silky skin as his fingers delved beneath it, searching for the damp heat guaranteed to drive him over the edge.

Fingers skimmed, once, then twice, along the lacy edge of her silk panties. Delaney's own fingers stabbed into his shoulders, and one hand flew down to grab his wrist in protest. As his dick pressed in painful demand against the fly of his jeans, Nick slid his tongue along the edge of her lips, soothing her with soft, gentle kisses until her grip loosened.

Slowly, so slowly it was killing him, Nick slipped his fingers under the elastic lace of her panties. He gave a soul-deep sigh of pleasure as he found the damp curls awaiting him there, her heat offering an erotic welcome.

He felt her gasp against his mouth, her body stiffening, even as she scooted closer to his seeking fingers. Nick dipped his finger, just the tip, into her juicy heat and swirled it along the swollen oversensitive flesh his mouth watered to taste. Her whimper made his dick spasm in response. He needed her. Now.

But not here.

Regretfully, Nick slowly pulled his hand away and gripped her thigh again.

Tongues tangled, lips teased, teeth nipped. His senses filled with her. His hand twisted in her hair. The sane, domesticated part of his brain warned they were in public, and on the verge of putting on a show similar to the one in the downstairs alcove. The wild, horny part of him screamed it didn't give a damn. He needed to feel her body against his, to see how she fit, what she felt like.

He was going to go insane if he didn't. Soon.

Knowing if he didn't do it now, he wouldn't be able to, Nick pulled his mouth away from hers. Her soft moan of protest made him want to shoot that sane voice and go for the gusto.

"Let's get out of here," he said.

Huge brown eyes stared up at him, some indefinable emotion lurking beneath the desire. Then she blinked and it was like watching a window open. He could see the exact second her brain kicked back into gear, shoving the desire off to the side and reasoning through what'd just happened.

No wonder he was the one arguing on the side of lust. This woman was all about control, which only made him wilder for that moment when he made her lose it completely.

"Don't we need to order drinks? You'd mentioned a drink minimum," she asked softly, her voice scratchy and hoarse, like she needed to clear it but wasn't going to give him the satisfaction.

He was satisfied anyway, and knew his gloating smile showed it. Pulling away was hard, but he let go of her thigh and reached for his wallet. Extracting a bill to cover their unordered drinks, he tossed it on the table and slid out of the booth.

"C'mon, let's go," he said. He held out his hand, waiting for her choice. They both knew it was more than a question of if she was ready to leave the club. The bet—the only one he cared about at the moment—loomed between them.

He wasn't going to beg, but it scared him that he wanted to. He watched Delaney take a deep breath. Then she took his hand and slid from the booth.

"You're right," she agreed. "It's time."

CHAPTER SEVEN

IF NICK HAD figured on acting out a sex-in-the-back-of-the-limo fantasy, he hid his disappointment. Delaney wasn't doing nearly as well with her own emotions. She wanted to be pissed. Hell, she was pissed. He'd felt her up in a public place. Then he'd walked away, his fingers still damp with her juices, like stopping hadn't bothered him at all. Well, it'd bothered her. And now she wanted to prove—to herself and to him—that he damned well had been affected.

But even as she tried to talk herself into anger, all she could think of was his kiss. The feel, the texture, the power of it. She ran her tongue over her bottom lip, wanting to taste Nick again, craving the flavor. But she was afraid—terrified—if she gave in to a kiss, or a touch, she wouldn't be able to stop. Which would prove his point, wouldn't it? Lust will win out?

She almost laughed as she realized the only thing keeping her from semipublic sex in the back of a moving vehicle wasn't any sense of decorum or modesty. It was her ego, her refusal to lose the bet so handily.

That, and a bone-deep worry that despite all her research, she might fail her first hands-on test.

"I can see your mind working from here," Nick murmured next to her. "What's up?"

Delaney opened her mouth, intending to brush off the question. Then she shrugged.

"For you," she said slowly, "this is about a bet." He shook his head, obviously going to protest, but before he could say anything, she continued, "Even if the bet isn't the main reason behind your interest, it's still there. Won't our taking this step simply prove your point that lust is stronger than intimacy? At least, in your own mind?"

"Accepting the bet," he corrected, "isn't just about proving a point. It's about exploring this heated attraction between us."

He gave her a second to deny she felt it, but Delaney wasn't going to lie. She simply raised a brow, challenging him to continue. Nick grinned and, breaking their unspoken pact to keep their hands off each other during the ride, reached out to mesh his fingers with hers. It was like being plugged into a high-voltage heater, sparks started in her palm before zinging through the rest of her body.

"I wouldn't have issued the bet, Delaney, if I wasn't intrigued by you. Attraction isn't sufficient. At least, not to make me interested in a woman enough to back her into a corner and use a bet to get her to sleep with me."

"You're a clever man, and as you've said yourself, words are your business. I doubt you've ever resorted to a banal pickup line."

"For a woman who claims to believe in the power of emotions, you're awfully hesitant to trust your own," he shot back. "I'm guessing you're afraid. Is it of me being right? Or is it of sex itself?"

Before she could respond, the car stopped in front of

her apartment building. Ever the gentleman, Nick got out, then reached in to give her his hand.

Nick told the driver to wait, then curved his hand over Delaney's hip to guide her into the building. She used the silence, broke only by the staccato tapping of their shoes as they crossed the foyer, to gather her thoughts.

Afraid of sex, her ass. Her hesitation over giving him the advantage in their original bet flew out the window as determination filled her. He thought he'd won? That she was going to run from sex? Ha. She'd show him.

Now that she'd decided, her mind spun in a million directions. Was his chest smooth or lightly sprinkled with hair? Did he like it hard and fast and wild, or slow and sweet? Hell, which way did she like it? She didn't know, but she was sure both would be incredible.

She waited until they were in the elevator, watched the doors shut, then turned to face him. His gorgeous blue eyes warmed, but underneath the warmth were traces of annoyance. He was obviously a man well versed in burying his emotions. Or possibly used to being let down. She filed the question away to explore later.

Then she dived for him. His eyes flashed in surprise before her mouth latched onto his. A wild heat flared, hot and high. His hand was strong on her waist as he pulled her close, his other buried in her hair to tug her head back for his lips.

She moaned her pleasure as his tongue plunged deep to dance with hers. She met the moves thrust for thrust. Hands curved over the planes of his chest, pressing, stroking. She needed more. Wanted it all. Her fingers gripped his bicep, lust pouring through her like warm, sticky honey at the feel of the rock-solid muscle.

Antsy, desperate desire demanded relief. She pushed

closer, her breasts crushed to his chest. It wasn't enough. She wrapped one leg around the hard curve of his thigh, rubbing in slow undulations, trying to find relief from the pressure spiraling tight inside her.

Their passion took on an edge she'd never felt before. With Nick, she was free. She could demand anything she wanted and he wouldn't run from her. Wouldn't send her away. Instead, he'd meet her demands with a few of his own.

His kiss took on a rougher edge, teeth nipping. His fingers curled into her shoulder, giving her a gentle push back before skimming down to seize her breast. Delaney gave a keening cry of approval when he slipped the fabric away to find her aching nipple. Fingers tugged and squeezed, making her throb.

"More," she breathed against his mouth.

"Soon," he promised. Then he pulled away. Breath labored, he slid her leg from his thigh and nodded to the elevator door, open and waiting.

Delaney couldn't even find it in her to care that someone might have seen them. All she cared about was getting him into her apartment as fast as possible.

She scooped her purse up from where she'd dropped it on the elevator floor, digging for her keys as she hurried down the hall. She could feel Nick right behind her, but didn't meet his eyes. She couldn't, or her brain might reengage. She wasn't willing to risk it, to possibly ruin the mood.

At her door, she fumbled her keys. She bent to grab them and dropped them again.

Nick's hand closed over hers as he leaned down. Delaney let him retrieve the keychain. She straightened and, eyes closed, leaned against the wall while he unlocked the door.

As it swung open, she took a deep breath and faced Nick. From the look in his eyes, stubborn and challenging, he wanted it all. Physical and verbal capitulation.

"Come in," she invited quietly.

"You're sure?"

Fear, sharp and edgy, cut through the passion clouding her system. But it wasn't enough to stop her.

"Come in." This time she demanded. Not waiting for his response, she stepped over the threshold and tossed her purse and cloak over the nearby chair. Turning, she watched him pull his cell phone from his pocket and dial a number.

While he dismissed the driver, she held his gaze. Recalling everything she'd read about seduction, all the sex manuals, the romance and erotica novels—to say nothing of Nick's own books, she knew she had to take charge.

So she did. Burying her terror behind her fragile veneer of sophistication, she crossed her arms in front of herself then hooked her fingers around the delicate spaghetti straps of her dress and slid them down her arms. The silky fabric washed down her chest, baring her braless breasts to Nick's gaze. His eyes, a dark, intense blue, watched as if bewitched. She released the straps, letting gravity do the rest.

The dress poured like a waterfall down her body, leaving Delaney standing before Nick in a pair of skimpy black silk panties and her heels.

Without saying goodbye, he snapped his phone shut, tossed it to the floor and shoved the door closed. Two steps later and he was in front of her.

Delaney's breath whooshed out as he dropped to his knees. Nick's fingers wrapped around her ankles. When she started to step out of her shoes, he halted her with a tiny shake of his head.

He trailed his fingers up her calves, so gentle and light she almost whimpered at the move. When he reached the backs of her knees, he pressed his face to her belly. Actually thankful for her Olive Oyl body, with its long lines and lack of pudge, Delaney closed her eyes and her head fell back, her fingers curving into his hair as he pressed openmouthed kisses to her stomach.

She was pure sensation. The feel of Nick's fingers, now smoothing up the back of her thighs to grip her butt, the wet heat of his lips as he swirled patterns over her lower abdomen. When he traced his tongue the length of the elastic band of her panties, his fingers sliding under the silk to grip her ass and press her closer, Delaney gave a little cry.

"Like?" he murmured against her skin.

She nodded. Then Delaney's legs went to mush as Nick's tongue traveled along the inside of her thigh, working up, working down. She tried to lean back against the couch, but his fingers gripped her butt, forcing her to stay upright. Forcing her to focus. Her breath came in soft pants, heat curling deep in her belly. She'd had no idea pleasure could feel this sharp, this edgy. All she wanted, needed, was for Nick to end the torment, to do something about the need coiling tight inside her.

"More," she demanded in a husky whisper. "You're driving me crazy. I want more. I need you to take me higher."

"My pleasure," he promised as his fingers pushed

her panties down her thighs, his blunt nails scraping in erotic counterpoint to the soft slide of silk.

Eyes closed, Delaney felt, rather than saw, his reaction to her nudity. Her body, already warm and ready, heated even more. The curls between her legs went from damp to wet. Her nipples, already pebbled, sharpened to a painful hardness, needing his attention. Would he touch her breasts? Would he taste her moist center? She knew he'd do it all, but what would be first? Curiosity and impatience made her want to scream, but she didn't open her eyes.

Then he touched her again. The lightest whisper of a touch as his breath warmed her belly and his fingers trailed up her hips, to her waist, then higher still to cup her breasts. His fingers worked magic, both soothing and torturing her nipples. Delaney couldn't hold back her moan.

She squirmed, the pressure building tightly between her legs. Ignoring her unspoken request, Nick brushed soft, teasing kisses over her stomach, then down one thigh. Releasing her breasts, he pressed her legs wide open. She shifted her feet, teetering a little in the high heels. One hand clamped behind either knee, he continued to kiss his way across her thighs.

Delaney couldn't stand it, she had to look. Letting her eyes open to slits, she watched him as he watched her. His eyes were a bright, glassy blue, flicking between her face and his hand as he traced a line up her thigh, smoothing and teasing at the same time. When he reached her core, he locked his eyes on hers and traced one finger over her folds, swirling the damp flesh. A bolt of desire shot through her system, making her gasp. Satisfaction sparked in his eyes.

That look, the unspoken triumph that said he had control of her body, flipped a switch in Delaney.

"Do you want me to taste you?" he asked. "Do you want me to lick you, to pleasure you with my mouth?"

She had no problem with him having power in this little game, but damned if she didn't want it, too. Years of squashing her passion, her temper, were tossed aside. Delany took control.

She stepped back, grabbed Nick's shoulders and switched their positions. Still on the floor, he was up against the couch as she stood over him.

"I want you to drive me crazy," she drawled. "I dare you to make me lose my mind. To stop thinking. Are you good enough to make my body overrule my brain?"

His grin was fast and wicked. Obviously loving the challenge, he shifted. Taking her ankle in his hand, he lifted it so it rested on the back of the couch, right over his shoulder. His gaze, and his fingers, traveled in a slow, delicious slide up her leg. Over her calf, his lips pressed tiny kisses. When he breathed, moist and warm, against the back of her knee, Delaney would have lost her balance if not for hanging on to his shoulder.

"Taste me," she panted. She didn't want the sweet courtship of foreplay. She wanted a hot, edgy ride. And she wanted it now. "Use your tongue, Nick. Drive me crazy. If you can."

Playtime was over. Nick's eyes went cobalt, his hand released her leg so it rested on his shoulder. No longer gentle, he scraped his teeth up her thigh. Fingers and tongue, hot and skillful, worked her clit. Licking, sucking, nibbling. Those mythical fireworks flashed behind Delaney's closed eyes as she wrapped her knee tighter over his shoulder to keep her balance. Swirling and stabbing, his finger and tongue worked in concert to send her higher, drive her crazy.

More. She needed more. One hand gripping his hair, she used the other to tweak her aching nipple. The pressure built, tighter, more intense. Nick slowed his tongue, his fingers still swirling inside her, pressing deeper.

Then, without warning, he nipped at her clit. The shock, the sweet pain, hit like a hurricane. She gave a keening cry as her entire body convulsed, pleasure washing over her, taking her away.

Her orgasm kept on going. So did his tongue. Little flicks, soft laps. His hand had replaced hers on her nipple, since Delaney was holding on with both hands to the back of his head.

"Oh, my God," she gasped.

"Still thinking?" he asked, his breath hot and labored against her wet thigh.

She gave a little laugh. "Thinking about how good that felt," she confirmed.

"Not good enough. I want you brainless with pleasure."

She gave a shudder, letting her fingers trace the hard planes of his face. He was so hot, so sexy. *So* gorgeous. And for now, he was all hers. Any way she wanted.

"I want to feel your dick inside me," she told him. "I want everything you've got, and then I want it again."

In an instant, he was up and stripping. Clothes flew left and right, Delaney helping him with tugs and tears at the fabric. She needed to feel him, to taste his hard, silky flesh.

Before she could, though, he pulled her down to the floor. On their knees, he raised one brow in obvious question. The power and the choices were hers.

Damn, she loved this.

Delaney pushed him so he lay back on the floor. Then after a quick flick of her tongue over the straining head of his rock-hard penis, she slid up his body.

Her mouth took his in voracious need, tongues sparring for control. Just as Nick seemed to think he'd won, Delaney shifted.

One quick slide, and she took the hard, pounding length of him inside her. She groaned against his mouth at the pleasure of it. Nick shuddered, his hands gripping her waist.

Delaney righted herself, looking down at him. Slowly at first, she rode. Up. Down. He shifted his hands to cup her breasts, his fingers flicking at the turgid nipples in time with Delaney's rhythm.

Her breath coming in gasps, the orgasm just out of her reach, Delaney jerked, undulated, needing release.

Sensing she was close, Nick's thrusts intensified. Her legs gripped him, as if she could milk the pleasure from him with her thighs.

There, just there, on the edge, Delaney was about to come. Nick moved, fast and powerful and pulled her up his body. Her pussy spasming with pleasure, he sucked the juices, his tongue and fingers making her scream.

And Delaney's mind shut off.

EVEN KNOWING THE power of sex as he did, Nick was shocked at how intensely he reacted to Delaney's pleasure. His dick, already hard and wet with her juices, swelled painfully. He had to have her. Now.

He lifted his hand to his mouth, licking her essence from his finger.

"Delicious," he murmured as her eyes blurred.

Tormenting them both, he stood. He had to prove he could step away before he lost his mind. In an easy move, he lifted her naked body, damp with sweat, to the edge of the couch. His turn to take control.

He took his time, reveling in the delicious length of her leg as he caressed it from her wet thigh to the gentle curve of her ankle. He'd be dreaming of Delaney's legs for years to come.

He took one ankle, then the other, and wrapped them over his shoulders. The view alone almost made him lose it right there, all over her couch. Swollen and glistening, her lips pouted a welcome. Hands beneath her butt, he lifted her higher, giving those lips one last kiss. Her musky heat, the delicious flavor that was uniquely Delaney, filled his senses.

Her whimpering little cry of delight was all he could take. Nick grabbed the condom he'd set on the couch when he'd undressed and sheathed himself. Then, releasing her until only her ankles rested on his shoulders, he slid into her in a single, powerful thrust.

Her gasping cry filled the room.

Needing to move, to go fast, Nick set a quick pace. His hands on her hips, he held her still as he plunged in, out, back in. He watched her reaction through slitted eyes. He couldn't come until she did, and he was getting closer with each thrust. Her breasts, so small and perfect, rose and fell with her quick, shallow breaths. He wanted to touch them, to take the nipples into his mouth, but he was too far away.

As if hearing his thoughts, she strained against his hands. When Nick wouldn't release her, keeping her prisoner to his tempo, she clenched her fingers into the pillows, then raised her hands to her own breasts, swirling those long fingers around the pink tips.

Nick bucked, losing the rhythm. Her eyes opened and locked on his. She narrowed them, watching him closely as she pinched the nipples beneath her fingers. He groaned. She gave a tiny smile, then lifted one finger to suck it deep into her mouth.

Nick gulped as she returned the wet finger to her nipple, flicking and swirling faster and faster. Unable to do otherwise, he followed her rhythm. Faster, in and out.

Her breath came in pants now, her ankles pressing hard on his shoulders as her back arched. When she squeezed her breasts together, crying out her pleasure, he gave himself over to his own. Her inner walls contracted around his dick as he came, pouring into her. The power of his release ripped a bellow from him.

Damn. Nick could barely catch his breath, letting go of her hips to collapse on the couch with her. With a twist, he shifted them both so he lay flat on the cushions, her curled on top of him, his arms tight around her still shuddering body.

Nick rode the wave of after pleasure, his body coming down. He'd lost control. Totally lost it. She'd dared him to make her stop thinking, but had he? Oh, he knew she'd got off. But no question about it, she'd been calling the shots. Nick's breathing slowed to normal, but his heart rate took a little longer. Probably because his mind kept replaying pictures of Delaney as she came. He wanted more. He wanted to watch her come, to feel himself explode inside her. Again and again and again. Delaney gasped when Nick's dick, ready to play again, stirred against her leg.

"Oh yeah," he promised softly. "I'm going to spend the entire night making you lose your mind."

DELANEY'S BODY FELT FABULOUS. Warm, oddly achy and seriously sated. Her limbs were too heavy to move. Foggy from sleeping, her mind was much slower to awaken. Pleasure washed over her, a bone-deep emotional satisfaction at odds with her normal irritation at greeting the morning.

It was the unfamiliar hand cupping her breast that pulled her from sleep. Confused, she patted the hand with her own, noting the sprinkling of hair on the arm, the musky male scent filling her senses.

Nick. It all rushed back to her. Nick, and the most incredible sex of her life. Delaney blushed all the way down to where his hand lay in pseudo-innocence. Her nipple pebbled, poking at his palm like it was trying to wake him.

If he woke, he'd do something with that hand. And she knew firsthand the things he did were amazing. Memories of their night flashed behind her closed eyes, a wicked smile curving her lips. Emotions, sweet and tender, mixed with the sexual delight. She wanted to hug the feeling close and giggle.

She'd get up and make him breakfast. Maybe something sweet they could feed each other. She wondered if she had any berries. They'd be both healthy and sensual. With a deep sigh, she imagined serving breakfast in bed. A perfect morning after a perfect night.

Damn, they'd been amazing together. She had no idea where the wild wanton had come from, but she'd loved it. If Nick's arm wasn't wrapped around her, she'd have stretched and shuddered in delight. It was, she realized, like something out of one of his books.

Delaney's eyes popped open. Shit. It was *exactly* like something out of his books. Wild, erotic, intense. Lusty, even. Which proved his point quite nicely.

And here she was, giggling and thinking about making the guy breakfast. As if lust led to moony-eyed looks over orange juice. This was all about the bet. He hadn't sugarcoated his intentions, and while, yes, he'd been amazing in bed, it was to prove a point. That knowledge didn't keep the tears from burning her eyes, though. What an idiot she was, falling right in and proving both their points in one night. He was all about lust, and she automatically started weaving hearts and flowers into their experience, trying to pretty it up.

Delaney swallowed, suddenly very aware of how naked she was. And, she thought as she rubbed a finger over her cheek, she was without her mask. If Nick woke now, he'd see the real Delaney. The messy-haired, naked-faced, emotionally needy brainiac. Or, worse, he wouldn't see her. After all, she had years of invisibility behind her.

Neither was acceptable. And both were, she was sure, inevitable. She'd give anything to be wanted—really wanted. All of her—the brainy side, the newly found, sexy side and, she realized, the insecure little girl—just wanted hugs and assurance she was important.

As Delaney slid out of the bed, careful not to disturb Nick, she told herself it was for the bet that she was sneaking off to shower and put on her pretty mask. But her heart knew it was really out of fear that when faced with her real self, he'd simply look right through her.

CHAPTER EIGHT

THIRTY MINUTES, A shower and full application of makeup later, Nick found her in the kitchen. Show time. Delaney gathered her courage around her like a shield and pretended to be calm.

As she broke eggs into a bowl, he curved his hands over her hips and pressed an openmouthed kiss to the side of her neck. His hard-on pushed, insistent and ready, against the thin silk of her robe, but she forced herself not to reach around and give it the attention it deserved.

"Breakfast?" she asked in a chipper tone that should have gotten her arrested for its early morning use. "My secret recipe pancakes. I learned to make them at boarding school. Actually, they are my only claim to culinary fame, but I think you'll like them."

His hesitation was a physical thing. She could actually sense him pulling away, rethinking his morning plan. Then he shrugged, his shoulder moving against her back, and stepped away.

"Sure. I'm always up for pancakes." She glanced over as he pulled out a chair and dropped into it, almost drooling as she took in his appearance.

Only wearing his boxers, the chest she'd explored so thoroughly the night before was bare and tempting. Her fingers itched to feel the silky V of hair again, to follow the trail down his rock-hard abs to the elastic of his underwear.

"I'm up for other things, too," he said in a husky tone. Her gaze flew to his. The hypnotic blue of his eyes pulled her in, reminded her of just how incredible it had felt to slide down his body, to feel him inside her, to give over to their passion. Because she wanted to take him up on the sensual invitation so much, her words were harsher than she'd intended.

"Pancakes are all that's on the menu this morning, hotshot. You made your pitch, now it's my turn."

As soon as she said it, Delaney mentally winced. Why didn't she just give him his pants, slap him on the ass and send him on his way with a "nice job, stud"?

Nick's eyes narrowed. The cold calculation in them gave Delaney the shivers.

"Your turn, is it? How so?"

Tactless or not, she stood by her words. She had to. If she didn't, she'd lose the bet. She wasn't stupid enough to think he'd fall for her, but for once, she needed to prove to herself that she was strong enough to control a relationship. That she, masked or not, was enough to command the attention of a man like Nick Angel.

"Your point was that great sex is based on lust alone. You have to admit, we had great sex."

His blue eyes defrosted just a tad. "I was starting to wonder if you were going to claim it was one-sided."

"Lie?" Delaney was actually shocked. Facts were facts, after all. She frowned as she flipped the last pancake onto a plate and carried it to where he sat, all rumpled male frustration, at her cozy little bistro table.

"See, that actually supports my reasoning. We had sex—great sex," she quickly added when his eyes went icy again, "but physical pleasure aside, we don't know each other. Which is why I'm not taking offense at your allusion."

Delaney gathered syrup, butter and jam, not sure what he'd like, and placed them all on the table. Then she sat across from Nick and folded her arms over her chest.

"But I don't lie. Neither am I a pushover. Both of which are clear in my reviews, which is what started this. You'll realize this after I prove *my* point in our little side bet."

Nick gave her a long look, even sexier than usual with his shadowed cheeks and sleepy-eyed irritation. "Which brings us back to your turn, right?"

"Right."

"How do you plan to prove your point, then? To win the bet?" The obvious—to him—impossibility restored his usual affability. He gave her a grin and proceeded to slather butter and syrup over his pancakes.

Delaney waited until he'd taken a bite, watching to see if he liked the food. His look clearly said he did, which gave her a baffling sense of pleasure.

"For the remainder of our month-long fling, we're dating," she told him, hoping her tone sounded more implacable than apologetic. "We won't be having sex."

THE SHOCKED BURST of laughter hit him so hard and fast, Nick almost spewed pancake crumbs across the table. He had to cough, blinking to clear his watering eyes.

"You're kidding, right? Sex between us was incredible, and you think tossing it aside will win you the bet? Or are you banking on my death by sexual frustration as a win by default?"

She *had* to be kidding. Nobody walked away from

sex that good. A weird feeling he finally identified as panic hit Nick in the gut. He wasn't ready to end it, wasn't willing to give up the taste of her, the feel of her in his arms. Of his body inside hers.

Her lips quirked, but she shook her head.

"My point was that emotion makes for better sex. We've had great sex already as…what would you call us, acquaintances?"

Anger shoved aside the panic. Nick didn't like that term. She made it sound like they barely knew each other. Which was bullshit.

He knew her, dammit. He knew the sound she made when she came. He knew how she felt when her body gripped him, milking the last drop of pleasure from her orgasm. He knew her smile, her laugh, and thanks to watching her as she'd slept for an hour, what she looked like when all her defenses were down.

Beyond the physical, he knew she'd meet any challenge he threw out with intelligence and forethought. That she was probably smarter than he was, but so sweet with it he appreciated, rather than resented, her super-brain. He knew she liked chocolate and music and, though she'd surely disagree, she needed coddling and appreciation.

Nick didn't understand where the urge came from, since he rarely *chose* to spend time with women outside of bed, but he wanted to be the one to spoil and fuss over her. To bring her flowers for no reason other than to see her smile. To take her to the bookstore and watch her enjoyment, take her to a play and then listen to her analyze it afterward. Preferably in bed.

He simply wanted to be with her.

And that thought scared the hell out of him.

The pancakes turned sickeningly in his stomach. Nick was a loner on purpose. Because people let him down, because they couldn't be depended on. Especially women.

Like it had been sluiced with a bucket of ice water, his carefully honed cynicism shook itself awake. So Delaney wasn't that different from Angelina after all. Lure him in, get him hooked, then let the game begin. His ex had used sex to get a wedding ring. Hell, she used it for every damned thing she wanted. Only she called it love.

He should be thanking Delaney for putting the brakes on, not getting pissy. After all, one night with her had him thinking crazy thoughts, all gooey and emotional. This break was perfect. He'd never spent time outside of bed with a woman without becoming irritated over their demands. This would be no different.

"Okay, date it is," he agreed. His stomach back to normal, he polished off the last of the pancakes. "I have to run to New York for a few days, so how about Wednesday night? I'll pick you up around eight, we'll do a show."

Her look of shock at his easy capitulation was priceless. Better yet, it restored his appetite. Nick gestured to his empty plate and gave her his pitiful, starving look. "In the meantime, can I have another batch of pancakes? These are the best I've ever had."

Much like the lady who'd made them. A fact he figured he'd have no problem ignoring...after one more serving.

"I think sexual tension is almost a character in Ms. Duffy's books," Delaney insisted, leaning forward to make her point. "It not only moves the plot, but it keeps the reader, and characters, on edge."

Four weeks of "Critic's Corner" had given her enough confidence to ignore the red light on the camera and let herself get into the discussion. She still hated it, but at least now she could ignore it. It was almost like being back in the classroom. Except, of course, for the short skirts, male attention and fact that everyone here seemed to assume there was more to her than her brain.

"Don't you think it's frustrating to have that tension wind so tight? Not only for the characters, but for the poor readers who want them to just get on with it already?" Sean asked with a serious frown at odds with the topic. Delaney pressed her lips together to hold back a smile, since she knew he was trying to keep from snickering.

"I think we both agree that, in general, withholding the culmination of the sex keeps the reader flipping the pages. Of course, like you say, it needs to be done right so the readers aren't so frustrated they lose interest," she said. Then, holding up the hardcover book so the camera could pan in on it, she continued, "Ms. Duffy, in my opinion, does a fabulous job. I'd love to hear what our viewers think, though. Go to www.wakeupca.com and share your opinion on today's book discussion."

The camera light blinked off, letting her know her segment was finished. Sinking back in her chair, she let the book fall to her lap and let the fake smile drop off her face.

"You're getting better," the clean-cut blonde commented as he unhooked his microphone from the collar of his shirt. "I have to admit, I wasn't sure how you'd handle the ins and outs of a regular segment. Especially since you were so nervous on the air. But you've managed to keep it interesting and hold viewers' attention. A few more weeks and you'll be kicking butt."

Delaney stared. Her? Kick butt? More like fall on it. Even though she no longer felt physically ill before each episode, she knew she wasn't in control. Not like she was in the classroom.

"By the way, the producer wants to up the 'Critic's Corner' to twice a week starting Monday. He figures between the Nick Angel bet snagging so much attention and how the ratings take a jump when your segment's on, it'll bump our numbers even higher."

Twice? Delaney gulped. But the words *ratings jump* rang in her head, so instead of protesting she nodded her agreement.

Did ratings translate to charisma or whatever it was Professor Belkin wanted in his assistant head? This meant she was making progress. Her smile so big it ached, she thanked Sean and, after removing her own microphone, made her way through the chitchatting crew back to her dressing room.

When she got there, Delaney eyed her baffled reflection. So this was kicking butt, huh? Apparently it agreed with her, since, if she did say so herself, she'd never looked better.

Which made her laugh. She, who'd never cared about appearances, was rating her look. Of course, the credit for her grin, glow and weird habit of breaking into giggles all went to Nick. Or at least to the incredible sex she'd had with him.

A surge of excitement shot through her when her cell phone rang. A quick glance quelled the hopeful flutters in her stomach, but didn't squash her good mood.

"Mindy, hi," she said as she slid out of her skirt. As

much as she was starting to enjoy her fancy professional look, she was much more comfortable in the stylishly casual look she and Mindy had come up with that combined her old style—or what there had been of it—and her sexy new one. Nice-fitting jeans, kicky flats and fitted tops that made good use of Delaney's new favorite accessory—her push-up bra.

"Hey, how was taping?"

They chatted while Delaney changed, then wiped away her TV makeup and redid it with a surprisingly deft hand. She was getting good at this stuff, she realized.

"So I'll see you Friday night?" Mindy asked.

"What's Friday night?"

The silence made her frown. What had she forgotten?

"Faculty soiree. You didn't actually forget, did you?" Mindy asked hesitantly. Her voice was muffled, telling Delaney she'd started chewing on her fingernails. "That's the reason behind this makeover, remember? To show the dean and Professor Belkin that you're perfect for the assistant position, not that other gal."

Delaney dropped into her chair. Shit. She'd been so caught up in the TV show and her games with Nick, that she'd almost forgotten that it was all for the promotion.

It'd been a week and a half since she'd fed him pancakes and put conditions on their fling. Because Nick's business in New York had hit a snag, their date had been postponed until this Friday night.

Like a pouty child, she poked out her lower lip and sighed. She felt as if she'd just heard she couldn't play with her favorite toy. Or, in big-girl terms, her favorite boy toy.

Delaney winced at the thought, since it, and the con-

stant state of sexual awareness she'd been in since that
night with Nick, all supported his stupid lust theory.

"Are you going to attend?" Mindy's words were so
garbled, Delaney figured she was probably working on
at least two nails at this point.

"Of course." After all, the faculty soiree was what
counted. Her teaching, her career, her promotion. Those
were the real her, those would last. All the rest of this,
while wonderful, was only here for the summer. Come
fall, she'd be back in her real world. Albeit definitely
commanding more attention. "Like you said, that's what
this is all about."

It was, she assured herself a few minutes later when
she'd hung up. The makeover, the TV spot, even the bets
with Nick were all for one reason. To give her the edge
she needed to refute Professor Belkin's—and more importantly, her father's—estimation of her ability to command a classroom full of people in a way that would
boost the English department's numbers and prestige.

This—she looked around at the miniscule dressing
room—was only temporary. She needed to remember
that. She glanced at the book on top of her bag, one
of Nick's review picks. All of it, the bets, their relationship—if great, out-of-this-world sex based on a bet
could be called a relationship—was temporary. Step-
ping-stones to her real goal.

She thought of Nick, the way he'd smiled as he
stroked her body to a fever pitch, the way his eyes had
turned smoky-blue when he came. His place in her life
was as real as her cleavage. She needed to keep that in
mind.

If she did, maybe it'd make breaking her date with
him just a little easier.

NICK GLARED AT his laptop screen, tempted to slam it shut. But breaking the computer wouldn't help. Not with his hideous case of writer's block, nor the sexual frustration that was probably the cause of the writer's block.

He looked around the hotel room, trying to find a diversion. But other than ugly art and the bed, there was nothing. Deliberately nothing. As usual, he'd requested the TV be removed before he'd checked in, and had also had the Internet blocked.

His cell phone rang. He was so grateful for the distraction, he didn't even check the screen when he answered.

"Nicky?"

Son of a bitch. That's what he got for giving in to his frustration. Automatic resentment and anger twisted a tight, ugly knot in his gut.

"Hey, Mom."

"Sweetie, I need your help."

Of course she did. She wouldn't have called for any other reason.

"I'm getting married…." She gave an expectant pause for his reaction.

Nick stayed silent. Not because he was worried he'd say something ugly. Nope, simply because there was absolutely nothing left to say. The woman had more weddings under her belt than Nick had books published. Her marriages lasted about the same length of time it took him to write one, too.

"Jeremy is so sweet, Nicky. He's the perfect man for me." Translation—he was rich. "There's just one teensy thing. He's a writer. His manuscript is wonderful. Well, I assume it is. I haven't actually read it, of course. I mean, like I told the silly man, I don't even read yours."

Oblivious to the insult and, as always, not interested in his input, his mother babbled on about her future husband, her future plans and her many new purchases.

Pain he refused to acknowledge sliced through Nick. He swallowed and shifted his jaw, knowing a rebuke was useless. He'd never registered on his mother's radar unless she wanted something. When he was growing up, it'd been to get him to play the fatherless waif to her tragic single mother in another con to snag a new husband. Now, it was money and favors. Because she played him just as easily as the men she chased, he knew he'd give her whatever she wanted. Which only pissed him off more. Proof positive that emotions were only there for the woman's advantage. Guys were just screwed.

Nick eyed his laptop and ground his teeth. This was the price of procrastination. The writer's block he'd been mourning suddenly dissipated. As always, two minutes of conversation with his mother and he desperately wanted to lose himself in the safe, sane world of his stories.

"Nicky," his mother asserted at the end of her monologue, "I need a little favor."

Finally, the point. He hoped like hell it was a favor that would require his signature on a check and he could be done with it.

"I want you to get Jeremy a book deal. Maybe one like you have. You know, with a really big advance. We'll do public appearances, TV, media events. It'll be so fun. An author and his wife, the tour. Doesn't that sound perfect? I'll...we'll make a fortune."

"I'm not an agent or a publisher, Lori." The term *Mom* was only used when she was playing a role. Otherwise, she preferred her given name.

"I know that, Nicholas. I just wanted some help. It breaks my heart to think Jeremy won't see his dream come true. I never saw my dream, you know. I had to give up my biggest wish to become a dancer because, well, you know, because of you." Her sigh was a thing of tragedy.

More like because of a broken condom, but whatever. Nick's fingers itched for his checkbook. Why couldn't she just want money? It would have been a clean, bloodless favor. Knowing protesting would only incite more emotional blackmail, he sighed.

"Send me the manuscript and contact information. I'll forward it to my agent."

Having gotten what she wanted, his mother tossed off a perfunctory thanks, fast-forwarded through her goodbye and hung up.

Nick needed to write like an alcoholic needed a drink. Desperately, insanely, unthinkingly.

But instead, he gave in to the need to wipe away the ugly feelings left from the call. He lifted the phone again. Even as he told himself he was being ridiculous, he punched in the number from memory.

"Hello."

"Delaney," he said in greeting, adjusting the pillows behind him and leaning back on the ugly floral bedspread. "How's it going?"

"Nick?"

He pulled a face at her shock. What? He couldn't call? Shifting on the pillow, he had to give her credit. As a rule, he *didn't* call women.

"I got your e-mail about changing our date from Friday night. How about Saturday instead?"

"Saturday's good," she agreed slowly. He heard the

uncertainty in her voice and told himself it was because she didn't understand why he hadn't just e-mailed her the suggestion. It couldn't be because she didn't want to see him. He didn't think he could take any more slams to his already fragile ego.

"I also wanted to check and see how you are doing with the reviews," he lied, not sure himself why he needed to hear her voice. "Isn't the first one due up on the site tomorrow?"

Her hesitation was an almost tangible thing. As if she knew he was full of bullshit and wasn't sure if she wanted to call him on it or not. Luckily, since he had no backup excuse, she just made a humming noise.

That breathy little sound sent Nick's already edgy libido into overdrive. It was the same sound she'd made when he licked his way up her body.

"I've finished the review of *The Michelangelo Effect*," she told him. "As a matter of fact, I was just giving it a final read through before I send it in."

"Care to share?"

"Read the site in the morning."

"You sure? I could give you some pointers, maybe a few tips from a writer's perspective," he teased.

"Right. Because our opinions on what makes a good story are so similar," she shot back.

Nick considered that for a second. "You know, other than your romanticized view of intimacy—" which his mother consistently proved a nightmare "—they probably are."

"My views aren't romanticized," she protested.

He grinned. Perfect. He settled into the pillow and let himself get lost in the conversation. After a forty-five-minute debate on the topic, she finally admitted he was right. They did have similar ideas on what it took to make a story rock.

Nick wasn't sure how he felt now, though. Amped and enthused to write, definitely. But just a little worried. It had been a challenge to justify his view. Her opinions were well thought out and solidly backed by enough supportive arguments. It made them hard to refute.

Which didn't bode well for this bet of theirs.

"Did you finish your business there in New York yet?" Delaney asked after he'd gone silent.

"Almost." Nick hesitated, then, not sure why, admitted, "I need to take care of a few things for my mom, they'll require a painful lunch at least, a few miserable dinners at worst."

"I'm sorry," she said, her words soft and, well, sweet. Not judgmental at all, or even surprised. "Parent issues are rough, aren't they?"

Nick gave a bitter laugh.

"You've got issues with your parents?" he asked, not willing to admit how easily his mother could emotionally manipulate him. After all, he claimed not to believe in emotions.

"I suppose they could be called issues, although it's definitely one-sided."

"Your side or theirs?"

"Mine. I lost my mom when I was little. My father…" She trailed off. Her sigh was heavy enough to make him wish he could reach through the phone line to give her a hug. "Most of the time I doubt he's aware of my existence. He'd be shocked that I feel we have issues."

"So you don't see much of each other, I suppose."

What he wouldn't give to say the same about his mother. Or to not feel the guilt he did at making that wish.

"Actually, we usually see each other a few times a week, at least," Delaney told him, pulling him out of his dismal reflection of his family drama and back to their discussion. "Or, I should say, we're in proximity of each other. My father isn't known for seeing much of anything. To him, I'm pretty much invisible."

Invisible? Delaney? The concept boggled his mind. How could a woman so vibrant not be noticed?

"He must be blind," he said. Realizing the irony of their situations, he gave a bitter laugh. "You know, I'd give a lot to be invisible to my mom. Even for a few months. I could use the break."

"I can't imagine you ever being invisible," she said softly. There was an odd note in her voice, pained and sad. "There's an indefinable quality that some people have that commands attention. For others…not so much."

Nick didn't get it. Delaney definitely commanded attention, especially his. She must mean someone else. But to ask would delve into that emotional stuff he was so determined to avoid. So he kept his mouth shut.

"Your qualities definitely command my attention," Nick teased after the silence grew uncomfortable. He said it to relieve the tension, but he realized, he wasn't joking. "Why don't we talk about those for a while? Make my night, Delaney. Tell me what you're wearing."

CHAPTER NINE

DISTRACTED FROM HER self-pity over her relationship with her father, Delaney giggled. She'd never had a naughty phone call with a guy before.

She glanced down at her fuzzy red sweatpants and AC/DC T-shirt. She felt like a fraud talking to him in her normal, frumpy persona, but she figured she'd call it a test of how deep the makeover actually went. After all, he'd liked her fine naked, maybe he'd be just as interested over the phone if he didn't have a clue her sweats had a hole in the threadbare seat.

"I'm not wearing much of anything," she hedged with a breathy little laugh.

"Are you in bed?" Before she could answer, he made a noise and said, "Of course you're not. You said you were going over the review."

A twinge of guilt snapped at the back of her neck. Delaney had planned to read the first of his book picks in her office so she could keep it strictly business. But she hadn't been able to get Nick out of her mind enough to settle in and get serious about reading. Finally up against the deadline, she'd fallen back on the tried-and-true, and brought the book, her laptop and her Pepsi to bed.

Delaney glanced at the book she'd just finished reading. A rich jewel-toned cover, with the image of a famous statue, it was on the bestseller lists. It was an interesting choice for her first review, and yes, she'd been a little too distracted with thoughts of Nick to give it her full attention.

But she'd read it when it had first been released, so she was comfortable with her review. With a quick glance at her laptop screen, Delaney hit Send.

Now she could focus on more important matters... namely this intriguing discussion. Whether phone sex qualified as a step toward Nick acknowledging the power of emotion in a sexual relationship or not, she'd figure out later.

"As a matter of fact," she slowly told him, as she closed her laptop and set it on the floor before curling up on her side, "I am in bed."

"Exactly how little are you wearing?" His voice took on a husky timbre that sent shivers straight to her core. He'd sounded just like that when he'd told her how he was going to kiss her body, where he was going to kiss it. He'd had that tone as he'd told her how to pleasure him.

That tone made Delaney wet.

"How little would you like me to wear?" she countered. "Keep in mind, it's a little chilly in here. I need something to warm me up."

Delaney snickered at her dorky response, but hey, she'd never done naughty phone-talk before. Since Nick laughed, too, she figured she was doing okay.

"How about you?" she asked. "What are you wearing?"

"I'm dressed," he admitted. "I was trying to write and hit a brick wall."

"Sounds...hard," she said with a little laugh. "Maybe I can help you through it?"

"You want to help me?"

"Don't sound so shocked. I could be helpful, if you gave me a chance."

His laugh was pure naughtiness.

"You'd be surprised at how helpful you might be. I'm stuck on a sex scene. Wanna talk dirty with me?"

Delaney blushed. She couldn't help it. The man had pressed his face between her legs and made her come, but the idea of talking dirty embarrassed her. Crazy.

"You might want to get comfortable," she suggested to buy time while she tried to figure out exactly how one *did* dirty talk.

"I'm never comfortable around you," he admitted. "Especially when there's a chance of sex, even if it's only verbal."

She gave a little whimper, then winced. But he heard it and laughed.

"Just imagine I'm there, lying next to you," he suggested. "Pretend I'm watching you."

Nervous but already turned-on at the idea, Delaney rolled to her back and closed her eyes to visualize the scenario. "What are you watching me do?"

"You're combing your fingers through your hair. I'm watching the light glint off the silky strands." He waited, clearly expecting her to do it. Delaney licked her lips, then, with a sigh, unclipped her hair and ran her fingers through it. As she did, she imagined him next to her. Pretended his fingers were there, too.

"Your fingers trail down your throat and you arch your back." It was like he was reading to her, his writing voice coming through loud and clear. It made Delaney feel like she was listening to—acting out—one of his books. "With both hands, you cup your breasts. Lift them, Delaney, lift them for me to see."

As if in a trance, she did as he instructed. Her breath shuddered and she gave a moan as her fingers warmed her breasts through the worn cotton of her T-shirt, brushed over the pebbled nipples.

"Yeah, baby," he murmured in a hoarse tone. "I can picture you, your pale skin creamy warm. I'm imagining myself lying there, watching as you trail your nail around your nipple, circling tighter and tighter until you can scrape it across the hard pointy tip. I'm thinking of you giving me that look from your big brown eyes, the one that begs me to touch you, to taste you."

Delaney squirmed, pressing her legs tight together, and let out a sound at the images.

"It's an exquisite torment," Nick continued, "watching, knowing how your nipple would taste, but not letting myself touch you."

"What're you doing?" she asked in a whisper. "While you imagine me, knowing I'm touching myself, what are you doing?"

"What do you want me to do?"

"I want you to do the same thing." The images he'd painted vivid in her mind, Delaney tweaked her hard, aching nipples between her fingers, using the texture of her T-shirt to add to the exquisite torment. Her breath came in little pants as she imagined it was his fingers touching her. That he was there watching her.

"I want you to be hard thinking of me," she said in a husky whisper. She needed him to be as turned-on as she was. Needed to know she could make him feel just as wild. "I want you to be so turned-on you have to come."

Nick groaned. "Make me, babe."

"I need to touch myself," she groaned. "I'm imagining it's you, your hand, your fingers inside me." Desperate for some form of release, she smoothed one hand down her belly to the waistband of her sweats, then pushed aside the loose elastic and combed her fingers through her curls. As dampness coated her hand, she gave a soft moan.

"Tell me," he begged hoarsely. "Take me with you."

Delaney swallowed twice before she could get the words out. "I'm sliding one finger inside myself. Two, now," she told him. "I'm wet, hot. Swollen."

Nick's groan blew her inhibitions to bits. Delaney flicked her finger over her swollen heat, biting her lip.

"I'm pretending you're here next to me," she said, her voice strained, "I can imagine you, all thick and hot and hard. It's such a turn-on knowing that's for me."

"I'm hard," he admitted, his voice low and husky. "I'm wishing it was your hand wrapped around me, moving faster and faster."

"I want you, need you. My fingers aren't enough, I want to feel you. Tell me what you want to do to me," she begged.

Sentences got shorter, words became choppier. Delaney could barely keep enough focus to talk anymore. One hand working her nipples, she worked her wet core with the other, sliding her fingers over, around and inside, always imagining it was Nick.

When he gave a long moan of pleasure, she let it take her over the edge. Her fingers, slick with her own juices, flicked at her clitoris once, twice, then she flew. Color exploded behind her eyes, her pants became little mewling sounds of pleasure. From far away, she heard Nick's voice telling her how good she was.

Finally, like floating on a soft cloud of exhaustion, she drifted back down.

"You're incredible," he said.

She felt incredible. Empowered, strong, like she could do anything. She'd never been so aware of her physical self before this. Before the makeover and Nick. And not, she told herself, just because it was great sex. She could have that by herself, although Nick's coaching was obviously a good thing.

"You're not so bad yourself," she teased with a sleepy laugh. "And I have to ask, did that help?"

His laugh was rich and wicked. "Babe, that helped more than you know."

"I meant with your story."

He paused, gave a little hum, then said, "Yeah. Actually it did. I'm going to write, you sleep."

She was already halfway there, so she just murmured an agreement.

"Sweet dreams," he said softly, satisfaction clear in his voice.

"'Night," she mumbled as she clicked off the phone.

Delaney settled into her pillow, a smile on her face. With her body sated and warm, she knew she'd be dreaming of what had just happened. Over and over and all night long…which was very sweet indeed.

NICK WATCHED GARY'S face for any hint of what the agent thought, obsessing like he hadn't done since his first book. God. What was he thinking, trying to write this kind of crap? He knew better. But talking to Delaney, listening to her, he got this insane feeling of hope.

It would probably ruin him.

"Well?" he asked, unable to stand it any longer.

"Chill," his agent instructed. The older man pointed

to the minifridge in the corner of his office without looking up from the manuscript.

"It's rough," Nick explained. "I didn't polish or anything, I figured I'd get your feedback before I went too far with it."

He'd been so desperate to write when he'd gotten off the phone with Delaney. The desperation came from being inspired by her, rather than the frustration he often felt when he talked to his mother. He'd been blown away when he'd finished the scene. That, friend, was emotion. At least, as close as he'd ever gotten. Maybe he could pull this off? Have it all? Make his editor happy, pacify the fans and still keep Delaney around, screw the bets. It was a little scary how much the idea appealed to him.

When Gary didn't even acknowledge him, Nick got up and stalked over to the fridge. He rifled through the contents then slammed it shut. He opened the snack cabinet disguised as a file drawer and pawed through it until he found a Snickers bar. But he was too amped up to eat. He tossed the candy back in the cabinet and started pacing.

"Dude, what is your problem?" Gary finally asked when he tossed the printed pages to his desk. "You're more nervous than a virgin on her wedding night."

Nick pulled a face. "Cliché alert."

"Right, which is why I'm not the writer here." Gary poked one meaty finger at the stack of papers and lifted a bushy gray brow. "Want to talk about it?"

"No. I just want to know what you think."

Gary leaned back in his chair and stared at Nick over his steepled fingers. It was his thinking pose.

"I think…"

Nick wanted to beat the man upside the head with

his own desk blotter. But he knew from experience it wouldn't do any good, so he just growled.

"I think you're on the right track," Gary finally said.

"That's it? On the right track? I wrote…" Nick poked his finger at the manuscript and made a face. "I wrote emotion there. That's more than the right direction."

"No, Nick. You wrote one of the hottest love scenes I've ever read here. And I have to say, probably the first scene you've ever written that can be actually called a love scene, rather than sex." Gary shook his head and shrugged. "It's great. It's deeper than you've ever gone, it's strong. You've bridged that typical distance you maintain in intimate scenes, which takes your writing to a whole new level."

"But…?"

"But, it's one scene. The emotions, the promise of it, they aren't in the rest of the manuscript. Not yet. Put them in and we're in business."

Nick felt just as confident of pulling that off as he would have if Gary had asked him to give birth to a litter of rabid dogs.

FASCINATED BY THE play of the candlelight washing her face in a golden shimmer, Nick watched Delaney laugh from across the table. A weird kind of joy filled him at her pleasure. She was so different than the women he'd known. Honest, no games, what you saw was what you got. It was refreshingly seductive. Maybe he'd have an easier time weaving emotions, at least surface ones, through his story than he'd thought.

"Do you ever get fans stalking you, like movie stars?" she asked. They'd been talking about a *Wake Up Califor-*

nia guest with a habit of stalking her favorite TV stars until she got their autograph.

"Stalking?" Nick mulled. "No. I've had a few who write regular fan mail, that kind of thing. Once at a book convention I had a woman waiting outside my hotel room. But she just wanted me to read her manuscript."

Delaney gave him a long, considering look and shook her head. "Nah, I don't believe that was all. That might have been her excuse, but I'm betting she wanted more than your opinion."

She had, but Nick wasn't the kind to brag so he just shrugged.

He tilted his head toward the dance floor, where couples were wrapped around each other in the dim light.

"Dance?" he asked.

Her gaze wove over the couples and the band, then back to him. "We never did finish that last dance, did we? I guess I owe you one."

"I don't know about owing me, but I'd love to have you in my arms. And since you really seemed to want dessert, that's the only way it's going to happen in the next little while."

Delaney grinned and winked as she set her napkin on the white linen next to her plate. "The best of all worlds. Good food, decadent chocolate and you."

He stood and held out his hand. When she rose, he stepped closer, infinitesimally, so she brushed against his chest as she rose up. He gave her a slow, wicked smile to let her know it was deliberate.

"Isn't that one of those pre-sex courtship moves?" she asked in an offhand tone. He could tell she was affected, though, by the rise and fall of those delicious breasts.

"Is it? Does that mean we're going to have sex if I do it right?" Her hand in his, he led her to the dance floor.

She laughed as she moved into his arms. He almost groaned when he realized how perfectly she fit. This was insane. Her, the book, Gary, all demanding emotion from him. And him, wanting to give it to them. Insane.

"I meant it was the kind of thing, if you believe that lust drives relationships, that would fall by the wayside after the first sexual encounter. Don't you think?"

"I think I get turned-on when you talk all brainy like that."

"Ahh, then lust is still driving this relationship," she joked. Something flashed in her eyes, though, that made Nick drop his smile.

"You say that like it's a bad thing," he said, truly puzzled. "Why? I thought it was just my books you had an issue with. But now that we know each other, I can see it's not that. Are you really so anti-lust?"

"Are you really so anti-emotion?"

"Emotions inevitably lead to pain," he pointed out.

"Is that opinion based on personal experience?" she asked softly, her hand rubbing his shoulder comfortingly in what he figured was probably an unconscious gesture.

Deliberate or not, it did make him feel good. *Safe* was the word that came to mind, as stupid as that sounded. He tried to shrug off the weird feeling.

"Of course not," he lied. "I told you, I don't do emotions."

"Ever?" The look she gave him pierced clear to his soul, making further lies impossible.

Nick puffed out a breath and gave a one-shouldered shrug. "Let's just say I don't do them anymore."

She looked like she wanted to ask why. Nick steeled

himself, not wanting to go there but not sure he wouldn't answer *any* question she put to him.

But she just pursed her lips and nodded, then snuggled closer, her head on his chest as the music washed over them.

Good. Topic closed, with minimal poking into his wounded psyche. Wrapping his arm tighter around her waist, Nick still frowned. Why hadn't she pushed the subject? Because she was perfectly satisfied with the sex—incredible sex—and didn't care enough about him as a person to want to know more? He was going to ignore the fact that she'd put that incredible sex on hold. His fragile male ego proclaimed that was a maneuver to win the bet.

Or was she not pushing him because, despite his feeling closer to her than any other woman he'd known, she didn't think he had the emotional depth of a mud puddle.

Nick rolled his eyes. Shit, look at him. Open the door to emotions and he was off, worrying like a teenage girl in the dramatic throes of her first crush. Stupid, pointless and, considering the sexy woman moving so seductively in his arms, completely crazy.

Through with it now, he focused instead on how Delaney felt, as her slender body molded against his. His fingers smoothed the filmy fabric of her dress where it fell in a pleated waterfall over her hips. He raised the hand he held in his to his mouth, brushing a series of soft kisses across her knuckles. When she pulled back to give him a smile, he slid his tongue between her fingers. She gasped, her eyes going wide, then blurring. The desire in those brown depths sent his up another notch.

Nick steered them over to the edge of the dance floor,

where the lights were the most dim, pressing her close with one hand. The music changed, going darker, bluesier.

Still holding her hand to his mouth, he sucked one finger in, playing his tongue over the delicate length of it. At the same time, he loosened his hold on her so just a tiny bit of space was between their bodies. As they moved, they rubbed in counterpoint against each other. When her nipples, hard and pointed, slid over his chest, Nick wanted to groan. Yeah, she was as turned-on as he was.

Shifting just a little, he slid his leg between hers and gave thanks that she was so tall. Unable to help himself, he laid her hand on his shoulder, then wrapped both of his on her hips. He buried his face in her curls, nuzzling her hair until he reached the side of her throat and ear. Her scent, a subtle spice, filled his senses as he kissed her silken flesh.

DELANEY COULDN'T CATCH her breath. She knew she needed to be smart, to hold onto some semblance of control. But it was almost impossible with the way Nick was making her feel. The sensation of his body rubbing against hers, his chest pressed to her nipples, his leg causing such delicious friction against her damp core…

"Dating," she gasped as he pressed moist, hot kisses to her ear.

"Huh?"

"We're supposed to be dating. Getting to know each other. Proving…something."

God help her, she could barely remember her name, let alone what point she was trying to make.

"Lust versus intimacy," he responded. There was just enough humor in his voice to keep the frustration also in it from making her feel guilty.

Delaney swallowed, meeting his eyes when he lifted his head. She gave him a weak smile, relieved when Nick smiled back.

"Right," she agreed. "In my defense, I'm definitely feeling passionate right now."

He laughed and stepped away. As soon as he did, her body craved the heat of his like a drug addict craved a fix. With a desperate, biting need.

Breathless, almost thoughtless, she was glad of Nick's hand guiding her back to their table. As soon as he'd tucked her into her chair, the waiter was there with dessert.

Needing some satisfaction, Delaney dipped her finger into the rich creamy mousse garnishing the chocolate cake and sucked it into her mouth. The taste exploded on her tongue, almost as delicious as Nick had been.

She glanced over and caught the look on his face. A bubble of laughter burst out.

"You look like you're going to cry," she teased. "Did you want a bite?"

"Of you, definitely. Of the cake, not so much."

No longer frustrated for some reason, she giggled. Then she dug into the cake, this time with her fork. Delaney deliberately focused on the dessert, needing the time, to clear her mind. Or more correctly, to reclaim her senses. Not willing to think about what'd almost happened on the dance floor or figure out how that played into their bet—to say nothing of her personal belief system—Delaney looked around the restaurant.

Her gaze landed on a couple, probably a few years younger than she and Nick. They sat, holding hands with their heads together. Their joy in each other was clear.

She'd bet they never considered a choice between lust and love. It was obvious they'd simply embraced both.

She sighed, sucking the chocolate off her fork as she watched the guy kiss the pretty blonde's hand. It looked sweet when he did it, where as when Nick had kissed hers it had been an erotic hot button.

"Sweet," Nick said, unconsciously echoing her thought. He'd followed her gaze. She frowned at him, not sure if he was being sarcastic or not, given his views on the finer emotions. But he looked genuine.

He caught her narrow-eyed speculation and laughed. "Hey, I can appreciate romance, even if I don't choose to take part in it."

Delaney scooped up another bite of chocolate to keep from pointing out that a date that encompassed dinner, dancing and no possibility of sex might be considered romance in some circles.

There was an excited shriek, then a burst of laughter. Delaney and Nick both turned to see the couple they'd been watching wrapped in each other's arms. The blonde stared at her hand over the guy's shoulder, tears streaming down her face.

"Awwww, they just got engaged," Delaney gushed, stating the obvious. "Now *that's* sweet."

Nick snickered. With a flick of his finger, he summoned their waiter. Delaney couldn't hear what he murmured, but the waiter smiled and nodded.

"Sweet. Crazy, but sweet," Nick agreed.

"Are you really such a cynic?" she challenged. "Don't you know of any couples who have a solid, lasting relationship?"

He rubbed his chin as he considered the question. Then he shook his head. "Nope, sorry. I can't think of anyone I know personally who's escaped the emotional minefield unscathed."

"That's not what I asked," she pointed at, poking toward him with her fork to make her point. "Do you know anyone, at all, who is happy in a relationship?"

"Define *happy.*"

Delaney rolled her eyes. Before she could launch her lecture, though, their waiter approached the celebrating couple with a bottle of champagne. From the way the guy's eyes went wide, it must have been very pricy champagne.

When the waiter gestured to their table, her suspicions were confirmed. The couple mouthed "thank you" to Nick, who just smiled and nodded before turning back to face Delaney.

His eyes went wide at the look on her face.

"What?" he asked, his tone defensive.

"You're a fraud." Joy bubbled in her like the champagne the couple was currently toasting their future with.

"I beg your pardon?"

"You fake. You claim to be anti-romance, yet you send perfect strangers a bottle of what I'm guessing is the best champagne in the house? A totally unsentimental person simply doesn't do that," she declared, pressing both hands to the table and leaning forward to make her point.

Nick crossed his arms over his chest, the move stretching his jacket across his broad shoulders. The look on his face matched the stubborn tilt of his chin.

"Bullshit."

"Eloquent, Mr. Author."

"Total bullshit," he clarified.

"You don't say."

She could see him actually grind his teeth.

"Just because I'm a nice guy, and appreciate seeing other people excited even if it's for a totally doomed reason, doesn't mean I'm sentimental."

"Okay," she said agreeably.

He glared.

"Maybe I was just trying to impress you," he offered.

She couldn't hold back her laughter. Giggling, she just shook her head and raised both brows as if to say "yeah, right."

After a few seconds, Nick's stubborn look melted into laughter. "Okay, fine. Think what you like."

"I will."

"I could use it as a plot device, you know."

As Delaney finished dessert, Nick spun a story based on a bottle of poisoned champagne sent to the wrong couple. The more he spoke, the more animated the story became. When he stopped for breath, he gave a sheepish smile.

"Did you want to write that down while it's fresh?" she asked, fascinated to watch his off-the-cuff brainstorm.

"Nah, it's all in my head." He shot a glance over at the couple, their hands curled together as they gazed into each other's eyes. Then he gave her a wink. "You were right, in a way. Even if I don't personally open myself up to emotional land mines, I can still appreciate the beauty of the idea."

Before she could reply, the newly engaged couple came over to introduce themselves and offer their gratitude.

The beauty of Nick's actions shook Delaney. Not only

his kind gesture, but how friendly and encouraging he was with the pair. He might disdain expressing emotion in his stories, but he had so much of it inside him. She pressed her lips together to hold back tears. Because inside was where he'd keep it.

There wasn't anything beautiful about what she was feeling as she watched him accept the couple's thanks and chitchat with them. For them, falling in love might be sweet and fun. For her, she realized as her heart gave a sharp twist, it was pure hell.

Delaney's gaze traced Nick's features. The firm line of his jaw, his devastating smile. The laser-blue intensity of his eyes. He was gorgeous. But it was the sound of his laughter that did her in.

Didn't it just suck that the man she was falling for came with a bona fide guarantee to never fall—or accept—love himself?

CHAPTER TEN

"BUT…BUT, THAT CAN'T be right," Delaney stuttered. She stared at the bank of computers, her eyes flying from one monitor to the next as if the results would be different on one of them.

"I'm blown away, to be honest," Sean said. "I thought you'd win by a landslide. I mean, your review of *The Michelangelo Effect* snared you a seventy-percent approval rating. Your review of *Magnolia Summer* is at less than thirty percent."

"I can't believe it." Delaney dropped to the chair and stared off into space. Oddly enough, this book was one that after she'd turned in her review she and Nick had discussed and both agreed on. Delaney had originally been delighted at his pick. From a hugely prolific author of Southern fiction, the book should have been guaranteed to offer emotional depth and an intriguing plotline. But when Delaney had gotten an advanced copy, she'd been sick with disappointment. The emotion had been there, sure. But it'd been rushed and artificial. And even though she hated giving negative reviews she had to be honest. Her review had gone up on Sunday, the day after the book had hit the shelves. Today was Friday and it was clear the author's fans were rabidly loyal.

"Look, don't take it so hard," Sean consoled. "The powers that be are blown away with your segment, to tell you the truth. You're pulling in viewers, getting tons of mail. I just heard yesterday that they are probably going to offer you the spot permanently."

Her worry over the review's failure fled at Sean's words. Delaney burst into slightly hysterical laughter.

"No way?"

"Yup. It's not even about the Nick Angel angle, either. I mean, that's how you kept the job originally, based on the potential attention. But you're doing great on your own, bet notwithstanding."

Delaney gave a baffled shake of her head. TV? Her, full-time? Sure she was starting to enjoy the job. Why wouldn't she? She was finally able to focus on her true passion—commercial fiction.

"That's flattering, Sean, but I'm only here for the summer."

"Why? If they offer, it'd be a great contract. The show has a solid shot at being picked up regionally next year."

"I have to get back to my real life," she said with a shrug. A pang of regret hit her, hard and unexpected. She'd really miss doing the segments.

Of course, before she could get to missing it, or back to her old job, she had to win this review.

She might consider her private wager with Nick a purely wild gamble, but their original bet? The reviews? She'd made that with total confidence in her abilities.

She recalled her initial opinion that Nick had issued that side bet to distract her from their televised wager. Whether he had or not, it had apparently worked. *Had* being the operative word. Not anymore.

She had too much on the line to lose. Even to the man she was falling in love with.

BLACK NIGHT CLOSED around them like a shroud. The only sounds were the crickets' cheerful death knell and his labored breathing.

"But, I love you," he said, his voice ringing with the emotions he'd finally allowed out of that deep dark vault in his heart.

"I know you do," she said, flicking a strand of silken hair over her shoulder and giving him that smile that promised heaven. "But I can't let that change things."

"Change things? I opened up to you. I shared my world, my secrets." My heart, his mind yelled. But he didn't say it aloud. She already had too much power. Even as he reeled with the pain of realizing who— what—she was, his training kicked in.

Eyes flicked to the left. To the right. The forest closed around them. Escape was there, it was up to him to find it. To get himself out of the trap he'd walked into with open eyes.

"You were great, too," she told him with a wicked sort of laugh. "I'd heard you were a great lay, but you actually exceeded your own press. And the secrets, well, that's why I'm done with you. I've got all I need, and now we're taking you down."

"You're the black widow?" At least if he was going down, it'd be to one of the most notorious criminals in the country. His boss'd appreciate that.

This time her laughter was pure joy. That husky giggle of pleasure he'd fallen for. Amusement and pleasure mixed in those doe brown eyes as she shook her head at him.

"Hardly. I'm just a woman."

"I love you," he told her.

"I know," she said.
Then she shot him.

Nick slapped the laptop screen closed.

God, he'd been reduced to writing total crap. Garbage. He hated it. Hated the story, hated the pansy-assed emotional dreck spewing across his screen.

He got up and paced his office. The pewter-gray tones of the room failed to soothe him, as did the view from the floor-to-ceiling window overlooking the woods. Usually the sight of the rich dense foliage comforted him. It was his sanctuary. Now it sucked.

He considered going down to the kitchen for a drink, a snack. One of the large, sharp butcher knives. But it'd just be an excuse to avoid dealing with the trash he'd tried to pass off as writing.

He threw himself on the black leather sofa and dropped one arm over his eyes.

What was he supposed to do? Gary was nagging him to carry the emotions he'd put into his sex scene throughout the story. The guy had sent it on to the new editor for a look-see and he'd loved it. Raved, even. Nick wasn't sure how he felt about that. Praise was always good, but it meant he'd want more.

Could he do more? Not if that shit on his computer was any indication.

He'd never been as grateful to hear a phone ring as he was just then. He was even desperate enough to still answer after seeing the caller ID.

"Angel," he answered.

"Nicky? Get a hold of your agent and let him know he can throw away Jeremy's manuscript," his mother ordered. "The wedding is off."

"You're kidding, right?"

It was like turning on a faucet full blast. She spewed tears, lamenting the callous indifference of her newest love, the ruin of her life, the horrendous future ahead of her because of the broken heart she'd probably die from.

Nick sighed and headed downstairs. He knew he had time to grab an apple, maybe even make a sandwich, before she ran down. Exactly seven minutes later he set a plate of fruit and roast beef on rye on his desk, dropped into the chair and picked up the phone.

"What am I going to do?" she wailed, right on schedule.

This was, Nick knew, his cue to offer a few pitiful sounds of sympathy. Except he was sick of it. Sick of the roller coaster, sick of playing the same song.

"Quit playing games and go talk to him. Stick it out for once and give him a chance." Oh, shit. Was he drunk? He knew better than to offer an opinion.

Nick glanced at his soda. Nope, he was straight-up sober and obviously stupid. It wasn't his job to get involved in his mother's emotional drama. He was supposed to listen, make sounds and stay out of it.

"Look," he said, unable to back out now that he'd opened his big mouth, "you loved the guy enough to want to marry him and he can't have changed that much in the last couple days. It was obvious when we went to lunch that he worships the ground you walk on. If he wants you to join him and his daughter for brunch once a month, I hardly think it's worth ditching him."

"But—"

"Quit going through relationships like they're paper plates, Lori. If you want this one to work, unpack your suitcase, suck it up and do what he wants once in a while. He does it for you, it's only fair."

Silence.

Nick took a bite of his sandwich, the tangy mustard clearing the bitterness from his mouth.

"How'd you know I'd packed?" she finally mumbled.

"You always do. Ever since I was a kid and your second husband yelled at you for crashing his car into the garage door. You packed your suitcase and off we went." Her suitcase. Not his, he'd had to leave behind all his toys, his clothes and his first best friend.

"I didn't call to get lectured," she told him after she'd sniffled a few times. From her huffy tone, she was getting over the shock. "I was coming to San Francisco next week and wanted to get together. Can you fit me in?"

Great. More emotional crap. Nick almost said that if she needed money he could just wire it and save them both the time. But that would be obnoxious.

"How about lunch?" he asked instead.

Five minutes and all the pouting he could take later, Nick hung up and sighed. Head in his hands, he wondered if half past noon was too early to drink. His mother always made him feel this way. Drained, miserable and worst of all, vulnerable.

Nick frowned, flipped open his laptop and read the death scene again. *Vulnerable* was a good word for it. He opened himself to emotions and what'd he get? Shot in the gut.

With a sneer, he hit the delete key. If he lost the bet with Delaney, this was the kind of crap he'd have to write. No thank you. It was enough to bring emotion into his sex scenes. It would have to be.

He fingered tickets to the Erotic Exotic Ball on the

corner of his desk. He'd been thinking he'd skip it. After all, it was definitely not Delaney's kind of thing. But he had too much on the line. He had to win.

With a determined breath, he opened his e-mail program and sent Delaney a note, telling her to keep that night clear. He had a surprise for her.

"ARE YOU SURE I look okay?" Delaney asked, tugging at her skirt again. "Do you think it's too showy for the faculty soiree?"

Mindy sighed, but she stepped back and gave Delaney a thorough once-over. From the smooth fall of her hair, held back by a black quilted leather headband, to the brilliant royal blue silk shirt buttoned to her throat, to the black linen skirt that hit one exact inch above her shaking knees. When Mindy's eyes reached Delaney's feet, shod in black leather, high-heeled Mary Janes she sighed.

"You look great, and those shoes are hot."

Delaney glanced down and grinned. She'd discovered, much to her surprise, that she loved shoes. The fancy clothes, makeup and hair stuff were all okay. She was used to them now and had come to appreciate their effect. But shoes, those she'd actually started shopping for. On her own, for no other reason than they made her smile.

Then she frowned. "Are you sure? I mean, does this look say 'serious professor'? Or does it say 'idiot all dressed up'?"

Mindy rolled her eyes and grabbed Delaney's arm.

"Enough, already. Let's go. You want that position, you have to get in there and convince the board that you can command attention the way they want."

Delaney took a deep breath, then with her chin high, entered the hall. It was like stepping into a different world. One, she suddenly realized, she hadn't missed. The wooden panels were cherry, the floor marble, the atmosphere rarified and dignified. It had once been a haven. Now it was like that old brown suit of hers. Ill-fitting, uncomfortable and not very appealing. It had to be nerves, of course. This was her life, and as soon as she got back to it, it'd fit again.

Hopefully. The number of shocked looks coming at her weren't reassuring.

"Do I look that different?" she asked Mindy out of the corner of her mouth.

"You're great. Definitely not invisible. Just stay focused."

Focus. Right. She was here to make an impression, to prove her worth to her colleagues and the board.

With that in mind, she pasted a confident smile on her face and worked the room. Something she'd done hundreds of times before, but never like this. People wanted to talk to her. They came up to ask her questions, to compliment her new look. She was, she realized after an hour of trying to make her way to the punch bowl, the hit of the soiree.

"Your proposal is intriguing," Professor Mohs said after she'd cornered Delaney. They'd spent the first five minutes of their discussion on Delaney's shoes, the next five on her ideas for the English department. The other woman was a brilliant sociologist and looked like someone's favorite aunt. Black curls created a soft halo around her angelic face as she smiled beatifically.

"This is exactly what the department needs, if you

ask me. With this and your qualifications, I'd say you have an excellent chance when the committee meets."

It was all Delaney could do not to giggle and bend down to throw her arms around the woman's neck. As one of the hiring committee, her opinion was vital.

Five minutes later, the women separated. Delaney found Mindy by the buffet table and shared a happy smile.

"I'm hoarse," Delaney admitted. "I feel like I've talked more in this last hour than I do in a whole day of lectures."

"Different kind of performance," Mindy declared, popping a stuffed mushroom into her mouth. "You're more comfortable in the classroom. Right now, you're on display."

"Like I'd expected, everyone is asking what I've done to myself. I just said I had a little makeover, without going into any details." Delaney filled her plate with appetizers, then gratefully took a cup of punch from the student who was serving. She and Mindy made their way to an empty table and sank into chairs.

"I'm not sure how to answer the 'what have I been doing with myself' question, though. Apparently they all think teaching online classes barely qualifies as working."

"You were just saying the same thing," Mindy pointed out.

"That's because it is barely teaching. I mean, there is so much less interaction this way. I feel useless. A computer program could assign reading and grade essays." She shifted in her seat, tugging the hem of her skirt to cover an extra inch of bare leg. "Thanks to you and this makeover, though, there's little possibility of it being permanent."

"We need to go celebrate," Mindy decided through a mouthful of brie. "And hey, now that you've wowed the board, there's the man you really need to impress."

Delaney didn't need to turn to see who it was. She knew from the hushed tones that had settled over the room. Whenever her father walked in, people got quiet. Uncomfortable, almost. Or maybe she was the only one discomfited, which was pretty damned pitiful, all things considered.

But not anymore. Or, at least that was what she told herself. And like the makeover, if she faked it on the outside, maybe she'd start feeling it on the inside.

So she took a deep breath, lifted her chin and turned to scan the room. Her father stood, holding court at the opposite end of the hall.

"Go," Mindy encouraged, as if reading her mind.

"Right." Delaney took another deep breath and stood, crossing the room. Like water, the crowd parted to clear a path toward the dean.

When Delaney reached him, still in conversation with the head of the history department, he didn't seem to notice she was there. Professor Hail did, though. She shot Delaney a look of gratitude and tried to break off her conversation with the dean. But, oblivious as usual, he kept on talking. And talking. Delaney realized for the first time that her father's lack of awareness wasn't restricted to her. He didn't pay any attention to *anyone's* needs.

Now wasn't that an empowering discovery? Riding on it, she gave Professor Hail an answering smile and politely cleared her throat.

Nothing.

A few months ago, the look of sympathy the other

woman shot her would have fed her insignificance complex. But not anymore. She just rolled her eyes, and with an apologetic shrug to the other professor, tapped her father's arm.

"Wha—" Dean Conner turned, a frown creasing his red beetle brows. "Beg your pardon?"

"Father, do you have a minute?"

"Excuse me," Professor Hail said, and quickly hurried off.

"Delaney?" His frown deepened as he took in her appearance. From the disapproving look in his eyes, he wasn't impressed. Delaney wasn't surprised. "What on earth did you do to yourself? Is this why I haven't seen you lately?"

She was surprised he'd even noticed her absence.

"You haven't seen me because you reassigned all my coursework to online classes, remember?" she asked.

"Right." His frown eased and he settled his gaze on her left shoulder. For the next five minutes, he proceeded to discuss her online class results, grades and possible future courses.

That was it? No other comment on her makeover? Nothing?

She glanced down to make sure she was really wearing her fashionably fitted outfit instead of the baggy tweed of the past. Yup, there were her killer heels.

"Wait," she interrupted.

"I beg your pardon?"

"You're talking as if it's a given that my course load will be online next semester."

He gave her his patented "don't bother me with details" look.

"You said this was a temporary experiment," she insisted.

From the looks people shot her and the frown on her father's face, she'd insisted more loudly than she'd intended. After the horrible results of her one meltdown with her father, Delaney had always been careful to be the perfect daughter. To mold her personality to his expectations. Temper embarrassed him, loss of control was to be avoided at all costs. Shame at drawing notice to their dissension washed over her. Then, to her shock, anger sluiced it away. He couldn't send her to boarding school this time.

"You said you needed someone to bring excitement to the department," she insisted, feeling like a butterfly breaking out of its chrysalis. A very angry, very fed-up butterfly. "I'm that someone. My proposal is cutting-edge. It's dynamic, it's forward-thinking and would revitalize our English department."

"Now, Delaney—"

"No." She set her jaw, and for the first time in her life actually stood up to her father. "No, you can't 'now, Delaney' me this time. I told you before, I'm tired of being treated like I'm insignificant. Tired of being brushed off with a pat on the head and pseudo-praise."

Years of training kept her voice moderate, her words pleasant. After all, her father simply tuned out anything he deemed emotional. The irony of that being the basis for her bets with Nick occurred to her, but she shoved it aside to analyze later.

"I spoke with Professor Mohs earlier. She thinks my proposal sounds intriguing. Like it's a perfect fit for the direction the board has envisioned. *She* thinks I can do this job."

"I never stated I didn't think you could do the job, Delaney. But achieving that promotion will take more than one board member's opinion."

And he clearly didn't think she could get them. She'd known that he wasn't going to offer his recommendation. But she hadn't accepted it until now.

She couldn't maintain the even keel her father demanded, so she simply nodded and walked away. Not because she didn't want to embarrass him. Because she didn't want to embarrass herself. Barely able to see through the tears blurring her vision, Delaney made her way across the room.

Were the last four months all for nothing? Even with the makeover, she still didn't matter. Delaney's gaze fell on Professor Belkin, who'd just arrived. And with him was Delaney's competition, the brunette. She met Belkin's eyes and saw the message there. His choice was made and Delaney didn't stand a chance.

Her fingernails cut into the soft flesh of her palms as she tried to reel in the bitter anger surging through her.

She couldn't stand it anymore. Years of keeping her temper under control went out the window as she imagined the pleasure of kicking the smug-ass department head in the knee with her pointy-toed shoe. Or maybe she'd aim a little higher and deflate his ego.

Ready to rumble, Delaney started across the room. Before she got more than three steps, though, someone tapped her arm.

She glared, then, seeing who it was, smothered her fury with an effort. "Professor Ekco," she greeted the alumni chair and last member of the hiring committee.

"Professor Conner," he responded. "I wanted to congratulate you on your innovative proposal."

Ooooh. Delaney gave him a hesitant smile, his words doing more to soften her anger than all her deep-breathing exercises.

They spent the next few minutes discussing her ideas, Delaney becoming more animated and excited as she explained the various options for bringing more current fiction to the college.

Finally, the alumni head nodded. "You're right, Professor Conner, it's a fabulous proposal. One that will stand up nicely to the others we've received. Of course, Professor Belkin has backed a different applicant. I'm sure you can see that carries a great deal of weight."

Delaney ground her teeth to keep from growling in frustration.

"But…" He cocked a brow and leaned closer. She stiffened. The old guy wasn't going to hit on her, was he? She'd heard stories of that happening, but never at Rosewood. And never, *ever,* to her. "Well, I have to share a secret."

She steeled herself.

"I'm a huge fan of *Wake Up California,*" the old guy said in a hushed tone.

"What? How?" Didn't he have morning classes? And how was he getting a local San Francisco station all the way up here?

"My daughter recorded it for me," he said.

Her eyes bulged. *Oh, shit.* Who the hell did that? She'd never considered the possibility. So much for the best laid plans. She didn't even bother to sigh. She just waited.

"After discovering your alter ego as a reviewer, I've gone back and read your work. Impressive. And although

I don't always agree with your point of view, you present it quite well."

Delaney felt like asking if that meant the difference between an A and a B.

But she kept her mouth shut as he continued, "Now this bet with Nick Angel has been fascinating. Not only the basis of your argument, but the fact that you'd take such a risky stand. That," he said with a slow nod, "is what we need in the English department. Someone willing to take some risks, to stand behind a curriculum they believe in."

Her mouth dropped but no words came out. Excitement surged and she couldn't keep the delighted smile off her face. Interpreting her reaction, he quickly shook his head.

"No, no," he corrected. "I'm not backing your application, Professor. At least, not yet."

Excitement deflated like a leaky balloon.

"Not yet?"

He gave her an avuncular smile, patted her arm and said, "You win that bet against Nick Angel and I'll give you my recommendation. Especially if you can entice Mr. Angel to speak at the college. That would definitely impress the alumni." He nodded decisively. "Yes, I'm confident his appearance, along with your proposal and your academic reputation, will secure you the position."

Delaney gave him a weak smile of thanks.

How ironic. She, who'd been virtually invisible a few months ago, could snag her coveted promotion by winning one simple, high-profile bet.

Of course to win, all she had to do was nail the reviews, keep Nick from distracting her with his powers of lust and try not to get her heart broken.

She might as well try to convince her father to attend a daddy-daughter dance with her for Valentine's Day.

AT HOME THAT NIGHT, Delaney sat at her desk and pulled up the *Wake Up California* Web site.

She stared at the second poll helplessly. Still losing. Dammit, she couldn't lose. Before, beating Nick had been a matter of pride. Something between the two of them, even if the highly publicized poll was integral to the bet.

But now her future was riding on it. She'd taken the TV job to work on her presentation skills, to push the envelope of her makeover. She'd intended to use the proficiency she built there to aid her in selling herself to the committee. Not for her position on "Critic's Corner," and especially not her bet with Nick, to become the deciding factor in the future of her career.

Winning the bet was now vital.

With that in mind, she took the third book to be reviewed from the stack on her desk, and still in her skirt and heels, settled into her office chair, the nubby rich red silk giving her a sense of power. Notepad and pen by her side, she settled in to read the book, deliberately closing off all thoughts of Nick.

Instead of a Pepsi, she had a glass of ice water on the table next to her. Instead of soft rock in the background, she played classical as a reminder of what was at stake.

Three and a half hours later, she typed up the last of her notes and read the review. Was it enough to win readers' votes?

Nick had chosen a classic as his third book. Probably banking on the average genre reader shunning Jane Austen's work. Too many would read it and fall back on their high school English analysis, rather than really see the story's intricate message.

Her review challenged them to dig deeper. It was more than an opinion piece, it was the culmination of everything she was as a teacher. An ode to the work, written in such a way as to encourage the reader to decide for themselves what the story was about.

But was it enough? For the first time, she was beset with doubts about her ability as a reviewer. And as a teacher.

Finally, unable to stand doubt in the one area of her life where she'd always felt confident, Delaney closed her eyes and hit the Send button. There. Third review submitted. And she'd have to win this one to win the bet.

Exhausted, Delaney stared at the computer screen. She wasn't any closer to winning her private bet with Nick than she was to winning the public one.

Time to change that. With a determined jut of her chin, she booted up the Internet for research. It was time to figure out how to convince Nick that emotion, that *intimacy*—was vital.

After all, she had everything riding on winning.

CHAPTER ELEVEN

"A PICNIC," NICK repeated blankly. He had to have mis-heard Delaney. The point of her insistence on dating was to prove that emotions were more satisfying than lust. What would a picnic prove? How to intensify his frustration at not getting any? "You're kidding, right?"

Delaney shot him a wry look and kept on gathering stuff. Wicker basket, blanket, bag of what looked like... toys? Nick squinted, but couldn't tell. She really meant it. His incredulous gaze shot back to meet her laughing brown eyes.

"A picnic will be great," she assured him as she headed for the door of her apartment, blatantly ignor-ing his dismay. "Fresh air, relaxing atmosphere. C'mon, it's going to be fun."

The door open now, she cast a glance back over her shoulder and rolled her eyes. "What? You hate picnics or something?"

Nick searched his brain for picnic-related opinions, but didn't find any so he just shrugged.

"Have you ever *been* on a picnic before?" she asked.

"No," he answered, not sure why he sounded—or felt—so sheepish.

"Then come on, it's a new experience. I thought you were all about those."

"Sure. When they deal with sex or adventure. Not sitting on the damp grass battling bugs for my lunch."

Her eyes flashed at the mention of sex. Nick was glad to see the smoldering heat there, assuring him he wasn't the only one suffering through these stupid dates so she could try to prove her point. A point she'd been much closer to making with the dinner and dancing torture than with this picnic idea.

Then the heat banked and she gave him a friendly smile. Nick wanted to growl. Even more, he wanted to toss her on the couch and relive the incredible memories they'd created there just a couple weeks before.

Following her rules was killing him.

"I'll protect you," she promised, oblivious to his turmoil. She reached back to grab his wrist and pulled him through the door to the nebulous safety of their picnic.

An hour later Nick admitted, "This is nice. I wouldn't call it fun, but it doesn't suck."

He reclined on the blanket, the thick grass creating a cushy mattress beneath his back. A large mulberry tree offered shade as well as an intriguing pattern of dappled light playing over Delaney's hair.

Damn, she was gorgeous.

"Doesn't suck, huh? High praise, indeed," Delaney retorted with a laugh.

The sounds of the park, birds and children's laughter filled the air with a carefree happiness. Weird, how it made him feel lighter. Not passionate, though, so he still didn't see how this was working into her argument. Then it hit him. Maybe this was just what it appeared. A relaxing, comfortable outing between two people who were… What?

Nick frowned as he watched her gather the food

containers and restack them in the basket. Were they friends? He could talk to her about anything, actually looked forward to their discussions since she made him think beyond his comfort zone. They laughed together, had mutual interests, similar tastes. All friend-type things. How about lovers? That implied an intimacy that went beyond lusty sex, didn't it? But, as much as he'd like to claim otherwise, he wished they were. One night of incredible, mind-blowing sex hadn't been enough.

Nick's gaze traced the sharp line of her jaw, the sweet curve of her lips. He wanted her. More than he could remember ever wanting another woman. He'd suggested the bet be a month-long fling partially because a month was about his limit for relationships. While she'd definitely put a crimp in his timeline, Nick knew he wanted to be with her long after the month was up. He could have her every night for the next year and still not do all the things he'd been dreaming of with her.

Delaney pulled out a tub of cookies, distracting him from the other hunger gnawing at him. He groaned and pressed a hand to his stomach. Since this was the only appetite of his she was agreeing to feed right now, he promised himself he'd add another mile to his morning run and reached for three.

"Do you eat like this at every picnic?" he asked.

Her look was both shy and sad. He wanted to drop the cookies and give her a hug, but the tilt of her chin defied pity.

"Honestly? This is my first picnic, too." She shrugged at his look of shock. "I usually walk in this park for exercise, you know? I always see people picnicking. Families, couples. It seemed…special."

Ignoring her "don't feel sorry for me" air, he reached

over and took her hand. "If you wanted to eat in the park before, why didn't you just do it? You strike me as a woman who always goes after what she wants, even if it's as simple as eating on the grass."

She started to say something, then shook her head. "When I was a kid, my father was always too busy. Even if he'd had time to do things, the dean... I mean, Dad was definitely not the kind of guy for outdoorsy activities. He was more into a trip to the library."

The dean. Nice nickname for her father. Nick wondered what kind of uptight guy ended up being coined that by his only daughter.

"My family wasn't the picnicking type, either," Nick admitted, watching the play of their fingers instead of looking at Delaney's face as he confessed his deep dark secret. "My dad took off before I was born, and Mom...? Well, she wasn't into spending time with me at all unless there was a purpose in it. You know, impress the potential husband with her mommy skills. But she always picked things like ice cream parlors or pizza joints. Stuff that would keep my mouth filled so I wouldn't out her. This actually might be my first foray into a public park."

He met her eyes, searching for pity, but only seeing acceptance. She really was different than other women. Tension he hadn't even realized was there poured off his shoulders. Blaming the unwholesome fresh air for his urge to share, for the first time ever, Nick opened up. They talked about his childhood and hers. Compared growing up with absentee parents, meeting expectations, and their own forms of rebellion.

"So writing was your way of getting back at your mom?" she asked, her eyes huge with surprise. "How? I mean, I think of rebelling as running wild, breaking rules, doing things that bring embarrassment to the parent…."

Her voice trailed off and she frowned. Her gaze dropped to the blanket and she blinked a few times, then met his eyes again.

Nick wasn't sure why the thought had hit her so hard. He didn't know if it was that sad look in her eyes, or the odd serenity of the park setting, but he heard himself being alarmingly honest.

"It's a little hard to embarrass someone who doesn't realize you're there," he explained. "Writing was more of an escape. A way to step outside the constant emotional drama that my mother thrived on. Once I'd sold, it became a badge, in a way. You know, that I was… well, special."

Nick winced. What a pansy-assed thing to say. He waited for Delaney's laugh, but it didn't come. Instead she curved her fingers through his and lifted his hand to her mouth. A soft kiss over his knuckles and his insides melted.

"I'm so glad you found that affirmation," she told him. Her eyes made it clear she hadn't. "You're incredibly gifted and deserve to know it."

He wanted to tell her she was gifted and special, too. To show her how incredible he thought she was. Nick had no idea how to deal with the emotions slamming through him, demanding he share. They scared the shit out of him. It was all he could do not to get up and run.

"Did you want to write?" he asked, changing the subject in typical fashion.

"Definitely not. I'm a reader," she said, her tone adamant. "I admire, even revere the written word and am blown away by the creativity it takes to bring a story from imagination to paper. But my father views commercial fiction as the equivalent of crack for the brain."

"He must be ecstatic that you review it for a living then," Nick laughed.

The look on her face, guilt mixed with stubborn rebellion, assured him her father didn't have a clue. Nick laughed again. Good for her. Her moxie was part of what made her so fascinating.

"Just like I don't write my reviews looking for approval, I don't pick my reading material based on what he, or anyone else, thinks is appropriate. I'm just as likely to read Nick Angel erotic suspense as I am Homer, Jane Austen or J. K. Rowling."

"I'm honored you'd even categorize me with those authors," he said truthfully. The image of one of his books stacked on the bookstore checkout counter with their works was humbling.

"Well," she said with brutal honestly, "I wouldn't say you're at the same level that they are. After all, their works all focus on that one thing you're so determined to avoid."

"Emotion," they said together.

She giggled, the sadness gone from her eyes. Relief surged through Nick.

"Your stories provide an escape," she assured him. "They definitely fill a niche. But—" she shrugged one silken shoulder and gave him a smile that made him want to leap tall buildings and carry trains over his head "—you're so much more than that. Your talent is amazing, why wouldn't you harness it?"

"Why push for emotions, since they are such a part of the real world crap most people are looking to hide from?"

"But that's just it, I don't believe people are reading to escape emotions, they are reading to see emotions triumph. At least," she corrected, leaning forward to take a bite of his cookie, "positive emotions."

As he considered, Nick broke off another piece of the cookie and fed it to her. Her lips closed on the tip of his fingers. There was a crumb, a tiny one, in the corner of her mouth he wanted to lick away. But he wouldn't. Not because he was being some good boy following her rules. But because he figured the kids in the sandbox didn't need a graphic lesson on how to pleasure a woman. Realizing Delaney was still speaking he forced himself to listen to her words.

"Romance might focus on love, but other genres pull at emotions just as much. Read a war novel, they focus on the terrors, the triumphs. Horror focuses on fear, but the best ones use our emotions to heighten that fear, to build on it."

True. For the first time, Nick considered—really considered—her pitch to add emotion to his work. He'd always equated that to adding ketchup to a porterhouse steak. Pointless. But maybe, just maybe, there were ways to bring emotions into his writing that wouldn't be a sellout. Or pure fluff.

Not realizing she'd already made a breakthrough, Delaney reached over to tap his hip. He followed the thrust of her chin to see an elderly couple strolling along, hand in hand.

He looked back at her, sure he was focusing on the wrong thing. Nope. She was looking at the old people, a sappy look on her face.

Catching his skepticism, she rolled her eyes. "I'm not

suggesting you write octogenarian love. I'm just pointing out how enduring emotions are."

He cast another doubtful look at the white-haired couple, who were now seated on a bench a few feet away.
Gotta give the old guy credit, Nick thought as the aged
hunk leaned over and kissed his lady.

"A point for intimacy," Delaney said with a laugh.
"There's no way you can write them off to lust. I'll bet
they've kissed at least a thousand times, but he still slips
her the tongue."

Delaney snickered when he averted his eyes.

"You go to fantasy clubs and watch strangers do it
against the wall," she pointed out. "You've probably
watched more depraved acts than I can even imagine
in the name of research. Yet proof that intimacy—emotion—is enduring and sweet, and you look away?"

She gave him a long look under arched brows and
asked, "Why?"

Good question. Instead of trying to answer it, Nick
did what he did best. Took the opportunity.

Holding her gaze captive with his, he leaned closer,
until he could smell the chocolate on her breath, see
her eyes go wide. Heat, edgy and intense, flashed in
those dark depths. Her eyes flew past his shoulder and
she frowned.

"Trust me," he said as he slid his hand into her hair,
lifting her mouth to his. Teasing them both, he kept the
kiss light and easy. A soft brush of his lips over hers, the
gentlest stroke of his fingers. The taste of her tempted
him to delve deeper, to take her mouth with all the passion coursing through his body. But Nick forced himself to hold back. He only traced her lips with the tip of
his tongue instead of plunging it deep into her mouth.

He only rubbed his fingers over her silken hair instead of gripping it in his fists. It almost killed him, but he held back.

With a shuddering sigh, he pulled his mouth away and, with his forehead leaning against hers, stared into her eyes. Emotions, unfamiliar and not really welcome, wound through his system. All he wanted to do was hug her close while he tried to figure out what they meant.

She blinked, three slow flutters of those thick lashes. Then she pursed her lips.

"I'd say you have a pretty solid handle on passion," she said softly. "Even if you can't admit it yet, you've already proven intimacy's power over lust."

Pleasure fled as Nick's stomach knotted. Well, hell. Was she right? Nick looked into the laughing depths of Delaney's eyes. He'd have to hang out for just a little while longer and see.

DELANEY'S QUESTION POUNDED at Nick later that night as he sat down to write. He could recite, song and verse, all his reasons for avoiding that emotional claptrap in his writing.

But were they reasons, or excuses?

Did it matter? Whether he liked it or not, Delaney had pushed open a door. Now, the story that had been so solid and workable in his head was spinning in a million directions, and he knew the only way to regain control was to simply sit down and write.

As his fingers flew over the keyboard, the scene solidified in his mind. It looked like he was about to see, once and for all, if her pushing for emotions in his work would enhance his writing.

Or ruin him, once and for all.

"I THINK I'M IN TROUBLE," Delaney said as she shoved her chocolate cake around the plate with her fork.

"If you don't quit playing with that cake and eat it, the chef is probably going to come over and really show you what trouble is," Mindy warned with a gesture to the counter of the dessert-only restaurant.

Delaney looked over and caught the glower on the owner's face. Oops. She gave a wave with her fork and scooped up a mouthful of the decadently rich dessert. But halfway to her mouth, she sighed and set it back on her plate.

"So Nick's hot and sweet and beyond sexy in bed," Mindy said impatiently. "These aren't evil traits to have in a guy."

"They may as well be," Delaney said. She stared at the swirls and lines she'd made in her mushed-up cake, then met Mindy's gaze. "I think I'm falling for him."

"Shit."

"Eloquently put," Delaney said.

"But that's crazy."

"Hence the trouble I spoke of."

Mindy grimaced. Unlike Delaney, she dealt with worries in the time-honored way—she ate the chocolate. In big, contemplative bites. Delaney knew well enough to let her finish her mousse-filled éclair without interrupting. She went back to making food art out of her cake while she waited.

"Okay, maybe it's just great sex," Mindy said around her last bite.

"Better than great, but that's not it."

Mindy shook her head and, shoving her so-clean-she-could-have-licked-it plate aside, leaned her elbows on the table. "No, you've never had 'Oh, my god' sex before. It messes with your brain. Gets you thinking crazy, wishing on rainbows and crap."

Delaney paused in the act of forming her frosting into a flower to gape at her friend. "Rainbows and crap?"

"You know what I mean. Great sex, the kind that keeps you awake at night remembering how it felt, reliving it, that's the stuff that makes you think of happily-ever-after."

"Or maybe just about doing it again with upgrades."

"You could have upgraded that sex?" Mindy's mouth formed an O, her blue eyes bright and glittery with shock. "But… But, you said he was incredible. How do you upgrade that?"

"I meant upgrades on my part," Delaney admitted. "You know, toys, accessories, kinky fetish things."

Mindy's mouth opened and closed a couple of times, but nothing but squeaks came out. It amused Delaney enough to finally scoop up a bite of fudge frosting.

"Well, then," Mindy finally said. She puffed out a breath, then shrugged. "If that's what you want, what's keeping you from it? The bet?"

"I don't know. Maybe at first, the bet was to prove my point. Now, my career depends on it." With a curl of her lip, Delaney gave the frosting a vicious jab with her fork.

"Not that bet. The private one. Are you worried you'll lose that bet if you give in and have sex with him again?"

Was she? Lust versus intimacy. The line, once so clearly defined in her head, had blurred to become indistinguishable. Was she making her point by abstaining, as she'd intended? Or was it simply driving them both crazy?

"We'll do it again," she defended. "I mean, when I insisted we hold off and do the dating thing, that was to build up my point, you know? To prove that connecting, getting to know each other, would add an emotional element to the sexual encounter. I didn't realize it would be this hard to go without, though."

Since Mindy was currently going without herself, she just rolled her eyes. "How do you know who wins?"

Before Delaney could come up with an answer, the bakery owner swiped her plate away with a growl. Oops. She made a face at Mindy, who was trying to hold back a laugh.

"I don't know," Delaney finally said. She propped her elbows on the table, cradled her chin and considered the idea of losing. "I think it's going to be a hard call. The more I think about it, the less I think it's possible for there to be a clear winner."

"So why aren't you doing it like bunnies?" Mindy asked, throwing her hands up in exasperation.

Delaney licked her lips, dropped her gaze to the table, then met Mindy's eyes.

"I'm not afraid of losing the bet," she said slowly, "so much as I'm afraid of Nick seeing the real me. Without this makeover, this mask, he'd have no interest in me at all."

Mindy gave her that "what an idiot" look but Delaney just shook her head. "Seriously, would he have had any interest in me, in our side bet, if not for the makeover?"

"You can't ask that," Mindy insisted. "That's like asking which came first, the chicken or the egg."

"Huh?"

"Nick met you, hit on you, because he was attracted to you, right?" Delaney nodded, but before she could say anything, Mindy plowed ahead.

"He came on the show specifically to meet you, because of your review of his books, right?" Delaney nodded again, opening her mouth to clarify the point, but Mindy shook her head.

"You gave the review as a part of your makeover interview, just like you were on the TV show because of the makeover."

Delaney didn't even bother trying to say anything this time, just nodded.

"You did the makeover because you wanted your rightful share of attention, so you could get a job you deserve, right?"

Delaney just raised her brows, her head starting to hurt.

"And your job is something you love, right? You're a great teacher, you rock the lit courses. So, really," Mindy summed up, out of breath from talking so fast, "Nick has the hots for you because of who you are, not the color of your eye shadow."

Delaney counted to ten. Then, her head still spinning, she counted to twenty. Finally she shook her head.

"You might want to consider retaking that course in logical thinking and the development of the rational argument. I think you lost me in the first round."

"You just don't want to admit I'm right," Mindy said, undaunted.

"I couldn't even if I wanted to. I still don't understand your point."

The blonde heaved a long-suffering sigh. "My point is, you are who you are. Everything that brought you to this point, to this table having this argument with me, is all a part of the whole. It's the whole Nick's attracted to. Not just the packaging."

Delaney heard the words, but they were just meaningless sounds. She'd spent twenty-seven years feeling invisible. Being overlooked. Even her own father felt she was too insignificant to pay attention to.

Her current run of popularity, of attention, all stemmed from the makeover. Sure, she was smart enough to realize no amount of makeup or hair products, or even an awesome push-up bra, could transform her into a confident, strong woman. But... well...they did.

"Delaney?"

"I know what you're saying."

"But you don't believe me?" Mindy shook her head, confusion creasing her face. "How can a woman as intelligent as you think that a person's worth is really based on their physical appearance?"

"I don't question my worth," Delaney defended. "But you can't dismiss the results of the makeover, which *you* suggested. It's directly responsible for every change happening in my life right now."

"Do you think so little of him," Mindy challenged, "or just of yourself?"

"Neither, of course." Delaney had taken too many psych courses to be trapped that easily.

"Why not just let him see the real you, then? You're the same person with or without makeup, in that hideous tweed suit or in classy linen."

And take a chance at ruining their final round of hot, wild, prove-her-point sex? Hell, no.

"I think this is what the true basis of our bet comes down to," Delaney said instead. "Lust is based on the surface, on flaring attraction and quick burning desire. Intimacy is more, it's all that stuff you said. It's bedhead and morning breath. It's that flame that burns long and slow, that lasts past the initial flash of physical attraction. It's emotions." Delaney gave her a sad smile and shrugged. "The thing is, Nick doesn't believe in any of that."

With good reason, considering his upbringing. And as soon as she went back to being her real self and Nick found out she was a fake, he'd be gone.

So, despite the sexual frustration keeping her awake at night, it was just as well they would only sleep together one more time, in the name of proving her point, and then she'd go back to her real world and he'd continue with his.

She was sure that as great as the emotionally connected sex was going to be, she'd give anything for the lust-driven, do-it-just-for-fun encounter. After all, the next one was going to rip her heart to shreds.

CHAPTER TWELVE

"WAY TO GO," Sean hooted when Delaney left the stage. "Your last review is kicking butt."

"Yeah?"

Relief battled with surprise as Delaney scanned the printout he handed her. The online poll was definitely in her favor.

"The producer wants to bring Angel back next week," Sean told her. "He's thinking of doing a drawing at the end of this last segment of voting, picking two or three people who post on the blog to come be guests. You and Nick can do the whole debate thing again, we'll get some reader opinions, wind up the bet and declare you the winner. You really should reconsider taking the producer's offer, Delaney. The segment is growing, viewers love it. Last I heard, they were willing to go to three shows a week."

It scared her how tempted she was. Delaney had come to love her "Critic's Corner" segment. With only fifteen minutes of actual on-air time, the work she put into the reviews, the author interviews and reader interaction, it was so rewarding. It was like being a little kid in a toy store being told she could play with anything she wanted. Except, she had to keep reminding herself, she was a toy analyst, a teacher of the craft. Not a kid. She sighed and focused on the rest of Sean's news instead.

"Nick's agreed to reappear?"

"Not sure. I think that's something they were hoping you could nail down. Apparently he's not returning calls. His agent said he's busy writing."

Writing? She knew he'd be busy, he'd told her he'd be tied up for a week or so, which was why she hadn't thought twice about not hearing from him. But he was writing? Delaney's breath caught. What was he working on? He'd said she'd made him think. Had she really made a difference?

One more week and her bet with Nick would be over. And the side bet? They'd settle that, too. He'd sent her a note telling her to keep Saturday night open. She knew how the evening would end.

End being the operative word. As in the end of her and Nick. How did women do it? Go into a relationship knowing it had a limited shelf life?

"Delaney? Is this a bad time?"

She and Sean turned to see Mindy. Obviously liking what he saw, Sean puffed out his chest and introduced himself.

"Nice entrance," she told Mindy after they left the drooling host. "You know he's going to want to ask you out, right?"

"Ya think?" Mindy asked, glancing over her shoulder. "Guess the new dress paid off."

They laughed and made their way to Delaney's dressing room. Delaney's mouth dropped as they stepped through the door. There, on the table, was a huge bouquet of red roses. With a soft *oooh* of delight she fingered the lush, velvet blooms. They hadn't been there before. She spied the card tucked between the blooms and tugged it out.

You might have had a point…
Nick

A point about what? With a frown, Delaney turned the card over, but the back was blank.

A point about her reviewing ability?

A point about emotions?

"Well?" Mindy asked, poking an impatient elbow in Delaney's side. "Who are they from?"

She snagged the card from Delaney's fingers and frowned. "What's the point?"

"No clue," Delaney admitted as she looked at the roses, her smile so big it hurt her cheeks. A giggle escaped as she gave them a careful hug. Holding the card to her chest, she danced around the tiny room, laughing out loud.

Mindy gave her a baffled look of inquiry.

"I've never gotten roses before. Ever," Delaney explained as she looked at the card again. "Nobody's ever sent me flowers of any kind, let alone—" she counted "—three dozen gorgeous red roses."

"Since your hands are full, I guess this is the perfect time to say I told you so," Mindy announced smugly as she dropped into a chair.

Delaney just shrugged. She felt too good to argue, especially when her side of the debate depressed the hell out of her.

"A guy doesn't send roses for lust," Mindy pointed out. "Maybe you need to give yourself a little credit, Delaney. Look around, acknowledge where you're at and what you've accomplished."

After carefully setting the vase of roses back on the

table, Delaney took the seat opposite Mindy and sucked in a deep breath.

Once, she'd have laughed at anyone suggesting she'd be in a place like this. On TV, publicly acclaimed for her brains and still commanding attention. Being sent a dozen roses from a sexy man who was not only interested in getting in her pants, but also respected her brain.

Her. Dean Conner's mouse of a daughter.

Maybe Mindy was right? Maybe it was all a part of the whole. And, dammit, maybe Nick's attraction to her, his interest in her, was more than just a surface thing?

She hoped it was. She was so crazy about the guy, it was making her stupid.

"Well?"

"Maybe," Delaney hedged.

"What do you want? Really, really want?"

She wanted it all, Delaney confessed to herself. She met Mindy's gaze, almost scared to say it aloud, to make it real. As if doing so would take away this last month, make it all as ephemeral as a dream.

"Fine," Delaney admitted aloud, "I want it all. I want Nick, I want that promotion."

She wished she could keep the TV show. But she didn't say it aloud. Like having Nick, it was an impossible dream. Or at least improbable.

"Then get them."

Delaney bit back a hysterical laugh. What were the chances? Was there any way she could get Nick? Not just keep his attention for another week or so while they wound up the bets, but really get him. Like, for good? She'd be gambling everything if she tried. Because losing meant not just having her confidence stomped to hell, but her heart as well.

But some things, some people, were worth risking it all for.

"How?" she asked quietly.

"For a start, quit worrying about what's you and what's due to the makeover. Just be yourself. Spend time with the guy. And," Mindy said, nibbling on her thumbnail, "maybe you might wear tweed on your next date."

Delaney snickered, even though she knew Mindy was serious.

She definitely wanted Nick. And she'd have to share, eventually, her real job with him. But there was no way the man had to know she was a tweed-wearing geek inside. No, she'd keep that part of her locked away, hidden. Because no matter what Mindy said, Delaney was sure Nick would run, screaming, if he ever saw the real her.

NICK FROWNED, HIS gaze blurring as he pictured the scene in his head. It, unlike the screen in front of his face, was crystal clear.

What next? Did the guy take the emotional risk and lay it all on the line or did he keep doing what Nick's heroes always did, and kill the bad guy?

Like he'd done each time he'd found himself at a crossroads this week, Nick pictured Delaney's face and asked himself what she'd do.

Then he blinked a couple times, bent his head and dove back into typing, letting his vision coalesce into words on the screen.

WITH A GROWL of frustration, Delaney tossed the book against the wall and jumped out of her chair to pace the office. She was due to interview an author by phone for the next "Critic's Corner" segment and she hated the book. A thriller, it totally wasn't working for her. It should. The emotions were plentiful. So plentiful they were exhausting, actually. The protagonist swerved from emotional high to devastating low with enough speed to leave the reader worn out.

After reading three-fourths of the book she was totally sick of the emotions. Where was the action, the movement, the excitement? Just do something, for crying out loud, without the wallowing and introspection.

Was this how Nick saw emotion in writing? In life? When there were so many emotions assailing the reader, they simply shut down in self-defense. Had he done the same?

For a woman who'd always searched for feeling in stories, it was a slap upside the head to realize sometimes what made a story work for her could be just the opposite. Had she ever noticed that before?

Or, she wondered with a sigh as she dropped back into her chair, was Nick teaching her a whole new way to look at books, and at life?

NICK READ OVER his last scene and winced. Not because it was pure crap. That would be okay. He could fix crap. But this…it made him feel naked. For a guy who had never hesitated to strip physically bare, it was a bizarre feeling.

Nick shoved away from his desk, needing to stretch and move. He needed a distraction. Sex came to mind, which automatically brought Delaney into his thoughts. Not that she was ever far. He felt as if this story had been written with her sitting on his shoulder, tut-tutting any time he skittered away from that deep well of emotions she wanted him to tap into so badly.

The stiffness of his body made him look at the clock. It was midnight? So much for sex. Just as well, he needed a shower and sleep.

He glanced at the glowing monitor, the story screaming for him to return. He'd settle for splashing cold water on his face and a ham sandwich.

DELANEY GLARED AT the dreck she'd written. She had to nail her review and interview questions, and this wishy-washy noncommittal garbage wasn't going to do it. With a frustrated sigh, she hit the delete key.

Distraction. Maybe if she focused on something else for a while, she'd figure out a way to put her chaotic reaction to the book into words. She pulled up the college Web course and logged in. Might as well grade papers.

A half hour into reading first-year essays on the themes characteristic to Hemingway's books, an inter-college e-mail popped up.

Delaney clicked to open it, then groaned. Nothing like pressure.

To: Professor D. M. Conner
From: Professor Ekco
FYI: The hiring committee is meeting a week earlier than planned. As promised, I'll back your application as long as you've accomplished the goals as outlined. 1) Proven your reviews a success via the television show and online poll. 2) Secured an agreement from Nick Angel to speak at Rosewood College as a part of your proposed course study of modern literature. I wish you the best, as I see a great benefit to us all in this new endeavor.

Secure Nick? That wasn't part of the deal. Sure, she hadn't said no when Ekco had suggested it, but only because she'd been in shock over the rest of the conversation. His assumption was typical, though, and not, she knew, anything he could hold her to.

Shit. She pulled up www.wakeupca.com and clicked on the poll. Yes, she was winning, but her lousy second review had definitely made it a close contest.

Her gaze landed on the e-mail again and she sighed. She didn't have time for this. She had priorities and right now making her last few segments of "Critic's Corner" rock was top of the list. She needed to nail this interview, her viewers were counting on her for an insightful, focused look at the author and his books.

She wanted to call Nick. To discuss the story with him, to hear his ideas. To hear his voice. And, maybe, if she were lucky, they could even play a few phone sex games. But he wasn't available. She'd left him enough unreturned messages that she was starting to feel a little desperate and needy. She'd reached the point, she knew, of saying screw the bet, she didn't care about proving anything. She just wanted to be with him. In every way possible.

But first she had to write this review. Because her current methods weren't working and because so much was at risk, she was going to have to pull out the big guns.

The old Delaney. Geeky, plain and awkward, but hell-on-wheels at analytical reading.

She headed for the bathroom to scrub her face clean and tried to remember if her baggy-assed, threadbare red sweats were dirty or not. Time to let Dr. Conner back out one last time, since afterward Delaney planned to shove her in the back of a closet and hide her away forever. After all, she smiled as she scraped her hair into a knot and secured it with her pencil, she'd decided to keep Nick Angel.

NICK RUBBED THE grit from his eyes, then stretched his arms overhead. His back gave a satisfactory series of cracks, loosening the stiffness.

Done. He'd finished it. Oh, he knew it was only a first draft, written in a week of around-the-clock obsessiveness. It'd take him another two months to flesh it out, to add layers and details.

But the skeleton was there. And it was solid. At least, he thought it was.

Exhaustion wrapped around him, dragging at his body. But his mind spun in a million directions. He needed sleep. He needed decent food. More, he really needed a shower.

But all he wanted was Delaney. To see her, to touch her. He'd kill to taste her. But most of all, he wanted her to read his work. To tell him if he'd hit that emotional bar she'd set. To see if she was right.

With a glance at the clock, he calculated how long it'd take him to clean up and get over to her place. Was ten too late to drop in?

He considered, then hit the print button before shuffling to the shower. The promise of seeing Delaney wiped away the last of his fatigue.

He couldn't wait.

HIS TEETH NIPPED at her thighs, making her writhe in desperate need. The chains on her wrists bit at her flesh, reminding her she was his prisoner. His sex slave.

With a frown, Delaney pulled herself from the story

to figure out what had caught her attention. It took her a few seconds to separate the random pounding from the beat of the Aerosmith tune cranking from her stereo.

Her brain still enmeshed in the sex slave scene from one of Nick's earlier books, it took her another ten seconds to realize the pounding was at her front door. Company? She glanced at the clock radio on her bedside table and frowned. After ten at night? Mrs. Johnson down the hall must have had an emergency.

She threw off the covers and nudged her glasses back up the bridge of her nose. Hurrying to the door, she caught her reflection in the mirror and winced. Part of her hair was knotted around the pencil at the top of her head, the rest frizzed around her face. A face that, thanks to her moisturizer, glistened so her freckles reflected the overhead light. Baggy sweats and a ratty T-shirt completed her look.

Oh, well, her elderly neighbor wouldn't care. Leaving the security chain on just in case, Delaney tugged open the door.

Shit.

She stared in horror at the man on her doorstep. It was all she could do not to slam the door in his face.

"Nick?" Her vision swirled in a black mist of panic.

"You gonna let me in?"

Did she have to? Could she ask him to come back in ten minutes? Five, if she just did her makeup and stripped naked instead of finding decent clothes.

"Delaney?" he asked, his blue gaze sparkling with laughter. "Did I wake you up?"

"No, I was…" Getting hot and horny reading his book? Rather than sharing that little tidbit, she closed her eyes and tried to find a way out. Nothing. With a sigh, she closed the door, slid off the security chain and reopened it to let him in.

Fear, fast and furious, sped through her system. Her fingers gripped tight the nubby fabric of her sweats as she chewed the corner of her mouth.

She didn't want him to see her like this. Ever. She'd even made a list of kicky casual clothes and lingerie to buy if they ended up staying together and sketched out a plan on how to always be made-up and stylish.

"What're you doing here?" She could hear the horror in her tone, but he apparently couldn't since he just shrugged and gave her a quick peck on her cheek before crossing the threshold to pace her living room.

He shot a quick glance toward her, but then looked away so fast Delaney couldn't read his eyes. She clenched her teeth, rubbing a finger over the threads hanging off her T-shirt. Oh, my god, she must look worse than she'd imagined. Feeling raw and exposed, she took a couple deep breaths while she waited for him to explain why he was there.

But he just paced in silence.

"Um, can you give me a second?" she asked, eyeing the bedroom. Was it possible to save this situation? So much for her "ease him into seeing the real her and see if he was still interested" plan.

"I need your help," he said instead of answering her. His tone was edgy and just a little desperate.

"Okay," she agreed immediately. She didn't feel any less naked, but she couldn't turn him away. "What can I do?"

"I…" He looked around, then looked at the thick sheaf of papers held together with a rubber band in his hand. He held it out to her with a look so vulnerable Delaney's heart tripped. "Can you read this? I need to know what you think."

"Of course." Self-conscious paranoia forgotten, Delaney hurried forward to take the papers. Unable to help herself, she gave him a hug.

As her arms closed around him, Nick groaned and pulled her tight against him. Eyes shut, he pressed his mouth over hers in a rough, desperate kiss. Needy and wild, it sent tremors through her body as Delaney's tongue met his. His fingers unerringly found her beaded nipple beneath the threadbare fabric of her T-shirt. Delaney groaned and pressed closer.

More. She wanted more. Then Nick pulled away and, giving her one quick look, grimaced and shook his head.

"No. I need you to read that for me, okay?"

The worry in his expression told her not to take the rejection personally. He obviously had something major eating at him.

"Go ahead and sit down," she told him. "I'll just, um…do you want a drink or something?"

"I need you to read it like you would for work," Nick told her. She frowned at the implacability in his tone.

"What do you mean?"

"Not as my lover, but as a reviewer."

Damp heat flared deep in her belly at his reference to her as his lover. Her gaze flickered to the couch where he'd given her that first orgasm.

Maybe if she read fast, she could have another one tonight?

"My office?"

"Perfect."

DAMN. NICK FOLLOWED Delaney down the hall toward her office. When they passed the open door of her bedroom, he was tempted to grab her and haul her in for a quick, sweaty tussle on the messy bed. The tangled blankets and strewn pillows made him grin. Good to know she wasn't totally tidy, he'd been starting to get paranoid.

The sweet sway of her hips, barely discernable beneath the red, draping fabric of her sweatpants, distracted him. Usually when he finished a draft, he needed a physical outlet for all the pent-up energy he'd shoved to the side during his mental journey. In other words, sex.

Now was no different.

Except, for the first time he wanted something more. He wanted Delaney's approval.

He'd faced editors, his agent, hell, even the roughest reviewers with fewer nerves than he currently had battling in his gut.

"Can I get you anything?" she asked as they entered her office. "A drink, a snack?"

He almost asked for a Scotch on the rocks, but shook his head. Numbing his brain wouldn't make this any easier. Her frown, so pretty and confused, made him smile a little. He knew he was being all secretive and pushy, but he had no words to tell her how important this was to him. How much it meant to know what she thought. Of his words, his writing. His emotions.

"Can you just, you know—" he waved his hand toward the manuscript "—read it for me. Now, please."

"Of course. Do you want an opinion, or an actual critique?"

"What do you usually do when you analyze?"

"I make notes."

"Notes, then," he said with a nod.

Delaney gave him a long look, then nodded and settled into a chair. A part of his mind noted how the rich red fabric suited her, both strong and intense. Another part noted how young and sweet she looked without makeup. Her hair, all wild and unruly, made him thing of long, sexy nights rubbing over the sheets. He let that image entertain him for a minute.

Then she pulled a notepad and pen over from the small table next to her and started writing.

Nick's stomach clenched.

"That's the first draft, just so you know," he defended.

She didn't even glance at him. Just nodded and kept making notes.

Five minutes passed. Then ten. Nick paced. He couldn't even focus long enough to look at the titles of the books crowded in the bookcase except to note that most of his seemed to be there.

He tried to distract himself by looking around her office. Sensual and efficient, he decided. Sexy lines, enticing textures, clean surfaces. All typical of Delaney.

He shoved a hand through his hair and reconsidered her offer of a drink. Except for all the attention she was giving him, he doubted she'd offer again.

Nick's gaze lit on her laptop. Opened, the monitor was black. But he could tell it was booted up from the standby light.

"Do you mind if I go online, check my e-mail?" he asked her. "I've been buried the last week and haven't bothered."

She didn't even look up. Just waved her agreement and kept making those damned notes. Nick bit back the panic.

Familiar with her model, he pushed the silver standby button and waited for the monitor to power up.

She was already online. He reached for the mouse

to open a new browser, but before he could click, the e-mail on the screen caught his eye.

Professor?

Nick frowned, but kept reading.

Damn it all to hell. Betrayal slammed into him like a two-ton truck, stealing his breath. Black spots flashed in his vision, edged with a furious red.

She'd used him? Echoes of his ex-wife's and mother's half truths and lies whispered through his head. She'd straight up used him. And he'd let her. Hell, he'd made it easy for her.

She didn't want him. She'd only wanted to use his career. It was all for a promotion in a job he, who had opened his soul to her by handing her his raw, emotional manuscript, hadn't even realized she had.

Nick's gut clenched, his jaw throbbing with the need to rage. It was all he could do not to toss the computer across the room.

She didn't care about him. He was nothing to her except a means to an end.

Nick stood so fast, the sleek office chair flew back to slam into the wall.

Delaney's startled gaze flew to his.

"You okay?" she asked. Despite her furrowed brow, her tone made it clear she was only half-focused on him. The rest of her was focused on her freaking winning manuscript.

Hell, no, he wasn't okay. But he'd be damned if he'd give her the satisfaction of letting her know.

Which meant he had to get the hell out of here. Now.

"I've gotta go," he said, heading for the door.

"What's the matter?" She sprang to her feet, the pad and pen falling to the floor. The pages she'd already read followed, fluttering like confetti. Color swept her cheeks, as if she were embarrassed. How could she be, though? Anyone who could lie so coolly to his face would hardly be self-conscious of being a klutz.

"I've got to go," he repeated, ignoring her question. "I'll be back tomorrow night to pick you up for the ball."

"Ball?" Delaney asked, confusion clear on her face. Her gaze bounced between him and the manuscript pages still gripped in her hand, as if she didn't know which to focus on. "Wait, you're leaving? Don't you want to hear what I think of the story?"

"I got tickets to an erotic ball," Nick snapped, ignoring her question just as he ignored the manuscript she held out. Like he wanted it now? She'd just proven to him it was all crap. "I'll pick you up at seven. Don't forget to bring a mask."

CHAPTER THIRTEEN

"I TOLD YOU. Didn't I tell you he'd freak when he saw the real me?" Delaney ranted as she paced Mindy's office at eight the next morning.

She hadn't been able to wait for her friend to meet her for lunch, and this certainly wasn't a phone-call type of discussion. No, ranting of this level required in person, face-to-face time.

So she'd washed away the tears, only bothering to swipe on mascara and pull her hair back in a leather band. The jeans were pure defiance, since she'd known she was coming to her father's office.

"Maybe it was something else," Mindy said around her thumbnail. The poor blonde had been trying to eat her bagel when Delaney had stormed in. Chewing her nails was a poor nutritional substitute. "Maybe he was nervous about you making notes on his work? Maybe he thought you'd just, you know, read it and give him pats on the head or something."

"Maybe he was struck speechless at the sight of my baggy red sweats and oily face."

Mindy's eye roll forced Delaney to slow down, to push past the hurt and think.

"Maybe it's because my reviews are winning and he's pissed. I mean, he publicly stated if I won, he'd have to add emotions to his stories." Even as she said it aloud, she knew it couldn't be that. She'd read Nick's manuscript after he'd left—three times—hoping to lose herself in the story and forget her hurt over his abrupt departure.

He'd called it a rough draft. She called it pure brilliance. Emotions had poured from the pages, it had sung with a perfect blend of action and intensity.

"No," she murmured. "It has nothing to do with the bet. This has to be me."

"Oh, my god, you have to stop it," Mindy screeched, slapping her hands on her desk. "Seriously, why do you do this to yourself?"

Shocked, Delaney stopped pacing to stare at her friend.

"You're so paranoid about this mask, this fake you, that you won't accept that it's all just you. Professor Delaney Conner, sexy TV literary critic." Mindy's angry words hit at Delaney like blows. "You're not this phony with a half-dozen compartmentalized personas. You're a smart woman who finally let herself use the tools, the advantages, most other women use. Makeup, hair products, decent-fitting clothes."

"I'm not paranoid—" Delaney started to say, but Mindy interrupted her.

"Bullshit. You think that just because Nick saw you without makeup on, he's going to be all grossed out and run away? It doesn't work that way, Delaney. If he ran, it was because of something else. I'm sorry, but it was." Mindy's voice was softer now, almost consoling. "You're giving too much credit to that makeover. All it did was give you a few tools. It didn't change who you are."

"If not for that makeover, Nick Angel would never have noticed me. Never have pursued me, never have slept with me." Never have made her fall in love with him.

"Nick didn't see you before he came on that TV show, Delaney. He responded to your review. To your critique of his writing."

"He flirted, he teased and challenged me. He made those bets. He wouldn't have done that if not for the makeover," Delaney argued, using her worst fears to make her point.

"He wouldn't have had the opportunity if not for the makeover," Mindy agreed. "The makeover gave you the confidence to take that TV gig, to debate with him and to stand your ground when faced with a sexy guy you'd had a fan-girl crush on for years."

"You make it sound like he'd have been just as drawn to me if he'd met the frumpy me in tweed." Delaney rolled her eyes at the concept. Yeah, right. Nick Angel, the hottest, sexiest man on earth, attracted to the hideous mess she'd been.

"You're right. He wouldn't have looked twice at you in your frumpy persona." Mindy's easy agreement surprised Delaney, given the direction she'd thought the argument was going. Wasn't this supposed to be a build-her-back-up talk? "But only because you didn't deem yourself worthy of being looked at."

"Huh?" Delaney crossed her arms over her chest, tapping her foot in agitation.

"Delaney, you hid behind your tweed. You excelled in academics because it was expected of you, but that's it. Anything else would have been a risk."

The blonde lifted her finger to her mouth, then dropped it to her lap. She gave Delaney a commiserating look and shrugged. "Maybe it's easier to let yourself be invisible than it is to take a chance at being, well… rejected?"

Her immediate inclination was to sneer and suggest Mindy bone up on her psych classes. Next she'd be diagnosing an Oedipal complex and recommend Delaney reconnect with her inner child.

But she couldn't get the words out through the tightness in her chest. Tears—apparently she still had a few—filled her eyes.

Before she had to come up with a response, the dean strode into the office. She'd never been so grateful to see her father. Delaney opened her mouth to greet him, but he just gave her an absent nod and continued past her to his office.

Invisible, yet again.

"No," she said aloud. She looked at Mindy, who had a "well, what're you waiting for" look on her face. What *was* she waiting for? A miracle?

"Hold any calls," she told the blonde as she followed her father into his hallowed sanctum.

"Do you have a minute?" she asked out of habit when she entered his office.

The dean's startled look quickly changed to impatience. "Delaney? What are you doing here? Is there a problem?"

His tone made it clear if there was, he'd prefer she deal with it herself. Well, fine. She was dealing. Even though the well-trained part of her wanted to pacify her father, since that was the only way she ever earned his approval, the newly empowered part of her refused to back down.

"I need to talk to you," she told him.

"Did you check with my assistant about an appointment?"

"I'm here to talk to you *now*," she corrected carefully.

His sigh was heavy and loaded. Rather than her usual guilt at the sound, she only felt irritation. He was her father, dammit. But more, he was her boss and as a valued employee, she deserved respect.

With a lift of her chin, Delaney sat in the chair opposite her father, crossing one leg over the other. His disapproving look at her jeans didn't even faze her.

"Very well," he agreed. "What can I do for you?"

"I'm here to let you know I'll be coming before the hiring committee this week, and I intend to get the position."

Surprise apparently struck him dumb, since he just stared for ten entire seconds. Had she never stood up to him before? Delaney was ashamed to realize perhaps she hadn't.

"I've already made my recommendation," he finally said.

"And it's not me."

"I recommended the person I felt would best serve the college," he hedged.

Because he didn't believe in her? Delaney shook her head, her negative self-talk hitting her square in the face. This was exactly what Mindy was talking about. Usually, when her opinion or qualifications were questioned, Delaney stepped up to the plate and gladly proved her worth. But when her emotions were involved, like they were with her father or Nick, the smallest setback and she assumed she was lacking. Or, if she didn't quite measure up, she wrote off the situation, and herself, as a wash. After all, she realized, it was easier to reject herself before someone else did it.

But not this time. Mindy's words ringing in her head, Delaney nixed her habit of automatic self-rejection and stood her ground. If there was a buzzing in her head and her mouth was desert-dry, well, only she had to know that.

"I'd like you to reconsider," she said, her words soft but determined. "I've not only added to my resume, but I've acquired a number of skills that will serve me well in this position."

If she'd thought him surprised before, this bold assertion sent her father into total shock. Brown eyes, so like her own, stared. Then he shook his head and gave his patented sigh. "Delaney, you're simply not ready for the position. Experience aside, there is a level of confidence I feel is required to run the department. Age, authority and self-assurance are all working against you."

"But—"

"Present your application this week, let the committee decide."

She ground her teeth. Without her father's backing, she was left with only the bet on her side. And, as much as she wanted the promotion, she wanted it based on her qualifications. Not because of Nick's silly publicity stunt and her opinions on a few books.

"Is there any point in showing up to the committee meeting if you've already made up your mind?" she asked, falling back on her old pattern of not chasing anything she might fail.

"Perhaps your asking that question is something you should examine," he said slowly, his words obviously chosen with care. It reminded Delaney of her childhood, of his habit of teaching by asking questions in a way that forced her to look deeper for an answer. "That you'd ask it reflects the exact reasons I didn't recommend you for the position."

With that and a long, searching look, he ended their conversation. "I've got a meeting in a few minutes. Perhaps we can discuss this later?"

Delaney pressed her shaky lips together and nodded. Mulling over his words, she slowly made her way out of the office and back to the reception area.

"How'd it go?" Mindy asked, obviously trying not to cringe.

"He's already committed to back the other applicant, so nothing really changed." Mindy's face fell. Delaney shrugged as if it didn't rip her up that her father didn't have faith in her. "He said the same thing you did, in different words."

Mindy waited, giving Delaney time to shove back the tears so she could talk. "He doesn't feel that I've got enough faith in myself to be assistant head. He wants someone with a more authoritative persona for the position."

"I didn't mean to hurt your feelings," Mindy said softly. "I'm sorry for what I said before, okay?"

"You mean that thing about rejection?"

Mindy nodded.

"Don't be sorry. While talking with my father I realized you were right. This makeover pushed me outside my comfort zone, forced me to work through some confidence issues." With a grimace, Delaney dropped into the chair opposite Mindy. "But it's more than just prettying up the package. I have to believe in it, too."

Mindy reached into her desk, and with a furtive look toward the dean's door, pulled out a bag of chocolate-walnut fudge. She plopped it in the middle of the desk. Both women stared at it for ten seconds. Delaney debated the severity of this discovery, then with a sigh, pulled out three pieces.

"Can you believe in it?" Mindy asked as she unwrapped her piece.

"The thing is, I think I already do," Delaney answered around a mouthful of chocolaty heaven. "I can see my father's point. I'll find a way to correct the issues."

"Are you still applying for the position?"

A part of her wanted to scream no. Who in their right mind would when they knew they didn't have a chance? But when did she stop playing it safe? Now, apparently.

"I have to," Delaney realized. "Even if I know they don't think I'm ready for it, I have to give it a shot. I've always gone for the sure things. The ones I knew I'd get. It's like you said, I have to risk rejection."

The idea scared her so much she reached for another piece of fudge. Was her shaky self-confidence strong enough to hold up? As Delaney let the chocolate melt on her tongue, she realized that, confident or not, she was ready to make a stand.

"So, the big question is," Mindy said brightly, obviously changing the subject as she rubbed chocolate smears off her fingers, "what about Nick? Now that you're ready to take risks and know it's not about you being invisible, are you going to let this pseudo-rejection keep you down?"

"Nope, screw that. I'm not invisible, and I'll be damned if he's going to get rid of me that easily." Delaney licked chocolate off her knuckle and considered. "I'm going to need something supersexy to wear, though. And a mask, I guess."

Mindy gasped. "You're actually going to go to an erotic ball."

But was there a less visible way to prove her point? None that Delaney could think of. And, besides, she wanted to win their side wager. Not out of any spirit of competitiveness, but because she knew it was her one shot at the real prize. Nick's heart.

"Damned right I am. I have a bet to win. And in the process, I'm going to show him in very graphic terms just exactly what he's walking away from. If he won't accept the real me, fine." It'd suck, she'd be emotionally devastated, but dammit, if she went down, she'd do it knowing she'd tried her best. "But he's going to know before we end this just how incredible that real me is."

EVEN FEELING EMPOWERED in her own hot, visible skin, Delaney was still grateful for Nick's hand as he led her through the crowded entrance of the Cow Palace. It was proving difficult to show him how strong she was, given that he'd barely said a word since he'd picked her up. He'd ignored her inane chatter, grunted when she'd spouted facts about the variety of erotic balls held in Northern California this time of year, and offered one-word answers to all questions. She hadn't been able to pierce the wall he'd erected, so she still didn't have a clue what had set him off the other night. But the heated, eat-her-up-in-slow-slurping-bites looks he'd been shooting her more than made up for his silence.

They climbed the stairs and Delaney goggled at the other guests. She nibbled on her bottom lip, not knowing where to look first. Or in some cases, she realized as she averted her eyes from a particularly scary, very hairy almost-naked guy, where *not* to look. Even if her NetFlix queue was nothing but porn, she'd bet she'd never see anything like *this*. Oh, man, he was pulling out all the stops to prove his side of the bet. It was a good thing she'd overcome her insecurities and inhibitions so she could prove hers.

"Oh," Delaney gasped as she entered the huge stadium. Shock hit her like a sledgehammer. It was wall-to-wall kink. Like a circus for adults. Wild, raunchy and colorful. Noise filled the hall. It took her a few minutes to sort it all out. Voices, loud and raucous. Tinned music piped in from speakers and a dull roar seemed to be coming from behind the walls.

The huge room was packed with exhibitors. Everything from sex toys to lingerie to pornographic candy was on sale. The salespeople were even more intriguing than the wares they offered. Most were in S-and-M gear or lingerie. Quite a few had opted for the paint-as-clothing option.

Delaney cursed her fair skin as, despite her attempt at nonchalance, she turned beet-red. At least most of her face was covered by the leather studded mask she'd found at a fetish shop.

"Public nudity is allowed?" she whispered, inching even closer to Nick as she gawked at the painted breasts of a very well-endowed woman leading a very well-endowed man in a leather hood around by the…leash.

"The body paint skirts the nudity laws," Nick said, grinning at the couple as they blew Delaney kisses.

"She's in amazing shape. I had no idea…" Her words trailed off as she watched the woman walk, a leather riding crop clenched between her buttocks. Apparently she didn't have pockets.

"It'll get more interesting when we get inside."

Inside? She'd planned to prove her point to Nick in graphic detail, but she was starting to think she was out of her element here. How could she argue for passion when they were surrounded by the epitome of lust? All she could do was go with her emotions. With that in mind, Delaney swallowed her nerves and squared her overly clothed shoulders.

"Let's go, then."

NICK'S ATTENTION WAS fixed on Delaney as they entered the ballroom. Despite the careful distance he'd maintained to keep his cool, he'd been unable to stop staring at her since he'd picked her up. After all, she looked like his wildest wet dream.

Black leather cupped her breasts like a lover, her halter draping low enough to make him groan. Her skirt, some silky black fabric, swished and slid over her slender hips. His fingers ached to test the contrast of textures. It was like she'd known he was done playing, so to tempt him she'd reached into his mind to find his darkest fantasy, and had turned herself into it.

Lust, he reminded himself. This was to prove lust. He'd teetered on the edge, ready to believe in her. But she was just like his ex-wife and mother. A user who played emotions like game tokens. Now all he had to do was convince himself.

Nick leaned close, his arm curving around Delaney's hip to pull her tightly against him. Her hair brushed his mouth, the silky texture a floral-scented temptation.

"This is all about lust," he said in a low tone.

She shot him a startled glance. First confusion, then determination was clear in the eyes framed by the leather mask that covered the upper half of her face. She made a sweeping scan of the room, taking in the bands on the main stage, the fashion show on another, a contest of some kind that apparently involved a variety of dildos on the third. Then her eyes met his again.

"It does promote lust," she agreed. Then she nodded to the dance floor. "But not everything here is that simple, is it? Shall we dance?"

He'd thought she didn't like dancing in public. Nick frowned, but followed her to the floor where couples and singles all gyrated in wild abandon to a heavy throbbing beat. Lights and colors flashed off nude skin, Delaney's sexy leather ensemble looked sedate next to the rest of the crowd.

"Define simple," he challenged, grabbing her hips to keep her body close to his. There was a no-groping policy at the ball, but he didn't trust the drunk in the fishnet Speedo to keep his hands off Delaney's ass. He shot the guy a keep-away-from-my-woman glare.

"Simple is lust. Less simple is everything else," Delaney shouted back. Maybe she had a point. Her grin, the wickedly seductive shimmy of her hips and the way her hands caressed over the fabric of his T-shirt were all anything but simple.

The mostly naked women all around did nothing for him, but the feel of Delaney's fingers brushing his nipples sent his dick to full alert.

A fact she was very aware of, considering it was rubbing against her as they danced. She gave him a naughty smile, her eyes going hot and intense. Then she pressed her hands down his chest, over his abs until she reached his belt. Nick caught his breath waiting to see how far she'd go.

Her fingers slipped under the waistband of his pants, using it as a handle as she tugged him closer, her heels putting her high enough for his hard-on to fit perfectly between the juncture of her legs.

Bump, grind, slide. She had the rhythm down. Nick's hands slid from her hips to curve over her butt, wanting to control her moves. But Delaney was having none of that. Instead, she scooted away. Arms overhead, she shimmied up against him, down him. Damn, the woman had incredible thigh muscles. Down him, up him, back down. Nick's brain shut off, all reasoning, all memory of why he'd been pissed fled as she worked his body. Up and down, she shimmied. In and out, his brain begged.

Just when he thought he was going to go nuts, she wrapped those arms around his neck and used her hips to keep the beat against his straining erection.

"Remember how it felt," she said, her voice husky, her words a moist caress over his ear. "Remember what it was like when we were together. The heat, the wet, wild intensity as you came inside me?"

Nick damned near came again at her words. Astonished she'd say anything so bold, he could only groan and grab her slick, satin-covered hip with one hand as he trailed the other down the low neckline of her leather halter top.

"I want to come inside you now," he told her. "I want to feel you wrap around me, your wet heat taking me in."

She gave him a slow, wicked smile and looked around the room.

"Here?"

Afraid he'd misunderstood, Nick had to close his eyes before he spun out of control.

"Are you trying to drive me crazy?" he asked, desperately afraid there was a hint of a whimper in his words. He was supposed to be the one in control here. Not her. This was about proving his point, not succumbing to the damned emotions she'd stirred up in him.

"Do you want me?" she asked, her mouth tracing hot, openmouthed kisses over his jaw and down his throat. "Do you want me like I want you?"

"How do you want me?" he asked hoarsely.

"I want you so much. I want to feel you inside me. Hard, fast, intense. I want you to lick me, taste me, drive me insane. I want you and only you, Nick."

His breath came in faster, his pulse rapid. Nick looked around, wondering where he could take her.

"But…"

His gaze flew back to hers. Brown eyes, filled with smoldering desire, questioned.

"But what?"

"But you're in a room filled with almost naked, very horny women. Wouldn't any of them do for you just as well?"

He knew it was a trap. Her smile, amused and self-deprecating, told him she knew he knew. Nick laughed and shook his head. No matter what she'd done, why she'd done it, he couldn't lie to her.

"I want you. Only you," he admitted. Forever, he realized. Even as he cursed his heart for falling, he knew it was true.

"Then come on," she said, taking his hand and hauling him off the dance floor.

It took ten minutes and a hundred-dollar tip to score a private corner behind the stage curtains. The search didn't cool his ardor, if anything it amped it up even higher. Sheltered from the band by the thick fabric, the music was muted, more a feel than a sound as it pounded through the walls.

Without waiting for Delaney to offer an opinion, Nick grabbed her hands and pressed her back against the wall.

Anchoring her there with his body, he could feel the beat as it reverberated through her.

His mouth took hers in wild abandon. She gave as good as he did, pushing for more, demanding he give her everything.

Desperate need ripped through him. Nick had to have her. Now.

Without preliminaries, he scooped up her skirt and ripped tiny lace panties away. Nick lifted a brow at her gasp, then tossed them over his shoulder.

"You won't need those," he told her. He plunged a finger into her, groaning as her damp warmth welcomed him. She was panting now, her hands kneading his shoulders.

"Tell me what you want," he rasped against her throat as he lifted one of her thighs to wrap it around his waist, giving him better access to her juicy clit. "What do you need?"

"You," she moaned. "Do me now, Nick. Please, do me now."

In a quick move, he shifted their positions so his back was to the wall. Unzipping his pants, he barely remembered to use a condom before he pulled her to him.

He lifted her, his hands on her bare ass as he positioned her over his throbbing dick. One quick thrust and she was riding him. Hands lifted, bodies strained. Quick, hot, desperate. There was nothing sweet, nothing gentle about their coming together.

It was hard and fast. He had no control, but she didn't seem to care. Her hands braced against the wall on either side of his head, she took his mouth with hers, signaling her release with tiny, panting mews.

The sound of her coming, the feel of her body spasming around him, was all it took to send Nick over the edge. His fingers digging into her butt, he ground himself against her, and his body went rigid with the power of his orgasm.

"Delaney," he yelled, his voice a guttural cry of triumph.

Her. It was all about her. He knew he'd never felt anything as intense, as incredible, as what she gave to him. Because it wasn't just a physical release. Sex didn't feel this good. It was more than that, it was the way she offered herself, the trust, the power she demanded he share.

Damn her, it was the most amazing thing he'd ever felt. And he knew he'd only feel it with her.

With a shuddering sigh he felt Delaney's leg slide down his body. Nick, barely able to catch his breath, let his head fall back against the wall behind him.

"That," Delaney said, her voice soft and husky with pleasure, "was based on intimacy. Lust would never feel that good."

Her words snapped him out of his sexual fog. The bet. While he was waxing poetic over how she made him feel, her focus was on winning the bet. He bit back a self-derisive laugh. Here he was thinking all this emotional crap, and she was still all about what she could get. Served him right. He opened his eyes and glared at her.

"Intimacy? Felt just like lust to me. *Professor*."

CHAPTER FOURTEEN

PROFESSOR?

How'd he find out? And why the hell was he so angry about it? She shifted so her skirt fell back down to cover her bare assets. Seeing the ice-cold anger on his face, she desperately wished she had her underwear back.

Suddenly the crowd, so distant moments before, seemed to be pressing in on them from beyond the stage curtain. When they'd arrived, she'd been sure of herself, ready to embrace the sensuality of the event and to show Nick the passion between them. Now she just felt confused.

"I realize it's semantics, but I didn't hide my occupation. I simply didn't share it."

"Semantics, my ass. You know everything about me. The ins and outs of my career, my family, my life. All you shared about yourself was a carefully presented sham created to snag you some promotion." He bit the words off in a low growl.

"Sham?" Delaney knew her laugh was bitter, but she didn't care. Her shock was fading, leaving behind the realization that he'd done this on purpose. He'd deliberately tried to make what they had into something ugly. Anger sputtered in the back of her head.

"I didn't seek you out, Mr. Famous Author with a point to prove. *You* came after *me*. You proposed not just the first bet, but the second as well. Don't try and claim I used you, since you're the one who walked in with the self-serving agenda."

"Oh, no," Nick said, his face a rigid mask of ice. "You're not turning this around. You're the one who pushed emotions, left and right. Harping on and on about how they make a relationship, how important they are. What a bunch of bullshit, considering the whole time you were using me. Using our bet, our relationship, to further your career. We won't even get into what you did to my writing—"

"Oh, no, you don't," she interrupted. "Whatever changes are in your writing are from discoveries you made. It has nothing to do with the fact that I teach English."

"Discoveries? You mean lies, don't you?"

The anger, flickering embers just moments before, flamed to a blaze. "Lies? You couldn't write a lie if someone held a gun to your head. You wrote that story. My review, our time together—even the sex we had, as incredibly amazing as it was—had nothing to do with what you put on those pages."

Self-righteous fury coated her words, but Nick wasn't listening. He glared and held up his hand.

"I don't want to hear another thing about my writing. Forget I mentioned it. Forget you've ever read my work. I refuse to hear another one of those cries for emotion from someone who can't even be honest about her own."

She wanted to refute his words. To throw them back in his face. But she couldn't. Because, for all that he was dead wrong about her honesty about emotions, or about his writing, he was still right. She'd hid behind the makeover, tried to manipulate the situation to keep his interest. To keep from losing him.

And now? Delaney realized trying to tell him differently was pointless. Unlike her father, who was simply unused to expressing emotions, Nick refused to open his heart. He was using her job as an excuse to destroy any possible bond between them.

She might have worn a mask, but at least she'd realized who she was under it. He couldn't let his go.

"Perhaps you're right," she conceded miserably, bending down to pick up her purse from where it'd fallen on the cement floor. "I didn't tell you about my job. Not for the reasons you think, although you probably won't believe that."

She met his eyes, her heart aching at the anger in their blue depths. "To be honest, I don't know that I'd do it differently, either. Because I was afraid. Not of your reaction to my occupation, but of your reaction to me. I was afraid you'd look right through me. That I wouldn't measure up, that I wasn't enough of a woman to hold your interest."

She was naked now. Mask off, emotions bare and wide open for his inspection. For the first time, Delaney wished for even a portion of that invisibility she'd spent her life hating. But she'd asked for this. Her stomach churned. She wanted to be seen, which meant she had to let him look. And to accept his reaction.

Except he didn't say anything. Nick just stared, stonefaced, his hands shoved in the front pockets of his jeans.

"As hard as I pushed for emotions, I was afraid to trust them," she admitted. "But I'm willing to try, now. Are you?"

His glare was answer enough.

"Too bad," she murmured, trying to keep the sound of her heart breaking from seeping into her words. "You have so much to offer, and I'd bring more to your life than you can imagine. If you get over this fear of yours, come find me." Delaney took the risk, put it all on the line, even though she knew rejection was inevitable. "I'm the best thing that could ever happen to you, Nick. And you know what? I'll bet if you gave us a chance, you'd be amazed at how awesome we are together."

"Another bet?" He gaped at her, clearly shocked. "You're shitting me. How stupid do I look?"

"From where I'm standing?" Delaney gave him a pitying look. "You really don't want to hear my answer."

His sneer slapped at her heart, but she lifted her chin anyway.

"Since I met you, I've come to realize I used to be afraid," she told him softly. "Not of sex, but of rejection. Of opening myself, my *real* self, to you and having you turn your back. But as hard as that would have been to deal with, it's even harder realizing you'd rather reject emotion for its own sake than take a chance and see what we could be to each other."

She checked her purse to make sure she had cash, then gave Nick her best TV smile. The plastic one that said she knew he didn't give a damn what she said and she didn't care.

"Well, it's been lovely, then. Thanks for the evening. I'd say I proved my point here and won our side bet, but I realize you're too much of an emotional chicken to admit it, so we can call it a draw."

She ignored his growl and turned to leave. She knew her heart was in her eyes when she looked over her shoulder, but she didn't care. If he wasn't smart enough to treasure the love in her gaze, he wasn't worth it. "I'll take a taxi home. Give me a call if you're up for *my* bet."

She swept the curtain aside, the pulsing lights momentarily blinding her. Delaney blinked and kept going. She made her way through the crush of bodies, skirting around the occasional extra-large dildo in her way, and hurried to the exit.

It took all her courage, and a constant stream of mental lecturing on her self-worth, to get Delaney out of the Cow Palace and to the taxi line. It wasn't until the cab driver gave her a questioning look that she realized her face was covered in tears.

And that she'd lost her mask somewhere inside.

TWO DAYS LATER and Nick was still reeling from the intensity of their encounter and Delaney's audacious parting shot.

He'd bounced from anger to disdain and back again so often, he felt like a Ping-Pong ball.

Emotional chicken, his ass. Just because he'd called her on her lies and refused to keep playing her game, that didn't mean he was afraid.

"Nick, what're you going to order?"

He glanced across the table at his mother, then at the waiter.

"The fried chicken," he ordered with a self-derisive sneer.

The last thing he'd wanted to do today was meet Lori for lunch. But he'd reasoned that her drama might help banish his memory of that heart-melting look in Delaney's eyes as she walked out on him.

"Nicky, you keep spacing out," Lori accused with a frown. "Are you thinking of one of your stories again?"

He shrugged and tried to focus on the woman across from him. She looked good. Hardly anyone's vision of a mother, she was slim, toned and sporting platinum curls that swept her cashmere-covered shoulders. Moneyed and pampered, she definitely didn't look old enough to have a son his age. She'd love hearing it, so he kept it to himself.

"You don't look anything like the crying mess I talked to on the phone a couple weeks ago," he said instead.

Lori gave him a dirty look. "Just because things like betrayal and an ugly divorce don't faze you doesn't mean they don't hurt real people who have hearts. I was having a bad time, but I'm over all my issues, now."

Nick sneered at her comment about his lack of a heart. Didn't he wish that was true.

"Sure you are."

"Don't be a jerk, Nicholas." The pouty look on his mother's face let him know she'd start crying next.

"Fine," he muttered the empty word, simply to keep her from tossing a fit at the table. "I was wrong, I'm sure you're in a great place and don't have any relationship issues to get over."

As if.

"No." Lori looked down at her lap, then gave Nick a shamed look. "You were right. I do have issues, of course. But when I called I was being unreasonable. I was afraid of Jeremy's daughter's hold on him, that he'd pick her over me. But I love Jeremy. I don't want to screw this up. I took your advice and unpacked my bags. We talked. Things are good."

Nick could only stare. Had all the women in the world gone crazy? His mother making mature relationship decisions? Delaney screwing his brains out in public, then daring him to man up and face his emotions?

Was eleven-thirty too early for Scotch?

"When did you get so smart about all that emotional

stuff, Nicky? For a guy with no heart, you definitely know what you're talking about."

"I'm not heartless," he said, unable to stop himself.

Two months ago, Nick would have shrugged the comment off with a vague agreement. But now the idea that his own mother thought him heartless hurt. He rolled his eyes. Chalk another win up to Delaney—now he was a whiny prissy-boy getting his feelings hurt.

"I didn't mean heartless," Lori said absently, her attention on the lunch their waiter was setting in front of them. "I meant you don't let things hurt you. You've always closed yourself off. You don't get all emotional or invest yourself in relationships. I'd go crazy if I were that lonely. I'm afraid to be alone, of course. But you? You embrace your solitary life."

Nick barely heard her, focused only on the phrase *afraid to be alone*. Was that why she ran from relationship to relationship?

Nick frowned as Lori dug into her pasta. Why hadn't he ever seen that before? He'd been so busy blaming her for his emotional scars, he hadn't bothered to notice she was sporting her own.

The realization did nothing to ease his frustration, although it did numb his anger. He was empty without Delaney, but he couldn't risk reaching out. He'd opened up and gotten screwed over. Why did that just make him sad now, instead of pissed? Pissed had been a lot easier to handle.

STILL MULLING OVER his lunchtime epiphanies, Nick arrived home and headed straight to his office. There, he tossed the large envelope he'd found on the porch to his desk and booted up his e-mail.

Nothing.

He checked his answering machine.

No calls.

For a woman so devoted to emotions, you'd think she'd try harder to force him to work through his. Sure, he'd shoved her away. And if she'd tried to reach him yesterday, he'd have probably made a show of hanging up on her. But dammit, why wasn't she calling?

Nick rolled his eyes and dropped his head against the leather back of his chair. God, this emotional crap was turning him into a teenage girl.

He eyed the envelope he'd brought up with him. No return address. He ripped open the packaging and read the note paperclipped to what he recognized as the manuscript he'd left with Delaney.

You asked me to read it as if I were reviewing. I thought you'd like to see the results.

He stared at her handwriting. It was surprisingly simple for such a feminine, sensual woman. He traced his finger over the loopy *D* she'd used as a signature.

Realizing what he had done, Nick snorted. Oh, yeah, total teenage girl. If he wasn't careful, he'd be getting himself a subscription to *Seventeen* and watching Orlando Bloom movies.

To torture himself, he took the rubber band off the manuscript and started reading. He left the yellow legal papers filled with notes for last, focusing instead on the comments she'd made on the pages themselves.

An hour later, Nick read the last page and realized he was a total dick. Whatever Delaney's reasons for not telling him about her job, they hadn't had a damned thing to do with her bet to add emotional depth to his writing.

He'd been so paranoid, so worried his words and his emotions might be found inadequate, he'd done exactly what Delaney had accused. He'd run away. Rejected her before she could reject him.

Pretty sad.

He looked at the notes she'd scrawled in the margin, each page filled with insights, comments, reflections. Delaney had found depth in his words. Interspersed amongst the analysis were sexy propositions, suggestions of things she'd like to try with him, and once or twice she'd even offered ways to make a scene even kinkier.

Was it any wonder he loved her?

Love. Nick puffed out a breath and accepted the truth. The realization, instead of making him feel suffocated, was freeing. All the anger, the doubts, dropped away. Delaney and his feelings for her, made him feel like he could do anything.

Nick flipped to the last page of her notes. Instead of comments, it was a copy of the *Risqué* magazine make-over story he'd read the month before. A small paper fluttered to the floor. He retrieved it and stared. A photocopy of her teacher ID card.

Dr. D. M. Conner, PhD. Rosewood College. He eyed the hire date on the card and raised a brow. Obviously she'd put that brainiac tendency of hers to good use to be a fully credentialed professor so young.

He frowned at the photo. They sure used lousy lighting. Her skin looked pale, her hair washed out. But the humor in her gorgeous brown eyes was clear. His gaze traced the sensual curve of her bottom lip, remembering how it felt to run his tongue over that tender flesh. Her mouth fascinated him, whether it was glistening with that glossy stuff she used or bare and tempting like it was in this picture. He wanted—needed—to taste her lips.

She was beautiful. She was smart. She was honest.

Painfully honest. If he hadn't been so busy running, he'd have admitted it sooner. Whatever that e-mail had said, he knew she wouldn't have manipulated him. She might have used their bet to her advantage, but hadn't he as well?

Or, he acknowledged as he glanced at the manuscript, wouldn't he have used it if he'd won? Except she'd won on both counts, the review bet and their debate over lust versus passion. Because passion had sucked him in one hundred percent.

Nick pulled his laptop over and with a few quick strokes, put together a note to Gary.

Lost the bet, worked in the emotions. It's a first draft. It should work, but if not, I'll go even deeper.

He attached the computer file containing the pages Delaney had read.

That taken care of, he fingered Delaney's card again.

Rosewood College, huh? Maybe it was time to pay her a visit.

DELANEY SAT BEFORE the dean and the head of the English department, waiting for their verdict. Her hands beneath the desk were still, although she wanted desperately to twist them tighter. She'd learned in her TV stint to show outward calm, though, and it was paying off. She'd given it her best, putting every bit of presence and charisma she'd learned on the TV show into effect.

From the looks on their faces, it hadn't done any good.

"Well," her father began. Then he sighed and fiddled with some papers on his desk. Impatience made Delaney want to scream.

"Well," he said again, this time meeting her eyes, "I have to say I'm actually surprised. Professor Ekco was sure you'd have something extra in your presentation that would sway the committee."

Delaney bit her lip and debated. Then she shrugged. "He'd suggested I take a different direction with my proposal. He felt I should include recent job experience and a new contact and possible guest speaker."

"You chose not to," her father said, stating the obvious. "Why?"

Was it failure to want to win on her own merits? Not in her opinion. But her father's? She glanced at Professor Belkin. She didn't know why he looked like he'd been sucking lemons.

"I felt my qualifications and proposal were strong enough to stand on their own. If I'd gotten the position, I wanted it on my merits alone."

"Good choice," her father said with a nod. His words, faint praise though they were, brought a glow to Delaney's cheeks.

"Of course it's a good choice," Belkin spat, erasing her glow. Delaney and the dean both frowned at his hateful tone. "Trash books would have no influence on the hiring committee."

Delaney's jaw dropped. She'd be hard-pressed to decide if it was over Belkin's angry words or her dignified father rolling his eyes.

Her father said nothing though. He just gave her a long, expectant look. Delaney knew that look and with a deep breath, took the unspoken command and stepped up to the plate.

"Could you define what you mean by trash books, Professor?"

"Oh, please, don't play coy. Commercial fiction? Especially that romance and erotic stuff? You've been promoting pure trash. Everyone here at the college knows about you, Ms. Conner."

Delaney went cold. Everyone? Her eyes flashed to her father's. His gaze was steady, his expression contemplative. Oh, yeah. He knew.

Now what? The old Delaney would have cringed and tried to appease the people facing her. But...she frowned and took a deep breath. Not now. She was proud of how far she'd come.

"I'm aware of the snobbery that blinds many literary circles to the possibilities available in modern fiction," she said slowly. Belkin gaped at her unapologetic words, and her father just raised his bushy red brows. "That wasn't my reason for not including my recent ventures in my proposal. My time with *Wake Up California* is, in my considered opinion, a strong learning tool that's only improved the skill set I bring to my job here."

"Promoting fluff fiction?"

"Promoting the art of reading," she said, tossing the motto of the English department back in his face.

Belkin turned magenta and sputtered something rude, but shut up when the dean gestured.

"Delaney, we're not casting judgment on your extra-curricular job decisions." Delaney quirked a brow toward Belkin. The dean grimaced and gave an infinitesimal shrug. "We're here to discuss the promotion and your future in the department."

Her stomach clenched. Future? Oh, hell. Had this all been a mistake? She swallowed the fear clogging her throat and took a deep breath. Two more in and out, and she was back in control.

No. The makeover was the best thing that had ever happened to her. The TV show was the best thing she'd ever made happen. And Nick? She wouldn't trade Nick, their relationship—even if it was over—and, yes, their bets for anything in the world. She'd learned to value herself. To stand up and be noticed. To be visible, in more than just a physical way.

"Do you, personally, have an issue with my reviewing?" Delaney asked.

Her father frowned at her taking control of the conversation. He stared, respect slowly taking root in his eyes. Then he shook his head. "No. As you know, I don't watch TV myself, but one of the professors had—what do you call it? used TiVo to record a few segments. Just as I am when I watch you teach in the classroom, I was impressed with your passion and ability to bring the student, or in this case the viewer, into your excitement for the topic."

He was proud of her? Shock kept her silent for five seconds.

"What are your feelings about this particular topic?" she dared to ask.

"Popular commercial fiction?"

She nodded.

"As you said, it serves a purpose. And you make that point quite skillfully. Unfortunately, your name is so well known in the commercial field now, Professor Belkin is concerned it will detract from your ability to teach your classes."

Of course he was. Delaney spared the snob a glare. "Do you agree with him?"

Delaney realized that while her father's opinion mattered, it wouldn't make a difference in how she felt. She was proud of herself.

"Actually, no. I'm of the mind that your sideline causes no issue. But that isn't my decision to make. It will be yours, though." Irritation was clear on his face when he looked at Professor Belkin. Then, with a pride-laced smile, he nodded to Delaney. "The hiring committee has chosen to offer you the job as assistant head of the English department."

Shocked triumph surged through her as Delaney bit back a shout of excitement. Her father raised a brow, then continued, "On the condition that you agree to desist any and all reviews, television programs or the like."

Her stomach sank. Give it all up? Her reviews, everything? Delaney looked at the man who she'd spent her life trying to please. For the first time, he was giving her his entire attention. And it wasn't because of her makeup or her reviews. It was because, simply by believing she deserved it, she'd commanded that attention.

For the first time in her life, she was in total control. It was the wildest feeling. Delaney swallowed a triumphant laugh and flicked a dismissive look at Professor Belkin. Him, she didn't need. But her father? They were about to come to an understanding. One she'd always wanted and now knew she'd have.

It was time to be proactive and turn her life into exactly what she wanted.

"It's an honor to earn this promotion," she told her father. "There's no decision to make. My choice is clear."

CHAPTER FIFTEEN

MONDAY MORNING DELANEY sat in front of the blinking red light and smiled at Sean.

"Delaney, we're thrilled to have you as a regular part of *Wake Up California,*" Sean said. He looked at the camera and gave the viewers his boy-next-door grin. "Not only is Delaney signing on permanently, we'll be expanding 'Critic's Corner' to five days a week. Stay tuned after the commercial break for the results of the Delaney Conner and Nick Angel bet."

The light went blank and Sean gave Delaney's knee an absent pat before hurrying off to answer the producer's summons. Seated on her now permanent set, Delaney smoothed a hand over her Burberry skirt, the soft gray plaid a sedate curve over her hips. She'd paired it with a stereotypical white button-up shirt, but hers had lace at the cuffs and on the camisole peeking out over the top button. Black suede boots hugged her calves, giving her a sense of fashion and control.

A far cry from brown tweed, yet still her.

Just like this job. She'd been amazed at how her father had taken her decision. He'd actually grinned. Six months ago, she'd have told herself it was because he was glad to be rid of her. But she was over the self-pity trips and knew his smile had been pride, pure and simple.

Now she had it all. Or—she glanced at Nick's latest book displayed on the table next to her—almost all. The only thing missing was Nick. And that was her own fault.

She'd finally admitted to herself when she'd arrived on set this morning that she'd used Nick's anger, his hurt, as an excuse to run away. Sure, she'd left in a grand show of bravado, but the reality was she'd figured she was better off leaving than waiting for him to end things today when they officially announced the bet results.

But that was before. Now? Now she was Delaney Conner, Super Reviewer. Savvy, sexy and commanding, she'd be chasing her man down as soon as today's taping was over.

Feeling like she could take on the world, Delaney smiled at the blinking red light and welcomed the viewers back. Three minutes into her spiel, there was a flurry of whispers and rustling of people on the set.

"What spurs change, in life and in fiction, is action. We see powerful examples of this in both modern and classical literature," Delaney continued without a hitch. "Take *Wuthering Heights,* for example. It was Heathcliff's love and loss of Cathy that turned him into a man of action. Dark actions, granted. But actions all the same. His primal response to her death pulls the reader into his psyche, lets them feel his pain. It shows, better than any inner monologue the writer could have sketched out, the depths of his emotion."

Not breaking verbal stride in her lecture, Delaney scanned the set.

Well, well. A slow smile curved her lips as she took in the most welcome sight she could imagine. Delaney took a deep breath, but knew it wouldn't stop her pulse from racing. Not when faced with the sexiest man she'd ever met. Gorgeous. Pure male perfection.

Nick Angel.

His midnight hair waved back from a face that she saw in her dreams. Piercing eyes, a vivid blue that saw clear through to her heart, narrowed when they met hers. He quirked his brow in challenge, letting her know that he might be here, but she wasn't off the hook.

He'd come, his gaze said, ready to rumble.

Delaney swallowed. Then she lifted her chin, her message clear. *Bring it on.*

"I'm delighted to announce we have a special guest today," she said as he came close. The camera panned back to get them both in the frame. "*New York Times* bestselling author Nick Angel. Let's see if we can get his take on the subject."

His look assured her he'd have a great deal more to discuss. Anticipation made her grin as he took his seat and clipped on a mic.

"Do you mind if I ask a question, first?" Nick asked, his tone making it clear he'd ask anyway. He leaned back in his chair, a wicked grin on his face, one arm along the back of the seat as if he hadn't a care in the world.

Delaney knew better. The sharp blue of his gaze told her she'd better stay on her toes. Fine with her, that's why she'd worn the killer heels.

"Ask away," she told him.

"You talk about these darker actions as if there is no choice. Don't you agree that we, as humans, are always free to accept or reject those unsavory urges." With a taunting grin, he added, "Or, to make it simpler, to accept or reject *any* emotion."

Delaney narrowed her eyes. She'd ask what he knew

about emotions, but the depths he'd tapped in his last manuscript said he knew plenty. Yet he still ran from them.

"I agree there are choices. Usually. But not always. Fear could be considered a darker emotion, couldn't it? And our reaction to it is instinctive."

"Fight or flight," Nick agreed with a nod. "Yet, even in that, there's a clear choice. Run or stand your ground."

Delaney pursed her lips. Which one, exactly, was he accusing her of?

"So in your opinion, there is always a choice?" she countered. "Most would say that one doesn't choose to fall in love, it simply happens. Usually at a very inopportune time."

A small smile played at the corner of Nick's mouth, sexy and teasing.

"Again, there's a choice. A character can walk away from love."

"I agree to a point," she said slowly. Her eyes searched his face for a clue. Was he here to tell her he was choosing to walk away or face love? There was so much riding on this debate, her brain was stumbling over words. "Choices are mandatory in fiction. A character that refuses to act is a character that the reader quickly loses empathy for."

"To throw your own example back at you, what if the character is afraid to act?"

"Growth comes from facing those fears, from overcoming our personal conflicts," Delaney pointed out. "Or, of course, accepting that we're too weak to face it," she said with a taunting smile of her own.

The producer hopped up and down, practically doing the potty dance as he pointed to his watch. They were almost out of time. He mouthed the word *bet* and Delaney nodded.

"You say that like you're an expert," Nick commented.

"An expert on what works in fiction, yes. Unquestionably."

"I suppose you'd say your reviews support that claim," he said after a glance at the producer.

"I think I've shown that to be true, don't you?" she asked. A part of her worried that he was irritated at losing. But she couldn't back down. She couldn't ever be less than she was, less than important. Not even for Nick.

Delaney paused while the producer indicated they were showing the review results to the viewers. The voters on *Wake Up California*'s Web site had agreed with four of the six book reviews she'd posted. Not a landslide win, but it definitely proved that she did, in fact, speak for the average viewer. Or at least 66.6 percent of them.

Her eyes met Nick's, trying to read his reaction. But he was an expert at hiding his emotions, and his face was blank. She sighed as the producer pointed to her, indicating she was live again. She loved winning, but not at Nick's expense.

"I'm sure you've all followed my bet with Mr. Angel on whether or not my reviews hold weight," she stated, looking into the camera as if she were talking to a group of friends. The entire set was silent, everyone staring intently at the drama unfolding in front of them. Delaney noted a few snide looks aimed at Nick, but there were just as many lusty, drooling ones. "And as the poll shows, viewers agreed with four of my six assessments. Which, according to Mr. Angel's parameters, should confirm that my views represent the average reader."

Nick's eyes gleamed and a small smile played at the corner of his mouth, but he didn't say anything.

"What you don't know," she said slowly, "is *my* summary of this exercise."

All eyes were on here again, including Nick's.

"While the reviews were the basis for the bet, the actual topic of debate was emotion versus lust." She met Nick's gaze. "In examining Mr. Angel's views on the topic, I've come to realize that despite the obvious lure of emotions, lust is just as empowering."

Nick frowned. She didn't take her eyes from his.

"Lust, especially as portrayed in Mr. Angel's writing, requires an element of honesty. Real lust isn't just a quick, simple urge. It isn't easily slaked, nor is it something that fades quickly. Real lust has power. It requires intimacy. It's dark, real, intense. It is, I've come to find, just as real an emotion as the ever-touted love."

Delaney hesitated when Nick frowned. But, unable to give up now, she continued.

"Emotions—especially the grander ones like love and intimacy—make us feel good. As humans, we're hard-wired to seek connections, to find reflections of ourselves in others. It makes us feel good to give nice names to those reflections. Lust, obviously, isn't a nice name. We want to pretty it up, make it sound good, but sometimes, in life and in fiction, lust is the answer. Thanks to Mr. Angel, I learned the power of lust this last month. In literature of course," she added.

"And what about in real life?" he asked. His tone was matter-of-fact, as if it was just another question to debate. But the intensity in those blue eyes, the tight set of his jaw, told her the answer was crucial.

Delaney stared, her heart beating wildly. It took her five seconds to realize the producer was gesturing to cut.

"And with that," she told the camera, "we'll break for commercial."

"Cut."

Without a word, she and Nick unhooked their mics, and he silently followed her as she headed for her dressing room. Her permanent dressing room, she noted as she saw her name on the door. She'd come a long way. As she opened the door, she tossed a look over her shoulder and asked, "So? You're here to take me up on that bet?"

His grin was fast and appreciative. His steps into the room were slow and measured. Delaney felt as if she were being stalked by a very sexy, very powerful cat. One that planned to eat her up in slow, savoring bites.

"Why don't we conclude our last bet first, hmm?"

"Lust versus intimacy?"

"That's the one."

Delaney swallowed hard when he stopped within touching distance. It was all she could do to keep her fingers to herself instead of letting them trace the hint of stubble darkening the curve of his jaw.

"I've already shared my views on that bet," she said slowly, trying to quiet the nerves in her stomach. Everything, she knew, was riding on this confrontation. Earlier, she'd been impatient to hunt him down and force the issue, but now that he was here, she wished she'd had more time to prepare.

"Then it's my turn to share and your turn to listen, isn't it?" he said, taking that last step to close the gap between them. The hard wood of the makeup table dug into her back as Delaney sucked in a shallow breath. If she so much as moved to the left or right, her breasts would brush against his chest.

Pure temptation. But one she knew she needed to ignore. At least until he'd made his point.

So she kept her body still as her eyes met his.

"You were right," he said. Then he stopped, either for her to take over, or to gather his thoughts.

She raised a brow, waiting. He grimaced. His shrug sent tremors of desire through her body as his chest brushed her breasts.

"I was chicken. I was afraid to accept the emotions between us, to trust them or you. Or, actually, myself."

Her jaw dropped. Holy shit. When he'd admitted she was right, she'd figured he meant her critique of his manuscript. Delaney's stomach climbed into her throat, nerves shivering down her spine.

"And now?" she asked in a whisper.

"Now, I'm still afraid," he admitted, reaching out to finger the collar of her shirt. His eyes met hers and he pulled a face. "Like you said, opening up means the possibility of rejection. It's one thing to put my words out there, my stories. But putting my heart out there is harder, you know?"

Her breath caught in her chest at his admission. What did that mean? That his heart was involved? With her? A little or a lot? Was there an etiquette to asking someone for clarification when they were pouring out their emotions? She almost laughed. For all of her pushing for the concept, she had no idea how to deal with it.

"Rejection scares me, too," she admitted. She met his gaze, her eyes tracing his features. He was so gorgeous, would he even understand? Did it matter?—she had to be honest. "You were right, I was hiding things from you. I didn't want you to turn away. I didn't know how you'd react if you knew the real me."

"How could you think you wouldn't measure up, Delaney? You're not only one of the smartest women I've ever known, you're the most gorgeous. I can't believe you'd think I'd care if you were a teacher instead of a TV personality."

"It goes a little deeper than that," she admitted.

"Honestly, after I got past the anger at feeling used, I wasn't surprised by your job," he continued. "Your brain is one of the most beautiful things about you. It's a turn-on to debate with you, to watch you think."

She wanted to grin at the warm, fuzzy feeling his words gave her, but she was stuck on his first statement.

"You thought I used you? How?"

"For some promotion." Nick explained how he'd read her e-mail that night. Realization dawned, like a smack upside the head. He'd been pissed over feeling used, not freaked to see her in her red sweats and greasy face. Delaney couldn't hold back a slightly hysterical giggle.

"I didn't use you," she told him. "At least, not like that. The only things I took before the board were my teaching qualifications. I didn't bring in our bet or my stint on *Wake Up California*."

He nodded, his expression making it clear that it really wasn't an issue. "We had a bet, a very public one, which you could have used without compunction," he told her. "I jumped on it as an excuse to justify my fear, to push you away and deny how I was feeling."

Then, as if unable to hold out any longer, he slid his hands down her waist and grasped her hips to pull her against him. He gave her a wicked grin and asked, "So if not that way, how *did* you use me?"

"For the great sex, of course."

Nick's laugh filled her with joy. Delaney wrapped her hands around his shoulders, loving the feel of him back in her arms. Before she could let herself sink into the sensation, though, she had to know.

"I was worried…" She took a deep breath and opened up completely. "*Am* worried about your reaction to how I looked before the *Risqué* magazine makeover."

She felt like she was waiting for the guillotine blade to slice her open as she watched his face for signs of distaste.

"That magazine thing?" He gave a disinterested shrug. "Why would that matter?"

She squinted, trying to discern if he was being nice. But he just looked confused.

"I gave you my picture," she said slowly. It had taken all her nerve to do it, too. Especially that shot, but she hadn't had much choice. She purposely had very few pictures of herself. Her faculty shot was horrible, a makeupless frump. "Didn't you get it?"

"Your ID card? Yeah, I have it." He shrugged, then gave her a sheepish look. "I framed it and keep it on my desk. I never got that kind of thing before, but I do now. Just seeing your face, it makes me feel good inside. I spent the last few days working on my book. Using your notes, your suggestions, to make it work. I like to imagine you're watching me write, pushing me to take it deeper, to go further."

Delaney pulled her mouth shut. "You framed it? That picture? But…it's horrible."

His blank look said it all. He didn't see the makeup, the hair. He saw her.

"I love you," she blurted out. As soon as the words

escaped, she wanted to slap her hands to her mouth to shove them back in. But she didn't. Because, for once, she was putting it all out there. Rejection be damned, she was making a choice.

Now it was his turn. He could be a coward and run, or be honest and admit he loved her back. Her shoulders knotted tight as she waited to see which he'd do.

NICK GAVE A huge sigh of relief as Delaney's words washed over him. Unable to stop himself, he pulled her into his arms. "I love everything about you. Your brains, your looks, that sexy little sound you make when you come. I love that you're not afraid to stand up to me, that you're not afraid to stand up for what you believe in." His mouth against hers, he murmured, "I especially love that you love me, too."

Thank God, was all he could think. He'd hoped she cared. He'd lain awake at night remembering the look in her eyes as she'd left the ball, hoping what he'd seen there was love. For a guy who'd dissed the concept for so long, he'd been on shaky ground.

Unused as he was to emotions, let alone to trusting they'd last while he worked through his issues, he'd been terrified she'd changed her mind. Or, at the very least, had spent their days apart building a nasty case of anger against him.

As usual, Delaney had shocked the hell out of him. Instead of anger, she'd publicly argued for lust in his favor. Instead of gloating over her win, she was sexy, passionate and fair.

She got his writing, saw in it and him more than he'd even hoped for. She took him from happy to horny with just a smile. And she'd given him her heart, just like that.

Was it any wonder he loved the woman?

"So we've settled our bets, right?" he said, pulling back reluctantly.

Her considering frown made him laugh. Even now, in the middle of his declaration of love, she ran it all through that super-brain of hers. "Yes, I suppose we have settled them."

"Right. You won the review bet, and the prize was my writing more emotion into my books. Which, actually, I've already started paying off."

She nodded, her head tilted like she was trying to think a few steps ahead of him and see where he was going.

"The lust-versus-intimacy bet was a little more challenging, since I'm saying intimacy wins hands down, yet you just argued for lust here in front of all those impressionable viewers."

Her face lit up at his admission, then she winced and laughed. "I did give a mixed message out there, didn't I? How about we say I was playing devil's advocate, since we both know I believe intimacy outlasts lust."

"Right. Then I'd have to say you won," he mused. He nodded, his face as serious as he could get it even as nerves jangled through his system. Damn, this wasn't easy. "Since we'd left the prize for that bet open, I figure I have to ask you to marry me. If you'd lost, you would have had to ask me."

Her jaw dropped, shock clear on her gorgeous face. Three times, Delaney blinked, trying to force words out. Nick laughed. Suddenly, it *was* easy. Simple even.

"What?" she finally squeaked.

"I want a commitment. It's that choice thing. I love you. You love me. I believe in those emotions between us, and I believe they're strong enough to last. I want it all. And I want to prove to you I believe it's real."

Her laughter was a gurgle through the tears streaming down her face. Nick hoped they were happy tears. When she launched herself at him, her arms wrapping tight around his neck, he figured they were definitely happy.

"That's a yes?" he asked, breathing in the flowery scent of her hair as relief surged through him. He hadn't realized how worried he'd been about her reaction until the tension melted from his shoulders.

"Yes," she told him, lifting her face to blind him with the brilliance of her smile. Joy, simple and pure, filled Nick. "Yes, I'll spend our life exploring lust, passion, love and even those fears. Yes, I want to be with you, to take chances and to grow together. Yes… To everything, yes."

Their mouths met in a kiss filled with everything she'd said. Passion, lust and love—all mingled as their lips and tongues danced together. Nick's body reminded him, in hard graphic detail, how long it had been since he'd had Delaney in his arms.

"I want you so much. I need to feel you wrapped around me, hear you cry out my name." Nick buried his face in the curve of her neck and groaned. "Are you done on the set? Can we go?"

She forced her eyes open to glance at the large round clock on the wall.

"My door has a lock," she said softly. "Ever done it on a makeup table?"

Nick grinned, loving this naughty side of her. And he'd thought lust would scare her away? Damn, he'd been stupid.

"Sex at work?" he teased. "Aren't you the naughty one?"

"I plan to be," she told him with a grin so wicked his dick throbbed in desperate response. "After all, you're going to need me for research."

"You're my perfect woman," he breathed in gratitude.

"Yes," she agreed with a laugh. Humor lit her eyes with dancing lights of pleasure. Nick stared, amazed to realize she was just that. Perfect and all his. She knew him, the real him, and wanted him anyway. Not for his success, not for his connections. Simply for him.

Kinky books, emotional baggage and all.

"You're like my very own storybook heroine," Nick said softly as he traced a finger over her shoulder. Her eyes widened, then filled with tears, making him feel like an ass. But he had to say it. "You're amazing. Strong enough to accept me for who I am, and caring enough to push me to open up, to be more."

"That's my line," she said with a tremulous smile. She blinked fast to clear her eyes. "That you see me, the whole me, and love me is amazing. It's almost as much a turn-on as what you do to my body."

With a laugh, Nick took the hint. His mouth took hers on a wild ride of pleasure. This was intimacy. The delight of her body under his and her eyes staring, lovingly, back at him.

Six months ago he would have said it was impossible. But thanks to Delaney, he finally believed in Happy Ever After. And damned if his wasn't going to be a wild, lusty one.

* * * * *

We hope you enjoyed reading
SCANDALIZED
by *New York Times* bestselling author
LORI FOSTER
and
RISKY BUSINESS
by *New York Times* bestselling author
TAWNY WEBER.

Both were originally **Harlequin®** series stories!

You like it hot!
Harlequin® Blaze® stories sizzle with strong
heroines and irresistible heroes playing the game
of modern love and lust. They're fun, sexy and
always steamy.

ⓗ HARLEQUIN®

Blaze

Red-Hot Reads

Look for 4 *new* romances every month
from **Harlequin® Blaze®**!

Available wherever books are sold.

SPECIAL EXCERPT FROM

HARLEQUIN

Blaze

*Kennedy Duchane and Asher Reynolds have been
fighting their attraction for years. But when she has to
help him overcome stage fright, a little sexy distraction
may be just the ticket!*

*Read on for a sneak preview of
UNDER PRESSURE,
the final book in **Kira Sinclair**'s sizzling trilogy
SEALS OF FORTUNE.*

The sweet scent of vanilla tickled Asher Reynolds's senses.

Cracking one eye open, he stared up at Kennedy Duchane looming above him. Her thighs were spread on either side of his hips.

"I could get used to waking up to this, Cupcake," he rumbled, threading his fingers through her hair and pulling her closer.

Something soft and wet swept across his cheek.

"What the hell?"

She grinned wickedly, and for the first time he realized she held something in her hand. A pale cupcake with a thick swirl of bright pink frosting.

Eyeing it, he asked, "What is that?"

Her grin widened. "Payback."

Before he could even twitch, the thing was top-down in his face. Kennedy smeared the sticky mess from his forehead, down his nose and across his chin.

There was no question, he was under siege.

Asher grabbed her by the waist and flipped her onto her back. He wasn't about to make this easy.

With one hand, he captured her wrist, holding her arm above her head and immobilizing her weapon of choice.

She hadn't just brought one, but a full dozen of the sticky pink things.

Stretching out, he grabbed some ammunition of his own and struck. She yelped in surprise and tried to wiggle away. But he had her well and truly pinned.

"Nowhere to go, Sugar," he drawled.

Kennedy glared up. "Calling me Sugar is no better than calling me Cupcake, you Southern-fried Neanderthal."

Dipping his finger in the pink confection, Asher spread a smear across her collarbone.

"I only use nicknames with people I actually like," he murmured.

She squirmed. "Why Cupcake? It sounds so…empty-headed and pointless."

"Hardly." Pushing up onto his elbows, Asher gazed at her, his heart thumping erratically.

"*Cupcake* is the perfect description for you, Kennedy. The kind of treat you know you shouldn't want, but you can't seem to stop craving… Besides, I always knew you'd taste so damn sweet." He brushed his lips over her frosting-covered skin.

Don't miss
UNDER PRESSURE by Kira Sinclair
available November 2015 wherever
Harlequin® Blaze® books and ebooks are sold.

www.Harlequin.com

HARLEQUIN®

Blaze®

Red-Hot Reads

Save $1.00

**on the purchase of
UNDER PRESSURE
by Kira Sinclair,
available October 20, 2015, or on
any other Harlequin® Blaze® book.**

Available wherever books are sold, including most
bookstores, supermarkets, drugstores and discount stores.

Save $1.00

on the purchase of any Harlequin® Blaze® book.

Coupon valid until December 31, 2015.
Redeemable at participating outlets in the U.S.A. and Canada only.
Not redeemable at Barnes & Noble stores. Limit one coupon per customer.

5 2613151

5 65373 00076 2   (8100)0 12106

NYTCOUPI015

Turn your love of reading into rewards you'll love with

Harlequin My Rewards

**Join for FREE today at
www.HarlequinMyRewards.com**

Earn **FREE BOOKS** of your choice.

Experience **EXCLUSIVE OFFERS** and contests.

Enjoy **BOOK RECOMMENDATIONS**
selected just for you.

PLUS! Sign up now
and get **500** points
right away!

MYR16R